Praise for *Color for Canvas*

Color for Canvas opens in the 1820s on the Kansas prairie, where Running Feet, now running for her life, is the last of her tribe. Suddenly, her Comanche pursuers halt. On the cusp of her capture, she's apparently become invisible. Is the land protecting her ... or something else?

The girl has survived to dream of good in the secret place of thunder.

This legacy and mandate are handed down and expand when they reach a future in which "Plain Jane" receives a gift delivered with a directive: to capture, on canvas, the good in the world for the generations to come. Fast forward to 1982 New Jersey, where elements of supernatural influence appear in Jane's life:

In spite of an otherwise lackluster life, the girl recognizes a universal force at work, one intent where she is concerned.

Transported to an extraordinary world via a dream that awakens her hope, potentials, and new possibilities, Jane's artistic focus grows new pathways of light not only for her own life, but in those around her.

The timeline swings between 1800s Kansas and modern times, clearly defined by chapter headings. Readers move easily between seemingly disparate times, places, and lives while absorbing connections between forms of spiritual insight and light that mark the choices and observations of Agnes, James, Jane, and a host of others.

Jane begins to confront the underlying meaning of these figures in her life:

"The things you show me. The Land, The House, the people here...is all of this a replacement for what is lacking in my own life, or a method by which I am to learn something?...is Agnes allegory for who I am?"

The fact that Jane and this girl paint and reflect their worlds from different eras and viewpoints adds to important inspections and revelations. Readers come to understand, alongside Jane, not only why these experiences are connected, but just how they impact the world through symbolism, creative representation, and acts of kindness.

Much more than a spiritual, psychological, or artistic journey, J.M. Huxley crafts a hard-hitting novel of discovery which entwines many revelations via threads of positivity which ultimately emerge from the characters' lives and choices.

Her ability to show how these individuals rise above their circumstance, chance, and choice to bring light into the world via their disparate efforts is a message especially needed in modern times.

Libraries looking for inspirational novels that celebrate and meld art, purpose, and spiritual reflection with a supernatural overlay and time-travel discoveries that are alluring and unexpected connections will welcome Color for Canvas into their collections.

Readers looking for fiction that is thought-provoking, uplifting, and perfect for book club discussion, Christian inspection, or personal reflection will also find Color for Canvas a compelling read. It reflects its own aura of hope and possibility while delivering an important message about creating the most from one's life.

—D. Donovan, Sr. Reviewer, *Midwest Book Review*

J. M. Huxley has created a masterpiece canvas of words painted with the lives of generations of women artists who paint what they see, but what they "see" is often generations before they lived on the earth or generations after they lived out their lives. You will be drawn into the mystery of these women's encounters, their legacy of artwork, and a thrilling climax when everything falls into place and the master canvas comes fully into view.

—Diana Larkin, best-selling author of *The Rescue of the Ages* and podcast host of *A Watchman's Journal*

"Color for Canvas by J.M. Huxley was a vivid, emotional journey from start to finish. Every character breathed with nuance and authenticity, their inner worlds painted with a masterful brush. The story swept through different time periods like a silk thread pulling together vision, meaning, and mystery, each moment smart and rich with purpose. I found myself caught in a tapestry I never saw coming, one moment holding my breath, the next deeply moved. It was more than a book—it was an experience. A stunning blend of emotion, revelation, and surprise. A true joy to read."

—Missy Maxwell-Worton, award-winning author of *Don't Mess with This Mama* and CEO of Warrior Writers Training*

One has to have a brilliant imagination to create such a piece of artistic fiction as *Color for Canvas,* and JM Huxley definitely has it. Janet's literary intelligence brings the reader into her world, where a mix of make believe and reality will keep you in suspense. I literally could not put the book down! I can't wait until she writes the sequel to this incredible journey of many generations that come to life on the pages of this novel. Grab a cup of your favorite hot beverage, curl up on your favorite chair, and get ready for a fantastic journey! You will be so glad you did!

—Carolyn Searcy, artist, inner healer minister, magazine contributor, and featured author in *Resilience: Women Rising to Their Greatest Moments*

I got to know Janet through my friend Diana Larkin, and Janet has interviewed me a few times on her podcast, COLOR SPEAK. Janet is a kind and creative woman who is motivated to help people on their journey of life. What stands out to me is that she is so willing to share of her own experiences, not to bring attention, but on the contrary, to be of help with the knowledge she has learned. The scripture 2 Corinthians 1:4 reminds me so much of her where it says, "so that we can comfort those in any trouble with the comfort we ourselves have received from God." To me, this verse defines Janet. So, when I read her manuscript for *Color for Canvas*, it clarified who she is; this book reminds me of a tapestry that is being woven. Unanswered questions create a desire to read on, to know the outcome of generations. On one side, it's rather messy with knots and yarn interwoven through the stitches, no rhyme or reason in design. On the other side is a masterpiece in the works. Often that's what happens in our lives when we don't have a clue how things are going to work out, and then there comes a connection with a certain person with a different perspective than what we're used to that leads us out of the cobwebs and uncertainties. Throughout this book, there is an underlying knowing that there is a God, and He is leading us through the maze of life.

—Patty Teichroew, blogger, podcaster, and founder of His Mouthpiece Ministry

Light WARRIOR
PUBLISHING
TM

COLOR

for

CANVAS

J. M. Huxley

For Henry

I wrote it just like you told me to

"The white canvas—
it's like a layer of dust that covers up the real painting.
It's just a matter of cleaning it.
I have a little brush to clear away the blue,
another for the red, and another brush for the green.
And when I've finished cleaning, the picture is all there."

—George Braque, 1882-1963

Prologue

THE PLAINS OF KANSAS, 1820

She runs west through the wind and summer grasses, over the earth baked to brick, away from the hunters.

She moves fast, as if she might take flight, long hair flying behind like a mustang's sable tail in motion, every one of her muscles working in unison to give her lift. If only she could be a falcon now and rise above this place! Blue Eagle had once told her falcons, though not as big or strong, were faster than eagles.

But desperation sounds nothing like the beat of freedom's wings, where fast flight looks smooth and easy.

Behind her, the breathing of her pursuers is labored too, something she easily discerns as they close in, their own exertion evident in furious, audible bursts. She senses their outstretched arms at any moment could wield weapons close enough to meet her flesh.

Close enough to break her open, too.

Their murderous breath remains thick in the air, a frenzy begun in the killing time just a short while ago when her family was stolen from her, and now heaviness feels entirely triumphant. And consumed with shedding every last drop of her tribe's blood. What had begun under the direction of evil spirits had fomented sick glee.

The hunters whoop and call out in their feverish run, but soon any vocal clamor gives way to necessary focus and the vastness of the prairie. The rush of the winds and the parting of grasses and a big, seemingly passive sky appear either cruelly disinterested or passively complicit as the darkness chases the last member of a human party already obliterated—one lone, insignificant girl.

The girl is small, the grasses tall this time of year, and she runs like she's one with nature, one with the light, as if her feet are spirit and the sky isn't passive after all. As if the prairie is her friend, the land her guardian. She runs like destiny, as if this very moment had always been foreknown.

Maybe it had.

The very moment in which her life could end. Or the one she could very well have been named for.

Running Feet. The name she has always begrudged. She'd have preferred Dancing Feet—her oldest sister's name—which seemed much more whimsical, or even Skipping Feet—her youngest sister's—which, all things considered, wasn't the best, but it wasn't bad either. It was definitely more interesting than a name like Running Feet. Running Feet was unexciting. Definitely not like those given her siblings and especially not like her brother's. His was the best of all. Blue Eagle.

But none of those names matter anymore, as if they ever mattered, she considers wryly. Those names died with the people they'd belonged to just a short time ago. The girl's family, the hunting members of her tribe, now all returned to the earth from which they'd sprung. Brave Cougar and She Sings, her parents, delivered back to a thirsty ground, too.

Leaving her here all alone.

In this world, death seems almost to eclipse everything else, and names are but whispers in time, and she knows this as she runs. All of this is to be expected, really. And as she runs, her mind runs, too. Even now, her mind explodes with the life inside her, the one given by the Great Spirit. It causes hard lungs prickly stinging, a wild heart fierce drumming, and legs fast driving, nearly beyond what is humanly possible for a girl of twelve.

And thoughts—that may be the last to pass when her own physicality reaches its time—dictate grieving must wait.

In this moment, there is only life, and she runs as if she can outdistance her mind, for that time when it will no longer be attached to the material. As if she can outpace the Great Spirit, too. As if the winds of the ancients are behind her and always will be, and there is only going forward, not back. Fast, like a wild horse the girl runs, not daring to look over her shoulder.

It will be night soon, and even if her hunters give up to return to their party, the wolf packs could take their place. They are probably already celebrating the night's hazy, pink rebirth.

Her running feet begin to ache in protest; each sole's repetitive thump on the ground booming to her mind, a rhythmic cadence that only calls attention to the weakness growing in each knee.

She wonders how long she can do this, how long she will be able to outdistance herself from her enemies, how long it will be before her legs wobble and give out. And any physical pain is overcome with a conscious effort to focus on overshadowing what really is too tender to consider in flight.

Her family.

What must come next.

Being alone.

No!

She can't fly, but she can run, and fast, she reminds herself. She was born for this! She needs only keep this focus. *Don't stop!* she tells herself. *Don't look back!*

And suddenly, an energy unlike any she's known before fuels her beyond her own limits. She runs faster than she's ever run before, and she's the fastest runner among her people. She resolves to run fast until the last rays of the sun settle into brown, until the sky is black and the stars are out. She'll run fast to the horizon and keep running until she falls off the earth, even if Manitou isn't there with open arms. Even if he has never been there and her people have gotten the Great Spirit all wrong.

But maybe, just maybe, He will be. Maybe there is a Great Someone who is helping her now.

If she can make it through this day alive, only then will she consider a Strength that could very well be running beside her. But are those braves still behind her? The girl slows to have a look.

Steeling her nerves, she stops at last, crouching low to the earth. She bends over to steady her hands on her knees while gulping air, trembling as she makes ready to look.

She remembers what her father had told her about making herself a warrior. What he said about being like the cougar. Steady. Aware. Ready. She re-positions herself with this in mind, making herself smaller yet larger all at once and pulling up slowly until she is eye level with a sea of golden tassels, allowing her vision to adjust, scanning across the tops of the waves.

A thin, blushing blanket of color lays across the hot, gray sky, deepening shadows in the low places. Soon, it will be impossible to see. Will they pursue her into greater darkness?

From left to right her eyes wander the prairie, daring to look for signs of their approach. She believes she's managed to create a good distance, but it's hard to know for sure.

It isn't long before she discerns solid heads and broad shoulders in forward movement. As the murky outlines of men come into focus, she senses dark eyes looking her way. She gasps and falls to the ground, trying not to cry. Warriors don't cry.

Blue Eagle would never cry!

Suddenly, a small blue bird appears, dipping and fluttering around her. "No! Go away," the girl orders the bird under her breath, for the menace will surely give her whereabouts away. "Shoo!" Undeterred, the bird continues to hover above her. "Stupid bird," she starts to shout, but catches herself, watching it alight to the east where it flies into deepening shades.

The men are close now! That bird has probably led them straight to her! They're so close, she detects the murmurs of their beads and trinkets, the soughing of the grasses around their limbs. She hears their labored breathing and tries again to steady her own, but it's impossible. Her heart is still hammering a barrel in her chest. Her limbs still tremble, weaker now. The bird returns to soar overhead again, this time heading west into the colors.

Then suddenly, it is back again, swooping down in front of her before climbing high, accelerating as it does, as if trying to send a message. Trying to ignore alarming thoughts of exposure, the girl gives in and follows the bird.

Could this be the Great Spirit come for her?

The sounds of the plains diminish in the wind, which is all that can be heard now. There is no discernible movement in the grass. No stamping the ground. No exaggerated breathing.

Have the warriors come to a stop again?

She doesn't see the bird.

She must take another look!

But her heart nearly freezes when she sees their eyes follow the very path she'd taken to her current location. She is fooling no one. No farther than the span of a dozen horses, they'll be upon her soon.

And just then, a pair of eyes lock on hers.

She gasps and falls to the ground, unable to inhale. Even in the low light, she notices her left heal is bleeding. She rolls onto all fours and begins to make her way further into the tall stems that surround her, crawling north for a few minutes. It is only seconds before she can no longer stand this position. She pops back up to break into a gallop, continuing west, wishing the wind was her friend. Still following the path of the bird.

Back at the campsite, the Comanches are probably celebrating their bloody victory. She knows they'll plunder what little her own tribe possessed and hopes it will at least include the buffalo meat her family had secured in their hunt. There is no reason the beasts' lives should be wasted. Surely her family was killed for such. Hunting grounds fought over mean nothing if not that. There can be no ruin for sport. No life taken without cause.

Until now, perhaps.

Storm clouds gather overhead, thunder claps in the expanse, and soon a steady rain begins to fall. But oddly, a clearing appears in the sky ahead, where a startling slab of turquoise blue appears to poke a hole in the bleakness. Leaden twilight is broken through, revealing an opening which widens to the most radiant beam of sunlight the girl has ever seen, as if Manitou himself is casting his glow down from above. The light illuminates a rare, thickly trunked tree with heavy branches. Such a giant on the prairie is as remarkable as bright wildflowers on a blanket of snow.

The bluebird heads for it as the sound of thunder increases in warning.

The Great Spirit is surely beckoning her there!

The girl sprints for this spot, knowing as she does she will be safe. If only she can reach the tree in time! She must continue to widen the distance between herself and the weapons raised behind her, the tomahawks and spears and bows with arrows, all so very close.

And as she sees peace in the distance, she starts to fall in on herself, as if such a thing cannot last, as if it is too much to hope for. As if what she sees is only a mirage and out of reach. The pain produced by these thoughts is so intense, it threatens to burst and drown her like the flash of many waters now rushing across the flood plain. Her knees begin to liquify.

Don't stop now, urges a voice within her.

She keeps her eyes on the light.

She fights against images of the tomahawk wedged in Blue Eagle's chest, as well as recollections of how she'd fallen off the back of the horse they'd shared, her arms knocked from his waist, the air from her chest— what happened in so short a period of time as to change what lay long before her. She banishes thoughts of her brother's spirit already gone by the time she reached him again, the sight of her sisters bludgeoned to death and laying side-by-side, face-up to the sky with their eyes and chests open, and of her parents face down in the dirt, split apart.

The tree before her represents refuge. Provision. And when the girl reaches it under the light, she knows she is safe. She has made it! She lovingly touches the rough bark wrapped around its base while boldly turning to stand her ground. As she dares to look behind her one last time, she finds herself in possession of a strength she hasn't known before. She resolves she won't look away, no matter what she encounters.

In the short distance, she finds all three Comanche braves staring at her. Only they don't advance. They don't move. Actually, they don't even seem to *see* her. They appear to look right through her, bewildered, as if she has just disappeared before their very eyes.

They wander about a few minutes more, walking in circles and shaking their heads as Running Feet watches. Finally, they give up. Visibly irritated but worn, too, and undoubtedly hungry, they turn around to jog back the way they've come, undeterred by the rain but evidently buoyed by festivities surely underway.

"The wolves will get her anyway," one shouts through the shower's hum.

"But I'd have gladly taken her before them," agrees another.

The third chuckles devilishly and adds, "Let's feast."

The girl sighs in relief. She's safe! They hadn't seen her here! It's as if the land is protecting her.

Or something here is.

Something that causes the tall grasses and big sky and blue birds to agree, and maybe there is such a thing as Manitou.

If so, Running Feet isn't such a bad name after all.

As thunder rumbles and lightning explodes and the wind runs a fast pace, the girl collapses and curls up to sleep, sheltered and dry under the boughs of the giant tree. There the wind exhales, and the rain relaxes to subtle sound, exposing lullaby notes in soft grasses—wind instruments in concert with hidden orchestras. A gentle symphony just for her.

The girl has survived to dream of good in the secret place of thunder.

There, under the tree as sentinel, where nature plays music and light makes unusual color, good dreams rule over the bad.

And the unseen rules over what is seen.

Chapter
One

CAPE MAY, NEW JERSEY—DECEMBER 1982

The funny business begins the moment the girl's twelfth birthday arrives, precisely, as if both second hands on the clock know what is happening when they join together in unison to point up to the heavens this day. As if they, and all things related to time, could work in unison on such an occasion.

And this stands to reason, given she was born on 12-12 at twelve noon straight up—exactly twelve hours from the beginning of a new day.

Now, it's December 12 at midnight. Another 12.

Happy birthday to me, she thinks.

Given her wild imagination, it isn't odd in the least that so much of her world involves the number twelve. She wholly embraces it. Her address is 1212 Eagle Road. Her home telephone number ends in 12. Nearly every time she looks at a clock, it's 12:12. And so it goes.

In spite of an otherwise lackluster life, the girl recognizes a universal force at work, one that makes her feel different. Since 12 is a symbol of cosmic order, time measured in two groups of 12 each day with 12 months in the year, it's safe to say there is something beyond what she can see that's trying to get her attention. However, any mystical messaging that could be encouraging has yet to provide assistance in the real world.

In school, the girl's grades are mediocre, not because she isn't wildly brilliant but because she's wildly imaginative; she never excels except in her own mind. She can't sing or dance or play sports—nothing that causes anyone to notice her. She does play the piano but under duress. And not well. Her parents insist upon it.

Her parents insist upon a lot of things.

They don't, however, insist she is beautiful. In fact, they don't affirm her in any manner except indirectly, and that's at a stretch, and if everyone is being completely honest, she is and always will be Plain Jane.

Their passivity confirms this.

She is a Plain Jane who always has been, always will be, just plain average unless you count a small claim to fame thanks to the number 12.

Her own imagination affirms this.

So, the first time the stranger with the long, white hair and equally impressive, neatly trimmed goatee appears to her, she is 12. Not only that, it's the very day she celebrates this milestone. Rather, she will once daylight appears. Technically, it's still dark, and she's still asleep. Or is she? Anyway, it's her birthday. *It figures*, she will later conclude.

"Jane," the stranger says to her because, wouldn't you know it, her name really is Jane, as if to beg the rights to plainness from the very beginning. "It's time you see."

Those were his first words to her. She'll never forget them.

In a dream you don't hesitate when there is no threat looming, and sensing none, she glides easily into a response. "See what?" she asks. In truth, the stranger's looks are disarming. They certainly help persuade.

He is absolutely splendid.

She can see that. And so is the place he has transported her to.

It's beyond-words spectacular! Unlike any remarkable spot on the planet; it seems, well, out of this world! What she sees exists beyond her own imagination.

"If only I could dream like this every night!" she muses aloud, tingling with excitement.

A sea of grasses stretches to the horizon, surrounding her under the biggest, most beautiful blue sky she has ever seen. Slowly rotating a full three hundred and sixty degrees, she finds the same view in all directions, and far from bland, isolating, or mediocre even, there is something about the colors here that make her feel more alive than she ever has before. They appear deeper and more vibrant than color can be. In fact, here color seems to sing! Can that be? Or is it the wind that produces music?

Water droplets cling to the tops of grassy garnishes, and she thinks she can hear them. They shimmer and vibrate, making the smallest of sounds, stretching the fields to melodious sparkle. When touched by the light, it's as if fistfuls of diamonds that rained down from the sun have been scattered to play. Purple clouds gather themselves together in the distance and move closer. A lovely floral bouquet settles in, and she inhales deeply.

This is some dream! the girl thinks.

Could this be heaven?

Wherever this is, it resonates within the deepest parts of her in a way that feels outside of human ability and certainly apart from what one could reasonably expect from any place on earth. She suddenly feels profoundly connected to something bigger than her own simple imagination.

But where am I?

It could be the Great Plains, but who knows? She couldn't identify grain from grass. She's never been west of the Mississippi, and her aptitude where geography is concerned is lamentably insufficient because she's been lamentably unconcerned about the subject, she realizes. Wherever she now finds herself, she understands an unusual connection to it, as if there is an electrical current running through her and into the soil. As if it is alive and she is a part of it.

As if she always has been.

It doesn't feel like a dream. It feels real. And so otherworldly.

So is the stranger.

"Where are we?" she asks but the stranger only smiles.

There is so much beauty here, all around.

He appears a product of the land. Somewhere in his mid-thirties, his smooth, olive skin looks like it's been painted in a bronze highlighter. His dark, melodious eyes, set the perfect distance apart from one another, appear enhanced with a strange illumination, as if starbursts of purple and gold are in the process of continual explosion in each pupil. In fact, the whole of him seems to glow, and the contrast of snowy white on his head and a well-manicured face against dark, flawless skin makes impossible any hard evidence of experience rooted in time.

His dimpled smile is impossible, too.

He wears a suit of fine, white linen, tailored to a sleek, slim fit. Complemented with leather loafers, he embodies the comfort of class and elegance. Though not in keeping with the current 80s trends in style, it works for him.

She then takes notice of her own attire. No longer in her cotton nightgown, she is wearing her standard baggy blue jeans and a plain white T-shirt.

Suddenly, the atmosphere changes, the air streaming with greater power, Jane's own senses accelerating. It rushes the tops of the waist-high stems surrounding her, pressing her into movement, which causes her toes to curl in her shoes as if she were barefoot in the sand, the tide pulling her out to sea. Fluttering tassels move together like ripples on the ocean, stirring scents of gold, or what she imagines to be the scents of gold if there were scents to be found in precious metals or gems, and shouldn't such treasure smell like jasmine and summer sage?

Bigger still is the sky above, bigger than she can ever remember a sky being, bigger than the land itself, which is big, too, spread out in all directions endlessly. It's turquoise all over now. Could it be growing larger?

Turquoise becomes azure and deepens to plum, emerald softens to yellow, which mellows to gold. This light show is not one she will soon forget.

The extent to which these scents and colors are tied to forever and unseen things she doesn't know; however, she now understands one's senses can be liberated from reality for augmented experience. It's as if life could be encountered in a bigger way on some gigantic, IMAX movie screen set with surround sound to magnification for better focus and enhanced mortal ability.

Is this for real?

Every cell of her being, each little hair on her arms, is swept up in goosebumps that climb the back of her neck. And heart excavation, like the unburying of years of sand over treasure, exposes strange, mystical desires she had previously been unaware of. From the most guarded, secret parts of her an alertness of what exists beyond, and yet within, begins to build.

The supernatural does exist.

She is connected to it. And to this magical place.

The girl, known as Jane, inhales deeply.

And what about this beautiful stranger? He'd been waiting for her. Why?

He's big himself—he must be well over six and a half feet tall and as wide as a linebacker, and once again, she is stunned by what she sees as she dares look at him. She finds him staring at her and returns his gaze, locking eyes with him boldly, her own neck clenching given his great height, but she can't look away. His soul is good. Jane knows this is true, because he seems to wear himself inside out with magnetizing authenticity, and—

Why had I been running to him?

He is still smiling but not mockingly. He appears only patient. And happy.

"Who are you?" she asks.

He doesn't answer but looks off into the distance. Switching tactics, she asks, "Why am I here?" Still nothing.

"I think I'll call you Mac," she decides impulsively. It seems right in a jazzy kind of way. He should have shades on. "Yes, Mac it is," she declares again, as if it matters.

At the same time, Jane is very well aware of the state she's in. If this —whatever this is—is a dream, she doesn't want to wake up.

"Happy birthday," Mac says, interrupting her thoughts. He says this with little inflection.

"Thanks," she answers smoothly, and she wants to ask him how he knows it's her birthday, but she doesn't. Something tells her she already knows how he knows.

"I'm twelve today," she offers, changing her tune, but she does try to say this as maturely as she can. She doesn't want to brag about her birth, but she is giddy for it because she has to claim something big as her own in a world where she feels so very small.

But she doesn't, of course. She does have manners that dictate birthday propriety, even though she's always thought the number 12 was special and that makes her feel special. And now, her golden birthday is like the explosion of the sun contrasted against other astronomical objects.

"I know," he responds without further inhale, and she thinks he must be waiting for her to say more.

"Where are we?" she repeats, this time pausing for his response.

"At the moment, I think it more important we address *why* are we," he replies. Still, without animation.

Still, she waits.

He continues. "Jane, some people must believe without seeing." He turns to the big sky and reaches out his right hand, and it seems the wind isn't the only one with power to change the heavens. The scene before her shifts to a new panorama. Gone is the gigantic sky and the vast plains.

"Believe what?" Jane now repeats, her voice trailing off to a whisper.

This is how Jane finds herself standing on the top of a craggy cliff overlooking an ocean. Overhead, clouds fall from position to disperse and become whitecaps at sea. She watches them transform again, rising into a gray mist that gathers to fall like rain all around. The scents of fresh air, salted and pine-laced, are as lovely as that summer jasmine that had been just out of reach but close enough to inspire, and everything is really, just so —perfect.

Jane awakens with a start and sits up in bed. It's still midnight. Still 12:00 exactly. Her twelfth birthday has arrived, and with it a new beginning. She knows this must be true, because whatever she just dreamed was definitely more than just a dream. It was a birthday gift!

As Jane returns to sleep, in her nightgown once again, she is only mildly aware of her damp hair and salty pillow. As her eyes close, she prays to fall back into that dream again where the world is full of only beautiful things.

Chapter

TWO

CAPE MAY, NEW JERSEY—DECEMBER 1982

"It was just a dream," Jane says to herself the following morning, the day of her twelfth birthday. After all, she's not irrational. Nocturnal wanderings are nothing more than what happens to the human brain powered down, when all sorts of thoughts collide for hidden reflection and imagination runs as if on film reel. On autopilot, the mind is released to float. Like the clouds out to sea, if she wishes.

Floating could cause a person to believe she is salty when she is not.

"It was just a dream, wasn't it?" she asks aloud of no one in particular.

But then that dream happens again. Now, she dreams traveling with Mac regularly. His appearances always involve the land on which they first met, a place vast and great at center stage. Though familiarity has nurtured in Jane an affection for the topography, she still doesn't know where it is specifically, or if it truly exists in her own world. In any case, Mac's visits always involve finding herself there with him, as if it's their home base. Before any subsequent journey can be made, it is from this location they begin, a "Go" space, like in the board game Monopoly, and this seems appropriate when getting out of jail resembles a longing in her own life. Moving forward, each encounter seems to validate the one before it. Each is more real, more vibrant, more liberating.

But how to define the encounters?

Dreams?

It's the best designation she can come up with. Even though they seem more interactive than dreams, and definitely more real; they are more like multi-dimensional experiences than anything else.

So, she can't talk about them.

Instead, she asks her mom for some art supplies, and she gets a few, but she might as well have asked her for cigarettes. Jane's mother wants her to crochet. If Elise is going to make a trip to the craft store, she'd rather pick up purple yarn, she tells Jane.

Nobody in Jane's family is crafty, so this makes absolutely no sense. No doubt crocheting is what proper girls do.

"I want to paint," she tells her mom. "I don't want to crotchet purple flowers. Couldn't I please have a little paint and some canvas so I can tap into my artsy side that way?"

"Wherever did you get such an idea?" her mother responds before asking Jane if she's practiced the piano and completed her math homework. Jane's parents choose her priorities.

As if on cue, Jane's younger sister enters the room. Jess is a snotty ten-year-old, so she adds her own unique commentary whenever she senses an opening for it. "I practiced over an hour today," she proudly announces before turning to Jane to mutter something their mother can't hear but Jane can. "Art is for hippies," Jess hisses sourly before exiting the room.

Why can't the brat just mind her own business?

Naturally, Jane fumes in reaction to the pious antagonism but ends up storming to her room rather than respond to it. She doesn't know why Jess can't be civil. Or truthful, for that matter. She knows Jessica didn't practice the piano. She's a pathological liar. Another one. Her life seems rife with them, considering the possibilities where Mac is concerned.

Could he be pathological, too?

Given Jane's elaborate imagination, maybe she's the pathological one.

Jessica is two years younger than Jane, and that's part of the problem. She seems to detest everything about her older sister, and Jane can't come up with any one plausible reason for her animosity. It's not as if they're competitors. They've completely different interests. They also couldn't be more different in appearance. Jane has wavy, dark hair and brown eyes when she isn't standing in the sun. When the light hits her just right, golden streaks stream through her mane from crown to end like comet tails, while gilded flakes that complement flicker in each pupil. Her skin is light but with olive tones to it, making her far from plain.

Jessica has fair skin with equally captivating, curly, auburn hair, and her green eyes are magnificent, too. But they're hard, like keys to the dark soul. There's even a coldness in her hair, the kind that dulls any heat that might otherwise be felt by the color red. Jane looks like her mother. Jess, like Father.

Jane is introverted in nature, which makes her easy to keep browbeaten. She's first and foremost a self-pleaser, one who's less likely to turn outward for help, but she's also swayed by the opinions of others, and she cares what her parents think. To a degree. Attempting to please unpleasable people is an exercise in futility, but where they're concerned, a part of her tries in spite of her failures.

Jess, on the other hand, takes self-pleasing to a completely different level and when it comes to others—especially family members—she has no desire for affinity. Oddly, that doesn't prevent her from feigning it with their parents, who reserve their hassling for Jane. They are blind to the ways of Jess, and certainly deaf to her lies. Deceit seems to be one of her greatest natural talents.

Again, unreasonableness everywhere.

Jess gets away with everything because she's the younger one. "You're the oldest," Jane's father always tells her. "I expect you to act like it." Which is why Jane is expected to set an example, to be held accountable in every situation. If ever Jane and her sister find themselves in a disagreement or altercation, their father's method of parenting is to focus the blame on one. "It only takes one," he says.

The oldest one.

Duty dictates Jane accepts this responsibility.

It's a lot of pressure, but there is no sense arguing with Father's rigidity. His heart is hard in the soft things. He can't possibly give Jane the affection she craves. This is why she calls him Father. Never Dad. And certainly, never Daddy. Daddies are supposed to love. They don't always blame and find fault.

And they give hugs.

Don't they?

You'd think Jess would be happy about the arrangement which gets her off the hook most days at Jane's expense. Jane always takes the blame for her.

Why can't Jess just be satisfied with that?

And so, indulgence is what has fostered, or perhaps even created, the monster in the house. Jess can do whatever she wants with impunity, and this grows more than one heart cold.

Mercifully, Jane has a pleasant diversion to focus on. One she is compelled to paint. Even if what she puts down in color remains outside her own conscious understanding.

Jane paints what she dreams. Or sees. Or knows—what she's felt beyond her own vision and concurrently understands deep down inside. Images that flash before her closed eyes in vivid color connect her to a world bigger than the one in plain sight. Not just of the Great Plains, but beyond.

The real outside of the real. In past, present, and future shades.

Just because an experience isn't real according to the world's standards doesn't mean it can't live tangibly in front of a person. It doesn't mean the people and circumstances seen and felt haven't been created, are imagination only, even if they do exist outside of time and space.

Neither does it mean they haven't already been drawn and painted before.

Besides, just because something isn't physical doesn't mean it doesn't exist. That what she recreates hasn't happened apart from what she feels compelled to do.

There is so much good to put in color!

More good than bad.

Good that causes her heart to beat with an insatiable desire to retell what she witnesses—what she comes to know personally outside of practical experience. Curiosity evolves into a need which turns into an obsession. She must express what she is witness to, what she lives, onto canvas; she must convey multidimensional realities she has no way of interpreting cognitively, because to hold them in would surely cause her to burst!

And fast. Before it is too late. Before the end of this world makes it impossible to do so.

She has so much good to brush across canvas before then.

Because that is what Mac had said, and sadly, he is the one person who seems more knowledgeable than anyone she knows. He is certainly more present than anyone she knows.

But he says it will all go away one day. He assures her he'll experience it, too.

"After your world comes to an end, I'll be here," Mac says.

"The world is coming to an end?" she'd asked, but he'd only tilted his head to one side.

Now? When?

Not for a really, really long time. Right?

Right?

"It won't be what you think. And Jane, you are far from plain," he says, stunning her further as he changes the subject.

How could he know she believed that?

"And, you have many gifts."

She looks at him quizzically. He gets her. Someone gets her.

So, Mac cultivates curiosity in Jane as if he's hooked her spirit to his narrative, as if every step back she attempts only affirms her connection to him and the places he shows her, as if her soul in shadow elongates, growing thinner and thinner by measure as she struggles for distance, yet remains steadfastly affixed to him all the while.

At any rate, that man has provided three concepts for consideration. First, he *knows* things. Things no one within her current frame of existence could know. Which means he could be right about the end of the world and all that. He could have some insider information.

Second, he's been able to show her things, reaching through her mind about them in her subconscious and while she is awake, too. He no longer waits for her dream states; she no longer calls them dreams. He certainly has extraordinary ability.

And third, these things are understood by her in a way that makes truth innate and the compass of her heart pointed toward it. She knows that she knows. Mac only facilitates.

These things are possible.

Jane is quite the dreamer, after all.

However, a still, small part of her holds out hope for the good truth, for him, despite the odds. Maybe there really is more to this planet than meets the eye. Much more. Perhaps her teacher was right when she suggested H.G. Wells was on to something when he wrote about the fourth dimension in *The Time Machine*, and perhaps Albert Einstein figured out more about relativity than he revealed when his theory broke new ground. It's likely we will never know the mystery of gravity this side of eternity, yet maybe there are some mysteries a few of us could be let in on, too. And maybe, just maybe, there is someone outside of what anchors us here who knows the truth of all of this. And wants to help.

Him, for example. Mac. And something makes Jane want to delight in the possibility of it all.

Maybe there *is* something more real than me outside of me, she thinks.

And maybe, just maybe, there is something I am supposed to do because of it.

At least there is power in this conflict. Because believing in possibility is infinitely better than staying anchored in reality. A family who doesn't see her world or even value her existence in it underscores this.

And so, she does the only thing she knows to do and something she didn't know she could. She paints.

She doesn't share her experiences with anyone; it's as if she is living two completely different lives. One in this world and the other, well, somewhere else.

With Mac, an ever-present tour guide.

It will be years before he no longer seems strange. Years before there is validation in all he has said.

Years before she will understand the significance of her own work.

And years before she will find the mysterious portrait of herself, painted by another hand in another time, long before her birth, that will tie everything together.

In the meanwhile, the only truth that exists in her present world is what is transferred to canvas.

Though she has no way to define it presently, promise is what clings to brushes dipped in colorful paints.

Chapter Three

THE PLAINS OF KANSAS—1804

It's a beautiful creation.

There is something about that land, something extraordinary that has existed from the moment it was formed and time began, fresh and new. It was made with purpose, and the people for whom it was intended recognize this. The people for whom it wasn't have felt this, too.

Mostly.

Whether passing through or experiencing it from afar, as in Jane's case, there is something that testifies to the unusual here, and even the hardest of human hearts knows this instinctively. From the beginning of things, neither the Great Flood nor any other distress to the land has changed this perspective.

The Land, then, exists in reality. In time past, present, and in the future, as if evidence of greater things to come, a glimpse of the impossible beyond the possible. This understanding stretches out for great distances under the sun and infinite, star-brushed sky.

This is true even now, before the soil has been formally claimed.

Because in the nineteenth century, as in all centuries, though humans have not yet staked their claim officially, the mighty and the minor have used this land. Presently, buffalo thunder through unrestrained, and wolves run in great packs unfettered, while things that crawl along the ground shift about freely, and the ones that take to the air roam loose above it, too. And sometimes the skies are dusty and full of menace, and sometimes the soils are soaked in blood and full of sorrow. Sometimes, the weather cycles with the hardened hearts of men. When great currents race across the great land to crush all in the way, and when great winds coil into instruments of destruction and the balance of great power on the Great Plains seems tilted away from humankind, the fight to survive is a part of this legacy.

But humans are mostly good and tenacious, designed to fight with grit, to delight in righting scales for posterity. They were meant to triumph on land loaned them and to know peace there, each generation imparting encouragement to the next, passing baskets of hope like warm bread and sweet jam distributed to hungry people at a cold dinner table.

And so, The Land is a place worth sharing, though it seems impossible at times to do so adequately, and promise is something inside and outside of time.

On July 2nd in the year 1804, men whose names will become known across a planet sit around a campfire here, feeling the depth of nature. The visitors are Lewis and Clark and their company, and they've met with the local people, the Kansa. These humans record the splendidness of The Land and its people in their journals, including mention of a grove of pecan trees and great quantities of raspberries, but they don't write about the large tree in the middle of the prairie that stands alone. They pass by it and wonder at its particular majesty, the way it flourishes here and the way it makes them feel, just a few years before a little girl named Running Feet will enter the world to ultimately find it.

It is the first time observations of this nature are recorded in print and not just handed down by word of mouth in this place.

Unbeknownst to those who live and visit in this time, there are others who know this spot of earth, too, including another girl from an unfathomable distance. From far away in a different time and place, Jane witnesses it in pieces and delights in each of them, though she can't say why. All she knows is how The Land makes her feel as it is revealed to her, and what she feels is only good.

In the beginning.

Naturally, she understands there is always the other side of things, though she hasn't yet come to terms with the imbalance of it. She hasn't yet known firsthand the struggle.

For now, Jane is content to witness the wonder of it, pondering her own connection here. Believing she must be the only one in the world to love it so.

Chapter
Four

CAPE MAY, NEW JERSEY—1987

Jane Campbell, now seventeen, has always been a dreamer.

As a kid, she envisioned herself in impossible scenarios and ever-changing scenes which, in her own opinion, far exceeded anything Hollywood could drum up. She was a superhero and a philanthropist, a remarkable athlete and scholar. For example, by the time she was twelve, her fancy had earned her the gold medal in women's figure skating with triple jumps no other competitor could come close to (quadruples would come later), and the top honor in the National Spelling Bee contest by spelling the word *staphylococci*. She had also soared to the top of Country Billboard charts with a hit single about an emblazoned saddle worn by a horse named Diamond. She had a beautiful voice. Her family was proud of her.

By the time Jane reached her teenaged years, her imagination had won her the discovery of a cure for diabetes, a Pulitzer Prize in both fiction and non-fiction, the nightly network news anchor position on all three channels (at various times, of course), and an Oscar for best actress in a hit box office film—one where the heroine courageously saves humanity from itself. Imagining herself as Jane next to Tarzan is as easy as waking up each morning. As easy as believing her family believes in her.

She now also believes what she experiences outside of real life might be more exciting than all of those things.

Reality hasn't been kind to Jane. Or maybe she really hasn't been kind to herself. Perhaps she's been content with fantasies. Not only does she have hard-hearted parents and an icy sister to thank for this, the bullies at her elementary school too—the ones who never invited Jane to their get-togethers, the ones who were much too popular for Plain Jane. They planted and watered the seeds that eventually grew the jungle cords from which she swings, if not the tight cords she balances on.

It's possible she needs to move beyond pretending to vision, which shouldn't suffer loss at the expense of fantasy.

Enter Mac.

She can't seem to break the connection! Not that she has an inclination to.

Some of what he reveals seems familiar, as if he's scraped inside the deepest parts of her to release what's innate, what was there all along.

Especially where The Land is concerned.

Naturally, she continues to paint it, and this desire grows with each day, for most of what she recreates allows her to escape there whenever she wants to. It's her own magic wardrobe of sorts, a sanctuary like the one C.S. Lewis wrote about.

Interestingly, as the visits with Mac increase, Jane's fantasies decrease. They just aren't as useful anymore. Neither can they compare. Besides, in Jane's wild imaginings, she had always been the star of the show. Now, a shift in focus. A lack of attention from the people in her own life doesn't present the problem it once did.

There is so much more beyond herself.

Her parents are as unaware of Jane's other life as they'd been of her fantasies, and certainly, her younger sister is, too. Not that Jane has been inclined to mention what could indeed be fantasies grown bigger. No, she can't breathe a word. Not even with her best friend, Sam. Mac prefers it that way, and she respects his reasoning. "There will come a time for it," he said, on the few occasions she attempted to broach the subject of sharing.

He can be a little difficult at times.

It's been a five-year balancing act, keeping Mac her little secret; a seesaw seventeen-year-old Jane stands on with feet spread wide between her present reality and whatever exists outside of it.

So, she continues to paint what she sees, the supernatural attached to canvas. It's one way to channel pent-up energy into relief for safe exposure, great therapy for what she can't talk about. Which is pretty much everything.

She believes she's getting fairly good at painting, but what does she know?

She's never been outstanding at anything, so maybe she doesn't know.

School is droll, the teachers uninteresting, and her fellow students even less captivating, but she does try hard to learn and sometimes to connect with people, which is about as easy as walking out on the end of an unstable tree limb high off the ground. Hundreds of feet up.

Fortunately, there is Samantha. There is common ground between them. Neither girl is active enough to be popular, pretty enough to be a threat, or exceptional enough to get noticed, so they slip right through cracks to be left alone. In short, Jane and Sam are as content as a couple of plain juniors enduring life can be. At school, at least. Sam's parents leave her alone. Jane's do not.

Jane's parents are demanding from their arm's length position, a contrast noted from a general mode of detached operation.

"Have you thought anymore about your future?" Father asks one night at the dinner table. At the other end, Jess, a freshman living a double life herself, if the rumors Jane hears at school are true, casts a hateful glance Jane's way and rolls her eyes.

What is *her problem?*

"Of course," Jess intrudes enthusiastically. Father had been addressing Jane specifically, and they all knew it.

Good grief, it's not as if Jane is in her sister's way. Jess hangs with a totally different crowd. The wrong one, in Jane's opinion, though what does she care? She doesn't give a crap about cheerleading, or the Tanda's club, or championing any of Jess's weird causes, like TAVA, Teens Against Video Arcades. Jess is entitled to live her life, and as far as Jane is concerned, more power to her. Jane just wants to live hers, and she doesn't want to pretend she's somebody she isn't while she does.

Except in her own mind.

Jess, who is all about pomposity at home, is a completely different human away from the house. The only commonality between the sisters is their living of dual lives.

Outside of the occasional attention of Everett and Elise Campbell, Jess is the poster child of rebellion. Inside the perimeter of home, she plays the game of industrious student and familial conformist. For reasons Jane can't fathom, Jess placates Father with assurances she'll follow in his illustrious career footsteps, something Jane doesn't believe for a minute. And maybe Father doesn't either, what with his uncharacteristic razor focus on Jane's future career; he is completely uninterested in any other aspects of her existence. If he believed Jess, you'd think he'd be content with one civil engineer in the family willing to take over the family business.

But engineering is engineering. To Father's mind, the only lucrative career in a pedestrian world. His offspring must pursue the same career path to be deemed worthy.

Fat chance of that happening.

For either of us.

The fact that Jane also has zero interest in law school (a white-collar second for eligible career choices and one her mother excels in) is further cause for consternation. Neither of her parents appreciate indecision against mediocrity. They allege they knew what they wanted to do with their lives about the time they landed in middle school. Modest was never part of the vernacular.

But Jane has also known since about her twelfth birthday what she wanted to do. She just can't share it with them to any satisfaction. What she really wants to do is paint. She'd settle for graphic design even!

They know she's an aspiring artist, especially when art supplies have been on every birthday and Christmas list for the last five years. Sure, they were surprised she showed such a knack for it, not that they'd admit it. When the requests became persistent, they couldn't help but comply. Marginally. Much to her family's dismay, Jane didn't lose interest.

But one doesn't make a living from art.

Art is for the eclectic, the wanderers. It isn't for the intellectually gifted, by any means, and it certainly isn't what the teenaged daughter of an elite (to their minds) East Coast family does for a living.

Why use one's hands when the mind is so much more profitable?

"Well?" her father demands, looking Jane's direction as she shovels another bite of food into her mouth, navigating the end of a large piece of iceberg lettuce failing to clear her lips. She finishes chewing and quickly swallows to respond, feeling heat rise up her neck and into her face. Couldn't they just react to Jess' interjection?

Looking down, she stabs another piece of lettuce heavily laced in Caesar dressing while considering an appropriate response. "Father, we've talked about this. I don't know yet."

"You need to be giving this some serious thought. And now," he booms, his voice louder than usual. He picks up his glass and takes a long pull of amber liquid without taking his eyes off Jane. She knows this without having to glance up herself.

"But why? Why do I have to know right now? There is plenty of time to decide," she pleads as she continues to eye her plate. She moves her food around with her fork.

Her mother cuts in. Always rushing to support Father. "There really isn't. You should be getting test scores back any time now, and planning your educational future needs to happen in this junior year if you are to get into a good school."

"Define good school."

"Jane!" Father roars, slamming his drained glass down on the table. "A healthy future depends on a reputable school, something you must think about!"

She's long past weighing her responses now. "I suppose that would be true if I wanted to be a surgeon, a corporate lawyer, or God forbid, a civil engineer. But I'm heading in a different direction than you two," Jane replies, evenly at first, hearing her own voice gaining volume with each syllable. She hadn't meant to give her hand away just yet, but the timing of an empty cocktail glass on the other end of the table is motivation.

There's no time like the present.

She'd been honest when she'd said she hadn't given it some serious thought, but now that her words have slipped out with the flow of whiskey, vocalized to collide with her brain like a morning hangover, she's forced to concede, to herself as much as to them, what she's known all along.

She wants to paint. She can't think of anything she'd rather do.

She doesn't want to go to college. And really, this should be no surprise to anyone. A bedroom closet full of sketches and paintings in all mediums should have been evidence enough of her trajectory. Not that anyone in this house has ever really taken notice of them. They've been relegated to the back of her closet for years now.

She's done everything else they've asked of her. She's been a model daughter! Okay, so maybe she didn't practice the piano as often as she should have.

And she never crocheted any purple flowers.

An affected chuckle from the end of the table causes Jane to glance at her sister, who shakes her head in exaggerated disbelief. Angrily, Jane looks away. Jess' effort is pointless. She doesn't need to remind. She's already won.

Thank you, Judge Jessica.

But it's not a contest! For Jane anyway. She doesn't care to compete. She's not focused on what happens here. Even when *here* seems terribly unfair and in favor of others. Oh, Jane knows life is unfair, but it seems as though it's more so inside her own home.

Her parents take injustice to a whole new level.

Take, for example, the dog. She'd begged her parents for one. Jane wanted a dog so badly she'd practically cried her heart out over it. She'd go to sleep thinking of it, and behind closed lids, she'd loved it. That German Shepherd always bounded straight for her, tail wagging, tongue rolled to one side, ears up at points to the sky. Where that dog lived, fields were green and dandelion parachutes floated aimlessly by the millions. Oh, to be so carefree!

"Absolutely not!" her mother had said. "We are not going to have a dog in this house. I won't hear another word on it."

Not a week later, Jane's sister brought a dog into the house. She had marched him into her bedroom and lodged him there. She'd named the bulldog Bud for Budweiser, much to their parents' blissful ignorance. And then she'd gotten a calico cat for her bedroom, too. The one she called Coke. How charming. How she convinced their parents this was acceptable

Jane could only guess. When Jess had tired of them, the animals had vanished as fast as they'd appeared.

Though Jess pretends at home to be the model daughter with noteworthy school activities to persuade and grades that are good enough to act as subterfuge against an opposing narrative, the real Jess includes smoking weed behind the local 7-Eleven and going to raging parties in no short supply at homes absented by constantly traveling parents. Even trips to the arcade at the mall to participate in an activity she has vocally protested.

Maybe the parents are on to Jess. Maybe they care, a little. Or maybe after all the energy they've expelled on expectations for their eldest child, they don't. Maybe their very little real interest, which seems to be rapidly dissipating, university discussions notwithstanding, has left them little ability to parent their youngest. Jane is used to it now. What else can she do but let it roll off her back? The less mental space she relinquishes, the more space she has for the things that matter.

The Jersey Shore is Jane's favorite place in her own world, especially during the summer when she can escape to soak up the sun. Today, as she pretends to snooze with Sam by her side, Jane can't help but reflect upon the previous night's dinner experience. She'd managed to maneuver her way out of the uncomfortable conversation regarding her future, but she knows it's only a matter of time before it rears its ugly head again.

Her parents are not people who give up easily. Or at all, for that matter. Things are going to get real, Jane thinks. Realer, and it just stinks. Why couldn't she have been born to a different family? Why did everyone around her have to be so difficult?

Why couldn't The Land on the prairie she loves so much be hers, even for just a short while? Perhaps one day she'll figure out how to go there. Perhaps she won't leave.

But for now, Cape May is wonderful, too. Even with the seasonal heat, she's always loved the seashore. Her hometown is fantastic all the year through but especially in late spring and summer when it comes alive. Until unusual adventures pervaded her real world, she'd been determined few places existed lovelier than the Atlantic shore with its new and renovated Victorian architecture.

Enchanting delineation highlights storefronts with unique window displays, including surf shops and touristy trinket offerings, candy stores, and ice cream parlors, and the most wonderful pier on the shore's first boardwalk.

"Let's meet early for a coffee and a scone," Sam had suggested. They spend most Saturday mornings at the beach together.

This morning, behind the large front windows paned in white, their favorite boardwalk bakery boasts a gigantic loaf of bread in the form of an old, masted ship.

"However do they do that?" she'd wondered aloud.

"Magic," Sam had replied casually, not giving the display another thought as she pushed open the front door to release an explosion of mouth-watering aromas.

"Maybe," Jane said, inhaling deeply as she followed her friend inside. "Because everything here tastes as good as it looks."

"Worth a few minutes longer at the gym later," Sam said over her shoulder, though Sam always seems to have a million reasons for avoiding exercise.

A few minutes later, the girls had walked out of the store with the best lemon scones on the planet, and as Jane trailed her friend to their usual spot on the sand, she had magic on her mind.

What is magic, exactly?

Now comfortably positioned on her beach towel, she considers this as she admires her surroundings. Always intrigued with architecture, homes in the surrounding residential area come alive again to Jane. They boast enticing finishes with lacy turrets decorating a coast frosted to her mind like icing on an exquisite wedding cake or the sand castles she used to create when she was a kid with wet sand dribbled down from small fingers in steepled patterns along molded walls.

As always, there are plenty of tourists out sunbathing and strolling, and this life, really, could be so very nice, the Jersey Shore a fine place to live.

If.

And yet, the sand itself seems a friend that begs to touch, to embrace every inch of skin with a blanket of tiny pebbles before the vying sun can stake too much claim, the salty moisture sticky in affection. And just when Jane begins to take greater notice of the sand she has, indeed, painted herself in, as well as her friend's quick escape into a midday nap beside her, a sudden rush of fragrances alerts her of an impending change. Or is it the hot oil and sweet sugar from somewhere close by she detects? No, scents of wild sumac and jasmine float her way, a signal the shift is coming.

Mac is more persistent now. He doesn't wait until cover of night to show up, squeezing himself in between her dreams like a movie trailer for attention. As on so many other occasions, he has no need to dialogue either, and this is fine by Jane, now familiar with his ways.

He's brought his own background along with him again—one that overpowers the shore and all around her. Or could it be that she is the one who has moved? Regardless, Jane knows she has no risk of exposure. In the blink of an eye, she's standing by his side in tall grass.

Mutual affection is comfortable, and she smiles. Honestly, her own neediness is understood by the both of them. A family like Jane's underscores Mac's faithfulness and he visits at least once a week now.

She finds herself standing on a plain that stretches out to the horizon, with long prairie grasses dancing as if on toes, a million white flowers materializing to bob like gulls on a moving sea.

Now this is magic.

Detached from disappointment to stand where the prairie is tall and the sky big and personal, is restorative. How long she is away is immaterial. When she returns, no time will have passed in the present, though her heart will have grown by centuries.

I can take my time.

And yet, speaking of time, it's never truly hers, because if it were, she'd be in charge of scheduling.

Mac's timing is sort of a drag.

Does he have to show up with a view to the other side whenever *he* pleases? When the world is lovely here, and unpleasant things are packed away and sitting at that stifling dinner table at home?

Mildly irritated, Jane thinks Mac has no consideration for her schedule.

In the distance, the sound of a far-off train whistle sounds, taking her back in time. She feels the air around her turn chilly, and she shivers, folding her arms into her chest to create warmth. Sweet summer scents give way again, this time to the earthy smells of autumn, aromatic and spicy.

The Great Plains fade to a forest where the scents of a wood fire burning are evident. She sees a plume of smoke come into view just beyond a gathering of pine trees. It moves skyward before reaching a plateau, then rolls flat into a blue background rapidly fading to gray.

No longer in a swimsuit, she pulls an open cargo jacket together in the front and zips it closed as she begins to walk to the top of a small hill. Her feet are in warm, woolen socks and boots, laced up.

"Helpful," she mutters, taking note of the appropriate provisions. Just when she's about to reach the top of the crest to find the source of the smoke, Jane finds herself back in the baking New Jersey sun, the sound of waves crashing on the shore, the scents of summer restored. The jacket, socks, and boots are gone.

Well, that was productive.

"Thanks?" she calls out questioningly to Mac, but he's already gone.

She looks over to Sam's fluttering eyelids and lifeless form and thanks the heavens, or fate, or whatever might be on her side, which given her life is very little, for her friend's still-slumbering state.

Despite Mac's unpredictability and apparent disregard for Jane's perfect timing, his visits are proof someone actually gives a real crap about her. And they are proof that senses can sometimes overrule sensibility. Maybe that's the real magic.

Sitting now, Jane begins to dust the sand off her arms but the tanning oil she's slathered all over herself makes it nearly impossible. It clings to her like Mac, she thinks, amused. Or is it the other way around now?

Giving up on the sand battle, she hugs her knees up to her chest, watching the waves roll in off the shore. She allows them to hold her captive for a moment.

The rhythmic sounds never fail to impress, and she thinks there isn't anything more balancing than the sound of water rolling over itself to break and re-group, and maybe that's because the human body consists mostly of water, and aren't we constantly doing the same—breaking and tumbling over ourselves only to regroup and build strength to repeat the process? Maybe that's why the shore feels so hypnotic, so much a part of herself, as if it's her own heartbeat outside of her chest.

It's like the vastness of the prairie, it occurs to Jane. There, thousands of miles away, exists another sea of sorts, where she feels a connection in a different way. If only she could process this with someone!

What if I'm not mentally well?

What if Mac is a figment of my overactive imagination?

Worse, what if he is real?

Chapter
Five

CAPE MAY, NEW JERSEY—1987

Things are going from bad to worse at home.

Jane's father and mother seem completely checked out emotionally. Then, there is her hostile sister. Jess' constant antagonism and sucking up to disinterested parents wears on Jane's last nerve.

For the love, Jess doesn't need to continue to fight with Jane for superiority.

What she doesn't know, what Jane won't admit, is that Jane already feels inferior. She's always felt inferior.

So it goes that several weeks after Jess' rumor that Jane has no interest in boys, a conviction needing no proof in an environment that happily sucks up such gossip to blow with the winds that will carry it, Jane finds herself without a date for her senior prom. She's disappointed. Heartbroken, even. Alex, Jane's crush and the cute boy she was hoping would ask her to the dance (and so much more) won't look at her now, and worse, even Sam is keeping her distance. How *could* she?

Okay, she thinks, if Jess wants a fight, she'll get one. Jane thinks of dozens of ways to get back at her sister, dozens of ways to punish her, for she deserves it! No more complacency! However, nothing comes to mind that Jane doesn't already regret considering. She just can't.

What's wrong with me? I should be a better fighter. I should be more conniving. I should be more—normal.

Jane knows she isn't a perfect sister, but she's never done anything to encourage such sibling rivalry. Except, perhaps, to effect detachment.

And to be born first. She wishes that part weren't true, that she could have allowed Jess the elder perspective, if it would have helped. Jane isn't looking back, only forward! Furthermore, if only Jess knew how plain Jane really feels, she wouldn't bother with all the competition nonsense. Plain isn't just a label Jane's believed; it's one she has fully embraced.

But she swallows the knot of fury she feels in her throat and works to make things right. "I'm sorry for whatever I've done," she says. "We're sisters. Couldn't we at least try to be friends?"

"Why bother?" Jess snaps.

"Why do you hate me so?" Jane affects a calmness she doesn't feel, forcing back tears.

"You know!" Jess snaps.

"Why did you start the rumor about me?" Jane redirects, praying Jess will deny it.

She doesn't.

How could she be so cruel?

"I hate you!" Jess shouts before slamming her bedroom door, anger still floating the distance between them.

Jane's heart falls. Jess isn't her favorite person, but her response stings. Jane had put herself out there! *Way* out there. She should have known it wouldn't work. She should have dealt with this the way her sister would have!

However, when an opportunity presents itself one afternoon soon after that, retribution is the last thing on Jane's mind.

Jane slams her locker shut after school when, as she turns to leave an already empty hall, she finds Pete quietly standing behind her. She recognizes Pete as the guy Jess is currently dating, but Jane has never actually seen him up close. Now, proximity does him no favor.

What a creep.

He's about a year younger than Jane and a year older than Jess, and the fact that Jess would give him a second look is unbelievable.

Pete is tall, lanky, and unattractive. Highly unattractive. And unwashed. He wastes no time in sidling up beside her. In fact, he is so close, he is nearly on top of her in a moment. This would be troubling enough even if he didn't smell feral.

Gross.

Thrusting his face toward her, Jane notices a prominently placed pimple trying to break the skin on his blotchy, white chin, but it's less threatening than his unnatural, greasy black hair and the wrinkly black T-shirt he wears to match. On the front is an ironed-on picture of Gene Simmons with his tongue hanging out of his mouth. The lead singer of KISS looks as demonic as Pete to Jane. She shudders. There is something dark there.

If Jane were Jess, she'd turn on all the charm now. Make her sister crazy with jealously. Instead, feigning nonchalance, she attempts to step around him. "What can I do for you Pete?" she asks impatiently.

"So, you know who I am," he says, pretending coolness himself. But something in the air makes Jess feel as though the atmospheric pressure around her has dropped significantly, and this causes her stomach to tighten. There is no way Jane could ever pretend to be interested in this.

Putting aside all thoughts but the ones that will allow her to remove herself from the situation—and fast—Jane's mind races toward flight, her heart rate accelerating as she realizes the difficulty of gracefully making this happen. The hum of traffic and the twitter of a few birds sound off in the distance.

Sensing her hesitation, he moves in closer. He places a forearm above her head, pining her up against the locker with his chest. She attempts to push back, but he only leans in harder, bringing his other arm up to her left side. The locker latch is now digging into her back and she begins to panic, losing the grip on her books, which manage to slide down the confined space to the ground as she wriggles to get free.

Pete snickers. He's a few inches taller than Jane, and though he presents no hard evidence of a commitment to athletics, his chest feels like concrete cinder blocks pressed up against her own, his arms like a vice grip against her. She tries to turn her head to one side, but with little room for movement, she only succeeds in panicking. Pushing up on her tiptoes and feeling faint, she attempts to look beyond his right shoulder.

Is anyone else around? Is anyone seeing this?

"Let me go!" she hisses.

Where is everyone? How could they have disappeared so quickly after the last class period?

She'd only stopped by the library to pick up a couple of books before heading straight here. Her fellow classmates obviously didn't mess around when it came to fleeing campus on a Friday afternoon.

Impervious, Pete presses in, his mouth hot and up against her ear. "Not a chance," he whispers.

"I mean it. Get back!" Jane yells in the closed space between them.

"I wanted to see if it was true," he says menacingly and without slackening his position. The combination of his foul breath and moldy clothing makes her think she will vomit.

What a catch, Jess.

"What's true?" she asks, attempting to distract him. Managing to twist her head in the opposite direction, she frantically searches for fresh air as he places a knee between her legs.

This can't be happening!

"That you aren't into men. Just had to see for myself," he says, tearing the top of her blouse open. He forces an angry kiss on her mouth.

A variety of emotions rush Jane, but her presence of mind screams, *You are my sister's boyfriend!*

How could you?

How could she?

She attempts a scream from her covered mouth, but suddenly Pete pulls away, evidently satisfied with himself. He leaves quickly without another word or look over his shoulder as Jane quickly gathers her fallen things. When she thinks of his mouth on hers, she spits on the ground. When she considers how un-ladylike this is, she nearly laughs out loud. What irony.

Inwardly shaking, and pretending her limbs don't feel like jelly, she presses her books against her chest to conceal the state of her blouse and sprints to the student parking lot. Fortunately, she doesn't run into anyone along the way.

She manages find her keys in her bamboo handbag quickly and to insert the correct one into the lock of her Honda Prelude. Still trembling, she falls into her seat and starts the engine, accelerating out of the lot before yanking the door fully closed. There still isn't a soul in sight.

How can that be? There are a thousand students in the senior high class alone. Not all of them should have disappeared from sight.

As she drives home, she replays what has just happened in her mind. Should she tell someone? Would anyone even believe her? There were no witnesses. And how on earth could she even begin to talk with her sister about this? That would almost be easier than having to discuss the matter with her parents.

She could certainly get back at Jess now, clue her in about what her cringy boyfriend is capable of. At the very least, warn her. In Jane's favor, there would be some humiliation attached to it. In Jess' favor, Jane can't do it.

Jess would never believe her! And God knows what she'd do in retribution. No. Things could only get worse. And besides, she'd have to admit her own weakness. Especially to herself.

Once again, Jane vows to keep what she knows hidden.

Jane assumes Jess is unaware of what happened with Pete when, after two weeks, Jessica hasn't said a word about it. And Jessica definitely would have had a word on the matter if there was one to be had.

That didn't mean, however, time had been given over to Jane as something in her favor, even if she had decided to move forward with exposure, which she is decidedly determined not to do. Where her sister is concerned, risk assessment dictates she remain silent. So does trauma.

Real time never seems to be in Jane's favor! Because real time should have allowed petty differences to pass, should have afforded opportunity for any friction to float like water under a bridge, but the only thing floating had been Jane's homework, found drifting in the family swimming pool. Along with her favorite leather Nine West boots. Actually, those had sunk. She'd saved a year for those boots.

How *could* she?

Mac never addresses the Pete incident with her, assuming he knows. He hasn't broached the Jess situation, either, and why would he? Though the years between them seem bonding, and there is nothing they shouldn't be able to discuss, family is off-limits. Come to think of it, all things are. Everything in reality, anyway.

Except the end of things. There is that. But for now, it's only on the way, off in the distance somewhere.

The present is an arrangement she understands in implication. What Mac shows her, what they discuss, isn't so narrow in scope as to allow focus on her personal life.

And so, later when Mac pays her a long-overdue visit, Jane doesn't bring up the subject. She is much more concerned with the fact that it has been weeks since she has seen him, and this delay is mildly infuriating. Mac never really adheres to any precise structure, so she can't fault him for not ministering to her sooner. It's just without the support of her parents or sibling to connect with, Jane is becoming more dependent upon his visits, and he'd been pretty regular before this.

Perhaps she's retreating into a place that isn't safe at all.

"Where have you been?" she begins, but stops herself.

I needed you.

She vows to let the situation with her sister go as well. And the one concerning the loss of her friend Sam, too. How could Sam have betrayed her like that? She'd been her only true friend! The fact that Sam has dismissed her so easily, and especially since she knew how deceptive Jess can be, shows false what Jane had believed true.

How easy it is to be deceived.

"Mac," she begins, but holds herself back again.

"Yes, love?" He says this tenderly.

Oh, goodness, he's never called me that before.

Startled by the term of endearment and his softened tone, the best she can come up with in the moment is the easiest truth on the tip of her tongue. "I'm glad you are my friend."

"Sweet friendships refresh the soul and lighten the heart," he responds, smiling at her in a way that makes her forget about the other stuff.

It has been six years, or half of twelve, that Mac has been unveiling other worlds to her, and never have they been anything but magnificent and supremely joyful. However, those scenes are beginning to change ever so slightly, as if they are being tweaked for accuracy, and Jane wonders if that's because she is changing, too. Is she now observing things differently?

Or is she being *shown* things differently because she is now ready for new information?

Jane picks up heavenly scents on the breeze, floral and herbal bouquets that have her feeling giggly all of sudden. Mac always seems to thin the air on his approach, as if a lightening of the atmosphere could pave the way for splendid revelation.

If only life could be like this all the time.

It isn't that she's lost the childlike optimism of her more youthful years, or now that her eighteenth birthday is here, her impending status as an official adult robs her of any of her extraordinary creativity. To the contrary, with each passing year, Jane feels she has come to greater understanding, honing an adept ability to distinguish between what is illusory and what is veritable. Her ability to dream with eyes wide open means imagination is never as exciting as the reality of keeping one foot in two worlds. One a place of mediocracy where no one gives a care, unless you count Jess' weird competitiveness, the other a place that gives her a feeling of importance, if only as an observer.

One scientific. One supernatural.

The Land is such a place.

Why does it matter? What's so special about a piece of land out in the middle of nowhere that may not even exist?

Will I ever have true understanding about this?

Mac has never suggested the slightest significance beyond experience, and it would do no good to question him anyway, but maybe she doesn't need to know in the present. Maybe she's not supposed to know; maybe she doesn't want to know. Why risk what works in blissful ignorance?

The dreams or visits or whatever they are must be taken for what they are. Enjoyment. Entertainment. Escape. For the time being.

But could what appears absolute also be arcane? It's the unanswered question she lives with. Definitively, anyway. Back and forth she goes, her thoughts vacillating like a ping-pong ball in volley.

It shouldn't be a surprise then that the scenes aren't static. With an expanding friendship comes expanding perspective.

And so, The House.

It appears out of nowhere to sit atop a hill on the beautiful land she's come to love.

It's magical, of course. Why wouldn't it be, given the allure of the land beneath it? Where the bluestem grows tall and runs to the sky sits an old, white clapboard house seasoned by a hundred years. She can smell the wildflowers that surround it.

"Wow," is all she can come up with.

"Yes," Mac replies and she can see that he, too, is admiring the structure.

The porch is wide, supported by four thick, white columns and graced with several white stairs that span the width of it. The front door is red and supported in symmetrical design by four floor-to-ceiling paned windows. The home's roof is red and decorated with two red brick chimneys at either end, east and west, and positioned right in the middle is one, lone gabled window paned in a white A-frame pointing to the sky. Two large oak trees grow on each side.

There is something unusual about this house, something that calls to her spirit. Such an impressive home *would* be on her dear land!

"I love it!" Jane exclaims.

"I knew you would," Mac says.

It isn't as if the home boasts extraordinary wealth or stateliness. It's old and out of date, especially to a 1980s post-modernist perspective. But its character is timeless! A unique landmark of triumph across generations, it seems a testimony to years of wisdom, the keeper of secrets. From the moment Jane lays eyes on it, she knows immediately this is true. She also knows if she never sees it again, its impression will last a lifetime. Just one look is all it takes.

She feels as if she knows this home already. She's been here before, and yet, this is the first time she's seen it. It's nothing like the homes she's known in New Jersey.

Blankets of emerald green covered in golden tassels surround the old home for what seems like miles. Beyond that is only sky. A big, cloudless, Aegean Sea sky. Which is why she can already see it on canvas. The House, whitewashed against its surroundings, bold reds to provide added contrast, blue to make the heart sing.

"I'll paint it."

"Yes," Mac replies. "Of course."

Jane has always loved old houses, as if each distinctive structure could have a life of its own, each one a memory holder in wood, brick, glass, and paint, with bones and skin and blood. Flooring and walls and roofs safeguarding stories, clothing generations, keeping the flow of time.

Yes, indeed, she can see it painted! The House. Her house. For it belongs to her, Jane reasons. And when she finishes recreating it the first time, it looks like the real thing. As good as a photograph, as good as any master's painting to Jane's mind, and she wonders how that's possible. She'd no talent that she'd been aware of before picking up a brush, but her ability seems to grow by leaps and bounds as the years pass. Now, she sees she's rather good, and this is rather surprising.

Finally, Plain Jane is good at something!

In bits and pieces, she transfers the colors to canvas: the long green grasses with golden tassels, the pink clouds held in the light of an early sun. The white coverlets and multi-hued buds and blossoms, brand new all over again. The tree patrols, east and west, and the big custodian that stands apart, as well as the wings that alight there, tens of thousands of them soaring in and out of the wind, brilliant calligraphy unleashed in great swirls and kite tails.

Oh, the vast lexicon revealed through nature!

Now, more! A house to take it all in! One grand masterpiece, and then the rest in portions to savor, too.

She may be overly sentimental, but she channels all the energy she once devoted to imagination and uses it to transfer what she actually sees. The chimneys and the stairs that climb the wide porch, and the front door, thick and hand carved. One lone window. A solitary brick or board or hinge. A collection of stenciled branches, the ones that tickle the house while scratching the skies.

She paints all of the pieces, as if each one is as important as the whole, but she doesn't paint the people inside. She hasn't seen them and won't imagine them. It's part of the mystery. They're like her own family, present but not.

Her renderings stack up in her closet, a collection for another day. But of all she has painted, she only does one complete reproduction of The House. She can't say why she only replicates it in its entirety once, but it's as if to attempt such a task more than that would be akin to trying to paint another Mona Lisa when there can only be one. One is significantly enough.

Which is why she is absolutely devastated when it goes missing.

Chapter
Six

CAPE MAY, NEW JERSEY—1989

Initially, Jane believed community college might pacify her parents. It hasn't. Higher education doesn't count unless it has the word *university* in the title.

A four-year plan was out of the question, however. Jane wasn't keen on furthering her education beyond obligation; she decided upon her current arrangement out of necessity. She figured a degree in graphic design would be a compromise they could all settle on because, unfortunately, she hadn't mastered the upper-level math necessary for excelling in architecture.

Or engineering.

There's no use in lamenting the past. Besides, she really just wants to paint landscapes, not draw houses or buildings.

And who knows? Maybe there is a promising future for the art-minded. There are rumblings design could soon go digital—whatever that means—and though it has something to do with a computer and it's nearly impossible to process how drawing and illustration might look on one, it's helpful to think of the future this way.

For electives, Jane takes classes in art history, which she devours, and especially a class highlighting drawing, painting, and sculpture from pre-gothic times to the Renaissance. The Renaissance! What an exciting time that was for celebrating talent! The Old Masters were something else.

What did Raphael's parents think about their son's work? He was so young when he died, he didn't have much time to prove himself. What might those painters and patrons think of her own art?

Probably not much.

She vows to go to Florence, Italy, one day and bask in the glow of great work and perhaps even to Paris for a visit to the Orsay, but as lovely as Impressionist paintings are in perspective, the fine detail and rich feel of clear delineation in oil on canvas is unsurpassed to her mind.

If only art were as relevant now as it had been during that rebirth in thinking, when creativity was a reflection of society and art was supposed to tell the stories words could not!

To tell her own stories, Jane spends as little time as she can at home. She takes her paint supplies over to Lucy's apartment where the two can work together. Lucy is a school friend, because Jane does have one of those again—an actual friend she met in one of her classes. One she hopes won't betray her.

Lucy paints a little, too, so she turned her extra bedroom into a studio. If it weren't for imposition and cash flow, Jane would have pressed her friend into allowing her to move in. She would have slept on the couch or even on the floor! It's past time to get out of her parents' house.

Please God.

In the meanwhile, Lucy is a godsend. It's great to know another human who understands her passion and can relate to her insatiable need to permit the soul a way to create. Or is it just a way to release pent-up frustration? Anyway, it's great to have an artsy friend. Any friend, in addition to Mac.

"You are always welcome," Lucy had said. Jane is happy to believe in someone again.

"I'll undoubtedly overstay my welcome, though, so you'll need to tell me when that happens," Jane had said, laughing.

"I will," Lucy had assured her, "but I am not a bit worried about it. I love the company and especially such creative company."

Jane works, of course, but she's not making enough to survive on her own. Her parents could certainly help her out with tuition, but their devotion is limited to the strings she allows them to pull. So, she pays for school herself by sleeping at home and working as a barista at a local coffee shop, and that goes over at home about as well as any declaration she might have made to live off the streets under a tarp for the time being. Or paint for tourists on the Atlantic City boardwalk.

As her father might say, it's *swell* to have so much support.

He thinks her a hippie, of course.

Father's degree is in civil engineering, the one career he feels is untouchable in any economic crisis. It's the one he values above all else, including his wife's law degree.

They both do quite well for themselves, which is swell for them.

Jess has decreed she'll do the same, even though she's still a hot mess. Coffee is a heck of a lot better than the substances Jessica ascribes to; Jane's time is better spent than the waste of it at the Pac-Man machines, which her sister is all about these days. So much for *Teens Against Video Arcades*.

Jane's coffee shop, Oliver T. Bean, is revolutionary. It's not your typical coffee shop peddling low grade coffee because the glorious beverage shouldn't just satisfy a basic human need poured from glass carafes left sitting on warming plates for hours. Coffee should provide a gourmet experience encouraging people to gather together for conversation and companionship. Oliver's fosters those things, offering rich espresso and drip coffee made from freshly roasted and ground beans on site, along with an assortment of wonderful pastry items baked fresh daily to complement.

Jake, the owner, said he'd done a lot of research before putting his life savings to work in beans. Jake cited the success of a coffee store chain in the Seattle area that began to sell espresso several years ago. He was excited about the prospect of operating a roasting machine on site to draw people in off the street with the intoxicating aroma of fresh, high-quality roasts, and the investment of tens of thousands of dollars in equipment was worth it. The shop is always busy; in fact, it's changing the way we all drink coffee, Jane thinks. It certainly isn't the Yuban Father consumes from his countertop percolator.

But Father isn't impressed with the coffee shop or its gadgetry. Oh, he likes coffee just fine. In fact, his caffeine addiction is above-average.

What he doesn't care for is a daughter who makes a living from it. "What in heaven's name is a barista?" he bellows when Jane tells him of her new job.

"A person who makes espresso drinks and pours coffee," Jane replies.

"So, you're a waitress," he snaps. "Wonderful. You've certainly exceeded my expectations for you."

"I was never going to be an engineer, civil or any other kind. It's not the way I'm wired. I want to do something with my life that makes me happy."

"Happy doesn't pay the bills!"

"Why can't you back what I want to do? It's my life!"

"You've evidently no idea how the world works. You can't pay the bills by painting it. Or by pouring coffee, for that matter."

Jane holds her tongue, though inwardly she's furious she's still having these conversations with her father. For crying out loud, she's an adult! Nearly living on her own.

Nearly.

But there's no point in arguing with Father. He won't hear of it—he's never wrong, and any *discussions* are generally one-sided. Jane understands it's best not to encourage any further word on it for now. She vows to find a way to move out on her own and to finish her college classes at the same time. God only knows how that will happen.

In the meantime, for some odd reason Jane can't wrap her mind around, Pete is still lurking about like an apocalyptic zombie. The wacko is, in fact, blatant in his skulking intimidation. He hasn't taken any further physical action but always appears to be on the verge of it, so Jane tries to pretend she doesn't notice him. When she's at the mall, he's loitering near the arcade. When she's at the local Acme grocery store, he's an aisle over. When she's walking to her car on the college campus lot, his car passes by. A handful of times when she'd been at the gym, he'd been there, too, acting like a phantom menace, drifting about without actually working out.

"What a loser," she mutters under her breath. Why can't he move on? I certainly have, Jane thinks generously.

Oddly, she isn't frightened by him. Just annoyed and strangely at peace. Hopefully he won't give her a reason to change that perspective.

Part of Jane wants to talk to her sister about it. The other part feels Jess could be behind it. Why would Pete be so intent after all this time unless he'd been put up to long-term bullying? She'd even seen him standing on the corner across from the coffee shop while she'd been at work.

Sure, she could report him or even get a restraining order, but what would be the point?

Who would believe her?

Thank the heavens for Mac, who whisks her away again to The Land she paints with an obsession, mostly in pieces—fragments evaluated at the end of many brushes dipped in many colors and laid across many canvases time and time again. Because in the strangest of ways, she sees every part of this special place on earth in ways she is incapable of in real life. Unlike so many other places she's been to and not remembered any details about (those in front of her she refuses to see, she concedes), each small bit and piece of her prairie land stays with her, as if-imprinted upon her mind. If someone were to ask her now to describe in detail the neighbor's house next door or to recall the color of the walls in her English classroom, she couldn't do it. But she can always remember the way the morning lifts off the prairie earth, how it casts its light across every stem and stalk, and how it retreats, too, leaving its many hues of gold to melt gloriously below the western horizon.

The real day had been long, and Jane is just settling into her room following school, a copy of the thick book she's only halfway through in hand, when she begins to detect trace scents of wild herbs and grasses, like those freshly cut on a summer day. She tosses Leo Tolstoy's *Anna Karenina* on her bed and sits down on the edge of her mattress, preparing herself for another trip. She's honed her awareness to a point where she can luxuriate in the anticipation of things to come. She folds her hands and takes another deep breath as perfumed aromas of the great outdoors grow stronger still.

It's dusk on the empty plains, and an early, pink night settles like a soft mist on a moor. There is no house in sight. Jane discerns she has moved back in time again. She inhales deeply and settles into the experience taking shape before her. She will enjoy this.

She's no sooner sighed, however, when the back of her neck begins to tingle with foreboding.

Something is different.

A gust of icy wind rushes her suddenly, stealing warmth, and she begins to feel herself back away in retreat, even as she senses this impossibility. There's no extracting herself. Less awareness of the real world had finally given way to full emersion, and now it's always as if she's captive until given permission to leave, as if she's stuck on a television channel that can't be turned with a knob on the set.

Jane has no choice but to wait and watch.

But just where is Mac?

The sun sinks lower and the light diminishes, lengthening shadows in real time. Whatever these visions or experiences are, they aren't stationary or one dimensional but dynamic and forward-moving.

Which is how the dark figures come into view. They approach on horseback with an evil fever Jane feels. She senses their breathing, their emotions, their hearts grown dark with murderous intent, like a plasm clotting the good atmosphere.

And there is nothing she can do but observe.

Chapter

Seven

THE KANSAS TERRITORY—1854

The Great Plains, where grass and freedom grow tall, is unsettled, but that is beginning to change in 1854.

Until only very recently, no deep thing had ever taken permanent hold of its loamy soil, no destructive thing had ever caused the earth to turn over itself in mass. Graves have been dug and seedlings have been planted, but its carpet grasses have yet to be torn out on a massive scale. No colors have been vanquished except in season, its topography unchanged for many centuries.

Kansas has always been tethered to eternity. It is said the state is an unbroken, undulating slab to the horizon and beyond.

Until now.

Thousands have begun the move here, both the willing and the resistant, all carrying certificates of entitlement in their own minds, the newcomer and the native in equal measure. Those whose stakes are tied to ancestors as one with this part of earth aren't the only ones to claim the land. New generations of North American natives relocated from the Great Lakes and the East Coast see this soil as theirs, too. It's been promised them! And now, nearly a century since the Kansa and Osage joined the Pawnee and Wichita, one could still argue any manmade permanency to the landscape in the form of scattered villages and nomadic living are only minor cuts in soil so pure angels still abide here.

The Great Plains once seemed too much ground to cover, especially when the sky discouraged such small thinking, however, perspective is in the midst of change. In Kansas alone, there are nearly fifty million acres of virgin grassland humans are eyeing with possession in mind.

What most don't realize, however, is emotion saturates the soil in deeply-rooted trenches—something that affects all who attempt to drink their fill, with the Comanches from the mountainous eastern Rockies now defending their hunting rights here, too.

The natural beauty is religion to the people who live here, particularly when the cycles are right and the bluestem wet. When game is plentiful and the grasslands are vibrant, and the latest cycle of "drouths" passed, the Great Spirit can swell here more intensely than elsewhere.

And when tracks are laid across the ground, humans see opportunity like never before. The ease of mobility across the continent entices faraway settlers in increasing numbers because Kansas is a place to reach the stars on tiptoes, and it's now easier than ever before to find out how true this really is.

Jane doesn't know it yet, but this land, her own beloved land, will soon belong to Seamus and Nell O'Donnell, and they will love it as much as one can love the earth, as much as Jane does, and more. They will be the first in a long lineage to own soil, traveling halfway around the world to claim it, as if it were an adopted child. One they'd dreamed of and fought for and held to their breasts.

The Land is their new beginning. Their promise.

What will belong to them is wide open and untouched, large and magnificent and sky-blending. And what no one but the natives wanted until only recently, because this was a place also once considered inhospitable by outsiders. However, when the area is opened to settlement in 1854, possession becomes obsession. Those night stars have inched closer, and the O'Donnells will reach them. They vow never, never to stop reaching.

"'Tis far more than I dreamed of," says Nell to her husband when they first lay eyes on Kansas.

"Aye, luv," Seamus agrees. "This'll be our new legacy for generations to come."

But they've no idea, yet, how hard they will need to contend for it. Though the Great Plains are roomy within the country's expanding economy, Kansas specifically will soon be a powder keg, their land a spark. A war is fomenting, a nation already divided, and Kansas hangs in the balance between slavery and freedom. Its settlers will suffer for trying to touch those stars.

Needless to say, Seamus and Nell are optimistic when they arrive in late spring following a long winter in New York City. They don't realize the exchange of hands the land has been through, the promises made and broken. The Great American Desert to some and Canaan to others will be right in the middle of a war zone.

There will be a fight to keep it. There will always be a fight to keep it. Because there will always be the darkness that exists along each cosmological wonder.

There will always be the unseen.

Such as the young woman named Jane over a thousand miles and a hundred years away in love with it, too.

How could Seamus and Nell know that? How could that woman so far away and in the future know what she does?

Seamus is used to battles. He'd lost his mum nearly ten years ago, and with no siblings, he'd spent the gap working to escape Western Ireland. As a lad of fourteen, he'd first lived with relatives, but then, sensing his own added burden on a house with little food, he'd left for good, foraging his way by working odd jobs and pinching pennies, and this was especially true after he married his best friend from childhood, Nell, and there were two to feed.

They'd used everything they had and borrowed to make the crossing, and once in New York City, Seamus had picked up a newspaper and read about land in a place called Kansas. Land that could be his own! There could be nothing more glorious to be had in all of life, and Seamus and Nell would be there to claim it if it took all of theirs. They'd both lived the oppression of tenant farming.

"All we have to do is work wi' devotion and determination," Seamus assures Nell upon arrival.

Nell smiles. "We can do it," she agrees.

It is said farming the land will bring the rain.

"Bring on the rain," they call out to God as they look to the sky, and they know he's heard them when the skies open up.

Once the first deed to The Land is acquired, Seamus and Nell O'Donnell purchase a few tools and build a sod house upon which prairie grass grows and small animals burrow, and when it rains too much, mud and water and sometimes mice and snakes find a way in. But it is theirs, and they get to doing all the things that have to happen so they can thrive here. God has done his part.

It is the first time their land has ever been cut into and sown, and the couple does these things with great reverence and even greater gratitude. A well is dug and a windmill placed above it to help in bringing water up to the surface; Seamus himself hauls a plow across the soil, pulling up the native grass for planting. A milk cow is purchased, and wheat begins to grow, and sometimes the sun is too hot. However, the little sod home is cool in the summer and stays fairly warm in the winter, and it is mostly attitude that keeps the temperature right, even when bitter winds whip across the plains and blow hard with nothing to restrain them. No matter the elements, no matter the season, the couple reads by candlelight from the leather Bible brought across the miles, and they find comfort there on the delicate pages.

And on Nell's twenty-fourth birthday in December of that year, she has a dream. In it, a beautiful man with dark skin dressed in white appears to her and shows her lovely things, and Nell is sure they are things to come, here on her very own land.

Chapter

Eight

CAPE MAY, NEW JERSEY— 1989

The sun is high over Cape May, but the campus library is chilly in the middle of a school day. Jane pulls her sweater around her.

She has secured her favorite reading nook, removed from interference of the normal kind because it's off more thoroughly-traveled areas. This one provides a corner window seat set in concrete and made soft with a cushion that allows her to look out across the better part of campus from the third floor.

She crosses her legs and takes a deep breath, congratulating herself for her speedy examination of the entire tray of slides containing the artifacts, drawings, and paintings she will be required to identify on an upcoming art history test. She had made good time to what is fast becoming one of her most beloved places to escape in real time.

Opening *Anna Karenina,* Jane leans back against a wall. The novel is proving to be a slower one than most, but she appreciates the way Tolstoy paints with description, and as one of his characters, Constantine Levin, discovers the joy of manual work in his Russian fields, she smiles. As Levin learns to mow grass with a scythe among his peasants and to delight in being fully, humanly present, Jane can almost smell the sweet scents of a summer rain blow in through the thick glass beside her.

She closes the book and inhales deeply. Is she so genuinely involved in her reading material her imagination has carried her away, or is another *experience* imminent? She glances outside to observe students rush off between classes, a few sitting on patches of green grass and under spindly trees, and she can smell the world around them, too. Or can she? Earthy fragrances continue to grow stronger. Jane looks about her nervously.

Can anyone else smell this?

No, of course not.

The library remains silent. Not a soul is in sight. Jane sets her book beside her and relaxes against the wall. She closes her eyes as her senses elevate, wondering if she will be given more information on the disturbing dark figures she had seen when she had visited last.

Like short stories woven together with the same thread, Jane's visions continue to arrive in vignettes, as if for browsing at leisure in small portions if not at her own small pace. She knows intuitively what is given her is not a tale as one might understand it, or a full-length story unraveled in chronological order, but a tapestry with different pieces stitched together. In no particular order, sewn fragments form a larger narrative, a collage of experiences arranged for unfolding revelation.

She opens her eyes to see a little sod house. It has been constructed on The Land and blends in with the earth, seems a part of it.

It's nestled in between the bright and bountiful, where billions of stems sway in the wind. They twinkle expectantly over the rooftop and around the walls of loam they're rooted to, moving in partnership with the emerging sun. Handfuls of light crystals appear generously scattered over each sprout, shoot, and blade.

Jane breathes deeper still.

This sod house must predate the big white house with the red chimney columns. She feels happy to know this. She's watching her land develop!

How this knowledge comes to her she cannot say, she only knows it to be true. She accepts the information unfolded for her.

"All things are relative," she hears herself say.

"*All struggle can be splendor,*" she hears another voice say. She looks around but sees no one, not even Mac. Her maestro is missing.

Who said that?

She finds herself moving close to the front of the dugout made of earth, where heat rises in the early morning. Suddenly, a small door opens to reveal a man and woman not much older than she is. Jane jumps back, startled. They appear to look right through her, unaware of her presence, and this makes her uncomfortable. She feels a trespasser suddenly, no longer a claimant of this land by association. "Mac!" she silently screams, but she's afraid to make an audible sound. Just because the couple can't see her doesn't mean they wouldn't be able to hear her.

The man is tall and fair, dressed in buckskin with a brown felt hat; the woman is a brunette but fair as well, clothed in cotton, with little pink flowers covering the material of her dress. Jane likes them immediately. They are lovely in the sunshine.

The man walks toward a yard fenced in by twisted wire where a thin, black-and-white spotted cow stands amidst patchy grass. A flimsy wooden lean-to up against the side of the dugout suffices for the animal's shelter. A pile of cut hay has been laid out for food. The man greets the slight cow with affection, and her long lashes flutter as he softly strokes her neck. "Okay, Penny," he says kindly. "Are you ready?" The cow seems to smile as she looks Jane's way.

Jane smiles, too. She's never seen anyone talk to an animal so tenderly. She's never met the eyes of a cow before, either.

Can the cow see me?

From the side of the small home, Jane watches the woman locate a tin washtub, and pulling it into position near the front door, she re-enters the small home to emerge with an armful of clothing which she drops in the tub. Jane watches her walk to a fire pit in the front yard to stoke the flames before grabbing another bucket. She heads to a well.

In the distance, a rumble of hooves can be heard, and Jane sees the woman look to the eastern horizon where a carpet of long, tasseled grasses holds uncharacteristically still. The man pauses his milking chores to stand and gaze out across the land as well. Soon, a group of men on horseback comes into view, approaching the homestead at a rapid pace. One of them is slumped forward in his saddle, struggling to lift his face from his horse's mane. He's obviously injured.

The four pull their steeds to a stop near the front of the home, and now close enough to be heard, the man at front inclines his head in the direction of the slumped rider. "We need you to treat this man," he shouts. The woman looks to the injured figure and then back again to the man who has just spoken.

"What's wrong with him?" her husband calls out as he steps out from the yard. His accent is foreign, Jane notes. He closes the gate behind him and walks over to stand protectively by his wife.

"Gunshot wound," the speaker firmly replies, offering no further explanation. He sports a scruffy beard and dirty face, but it isn't the elements that make him look hard. There is something about the man that causes Jane to shiver. Clearly, the other riders defer to him.

The woman speaks up, also in an accent Jane now recognizes as Irish. "Seamus, let me see what I ken do," she says, moving to touch her husband's arm.

"How'd he get hurt?" the man now known as Seamus asks.

"Never mind that," the hard man in charge directs. "Just fix 'im.'"

The men dismount at once and roughly pull their nearly-unconscious companion down off his horse, dragging him toward the house with little concern for his injuries. The woman rushes inside and returns with a thin mattress of straw she places on the ground in front of the home.

"It'll be much easier to see out here in the light," she explains, and the patient is laid on the mattress for examination. "Oh dear," she says, finally taking note of his shirt, saturated in blood. "What ken I do?" she asks, looking up into the faces of the posse, now towering over her.

"Take out the lead," the leader barks, still in his saddle. The other three men are already walking toward the well and soon begin helping themselves to water. The woman kneels to place her hand under the man's head.

"Seamus, get me a cup of water, would ya?" Her husband looks at her with concern for a moment before complying.

The woman is able to offer the patient a sip, which he refuses. "I will try to help ya," she assures him. He nods weakly before his eyes close again. Turning to her husband, she says, "Get the carbolic acid. We'll use that as an antiseptic. Oh, and me knitting needles and pincers." Seamus does as he's told, returning with the requested items without uttering a word. "And one more thing," she adds. "Grab the whiskey."

The patient comes around when offered a sip of the alcohol. Satisfied, the woman rips his shirt open at the buttons and tears a piece from the drier part at the bottom to use as gauze. Wiping the blood away from his chest and stomach, she finds the point of entry just below his right rib, but to his side, where it looks to have cleared vital organs. She sighs in relief.

"Help me hold him down," she commands the men who have just returned from the well. They comply begrudgingly. She then picks up a knitting needle to use as a probe. "This won't feel good," she tells her patient, and just then she has an idea to pour a little of the precious whiskey on the needle, something that causes her husband to flinch.

The men look away as she begins to work, but their leader is down off his mount in a flash and snatching the whiskey bottle from her side. He takes a long, thirsty drink. Seamus is noticeably displeased but still doesn't utter a word in protest.

The woman gives the injured man something to bite down on, and he moans until he loses consciousness. She continues her work until she locates the ball, and using pincers, carefully removes it. After setting the bullet and equipment aside, she tears another, larger strip of cloth from his shirt and soaks it in carbolic acid, placing it on the wound to apply pressure.

"I'll need me embroidery needle and thread," she says to Seamus, who rushes inside again to gather the necessary supplies. In his absence, she looks up to the leader, still positioned above her. "Why was this man shot?"

"Just attend to him," the leader replies gruffly. He doesn't remove his eyes from the woman.

"Aw, Tom, she has a right to know, 'specially now that she's helping Frank," interjects one of his companions, standing up to partake from the bottle of whiskey, too. The man identified as Tom appears to consider this for a moment before handing it over, still staring at the woman. "We was trying to apprehend some Jayhawkers when he was hit," he finally answers, wiping his mouth with the back of his hand.

"What's a Jayhawker?" the woman asks evenly, not taking her eyes from his. She thinks she knows, as she'd heard some talk in town.

"Does it matter?" roars Tom before glancing away.

"I should think it does," the woman says evenly.

"It ain't gonna do no harm fer her to know," adds the vocal one of Tom's companions again. "Prolly a good thing."

Another of the men speaks. "Clyde's right. I reckon these people need to know what they're up against."

"Which is?" Seamus says as he returns with the needle and thread to position himself near his wife.

Tom scowls at his men before glaring at Seamus. "Which is," says Tom irritably, "abolitionists. And the fires of holy hell for them that aid or abet 'em."

"We don't know what that means," Seamus responds evenly, plying Tom and the others for information. He knows very well what Tom is saying.

"It means," answers Tom, his anger mounting, "those who think this 'er territory will be called *free!*"

"I think ye'd better explain what you mean by that, sir," challenges Seamus, not taking his eyes from Tom.

"What it means is that this here territory ain't gonna become no free-soil state, and we ain't gonna put up with no Jayhawker or likewise that don't see the way things are, ya got that?"

For Jane's part, hearing this produces a long chill that courses down her spine. She knows her history.

These settlers have yet to live it!

"We've traveled from afar to work our own land and to live in peace with God here. We've no desire to be a part of any conflict. But if ye think we agree with ye on this issue, you're mistaken," the woman known as Seamus' wife responds bravely.

"And to clarify," Seamus adds forcefully, "keeping others from their God-given freedom isn't right."

Tom glares at Seamus before proceeding tightly. "There's nothin' you can do to stop progress, and though you don't look like the sort, I'm gonna tell you right now, you better stay back and out of its way."

"I don't know what sort ye think I am, but I will tell ye I won't stand idly by and allow injustice to happen without doing something to stop it."

"That could be a problem for ya," Tom says, the threat clear.

"How so?" Seamus challenges him, and giving Tom no time to respond, he continues. "This is my land. Maybe it's time you leave it." Seamus appears cool, intimating a strength that isn't to be trifled with. Though Tom doesn't react, he seems to have received the message.

"We should get outta here," Clyde says, interrupting nervously.

"Ye shouldn't move this man," the woman objects. "He must heal before he ken travel."

"Fine," says Tom. "We'll be back for him in a few days." At this suggestion, the woman looks to her husband, a silent agreement passing between them.

"He may stay here until he is mended enough to get back in the saddle. Leave his horse. Ye won't need to return for him," Seamus says. Tom doesn't seem to like that idea, but after thinking on it for a moment, gives in.

"Guess if I don't have to head back straightaway, that would be for the best. Just send him on 'is way when he's ready. But know this: I *will* be back here if I need to be at any point," Tom warns through stiff lips.

Neither Seamus nor his wife respond. The men also avoid further comment and within minutes are in saddles again, heading back the way they came. As they leave, shadows move across the land, blocking the light of the sun.

Jane feels the evil there and it terrifies her.

Meanwhile, time accelerates for Jane, moving her forward rapidly. In a matter of seconds, night descends. Her familiar herbal countryside now smells metallic and sulfurous. A new moon is just developing, offering little light under cover of darkness. Jane's throat tightens.

The settlers are worn after tending to the needs of their patient. They've been at nursing and chores all day and are now preparing for bed, settling their new houseguest comfortably into an arrangement of soft hay set away from the stove.

As they prepare for rest inside, outside a large pack of wolves gathers and approaches the dugout. The couple and their charge remain unaware. Jane sees clearly, however, as if she wears night vision goggles. She watches the beasts steadily approach and surround the little home. One wolf holds back from the pack and howls hauntingly into the night while the rest prowl about, noses high in the air, their forms opaque but troublingly discernible. Satisfied they've waited long enough, one begins to tear feverishly at the outside of the house, signaling his companions to follow suit. "No!" Jane yells, once again helpless to do anything but observe.

Fully aware of the trouble outside now, the man named Seamus grabs his rifle from above the doorframe and stands ready to guard his home. His wife moves to his side with a cast-iron frying pan as the beasts begin to breach the walls.

Scant traces of injury in warm air are enticing to the beasts, whose innate ability to thrive on the wild frontier seems to exceed that of the newcomers. The little home's earthen construction is no match for well-conditioned muscles and steel jaws. Even soil baked hard in the sun begins to crumble under such pressure.

The injured man, Frank, awakens but is so weak, he can do nothing to help. He falls back against the straw as the wolves tear and dig furiously to get inside. A scream pierces the night. Jane screams, too, when she sees a snarling muzzle has found a way in. As if encouraged by these sounds, more manage to break through the sod, biting and snarling, leaving bubbling saliva strung as webbing. Seamus fires off a shot and it hits its mark, leaving one predator partially stuck in the wall. The blast scares the pack off for a few minutes but after a brief scatter, they regroup to advance again.

"They won't give up!" the woman cries, near hysteria.

"We won't either, Nell," Seamus assures her.

"It's the blood," the woman now known as Nell yells. "They smell it!"

Her husband reassures her. "We won't let 'em in." He fires another round into the head of the next intruder as Nell screams again.

Jane also cries out again. "Make them stop!" she yells to no one in particular, but before she can say another word, she is back in the quiet of the library. She leans forward, her fists in knots, as she looks around her. Still not a soul in sight. She yells for Mac, paying no heed to the silence. Whether she disturbs anyone is of no consequence. "Mac!" she yells again softly, but he doesn't answer. "Why? Why did you take me there?" she demands. "Why did I have to be a part of that?"

He doesn't answer.

What happened to those people?

It had been no dream. For the first time since these experiences had begun, she knows this to be absolutely true.

What she experiences in the beyond is real. She had been present to live the horror.

And for the first time since she's known Mac, she begins to cry. For the first time what he's shown her of The Land isn't something that causes her heart to sing in color or her mind to relive it brushed across white.

Presently, all she can see is the darkness there.

Chapter
Nine

CAPE MAY, NEW JERSEY—1989

The strong, earthy smell of coffee warms and soothes Jane the following morning. Despite Father's perspective, Oliver T. Bean is making friends with the community. There are lines inside the café regularly.

However, as she works, she finds trouble concentrating; she can't shake off the terror of the previous night! The horrifying experience had even followed her into sleep as a nightmare and she'd tossed and turned, unable to find any rest. Now, she still can't get ruffians or wolves out of her mind.

The frenzy of those predators had been utterly petrifying!

She's steaming the milk for espresso shots when Jake walks in.

"Good morning!" Jane shouts over the steamer's strident efficiency, feigning lightheartedness.

Had last night been real?

It had to have been.

Jake eyes her suspiciously. He's on to her. Naturally. She focuses on her work.

Ignoring fleeting moments of temptation and well aware of parameters implied by Mac long ago, she still hasn't revealed anything to anyone, and perhaps this is more for her own well-being than for any other reason, for again, who would believe her? They'd think her mad.

Perhaps I really do need a therapist.

"What gives?" Jake asks pointedly as he hangs his coat on a hook by the door.

"Oh, it's nothing. I just feel—I don't know—unsettled."

Jake isn't taking his eyes off of her. "Unsettled?" he asks good-naturedly.

"I can't seem to shake a disturbing nightmare I had last night," Jane freely admits.

Shoot.

Exhaustion has spoiled her usual control of personal revelation. Exhaustion and Jake's blue-eyed scrutiny.

"I suppose that could ruin the start to an otherwise brilliant day," he chuckles, even as he continues to hold his focus suspiciously. "You want to talk about it?"

Ugh. He is not going to let this go.

Jane feels her cheeks flush. She should work on her filter.

We all have bad dreams, for heaven's sake.

But what she experienced overnight was overwhelming! She'd been there! She'd seen it. Felt it. Experienced all of it firsthand! The fury, the fear. How could she not be affected? Her hands begin to tremble slightly. "I'm okay," she assures him, hoping he won't notice. "It was just a dream."

How wonderfully awkward.

"When you're caught up, come talk to me," he says, heading to the back room.

"Sure," she agrees, feigning a grin. She reaches for a cup she sneaks into the queue for herself. On second thought, a double shot is the last thing she needs today. She puts the cup back.

Once the line of customers has died down, she heads to the back with a large ice water and pushes a chair to the small corner desk where Jake is seated. He looks up, laying his paperwork aside. "So, tell me about the dream," he says with concern.

There is no blowing it off, then.

"It was nothing, really. I shouldn't have mentioned it." She attempts a relaxed posture by leaning back in the chair but only ends up feeling awkward. She leans forward again.

"You know you can talk about it if you need to. Dreams can seem so real."

You've no idea.

Jane rolls her eyes inwardly. "Seriously," she says, trying to brush it off. She changes the subject. "Our bakery delivery was late this morning. The case was empty for the first hour or so."

"It happens occasionally." Smiling in a beautiful way, Jake leans back in his chair and crosses his hands behind his head.

"I wish I could be as relaxed as you are about everything." Jane sighs.

"I slept fine last night," he teases.

She returns his smile. "I'm glad someone did," she exhales, feeling lighter. There is always something about Jake that calms her. Despite the span of a decade between them, he gets her. Despite his casual good looks and dimpled cheeks, he is her dearest friend.

"Really, we can talk about it if you want to," he gently presses.

"Really, no, it's totally unnecessary."

"All right then. Would you rather talk about the late arrival of our pastries? Because heaven forbid our patrons miss a morning without a cheese Danish." He winks at her in an endearing way and she can't help but giggle. However, his attempt to hold her gaze for a moment too long makes her uncomfortable. She looks away quickly.

"Yes, we should talk about late pastry deliveries. This is a serious matter!" she teases back.

"But more serious than sweets, I've been meaning to talk with you about something," he says mysteriously.

"What could be more serious than coffee and sweets?"

"I'm serious about something else. Seriously." He laughs, but distractedly.

"Oh-kay."

What's he up to now?

Jake's operation in the world is unique. He actually *sees* it and reflects upon it and Jane considers this interesting, if not always comfortable.

"Your artwork."

"Oh dear."

"What would you say about exhibiting your paintings on the walls of the Oliver T. Bean Coffee House?" He waits for his proposal to sink in, knowing there will surely be resistance.

Jane immediately shakes her head. "No. No way," she says emphatically, holding her palms up.

"C'mon now! This could really work. I've been thinking about how to lift the vibe of the place. I need to add a little color here."

Why, oh why, did I have to tell him I painted?

"You've not even seen my work!" she protests.

"I'm talking about a mutually beneficial arrangement. Just think about it. This would be a great space for a showcase of your talent," he beams, and she can now see he loves her. So that is what this is all about.

She should have known. It's in the way his eyes rest on her, lids heavy and expectant, and the special interest he takes in her, and this worries Jane. She can't possibly return his feelings. It would be easy and undoubtedly marvelous if she could, but those emotions just aren't there. She can't force them for practicality's sake even if she does recognize his attractiveness. Even if she does see the way other girls look at him.

And it's a shame, because no one has ever really been interested in Plain Jane in a good way. No one has truly believed in her until now, unless, of course, she counts Mac, but he doesn't count, because their arrangement has never been about her. It's about The Land and the people there. Self-focus has diminished considerably in the time she's known Mac. Now, Jake is asking her to change that.

Jake isn't just her boss. He is a good man, like no one else on the planet. His friendship is grounding. She won't compromise it for the world. At twenty-nine, he's also nearly ten years older than she is, so he's more like a big brother than anything.

Alas, none of this would matter if there was chemistry in her heart.

She sighs. He wants to put her work up in the coffee shop sight unseen! She should offer him finger painting or rudimentary crayon drawings. He'd surely retract his offer then.

She can't do it, though. Not to a soul so gilded. He's so … good. Even here, in real life.

Real life.

He's a catch. That's for real. Just not for her. He's not only highly mannered, he possesses a pureness any doting maternal figure would scold a young woman for not responding to. Not that she has a doting maternal figure.

Although he dresses like a dork, with a closet full of button-downs and a few pull-overs, his light blue eyes the color of peace in a June sky and hair like spun silk produces a reaction in nearly every woman who enters the shop. In fact, it's nauseating how some go out of their way just to get his attention. God knows there are plenty of opportunities for him. Even though he is merely the owner of a little shop that pours coffee for people instead of designing structures to save the world or practicing the law that does.

Thoughts of maternal figures distract Jane momentarily as she considers the lack of any in her own life. Jane's mother couldn't be less interested in a relationship with her daughter, and Jane's only grandmother— her mother's mother—is unknown to Jane. She'd never met her father's parents, either. Both had passed away without warning, at the same time, or nearly so, before she was born.

The subject of her paternal grandparents was one Father had never seemed fond enough to discuss. All Jane knew was they'd been blue collar laborers and that her grandfather had passed away of a heart attack in a grain elevator. Her ancestors had been described by a single word that had stood out, a single color, and it wasn't favorable: *blue.*

Blue was what was used to describe laborers with little free will. Blue was physical. It was what collected on hands and knees and backs. In lungs.

Blue was a nasty word.

The color was something to surmount in a world where the sky was never meant to be limiting and where the absence of such was evidence of the ability to rise above it.

Jane turns away from Jake to diffuse the emotional impact she senses in this moment, knowing full well she will need to deal with his perspective later on. If she takes him up on his offer, honesty will need to prevail. There could be no strings attached. But how to do that, exactly?

Am I even considering such a proposal regarding my work?

She's never thought about unearthing her paintings from her closet out into the light of day so other sets of eyes may evaluate them. And yet, what Jake proposes should be her ultimate aspiration. Most artists would be thrilled to showcase hard work for hopeful validation, or even profit, but a lack of confidence has prevented her to even consider options. It's wild enough she's confided with anyone regarding her love of painting. Just Jake. And Lucy.

An image of her father comes to mind. Her sister, too.

God, no.

"I don't know," she tells him. "You haven't seen my work. It could be awful!"

He chuckles. "Well then, perhaps our customers will think *awful* artistic."

Jane tries to laugh, too. "That's a nice offer, but ..."

"I won't take no for an answer. I'll tell you what, just bring a few in to start with. Choose your top three to display here, assuming they're not too big and will fit on the walls!"

The idea begins to simmer, and sensing this, Jake takes advantage of it. "They'll be safe," he assures her. "And no one need know they are yours unless you want to come forward. That way you'll get feedback without having to suffer any potential mortification." Jane nods without realizing it. "Though I'm sure you won't hear it's anything close to awful!"

Hmm. No one need know who the artist is.

That much was true, she supposes. She hadn't even signed her work completely. She'd only put her first name in the lower right-hand corner. In very tiny, almost illegible cursive.

But it's risky! She can't bear the thought of her father being right, of hearing she lacks talent and can never hope to make a red cent from her effort. Of learning her paintings are blue after all.

On the other hand, perhaps bringing them out into the open will allow her to put her fears to rest. Or to put her paintings to rest, once and for all.

After all, she *is* beginning to put herself out there. She'd discussed her collection with Jake. That's huge! One small step for Jane, one giant leap for acknowledging—her intended path. Or is it intended? She realizes even this suggestion puts her at a crossroads. She could easily back off, keep painting in secret while finding a legitimate career path. Or she could move forward into what may be destiny by choosing differently.

Do I even have a choice?

But what she doesn't know, what Mac hasn't shown her, is her own fate where painting is concerned. What she can't presently fathom is that once her art hangs on walls, once they are out of the dark and exposed to the light, those paintings can come to life, changing everything in Jane's own.

Chapter
Ten

THE KANSAS TERRITORY—1856

If the territory known as Kansas could be a physical sword, unsheathed to sever the country in two, it couldn't be more precise. The breaking of a country is heralded here as opposing political ideologies escalate into the War Between the States.

Corruption finds its way into ballot boxes, organized gangs roam the countryside, and ruffians cross the Missouri border to terrorize. Sympathizers in the North and South fuel the debate with financial support and ammunition. Everything boils down to economy, and Missouri is a slave state. Nebraska is free. Kansas is up for grabs.

Seamus and Nell vow they'll stand for justice on their land. They didn't leave the prison of tyranny behind to put up with it here. They had fought off wolves, hunger, weather, and loneliness to live in this bleeding place and by all that is holy, they'll do their part as tensions stretch to breaking. They had never imagined it would be this way.

What they had known fairly early on was that a sod house could never be permanent, not here where wolves are so prolific and resolved. After another attack nearby, Seamus declared he would build a real house. Vowing not to leave his family, grown to three with their new baby, alone for long periods of time, he had first reinforced the insufficient dwelling, then planned for a more protective, permanent home, something that required travel for wood and supplies.

Now, the O'Donnell's new, one-room cabin is a luxury, the walls sturdy and sufficient, sealed with a mixture of mud and straw. They are grateful for a home that makes them feel safer.

Particularly from four-legged animals.

They don't get many callers at first, friendly or otherwise, but a Native American woman they don't catch sight of visits regularly. She now steps from behind a large tree to give a nod of approval as she looks toward the O'Donnell's new dwelling.

Meanwhile, while Jane is still having her visions, Nell is still experiencing her own. In them the man in the fine, white linen suit appears to her and shows her things outside the world in which she lives. He shows her things that feel real, unknown and known at once. It helps with her perspective here on the plains. Nell knows there is more than meets the eye.

Tonight, she pulls the covers up close to her chin. From far away she hears rain approach; soon it's pounding the roof. The air howls in accompaniment, but the rest of the household sleeps well. As thunder cracks like the clash of the gods, she fades in and out of slumber and the heavens give way to a bright sun. She's now where cotton-like clouds in puffs of white dot a deep, blue sky, and daylight plays vibrant color all around. She's immediately aware of sweet fragrances dancing around her, too—bouquets of herbs, florals, and grasses in concert—scents that sing in harmony. She's here on her land, but senses she is in another dimension of time.

As Nell continues to observe the scene before her, it changes. Unrecognizable trees appear—magnificent oaks and big cedars, hedgeapple and fruit trees, in rows and single lines and clusters. And then she sees a girl she doesn't recognize. She's dancing in tall grasses scattered with purple thistle flowers, her long, brown hair filling with wind like the mainsail of a fast-moving boat. She smiles a dreamy smile that makes Nell smile, too, and Nell feels a connection there. Then, she suddenly awakens. She wishes she could have stayed a few minutes longer, still feeling sunshine on her skin. Still admiring that girl.

Nell's heart is radiant because she knows what she will paint next.

She will paint that beautiful girl with the long brown hair and pink cheeks and remember what she saw in her eyes as she looked across their land.

Chapter

Eleven

CAPE MAY, NEW JERSEY—1989

I f good is capable of traveling in and out of time, evil can, too, and so it seems Jane has brought it forward with her from another dimension.

Her life hadn't been without conflict, but now it seems something greater, something tangible, has attached itself to her, as if some of the strife she has witnessed in other domains could trail her into her own. In spite of the beauty, mostly understood in another realm, overall tension remains.

Jane resolves to remain optimistic. That's what her childhood fantasies were all about. Now, however, that sort of dreaming is no longer useful, and truth is stranger than fiction.

Fortunately, a few nights after the haunting wolf attack, she receives a vision of the gunshot patient fully recovered, and the O'Donnells tending to their garden and milking their long-lashed cow. She breathes easier.

At home in New Jersey, life continues to be comparatively uneventful yet challenging, her sister's strange antics and parents' aloofness aside. It's been two years since her first encounter with Pete, but oddly, even he continues to bother her, and Jane wonders what's wrong with her.

Sometimes she catches sight of Pete as she's leaving the mall or finds him lingering by the magazine rack at the bookstore she likes to visit. He's been at the gym when she's been there and at the shore, too. She should be able to live her life without interference, so why the weird curiosity? It isn't as if she's all that interesting.

Her real life is really as plain as she is.

Pete's harassment could be a problem. Jane hasn't lost any real sleep over it, but she *is* mindful of his efforts and is not entirely blasé where he's concerned. She wouldn't call him a stalker. Necessarily. He's not really intimidating her. In fact, he sometimes seems to forget her. He hasn't attempted physical contact again, so she pushes any nagging thoughts aside. For now, he's like a pesky insect that comes out only in warmer weather.

Jane is strengthened by time and the growth in her own life. In fact, though she still views herself as Plain Jane, she also finally recognizes a unique power within, thanks to Mac. Oh, there are those that would say she's delusional. In denial. She should have reported Pete already. She needs to set better boundaries.

Don't be stupid, Jane.

Maybe she really does need professional mental help.

But that would be a terrible idea, for obvious reasons. And besides, most of the time what she really wants is the ability to talk with her mother about it.

Before school one day, Jane decides to reach out to her mom, vowing to make a legitimate attempt this time. She's already dressed in her comfiest jeans and a fluffy blue pullover sweater and making her way through a plate of eggs and toast when Elise taps into the kitchen. Her mother's annoyingly-loud heels accentuate a brisk pace. Time undoubtedly cannot be spared, but Jess has already left the house.

Jane takes a deep breath as she watches the crisply-suited Elise move to the cupboard for a mug, and as she begins to pour coffee, Jane dives in. What she'd like to discuss is the situation with Pete, but she chickens out at the last minute and opts for a safer subject. There are a few things on her mind from which to choose.

"Jake asked to hang my artwork at the coffee shop," Jane blurts out as she watches her mother fill her mug with the steamy liquid. Elise seems to startle slightly, but any reaction, real or perceived, is expertly brought under control in a flash.

Why is she so uncomfortable talking about the very subject that makes me happiest?

Without saying a word, Elise opens the refrigerator door and pours a dollop of cream into her cup, closing it without turning to look her daughter's way.

Really, the topic of art has to be a safer one than potential sexual harassment. Or strife between siblings.

Jane decides she might as well continue. "It was only a few pieces, but the largest one…"

"I have to run, dear. Attempts to contain the spill off the coast aren't going well, and our clients are naturally anxious," Elise interrupts, whipping around so fast, it's Jane who is now startled silent. Though it's no surprise, since her mother usually commandeers the subject matter, she's never been so abrupt before. "Thank God it's nothing like the Valdez disaster in March, but a catastrophe nonetheless, and animal rights activists are already having a field day, damn them."

Video footage plays through Jane's mind of wings and eyelids covered in black tar. Her mother's ploy is successful. The more disagreeable subject of Jane's paintings is off the table. On to more pressing matters.

Elise sets the mug on the counter and picks up her handbag, looping the handles, as well as a coat lying on the back of a kitchen chair, over her left arm. At the same time, she manages to retrieve a briefcase from the floor, slide the keys onto her pinkie, and grab the mug as she heads for the garage door. Elise is a great multi-tasker. As long as the tasks don't involve unpleasant things.

Or mothering.

Only then does she look Jane's way. "My legal team is meeting with the oil company's public relations group, and I need to be in New York by ten. I'll be staying in our apartment in the city tonight. If I miss calling your father, would you be a dear and let him know? Jess too?"

Elise doesn't wait for an answer. She's already out the door.

Autumn has dropped in early this evening, causing Jane to feel chilly as she steps outside. She regrets leaving her denim jacket with the puffy sleeves at home earlier. The sun, already escaped beyond view, seems another betrayer. Its last rays loiter weakly on what can be seen of the horizon, which isn't much, behind Oliver T. Bean's sleeping form.

A bitter wind stirs castaway leaves at her feet, and Jane shivers, thinking of the approaching winter. She dreads it. This is the one area in which Jane's optimism falls short. Fall colors only signal the approach to winter's monotone imprisonment. And death.

She gets into her car and starts the engine quickly. After waiting through a few minutes warm up, she maneuvers across the street to the corner gas station. As she pulls onto the lot, her mind is already snuggled up at home with a cozy blanket and a cup of tea, making the best of the blustery conditions with only an occasional flash reminder of the English homework due tomorrow. Fortunately, the bulk of the assignment is reading the next assigned novel, Alexandre Dumas' *The Count of Monte Christo*, which she is enjoying.

She glances over to the pump, momentarily weighing the benefits of waiting until later to fill her tank in order to avoid further delay and any insufferable small talk, but the attendant already approaches. She rolls her window down.

Fortunately, the station's employee isn't interested in banter, and the nozzle is soon in the tank. He's finished and walking back inside the building when she hears a vehicle with a distastefully loud engine approach rapidly and come to a screeching halt beside her. It's Pete in a classic, black Camaro. Her heart flutters. He quickly engages the clutch before revving it a few times for obnoxious affect. Whatever he'd done to the engine to make it piercingly loud had worked. In fact, the din causes the back of her eyeballs to ache.

What is it about some guys thinking loud is better?

Jane attempts to move her car forward to exit the lot but he is fast, angling his sports car in front of her. When she puts it in reverse, he does the same.

Great.

She glances over to the station's office building. The attendant has disappeared from sight.

Where does everyone go when this guy shows up?

Unfortunately, the adolescent and whatever muscled jerk he has with him move quickly. They're out of the vehicle in a flash. "Hi Jane," he taunts as they step up to her window. She hadn't rolled it up after putting her change away, and she now shivers in cold air.

She inhales, and reminding herself she's not the inexperienced high school student she once was, steels her nerves for confrontation. From the looks of his companion's intense scrutiny, Pete has already provided a riveting backstory where Jane is concerned. God only knew what that could be. What a jerk. It's been a year since Jess broke things off with him, for crap's sake.

Seriously, shouldn't he have moved on by now?

Jane takes the bait and answers him, but only to fire back a question of her own. "How's *high* school?" she sneers. She doesn't wait for a response as she begins to crank the window up.

"Cute," he says as he flashes a toothy grin. "I graduated last year."

"Fascinating," Jane says. "Now, get out of my way."

"It's been a while." He and his buddy remain in place, grinning menacingly.

"But not nearly long enough. Now, move your car." There is no way a couple of overly-hormonal, falsely confident boys are going to get under her skin now.

Pu-leeze.

"I'm serious, move!" Her raised voice through the partially opened window projects well because it attracts the notice of a middle-aged bald man in a pressed gray suit a few pumps away. He's out of his vehicle, evidently in search of that attendant.

Good.

"Just wondering if you like boys yet," Pete sneers.

Jane rolls her eyes. Regrettably, her previous inaction where Pete was concerned has troubled her. Not that she could have handled things much differently then, but the past months have made a world of difference where any cowardness is concerned. She's not about to show any now. "I like *men*," she says with emphasis on the word. "Boys like you, no thank you."

This doesn't sit well with Pete, who's stunned momentarily speechless. Maybe he didn't expect her to push back so boldly. She continues. "Don't you have some arcade to be in right about now? I mean, screw your future if you can play Pac-Man with your pointy-headed friends or Twister with some short-skirted bimbo. Oh, that's right, my sister isn't into you anymore."

"Your sister's right about you," he spits back. "You aren't worth the time of day."

"How refreshing. She's finally right about something then. Other than dumping you," Jane interrupts. "And, anyway, if you truly feel this way, why are you always lurking around me? I am not flattered, if that is your angle."

This hadn't gone the way he'd intended, evidenced by his hasty retreat. His buddy is already slinking back to the vehicle. Pete follows him silently but turns around and casts a hateful glare at Jane as he reaches his door.

Jane wastes no time in accelerating out of the lot quickly, revving her engine, too, but not so fast she doesn't catch the middle-aged bald guy smiling at her as he watches her go.

At home in an empty house, Jane thinks things through, ultimately deciding to have it out with Jess. One-sided, manipulative communication may be the way their parents' generation operated, but it serves no one presently. Jane has a sudden urge to break whatever weird cycle is in play.

Everett and Elise travel more than ever now and spend much of their time in the apartment they keep in Manhattan. For the most part, Jess stays to herself, and that's fine by Jane, who can't even feign a desire to interact with her only sibling. The only occasions for family relations are extended weekends or the occasional holiday, and even those aren't prioritized. For her part, Jess seems to keep any high school functions at arm's length, and their parents seem perfectly comfortable with this arrangement.

When Jess gets home later, Jane plunges in from her comfortable position on the couch. She sets her book down, any conflict avoidance heavily outweighed by a need to end the madness. "Can you please tell me why Pete still won't leave me alone?" She realizes immediately she could have at least begun her inquisition with a greeting. And maybe a little less force.

Jess' startles but regains her composure quickly, her mouth visibly tightening.

She may look like Father, but she certainly inherited that trick from Mother.

Jess wants to pretend she hasn't heard, but nearing the foot of the stairs she halts suddenly. Without glancing Jane's way, she hisses, "He isn't interested in you, you know."

"Then why does he go out of his way to engage me still?" This is not a statement but a legitimate question, Jane reasons.

"I can't help your delusions. Just because you think he's looking your way doesn't mean he's actually wanting anything to happen."

"*I* want nothing to happen, Jess!" Jane roars. "Did he ever tell you how he slobbered on me and pawed at my chest in front of my locker one day after school?" Jess' face seems to fall from its towering heights for just a moment, but she manages to compose herself quickly.

She certainly is her mother's child.

Jane doesn't give her a chance for further reaction. "That was when he was officially with *you*, and yet, he literally assaulted *me*, and when I was minding my own business. I could have pressed charges against him."

"He did not!" Jess shouts. "You're lying."

"He did! And I'm not!" Jane yells back.

"Then why didn't you tell me?" Jess demands caustically, finally looking at Jane with eyebrows raised high. "If it really happened like you say it did, why is this the first I'm hearing of it, all this time later? Huh?"

"Because I figured you wouldn't believe me! Or worse, that maybe you'd put him up to it."

"Now, why would I put my boyfriend up to making it with my sister? That's disgusting." She grabs ahold of the banister and begins to head upstairs as Jane flies off the couch.

"It wasn't a make out, it was molestation! I'm serious, Jess. He came at me again today while I was at the gas station across from work. He seems to be stalking me, showing up wherever I am. Whatever does he want?"

"I haven't the foggiest. But I do know one thing. It isn't you," she says emphatically before running up the stairs to her room where she slams the door shut.

"I'm so glad we are able to have civil, adult conversations," Jane calls up after her.

Twelve

KANSAS TERRITORY—1856

Thank heavens for her sanctuary, her land in all its changing forms, though she'd prefer to enjoy it apart from any force that comes against it.

Why does there have to be an opposing force, everywhere?

Now, standing on the property again, she sees a log cabin in front of her. Turning, she sees Mac by her side. "You didn't have much to say the last time we met," she says evenly.

"There was no need," he replies, still gazing forward.

Feeling emotion about to take the better of her, she steps in front of him, forcing him to look her squarely in the eye. "I don't understand you. Or this. What is this all about?" she says with a sweeping arm gesture. "Why show me such goodness only to follow with such darkness? Why nurture affection only to crush it with apprehension?"

She continues without taking a breath. "And why do you speak to me only on occasion, remaining silent when I need you most?" The last question comes from a heart that feels like the ruins of a crumbled building after a bombing when there is no one left to cry over it. Thinking of the ways people have let her down—her parents, Jess, Sam—even Pete's perpetual harassment—is devastating. She detests thinking of adding Mac to her list of disappointments.

Mac remains quieter still.

Jane has plenty more to say on the matter, but the rules of engagement generally found in normal human experiences, her own familial deficiencies aside, aren't the same with Mac. Communication between them seems to function in a dimension outside of practical understanding. Here, words need not always be exchanged. His minimalist approach is absolutely maddening.

And it occurs to her only now that perhaps she'd not *ever* actually spoken to Mac, but had conveyed dialogue by thought, thought he had heard and responded to.

Could that actually be the case?

She's growing weary of the mystery.

"What is happening here? The darkness, those shadows—."

"I show you only what you need to know in each moment," he interrupts gently. "Stay connected to the moment until such time as you are given the bigger picture."

"That tells me so much. Thank you," Jane retorts hotly. She doesn't mean to seem unreceptive, or ungrateful even, but her patience is thinning. She'd like to be able to communicate with him well—with anyone well!

She'd like to have a clearer picture of what exactly is going on.

Mac continues, as if reading her thoughts again. "Think of what you are given as an opportunity to evaluate pieces of a great puzzle. Weigh the value of each piece individually, then snap it into place as part of a masterpiece. You're already doing this with a brush. You re-create a panorama within a frame, then separately, each object within that frame. You paint each shape, texture, and color—close-ups, magnifying little things within the big, in order to understand it all."

"That's the thing, Mac. That's exactly what I am doing. I—."

Mac interrupts. "You are not understanding the bigger picture. So, focus by going in reverse. See the little details. Paint the leaf and petal, then pull back to show the flower it supports, and then a little farther to view the vase in which it sits on the table. Step back farther still to the table that vase is placed upon. Keep moving back to examine the room the table is positioned in and the house in which the room exists to the prairie upon which the house sits and the country in which that land lives, which is, of course, a part of the earth, which you may later paint."

Jane massages her temples with her fingers. "No kidding, Mac." She sighs and continues, as if her own explanation is necessary. "I paint what I see up close and from a distance, what resonates on so many levels. But then you go and change the composition. You alter the scenery, which changes the entire landscape on me. It is in those moments I don't know what to re-create. I don't know what to think about what I see; therefore, I can't make sense of it with a brush in hand, and I certainly don't want to paint it."

"Patience, my dear. I told you from the beginning you would need to persevere."

"You make no sense."

He grins. "But I do." And then Mac is gone again, and Jane is whisked into her painting, or what would become her painting in its better days.

In this moment, however, it is what she will *not* paint.

Again, the earth's fragrances come alive as its sun drops from the sky. However, this time it seems as if the orb has fallen permanently, giving the night an unusual power. Jane faces the little cabin alone now, its murky form in the encroaching darkness flanked by the outline of what appears to be tiny oak saplings as sentries. She shivers. The air is chilly and underscored by the pungent smell of decaying leaves and the smoke that consumes them. It's autumn here, too, but there are faint traces of sulfur and—what is that smell? Diesel fuel? Can't be. Not in the 1800s.

Can it?

Far from visional only, Jane's senses are becoming even more experiential, if that's possible. Concentrating on shallow breathing, she at once discerns the sounds of horses galloping a few hundred yards off as well as the muffled voices concealed inside the home, the lights long extinguished. Night deepens.

A half dozen riders pull up short of the cabin to regroup, their horses stamping hooves in displeasure. Agitated, they toss their heads and begin to whinny as Jane hears one of the men say, "It should be right here."

What should be right here?

"I say we don't need no cover of darkness. Let's come back in daylight," says another.

What are they looking for?

"I don't understand this. Y'all should be able to find the place in your sleep. It's not that difficult!" the first voice says, angrier.

"Don't start with me, Tom. You was here same as me. Find it your own damned self."

"Oh, I'll find it all right, Clyde, and when I do, I'll find you, too," Tom threatens, adding a string of expletives. He's been drinking. They've all been drinking.

"Now, don't get yerself all worked up, Tom," Clyde answers in a voice also slackened with drink. "I don't see why we should waste our time now. This ain't no fun. Let's get some rest first."

The men are looking for the cabin!

Or Seamus and Nell. Jane fears for the couple.

Why? What is it the Ruffians plan to do, particularly at this hour?

And how can it be they are lost?

She turns to ask these questions of Mac but then remembers he's already gone.

Of course.

The men can't find what's right in front of them. But the moon's paltry sliver of light is enough for Jane to discern the outline of the structure. Whatever barrier is preventing them from recognizing the very short distance from their target doesn't appear to limit her own perception. In fact, it's supernaturally potent in this moment.

How can that be?

Jane is suddenly overcome with a suffocating awareness of what's inside the hearts of these half-dozen men. She knows what compels them to ride under cover of darkness to a lone cabin on the plains at this hour.

Evil.

Jane wants to yell, to alert the O'Donnells, but when she opens her mouth, she freezes. As in a nightmare when a person turns to marble or finds limbs dissolved to dust, she is hopelessly incapable of action.

The horsemen begin to move again, slowly, at Tom's insistence. They ride back and forth for some time, looking for that house in the dark while Jane prays they won't find it. Inside the home, Seamus and Nell are praying, too. She can feel their good hearts.

"C'mon, we're just moving in circles," another of the group says.

"We could return with torches tonight and smoke them out," someone else snarls.

"Not a bad idea, only I say we use flame, not smoke," Tom slurs in agreement. His gang continues to defer to his inebriated authority despite an obvious inability to sit fully upright on his mount.

"I still say we return in the morning once we've gotten a little shut eye," continues Clyde, who begins to turn his horse away from the group now. Oddly, Tom follows, undoubtedly persuaded by his rapidly dilapidating state of mind. As he pulls in on his reins to conduct his horse home, he snarls, "One way or another, we'll get the traitor, and when we do, he'll be as sorry as hell he ever took a stand against us."

The party gallops into the dark night, and moonlight breaks free again to illuminate tender grasses.

Tom Crawford is functioning marginally better after a few hours face down on the lumpy straw bed he shares with his lean and haggard wife, who is tiring of his drinking. Tom could care less what she or anyone else thinks. Before his feet reach the floor, he polishes off a bottle of whiskey he finds under the bed, then stands and grabs his jacket off a peg by the door. Outside, he locates what's left of another bottle—about three fingers worth—under a pile of wood stacked up against the side of the house. He removes the top, takes a drink, then stuffs the container into his saddle bag, oblivious to the cry of a child inside.

Jane is still watching. She's been propelled forward in time.

The gelding under him moves about nervously, snorts warm mist into the cold air, and swishes his tail as if bothered by summer flies. Drunk or stone sober, Tom is a disagreeable human, and the animal knows it, but it also understands obedience is survival.

It's a short distance to Tom's favorite saloon in the middle of town, a fortuitous arrangement for the establishment's proprietor who likes the man no better than the horse does. Nevertheless, Tom's cash is as good as any, so he prepares to receive him by scrambling to put the extra glasses left out away. Who knows what sort of mood Tom will be in today.

Tom is no sooner headed inside, however, when a group of riders approach, calling him back. The saloon owner watches his best paying customer double back to untether his horse from the post in front. He is in the saddle again without appearing to utter a word, joining the group heading west. The saloon owner reaches under the bar top to put the glasses back up on the counter.

The posse stays on dirt until what serves as a road gives way to pasture. In the lead and desperately thirsty, Tom brings his steamy mount to a halt a few miles out of town, prompting the others to follow suit.

His head is pounding fiercely, and his throat is parched. He fumbles through his saddle bag and chooses a canteen of water over the whiskey bottle, taking several long swallows.

Momentarily satisfied, he wipes his mouth with his hand and tosses his head in a forward direction, motioning his men to follow. The only sound that comes from his mouth are the clicks he makes to nudge his horse forward, and those are unnecessary as he digs his spurred heels into the animal's side.

It's near an hour across grassland when the group slows to a stop. "It should be right over thar. 'Bout a hunderd feet, maybe two. Just over that ridge. Don't know why we couldn't find it last night," says Tom irritably.

Here the flat land sways and dips like a piece of soft fabric tossed to the wind. It can hide a dwelling in its folds, yet the men had known exactly what to look for and where to find it. It's a wonder the group didn't see the cabin last night in the light of a half moon.

"Last night, Will couldn't even stay on 'is horse fra'll the whiskey he'd downed," offers Clyde, intentionally leaving out mention of their leader's consumption. "It figures he couldn't make it today."

"Well, we'll make good of the daylight," Tom assures the men as he kicks his horse forward. "We don't need Will, or Hank for that matter. They can both sleep it off until they rot, for all I care."

The three other men follow, and as they come up over the top of a pleat in the earth, sure enough, there is the little cabin they were looking for tucked in just beyond a large tree, no longer under the cover of night and much easier to spot in the light of a bold sun. Though cradled by the prairie and thus partially protected from sight, the cabin is the only real landmark for miles in all directions.

The men ride into the yard and slide off their horses, Tom Crawford leading the charge. He stomps to the front door and begins to bang on it hard. After a few minutes, it opens slowly to reveal the slim, attractive Nell wearing a white apron tied around her waist over a long, rust-colored skirt and blouse. She doesn't appear to be rattled by appearance of the gang. Her rosy complexion and bright eyes should soften hearts of steel.

"What can I do for you?" Nell inquires politely, but Jane now sees her smile masks concern.

"Where is he, Nell?" Tom demands with great impropriety. He looks over the woman's shoulder.

"He isn't home." She isn't lying. Seamus had set off on foot before dawn, bound for Fort Leavenworth. He hadn't a choice, he'd told Nell.

Undeterred, Tom presses for information. "When do you expect him back?" Alarmed, Jane begins to silently plead to Mac for assistance.

Where is he?

"Where is he?" Tom demands.

Nell shakes her head. "I don't know."

"Well, now. Maybe we'll just wait." Tom is noticeably volatile, and his thoughts of Nell appear to grow more wicked. The other men move in closer to surround the woman.

"Mac!" Jane yells. "God! Won't someone stop this?"

And then, for a moment, Tom seems to hesitate, causing Jane to hope he might give up and turn around. But then she feels him change his mind again, shoving past Nell to enter her small home.

The sound of boots, harsh and intimidating on the wooden floor, frighten Jane. They frighten Nell, too. The door slams. A baby begins to cry.

Mac, where are you?

Seamus had left before dawn, making ready once he'd heard the drunken group leave in the dark. They were after his mind, and he'd already made it up. They could take his life, but there wasn't a man that would claim his thoughts, or his soul for that matter.

He'd known, of course, the Ruffians would return, but he'd hoped that wouldn't be immediately, and given no choice but to appeal for help from the Free-State men who'd planned to gather near Fort Leavenworth this morning, he'd left his family, hoping Tom and his gang possessed a little decency. The business of those pro-slavery fanatics was with him, not a woman or an infant. At least he prayed this was true. As he traveled, he recited Psalm 91 over and over again in his mind. Before leaving, he and Nell had read the verses by candlelight together from the family Bible they'd brought with them from Ireland. Then they'd continued to recite the verses out loud by memory.

> *"He that dwelleth in the secret place of the most High shall abide*
> *under the shadow of the Almighty.*
> *I will say of the LORD, He is my refuge and my fortress: my God;*
> *in him will I trust."*

They would trust in God. If there is a fight for justice and liberty here in Kansas, so be it. They will have help from above.

> *"Because thou hast made the LORD, which is my refuge,*
> *even the most High, thy habitation;*
> *there shall no evil befall thee,*
> *neither shall any plague come nigh thy dwelling;*
> *For he shall give his angels charge over thee,*
> *to keep thee in all thy ways …"*

Seamus hadn't made the decision unilaterally. It was Nell who had suggested he take the journey so as to best protect them all. Naturally, they both knew the thugs would return, but together they'd agreed it would be best if Seamus wasn't there when they did. She and one-year-old Agnes would be fine, she had assured him, and besides, she'd learned how to use the rifle to efficiency and was not afraid to demonstrate her aptitude. Nell knew how to deal with more than one kind of wolf.

"Please, God, take care of them while I'm away," he'd prayed, remembering the secret place of God and the rest to be found in His shadow, just like the psalm promised.

Now, Nell keeps an eye on the gun behind the open door, though it would be impossible to grab it for use against the four devils rummaging brazenly through her home.

For his part, Tom has no inclination of leaving. Hell, he might just settle in for as long as it takes for the Jayhawker to return. Make himself *completely* at home, delight in tormenting the wife. The baby's cries fuel a strange bloodlust within him.

The men go through the entire contents of the home, even Nell's wardrobe and bureau. As Tom unearths the woman's personal clothing items, he shudders with desire. Killing her, and the child, too, would give him a sort of wonderful satisfaction. But he'll not do that before thoroughly enjoying her in other ways.

Just as he's considering how to take his best pleasure, a different sensation comes to him, one that makes him feel as though he must get outside and away from this house, and fast. *"Leave now!"* he hears a deep voice order.

He shakes it off, but then feels his throat begin to close, as if hands have wrapped around his windpipe. At the same time, a terrible pain hits his head, as if he's been bludgeoned. It feels like his skull has been severed down the middle!

"Leave NOW!" the voice commands a second time, more forcefully.

Grabbing his head and cursing, Tom stumbles toward the door as the other men, currently in the process of stuffing themselves on Nell's food, fill their minds with other delights they might take. "Let's get out of here," he mumbles.

"What's the rush all of a sudden?" Clyde protests.

A gangly man with a sharp nose and pockmarked face picks up an egg from a basket, tosses it in his hand a couple of times, then heaves it against a wall, laughing as he watches the yolk begin a sticky course to the floor. He throws another while his companions help themselves to more of Nell's biscuits. Only recently removed from the stove, they are still warm. Nell reasons against protesting.

One of the men, his mottled beard dripping with stew, puts down the bowl he'd helped himself to and moves toward Nell, grabbing her by the waist. She recoils, the baby cries, and Tom barks from the door.

"Knock it off, Syl. I said, let's go!"

"Why?" he protests, tightening his grip.

"Yeah, what's the sudden rush?" the pockmarked guy agrees, tossing another egg.

"Because it's time to go," Tom snarls. "Move it, Hank!"

From somewhere another voice concurs. *"LEAVE. NOW!"* the voice booms loudly, and this time Jane, who is still watching, is certain all have heard it.

Tom certainly has. He has already reached his horse. Then, just as suddenly as Tom did a turn-about, the others do the same. Every one of them looks terrified.

Once the intruders have vacated, Nell quickly closes the door behind them and throws the latch down in place. It's a miracle the group never noticed the rifle propped up behind the door or the ammunition on the shelf above the stove. They would have helped themselves to those things, too.

She prays Seamus can return with a band of good men soon. She prays the Ruffians won't return. She prays wherever they go next, it will not be where her husband is.

When night arrives, Jane has returned to her own world, and Nell, left to hers, resolves to have peaceful sleep, protected against beasts of all kinds by the resolve of the unseen. Nell knows this to be true—the protection at work here, and because of this, there is victory. Even on days when the plains seem a vast and lonely place to do good on one's own.

As soon as she hears the honeyed gurgles of slumber coming from Agnes' cradle, Nell meets the dark-skinned man in the white suit. He takes her by the hand to a peaceful place by a steady stream where she can smell lavender and citrus. The young woman she'd seen before is standing there, in tall grasses dotted with purple milk thistle, the wind painting her long brown hair in garlands behind her. The golden light and domed sky are a different kind of lovely now, as if such a place—one that appears to be on Nell's very own land, or to look like it—could be a sign that overcoming adversity is not only possible, but promised.

The fulfillment of desire can be seen in the stranger's eyes, in the way they gleam as she gazes out across the meadows. There is triumph there, as if she has known great conquest in this place, and this causes Nell to feel needy and inspired at once. A mystical presence has settled across this land so similar to hers, evident in the way nature springs to life under its command, and the unknown woman's loving scrutiny testifies. Nell smiles. A picture really can paint a thousand words.

She vows never to take what she has here for granted.

There is allegory in the ways of God, for all he would have her do. And so, Nell recognizes the vision in its simplest form as love—a message from beyond of what she knows is the good already on the way to her. It affirms her family's destiny in this place, the white house on the hill in the distance she occasionally sees, a symbol of resilience. The woman as Nell's very own metaphor.

Nell feels she must continue to paint what she has seen, but she hasn't much to work with, so the next day she improvises further. She takes the canvas seed bag she'd carried with her from Ireland and cuts the stitching out so it stretches over her wooden table into one piece. She nails the four corners into place, and then begins to sketch an outline in charcoal. Later she'll gather a variety of seeds to crush for color paste, and when Seamus returns, she'll ask him to purchase linseed oil on his next run to town for supplies. She'll beg and plead with him to splurge for legitimate material on which to work.

Soon she will paint in oil outdoors where the light is best when her daughter sleeps and when she is finished with chores. When there is no other way to extract the images she sees from her mind but to paint them out and onto canvas, even when the canvas isn't much to work with and is burlap or bark or whatever she can get her hands on.

Despite her rudimentary artistic beginnings, Nell demonstrates an immediate and unmistakable talent as a painter, her paintings beautiful masterpieces. Her artwork allows her to communicate what she sees, but more importantly, to release what is there, if only in fragments. What she experiences with the white-bearded stranger is confirmation that there is more than what can be seen here, and that is comfort indeed. Even if she doesn't entirely understand it.

Chapter
Thirteen

CAPE MAY, NEW JERSEY—1989

It's missing! Jane's most beloved painting is no longer hanging on a wall of the Oliver T. Bean coffee shop.

She should have known. She had known! Why had she agreed to remove it from home? Though it made her smile as she worked at the espresso machine, it had been safest tucked away in her closet at home, out of sight.

It had been the only full rendering of the beautiful white house in its entirety.

The House.

The largest in her collection, too; it was the one she knew she would never sell or give away, which is why she'd overpriced it, assuring there wasn't even a remote chance she would receive an offer. The price tag was laughingly, embarrassingly astronomical. Ridiculous. Not that anyone would be that drawn to her work. Not that there was the unlikely chance anyone stopping in for a coffee would consider a painting on a wall, let alone think of suggesting a sale. But that is what artists often do—put price tags on the back of their work. A price tag on a piece means an artist is serious.

Valued.

She'd listened to Lucy. She'd believed Jake. Professor Randall, too, whom she'd reluctantly consulted apart from any viewing she might have permitted. Though Jane hadn't really wanted to bring any of her creations out into the light of day, something inside her had overcome her reservations, coaxing the piece into public view. Her own view! And she'd talked about it. With others!

Now, the white prairie house with the red roof and matching red door right in the middle, its happy white colonnades and wide-stepped entry is gone. The accompanying red brick walkway and matching chimneys, regal and colonial, too. That painting had captured the poise of the home, how it seemed inclined to tell stories, as if it really could, of the kinds of things that take place under wide skies and within big frames. Where grasses grow like trees and colors leak from heaven.

It had come to mean so much, that house.

Jane sighs audibly. She knew she would never paint another like it, but she couldn't say why.

"Where did it go?" she asks Jake when she enters the shop later. He'd called her as soon as he noticed it missing, catching her at home before school. She's no longer working mornings and now comes in after class around lunchtime because Oliver's thrives at all hours.

He shrugs, his expression heavy. He glances to the wall where it had been hanging. "I—I don't know. I'm so …"

"Someone has to know something," Jane yelps, wanting desperately to get a hold of herself. She's certainly not prone to hysterics, but her emotions regarding her artwork, and this painting particularly, run hot. Theft could push her past social propriety.

She could make a scene.

A total fool of herself.

She tells herself to calm down. To take a deep breath. She keeps her eyes on Jake.

"I'm sorry. I just don't know. I've asked the other baristas. They haven't seen a thing." Jake is clearly more upset now, seeing how distraught Jane is. He wouldn't cause her grief for the world.

"What do you mean, they've not seen a thing? They've been here, haven't they?" Jane says as she tosses her head in the direction of her co-workers. She's on the verge of tears. God help her.

"Nobody saw it removed, Jane. No one knows how it disappeared. Believe me, it was the first thing I asked when I got here, because *I* noticed. No one else did, though. Either it was here when they opened the shop early this morning and went missing sometime today while they were all at work, or it was already gone. Either way, not a soul here noticed."

"You've got to be kidding me. That piece is huge—thirty by forty inches! How could it have simply vanished without attracting the least little bit of attention? Did someone just walk inside in the middle of the morning rush and saunter out with it?" She tries to keep her volume down. She knows this isn't Jakes's fault.

"I don't know." He runs his fingers through his hair, exhaling loudly in defeat. He doesn't know what else to say. She had trusted him with her most precious possessions—possessions he had guaranteed! It's his fault one is now gone. "I'm just really sorry about it. I wanted to make sure I'd talked with you before calling the police."

"The police?" Jane exclaims, even more alarmed.

"Yes. We need to file a report. They'll undoubtedly want a statement from every employee here." Sensing her hesitation, he tells her not to worry, and again she sees the emotion there, which doesn't exactly help things.

"I don't know, Jake," she tells him. "It adds such somberness to the situation. I already don't know how to feel." Angry? Hurt? Exposed?

Devastated.

How embarrassing.

"Maybe they'll find it. It's a long shot, but maybe it isn't. I mean, how difficult can it be to learn something, given the limited space in which it disappeared? You said it yourself, someone has to know something. An investigation will at least alert everyone here we're serious about it."

"I don't know. Just give me a moment." She breathes deeply, realizing he's right. "I guess it's fine. It's just—well—it feels like I've lost a piece of me, like—I don't know—like a part of my heart has been taken, if that makes sense. Is that crazy?" She feels foolish for admitting this.

"No, not at all," he replies earnestly.

"Calling attention to its absence makes all of it more real. It's just so personal, you know."

"I can imagine it is," he says gently. He places a hand on her forearm, ignoring the customer now repeatedly checking her watch while waiting to place a drink order. "Wouldn't it help to know who took it so we could get it back?"

She considers this for a moment, especially the *we* part. It's the first time she can ever recall being included as part of a team of any kind, and it feels strangely wonderful, despite the circumstances. She's glad Jake is her friend, that he's on her side. His strength is reassuring. "I think it would," she admits. "I don't care who or why. I just want it back."

"I understand."

But then she feels a little silly again. Humiliated still. "Maybe I'm making too big a deal of it. Like, to be too serious about this is to think too grandly of my own skill."

"You shouldn't look at it that way. That's nonsense. Skill has nothing to do with it. The painting is your creation, a part of you."

Good grief.

"Skill has nothing to do with it?" Jane teases, trying to lighten the mood.

Jake laughs. "You know what I mean." He pauses. "In all seriousness, I don't suppose you'd have any interest in selling any of your other pieces now, would you?" he asks with a sheepish grin.

"There you go being serious again," she says, thinking he must be kidding.

"Because I'd love to own one of your paintings," he continues somberly.

Is this guy for real?

"Stop," she says holding her palms up to face him. "I know you're just trying to cheer me up," and forcing herself to chuckle, adds, "and it's working. But honestly, I don't know how I feel about you or anyone else actually purchasing …"

"I don't want to be insensitive at a time like this, but c'mon. You don't want to sell any of them, but you should, and we need to stop having this conversation. The one where you doubt yourself."

"I can't …"

"I'm sorry to interrupt you and I'm even sorrier that piece went missing, but maybe now is the time to think about it. Maybe now is a good time to consider parting with some of the others. Parting that could actually result in a little cash in your wallet."

Jane squeezes her eyes shut, weighing the truth of his words.

"Okay, so my timing is bad, but you had to know how I've felt, asking you to showcase some of your collection here." With a stiff smile he then turns to pick up the telephone receiver on the wall, affecting a coolness Jane easily discerns as a mask for anger, on her behalf! She watches him heatedly punch in 9-1-1 on the pad. It's as if Jake is as rattled as she is. Has anyone ever been so upset for her?

Wow.

"Wait, shouldn't you be dialing the local police dispatch? This isn't an emergency, you know."

"Oh, right." He hangs up and with greater control, reaches for the phone book on the counter. He locates the dispatch number and dials.

He seems nervous. What could be his motive? A feeling of responsibility, surely. But does he truly admire her work? Or is he just feigning a belief in her ability in order to soothe her feelings?

"Now you'll have me doubting myself again" Jane complains. He looks over at her quizzically. She continues, "Selling would mean confronting the quality of my work."

It's never been about quality, but truth.

"But knowing it's to a friend? I think that's a good start," he says, missing her point entirely as the dispatcher comes on the line.

"That's even worse," she protests. "I don't want to have to face anyone I know after they come to realize how amateurish my heart is," she says, attempting to lighten her mood.

"At least you'll know your heart is in good hands," Jake says laughingly as he covers the receiver with his hand.

Oh Jake, if only yours was.

The empty space on the coffee shop wall created by the removal of *The House* must be filled, so Jane chooses a landscape to hang in between the two remaining, smaller paintings, all of them in oil, which is the extent of her medium collection. She's been tempted to do watercolors, but the clarity she manages to produce in oil can't be matched.

Yellow is a single sunflower adorning the side of a dirt road; *Bells* are a collection of white wildflowers growing in a clump off a well-worn path. *When Leaves Are Red* is a group of ruby foliage contrasted against the gray grasses of a late autumn. All of those are smaller, eight by ten canvases. A little larger are *Blue Summer,* an ancient oak tree standing alone on a summer plain against a turquoise blue sky, and *Promise,* a cluster of tiny green shoots emerging from dark, dormant soil.

To replace the biggest painting gone from the center, Jane chooses a large landscape from the stack at the very back of her closet. She's given it the title *Twilight Mood.* This one, her second largest at twenty-four by thirty-six inches, depicts the settling of winter pastels at dusk. Fading tints brushed thin catch the receding light for color, while floating puffs like cotton hold pink against a silver sky.

Jane stands back to admire the painting in its new location.

"It looks good," she says aloud, sighing.

She has begun to find satisfaction in her least favorite time of the year. The colors of winter are restful, at least.

And on days when fear creeps back into her world again, because displaying her work for all to see still leaves her feeling exposed and the idea of selling as unprotected as standing naked in a snowstorm, it's the hope found in color that buoys her spirit.

Fortunately, she has plenty of inspiration, and just as the human body needs blood and a constant supply of water to go on living, Jane suspects she needs a constant supply of visions.

What if she runs out of this power? This water? This ... life?

Ridiculous. Even without another visit to The Land, she wouldn't forget it. For eternity she'll have the ability to imagine it, re-create it. Surely.

I could never empty out all of my heart onto canvas.

At least, she hopes this is true.

Meanwhile, the police have no leads, and her co-workers, if they know anything at all, are still playing dumb. It's likely she will never get that part of herself back.

And then, the strangest sensation occurs to Jane. Maybe she could actually do it! Maybe Jake was right when he timed his petition to allow him to buy one of her paintings because, strangely enough, now that she is actually breathing through and surviving the loss of her most important work, it occurs to her that perhaps she *could* sell other pieces of her collection. It wasn't as if she was ever going to hang them on her own walls.

Was she?

That would mean fully accepting herself beyond the criticism of others.

Okay, so maybe not yet.

But there are too many to even hang now. Her body of work is becoming too large to keep hidden in the back of a deep closet.

In the end she decides to risk it. After all, there *is* something about offering to sell that feels empowering and validating, and this would be true even if she didn't have a family who has never acknowledged her ability, a mother who isn't interested in it, and a father who sees no value there.

Until now, she has never known affirmation.

No, Jake was right. Exhibiting was the first step. Selling will be the second. The third if you factor in losing.

Thank God someone believes in her.

Chapter Fourteen

Someone believes in me!

It's what Jane reminds herself as her sister walks through Oliver's door with a group of her friends after school. Jessica has never entered the shop before, hasn't deigned to. She wouldn't give Jane the satisfaction without cause.

The grand entrance is marked with loud banter. Jessica tosses her long hair over to one side repeatedly and laughs forcefully, seemingly unconcerned with her own awkwardness, to say nothing for the disturbance of others. She's out of her element, but only Jane knows that. She catches Jess stealing glances at the menu high on the back wall as she talks with her friends, pretending not to notice Jane. Acting like she's in full control.

Ok, I'll play along.

"What can I get started for you?" Jane asks, now moving to stand behind the cash register in front of the group.

Jess squirrels to the back of the line, momentarily silent as the girls place their orders one by one. When it's Jess' turn, she's had sufficient time to deliberate. "I'll have a small latte," she says decisively.

"Sure." Jane smiles. "Hot or cold?"

"Hot." The word comes out with more force than even Jess intended.

"Great," Jane says, seemingly unperturbed. She gives her sister the total, making no effort to reveal their connection to anyone who may be watching, especially Jake. As soon as the register drawer is closed and Jess is handed her change with a "Thank you," the gaggle moves to the end of the bar to resume their private discussion.

As Jane busies herself, moving over to the espresso machine to prepare the drinks, she feels Jessica's eyes follow her. No one else in the group pays any mind to what's happening behind the counter, but Jessica is clearly keeping track of all movement in the shop, particularly Jane's. Jane pours and froths, handing each cup over in turn, her sister uncharacteristically quiet as Jane goes about her work.

Once all the drinks are delivered, an awkward silence settles in the café as every eye in the pack now focuses on Jane. It's unsettling—weird to say the least, but Jane resolves not to let the antics of her sister and her strange friends bother her as she cleans up the bar. She glues a smile on her lips until they begin to quiver.

The group giggles loudly.

Then, following a brief huddle, the girls take seats around the table closest to the bar, each making boisterous declarations in turn, each louder in volume than the one who speaks before her.

"This coffee tastes like instant Sanka," one of the girls trills.

"Right? Like, why do they have to charge so much?" says another.

By the time Jake emerges from the back room, their laughter has grown rowdy. "Hey Jake, could you grab me another bottle of vanilla syrup from the back?" Jane calls, hoping he won't notice the escalating situation. Maybe the posse will leave before there's any real trouble.

But he's already noticed. "Is there a problem, ladies?" he asks, ignoring Jane's request. Jake has never met Jess, but if he senses trouble in his café, he'll remedy it.

The blonde girl with hair like a poodle speaks up. "Yeah. There is. It took totally forever to get our drinks." The others giggle.

"I'm sorry to hear we didn't meet your expectations, *totally*," Jake calmly replies, speaking their vernacular. "What did you order?" The girls list their drinks in nasally, high-pitched voices. He offers a dry grin. "Your beverages were handcrafted with espresso shots. They take a bit longer than regular, brewed cups of coffee."

"Well, *that* employee seemed to be taking her sweet time," Jess retorts loudly, pointing at Jane.

"Again, I apologize for the wait. I know your time is *totally* important," he says sweetly. Jane giggles in spite of her fury. It takes every ounce of resolve Jane has not to intervene. How dare Jess take their family feud to her place of employment!

How mortifying!

Jake doesn't deserve to have his business subjected to any of her familial malfunction or nonsensical teenaged drama or whatever this is. He's simply a nice guy trying to run a decent business, not a venue for Jane's theater.

"Well, this stuff wasn't worth the wait," says Jess.

"Okay, well, have a nice afternoon!" Jake says as he turns back to walk toward his office. Jess has been summarily dismissed, but Jake has no idea Jess will not be made a fool.

He is nearly to his door when Jess trills, "Ooohh, would you just look at this décor?" Her warbly voice is several octaves above pleasant and loud enough to cut through the resumed coffee shop din like a fire alarm. Jess has everyone's attention now.

And she's looking directly at Jane's paintings.

So, there we have it. How did she know?

Jess continues, wrinkling her nose in affectation as she waves a hand toward them. "Isn't it just awful? So plebeian."

Does she even know what that means?

Jane feels the color drain from her face to pool in her chest. Jess hasn't so much as glanced at Jane's work at home—what little she's revealed—and she couldn't know about the closet stash.

Could she? Could she know?

She has to know.

Jane's pulse quickens as her blood readies for battle.

God help me, I'm going to kill her!

Before Jane can launch herself across the room like a feral cat, one of her companions pipes up to add her own commentary. "Yeah, stale and unexciting. Something you'd see in my old grandmother's sitting room." It's the circus poodle again. With too much blush on her cheeks and wearing jeans she's pasted herself into.

I'll bet she hasn't visited her old grandmother dressed like that.

The brunette with the wiry, teased hair, half of which explodes from the top her head like a fountain, chimes in, too. "I'm surprised a café like this would choose to decorate in this way. It's definitely odd. Uncultured. A little trashy, if you ask me."

"Ha-ha, *trashy* being the operative word," Jess agrees.

Have either of them looked in the mirror?

Jess has gone too far this time. She goes too far every time. And every time, Jane has been the bigger person. In fact, she's developed rather extraordinary self-control in responding to her sister's unsolicited commentary and blatant hostility throughout the years, mostly in an effort to keep escalation at bay. But there are limits to what one can endure. Now, she fears she will explode.

Instead, tears spring to her eyes, and she is forced to turn away from the counter, fighting the urge to take flight through the back door.

Missing nothing, Jake leaps into action himself, like a tiger pouncing on prey. "I'm the owner of this shop," he declares, "and my *grandmother* happens to be a wonderful interior designer." The trio is stunned awkwardly silent. "Moreover, she detests bad manners," he says eyeing them pointedly. "What is it about my décor you find unacceptable?"

"Um, well …" the poofy brunette begins, before finding herself also at a loss for further words. She looks down to the cup of coffee she's holding and takes a small, nervous sip.

"We were just observing," Circus Poodle says, equally uneasy.

"Just voicing opinions," Poofy adds, regaining confidence.

"Ugh. Trash all the way around," Jess exclaims, refusing to back down. "Taste to match the coffee. And the dumpy employees."

"I will not tolerate the harassment of my employees. And for what it's worth, I was the one who asked the artist to exhibit her work here. I admire it. Greatly."

Jess, now steely quiet, appears stunned by Jake's response. Jane knows she's not used to opposition. He's impressive.

Jane can barely breathe.

Taking full advantage of the group of ruminants now caught in blinding light, Jake continues amidst blank stares. "This immensely talented artist honored me with her willingness to allow her paintings to be displayed here. In fact, I recently bought one myself. Needless to say, I won't have her work disparaged any more than I will have my employees treated improperly or my business defamed by a bunch of ill-mannered brats."

Jane can see Jess's neck from across the room. Blotches of red in bursts reveal an angst Jane hadn't counted on, something that tickles her about as much as Jake's intervention, but not enough to assuage any of the hurt inflicted. There will be no getting over the insults this time. This time, they had action behind them.

Still, Jake is marvelous. There is that.

And he isn't finished yet. "I'm not sure what your game is, but you needn't play it here," he continues, walking toward the door. "This is an establishment offering warmth and kindness. You are no longer welcome." He holds the door open and stands waiting, an indication the group should take their leave, and they do, without another word said on the matter.

"Oh, and by the way," he calls after them, "We make GREAT coffee here!"

Once he steps back in the door, patrons get back to enjoying their discussions and beverages, and though traffic starts to pick up again, Jake orders Jane to the back for an early break. He helps out on the floor for a few minutes and then joins her.

"Do you want to tell me what that was all about?" he asks.

"That," she says taking a deep breath, "was my sister."

"Really? Which one?"

"The ringleader with the red hair she kept tossing around like a horse's mane."

"Wow. That was low. Why would she do it? Does she dislike you that much?"

Jane sighs. "She doesn't dislike me. She hates me. I'm convinced of it. And, honestly, I don't know why."

"That's rough. I am so sorry," he says gently, and Jane can see he truly cares for her. He's truly hurt for her.

"No, I am the one who is sorry. I'm sorry she brought this into your business. That wasn't fair to you."

"Jane, not everyone who enters this establishment is going to be fair or nice." He hesitates. "You don't think …" his voice trails off.

"I don't think, what?"

"Well, I mean, could your sister have taken that painting?"

"I don't see how. She's never set foot in here before today."

"I suppose you're right. Someone would have seen her," Jake agrees. "She's hard to miss."

"Don't try to work it out. It's impossible," she directs him. "I've been trying to figure her out for a long time, and speaking of figuring things out, I hope the police come up with something."

"I hope so too." He puts his arm around her, and she doesn't flinch this time. "Have you heard anything yet?"

"No. Not a thing." Pausing, she adds, "I appreciate you, you know." She pulls away to eye him earnestly. "I don't know what I'd do without you." As she says this, she realizes she means it.

Jake laughs in the relaxed manner she's become accustomed to, and she realizes again she does love that about him. He's the only one she knows that can tell a hard truth softly.

Could Jess have taken the painting to spite her? It hadn't taken Jake long after meeting her sister to come up with the idea. She *is* capable of it. And so much more. Jane remembers her boots at the bottom of the pool.

But if that were true, what could be her real motive? Spite? Jealousy? Jane is no competition. And why now? They don't argue nearly as much as they used to, and neither of them is home much to be in the other's way.

And then the only other possibility occurs to Jane. The one where her sister is right about Jane's lack of ability. What if Jane's paintings don't hold the lure for others they do for Jake? For her? What if they aren't as special as what she feels when she is painting them? What if they're bad? Jane feels she might be sick.

"Don't you dare," he says, eyeing her closely.

"Don't I dare what?"

"Don't you dare believe what those ornery girls said about your work."

"Of course I am going to believe them!" she admits. Her sister may have plunged the knife in too far this time, but truth hurts sometimes. This was deeply wounding. Devastating, actually.

"It's bologna. Complete BS. If you buy into that, you're giving up."

"I suppose," Jane says through trembling lips, determined to hold onto the fresh storm of tears now brewing behind her lids. She considers the episodes with Pete. Was it possible Jess knew all along what had transpired between them? Had she put him up to any of it? It could explain why Pete had suddenly backed off from harassing her just after she'd confronted Jess about it. Come to think of it, she'd not seen him in a while.

She forces thoughts of that loser from her mind and turns to Jake. "You're a good friend. A liar. But a good friend."

"I'm neither. I'm just a truthful chap."

"Chap, is it?" Jane asks, finally chuckling.

"Yeah," he says with the widest smile Jane has ever seen. "The chap who thinks your work is great. The one who *knows* it is. So much so, someone who couldn't afford it fell in love with it. That's probably the real reason it's gone."

In this moment, Jane isn't persuaded. In this moment, she is only convinced of the genuineness of the man in front of her.

He must be the most wonderfully kind guy in the world.

It's most unfortunate she can't paint him.

Worse that she can't possibly fall in love with him.

Chapter
Fifteen

THE KANSAS TERRITORY—1856

"It's your fault I paint," she tells Mac when she next sees him. They're standing on The Land in the green of a spring past. A soft breeze kicks up in intermittent rushes around them. "Not that I'm complaining," she thinks to add.

"What do you mean?" he asks innocently.

"Don't play dumb with me, Mac. You know exactly what I mean. You put me up to it. You knew when I saw the things you showed me I wouldn't be able to help myself. As proof of it, I suddenly found myself in possession of an unusual ability to do it. Talent I'd not had before. Where did that come from, huh?"

Mac remains unusually stoic. She thinks she sees a grin forming at the corner of his lips. He looks away.

"Yeah. That's what I thought." Jane leans forward to eye him squarely in the face, finding the confirmation she's looking for. But what she still doesn't understand is, why? And why would her parents be so opposed to it? Why would her sister find it so disagreeable?

Never mind the sister part.

Why does Jake love it so?

Never mind that part, too.

But why would someone take her favorite painting?

"Evil persuades. It works to disrupt what is good. But good overcomes evil." Mac answers as if he's reading her thoughts, which of course he is.

Could it be Jane is now reading Mac's thoughts?

He continues, "No matter how balanced things may look, good always outweighs the bad. Good is always infinitely more prevalent, always stronger than what is not."

Jane considers this philosophy for a moment. "And there are no gray areas."

"Exactly. There is only good or evil. Nothing in between. Choices are fully delineated, whether we realize it or not."

"I wish the good was more obvious sometimes."

"I'm sorry your sister rejects what she doesn't understand," Mac says.

"I'm sorry she hurts me," Jane replies.

"But you must not take it personally. The bigger issue is what she does to herself in the process. Her choices hurt her more than you."

"Knowing that doesn't make it any easier," Jane continues. "I don't want to live a life in conflict with her. Or my parents, for that matter." Jane leaves off the part about her sister's boyfriend's molestation. Surely she doesn't have to put her feelings about *that* into words.

"You need to persevere."

"What does that mean? I need to wait for them to get it? I need to be patient as they find fault with everything I do?" She pauses for a moment and continues. "Or I just need to get on with it, disregarding what anyone else thinks?"

"Yes." His eyes still twinkle with violet light and his teeth shine an unearthly white when he smiles big.

He really does have an amazing smile.

"Yes what?" she demands. "Yes, to all three?"

"Yes." He laughs out loud now.

"I fail to see this as a laughing matter. I'm completely serious, Mac. My parents are impossible and my sister openly hateful, if not downright vengeful. I am tired of feeling insecure about my future because the one thing I know I am any good at is cause for ridicule."

"That isn't true, and you know it," he replies, dusting dandelion wisps off his lapel with meticulous care. The prairie breeze is full of them this early summer day on the plains. "You're good at a lot of things. Like feeling sorry for yourself."

"No, I'm not!" she shouts.

"Not good at a lot of things? Or not good at feeling sorry for yourself?"

"Both. No. You know what I mean," she says, exasperated. "Did I see you roll your eyes at me? You rolled your eyes at me!"

"I did not."

"You did, too!"

"I did not. You have a responsibility to choose good. To fight against what is not, of course, but to focus on what is good. In this way, you will grow it to overcome what opposes it."

"Then why do you show me dark things? What happened to revealing only lovely things? What's the point? Don't you think I've enough dark things here and in my own life?"

"Have you had enough of the lovely, though?" he asks mischievously.

Turning her attention to their current setting, she now notices the cabin off in the distance seems to have materialized once again. She smells wild grasses.

"How are they?" she asks Mac. He shrugs and looks toward the house.

"Why can't you just tell me? Why must you show me? Why must I experience this firsthand?" But Mac is gone again, another question still unanswered.

"Why?" she screams more loudly, knowing he can still hear her.

The spring of 1856 is heavy with struggle, but Seamus and Nell O'Donnell hold on to it as one might hang on to the tail of a lion one is trying to tame. First, there is the very real issue of coaxing the land into cooperation for sustenance. Thanks to the cow, there is mush and milk on the table year 'round, and jackrabbits for stew now and again. Sometimes, if there are more than enough rabbits, Nell will fry up the meat and make milk gravy to go along with it.

It will be some time before the fields yield the produce hoped for, but the couple managed to get some field corn up last season, and that buoyed their spirits. The real harvests they dream of still drift on the winds of the future. Not so far out that they don't believe they'll blow favorably their way, and soon.

In the meantime, the corn helped. When they ran out of that, they used the dried stalks to feed the cow, which would have been great kindling in a place starved for decent trees. Nearby, Leavenworth has plenty, but other than the ancient, stand-alone sentinel positioned between their plowed rows, there is little to no wood here for decent fuel, and Nell saves every bit of what comes out of the field for nourishment, not heat. Fortunately, dung can be used as a fuel source until the next harvest when the fruit of their claim staked in the ground will surely be realized.

But they aren't the only ones to stake claims here.

The wolves and coyotes, the prairie dogs and the snakes, all vie for the right to thrive; the strong insects and flying things, the ones that arrive untethered and entitled, devour their share; the dirt and the sun that bakes it into cracks only to release it into the air have claims, too, as do the storms that run it back into rivers, sometimes sustaining, sometimes choking. Every creature, whether motionless or moving, settling or traveling, believes this place is theirs. The good. The bad. The afflicted. The afflicting.

Is harmony even possible where there is claim?

Kansas promises it for all that contend for it, and this is no easy feat.

It takes grit to live here, and people with grit don't quit. They work hard. They find contentment. They stay out of other people's business. They live their good lives for others, when necessary, but ultimately they live for themselves. Isn't everyone entitled to this? To live their own way in the pursuit of happiness without interference?

Jane understands the O'Donnell's perspective because history is one of the subjects she's been most drawn to. There is something about understanding the past that facilitates a remembrance of more, as if dusting off ancient volumes to touch old parchment could be transportive.

Understandably, she knows the ruffians who roam the countryside looking to harass and even harm anyone who runs counter to their objective aren't finished yet.

Tom Crawford emerges from winter's hibernation convinced inebriation allowed his mind to play tricks on him at the O'Donnell cabin last fall. He'd spent the cold months indoors listening to another voice urging him back out to the cabin to rid the county of that Jayhawker, Seamus. He'd spent even more time fixating on what he heard the voice tell him to do to Seamus' wife.

When Tom and the only other man he could convince to ride out with him this time, a redheaded, crusty newcomer by the fitting name of Rusty, arrive to pound fists against the door, Seamus is away again. This time, Seamus' trip into town is necessary to trade the butter and cheese Nell made for flour and salt; he will purchase the other supplies the family needs. Once again, his absence can't be helped. Nell must placate her visitors the only way she knows how. This time, however, her resolute hospitality is laced with more boldness than before.

"Where is he?" Tom Crawford again demands after having hammered against the door. This time he's stone sober, a rare condition for the man. He's taking no chances.

Nell opens the door resolving she'll again thwart escalation with the strength of feigned cordiality. Leaving off the specifics of her husband's whereabouts and realizing the fortuitousness of the moment, she gathers confidence, aware the timing of the town's bully here and not where Seamus is doing business alone is favorable. The military help her husband had sought in the past was limited to catching up with the opposition when it could be found, and there was a lot of opposition to catch up with. Like cockroaches, those bullies seemed to operate clandestinely, often retreating in the light of day, and it had been a small miracle Seamus and Tom had yet to meet up again. Nell wonders whatever happened to Frank, the man they had tended. Maybe he'd made better company since then.

"I really couldn't say," she says. "Will ye be comin' in and helping yourself to me food again?" She steps back and sweeps a free arm across the threshold to bid them enter. She knows she really shouldn't provoke them, but for some strange reason, she feels unusually brave. Maybe the visions she has regularly now embolden her, knowing the real beyond the natural.

What's unnatural is the way the men in front of her smell! Their odor isn't just sour, but sulfurous and metallic. The air around them seems odd too. In fact, it seems the temperature has dropped by degrees to downright frigid in the middle of a warm, spring day.

Nell isn't the only one to sense these things. From her vantage point, Jane does, as well.

"Maybe we'll just wait for him, then," says Rusty. Tom had told him the wife was pretty, and he was right. He runs a lizard-like tongue over his parched lips.

"If I'd known ye were comin', I'd have baked more biscuits," Nell continues impudently, but her sarcasm doesn't seem to register with the intruders. She glances at the loaded rifle behind the door.

Tom's eyes track with hers, and he starts to head for it, but just then, something stops him. As was the case on his last visit, he's suddenly startled by an odd sensation around his neck. It is as if hands are around his windpipe squeezing off his air! Rusty feels it, too, and both men begin to gasp for breath.

"This. Is. A. Waste. Of. Time," Tom sputters, frightened and racing for the door again. He's headed off by Rusty, who appears in more of a hurry to leave the cabin than Tom.

They certainly didn't stay long this time, think Nell and Jane together.

Both women are incredulous as they watch the men leave. The thugs hadn't eaten any food or torn the place apart. They hadn't rifled through Nell's personal things or threatened her. It had been a far different scenario, a completely different conversation, from the last witnessed here. It is only now Jane realizes she'd been holding her own breath.

And then Jane sees him. Mac. *With* Nell. Not standing beside Jane as he generally does in witness, and not vanished into thin air, either. He is there in the little cabin just behind Nell, his hands squarely on her shoulders.

And with him are at least a dozen others—beings of giant proportions, standing just behind Mac and Nell!

Jane's heart beats a drum inside her chest as she strains to catch it all quickly before they disappear, as her view is already beginning to fade. The scene is discernible but blurry, as if out of focus, and she blinks to steady her gaze as their forms diminish further. They resemble a troop of soldiers or a militia of some kind, but are the tallest people Jane has ever seen. Most of them must be ten feet in height, maybe more! She would be terrified if their benevolence wasn't so obvious.

The giants, whose faces are obscured to her, appear to have been defending Nell. Transcending the small cabin made from earthly matter, their superimposed images now give way, and they are gone.

Jane wonders if obscurity is her own shortcoming or someone else's deliberate attempt to shield her from total clarity. What she'd witnessed hadn't lasted long enough to reveal details for unreserved comprehension, but it had been enough.

Someone had wanted her to bear witness to this part of it.

Who?

Those giants had something on their backs, though Jane couldn't tell what that might have been.

What had it been?

"Mac, come back here!" she shouts. "Tell me what just happened!" She has no way to process what she's just seen, no frame of reference. Her mind feels sluggish, as if it's functioning in slow motion. The giants had disappeared quickly but not before Jane's eyes had transmitted woodland gods, half man and half animal.

No, that can't be the case.

But they were neither man nor animal.

Who, or what, were they?

And who had they been engaged against?

In a matter of minutes, the cabin is restored to peace.

Nell sits down on the bench at the table, smoothing her hair back as she does. The baby begins to cry.

"Thanks Mac. Thanks a lot," Jane yells, believing her words won't be heard by Nell. By Mac, though? Undoubtedly.

What had Jane just witnessed? Had she seen what she thought she had? If she had, she'd been the only one. Nell had been unaware. The thugs had been unaware. Or had they?

Mac?

He'd wanted her to see.

He'd made sure of it.

Jane pulls her sight from the house to the departing Ruffians, and what she sees next causes her to shiver. Though the sun will soon reach a high point, an eerie darkness surrounds the duo, forming a mass that clings to the men as they ride, like a thick mud, enveloping each in intervals. She watches as the darkness thins and shadows form individual silhouettes in agitated motion. They hover, ghost-like, stretching out from each rider before rejoining the larger inflammation, which coils itself around the bellies of the horses. Jane can see it really isn't a conglomeration but a collection of individual phantasms, and she shudders, frightened cold and suddenly sick to her stomach as malodorous scents reach her again.

Returning her gaze to the cabin and through the walls where Nell has closed and barred the door, it appears little is out of place as the woman lifts her daughter to kiss her long on the forehead. She transfers the toddler to her left hip and picks up a poker with her right, stoking a fire in the stove while humming a tune Jane recognizes but can't identify.

Why? Why am I being shown these things?

What is my purpose here?

Even as she ponders these things, she knows the answer to at least one question.

It is to believe everything is possible.

Mac wants her to know this firsthand. He's preparing her for something.

But what?

She would be foolish to consider anything outside of the very bold and highly-illuminated marquee that now shines from her mind's eye.

Who is their Commander in Chief, exactly?

There is definitely so much more to what can be seen visibly.

How much will He allow me to see?

And most importantly, what am I supposed to do with the information I've been given?

She dusts the dandelion puffs off her denim jacket, hoists her backpack to her shoulder, and heads out into a cold, snowy morning in her own world to start her car for school, thinking about Mac's words of perseverance and the end of the world and how it might be so much easier not to know.

In the 1850s, a young man by the name of Samuel begins drawing and painting what he sees on the plains of the Midwest. He is particularly interested in documenting his own role in the abolitionist fight for freedom in the territory known as Kansas. He creates not because he is a romantic but because he is a journalist, and there are stories to be told in color. If he doesn't accurately preserve for posterity what is happening here in illustrations of water and pigment and oil, who will?

He shares his finished perspectives with his fellow soldiers, the pencil drawings and the pictures done with brush, and those soldiers tell others about what they've seen. They tell their wives and children, too, and therefore, people talk about the soldier who is fighting for a good cause and painting it as well.

Because of Samuel, more people know about the Battle of Little Blue River and others in the Border War between Kansas and Missouri, and freedom for all means they know it is good to paint the world and what happens here. So naturally, when Seamus tells Nell of this, she is encouraged. She paints even more. But unlike some of her contemporaries, Nell paints only good.

And when Seamus joins the abolitionist cause officially, he carries one of his wife's paintings with him, the one she calls *The Shepherdess*. As he dedicates his life to the cause and fights in the skirmishes that will eventually pave the way to the War Between the States, he pulls Nell's favorite work from his rucksack and unrolls the twelve by sixteen-inch canvas to reveal a splendid landscape, framed in tall, wild prairie grasses and scattered with purple wildflowers, Queen Anne's lace, and little lambs. In the middle, a shepherdess in a long, white gown stands against the wind, her hair blowing in billows behind her. In the distant background is a lovely white house.

Seamus thinks the property looks a lot like theirs, but Nell wouldn't say when he asked her about it, and there were subtle differences even without the home he'd never seen before. He doesn't know for sure. What he does know is his wife has a marvelous imagination along with an unusual talent for painting.

But Nell needs no imagination to color the sky. It's ever-changing hues are the colors of her ever-changing heart, the earth a part of who she is, and Seamus understands this in some small way.

The painting is so lovely he must carry it with him, for it reminds him of his wife and makes him feel as though she is with him at all times. Not only does the painting appeal to Seamus' emotions, it captures the hearts of weary men whose lives are exposed and raw and worn as they fight against darkness. And perhaps that is why what Nell has created resonates within them, deep down under their weathered skin and rough resolve.

Pretty soon, that lovely maiden becomes a sort of mascot for the small abolitionist group. She exemplifies purity and all the beauty they uphold as sacred, a very picture of the good they hope to create in this world—a world free of oppression and tyranny. The land and its creatures symbolize what is promised to all beyond the fight. The Shepherdess foreknows their victory.

And why shouldn't soldiers nurture sentimentalism? Why shouldn't they embrace romantic notion? There must be something else to balance all of the ugliness.

At the end of long days, weary faces, weathered skin, and sore bodies not generally given over to frivolity welcome it. They ask Seamus to take out Nell's painting, and they gather around the campfires to gaze upon her picture of hope. They've never known a painting to make them feel the way they do—all warm inside, as if God himself had painted it. And He couldn't have created a more beautiful, inspiring human.

And then one day, the painting disappears. It isn't in Seamus' rucksack or anywhere in the makeshift camp hastily assembled the night before, as on every other night, for a troop on the move in places called slave states and free soil and soon to be known as Ruffians' Missouri and Bleeding Kansas. Seamus is heartsick, and so are the other men, who quickly spring into action to find *The Shepherdess*, but she isn't to be found. It's as if she has vanished into thin air.

Without her, a little hope is gone, too.

Reluctantly, Seamus returns home on leave to inform Nell, who tells him she cannot paint another. In fact, until her shepherdess is returned, she will not paint a replacement. Seamus thinks Nell mad at this point, her reasoning absurd. Why couldn't she paint another painting like the first one? Clearly, she has the talent to do so.

But Nell digs her heels in and refuses. She can't. It's as if that first one was her child, as if that shepherdess was her little girl, and she realizes now she's been in love with what she created, and in so many ways, the girl in the grass *was* her girl. The sister she's prayed might join Agnes, but God isn't answering those prayers, and Nell hopes the missing painting doesn't mean what she fears it does. Maybe that's why she is so melancholy over the loss.

Maybe she should have painted her real daughter instead of an allegorical one. She could have imagined her Agnes years from now as a young woman. She would be beautiful, too. Agnes Rose O'Donnell had been given her name because her mother had read Anne Bronte's novel *Agnes Grey*. Nell had later learned the name Agnes was associated with lamb in Latin, and this delighted her, given Agnes was Nell's own lamb. But when she'd painted "The Shepherdess," Nell wasn't thinking of Agnes Rose, or *Agnes Grey* for that matter. Her shepherdess was her own person, an allegorical representation of a caretaker of land and lambs.

Seamus should never have insisted upon taking her with him only to lose her. She doesn't know why she should feel as if a piece of her is missing, but she does. And seemingly unanswered prayers are to Nell what unkept promises are to the native people here.

To heal, she paints bluffs overlooking a vast sea and trees with rough bark the size of ships. She paints buffalo and endless horizons and wildflowers, too. But she never paints another shepherdess asleep in tall prairie grass. She never paints another lamb.

And she never paints the Native American woman who first recognized hope here, because Nell never sees Running Feet also watching her from a distance.

Chapter
Sixteen

THE STATE OF KANSAS—*1867*

A new form of violence sweeps across the Kansas plains in the summer of 1867 as the spirits of war refuse to let go. Although the official fighting is over, animosity remains draped across the land, friction substantially woven into stronghold. The Civil War ended three years earlier, but tensions are still high, and not just between the latest settlers. There are other places more peaceful to live than Kansas.

The O'Donnell cabin is far off any track beaten flat and etched deep by horse hooves and wagon wheels, but Seamus and Nell wonder if their land isn't a beacon pointing travelers far and wide to their location when strangers again show up on horseback needing help. This time a young man scalped and left for dead near the O'Donnell farmstead is found by a passing troop who places him on the back of a horse to ride for the nearest assistance.

Fortunately, the injured man's scalp has not been entirely severed from his skull but cut just above his forehead and pulled down over his eyes. Nell, a capable seamstress whose heart and flesh have grown strong in recent years, takes out a common needle and fiddle string to sew the unconscious man's head back together. She tends to him until his health is restored under the appreciative watch of the troops and Seamus, and after the man is sufficiently recuperated, he and the others are on their way. Like most women who live in this time and place, Nell has had no choice but to learn to care for the sick and injured and to expect the unexpected regularly. She grows braver all the while, as Jane does in witness, but oh, the struggles feel relentless.

Meanwhile, Seamus and Nell pray for peace, appealing to God for protection from a similar fate, vowing to keep their only child close to home. Containing Agnes Rose, however, who likes to wander and daydream, is a tall order. Especially now that she is twelve years old. Now that she has become an artist who likes to capture the big sky and prairie. Because on the morning of her twelfth birthday, Seamus and Nell's daughter suddenly develops a desire to paint.

With her pa home from war, painting the good things is easy, as if doing so will blot out the others—the fighting and the bleeding and the struggling. The young girl who laments disharmony like a wildflower cries over a cloudy day is mostly happy because she is able to memorialize what is beautiful.

Remembered in paint are the birds and grasses and cathedral skies, the sun as it melts in pink clouds across brown tassels, and the rain as it falls, purple-blue on the horizon, and this gives her joy, especially now that the girl's mother has put up her own paint supplies. Someone might as well use them. There is so much good to paint!

From afar, Jane understands. Jane chooses to focus on the light, too. Light is what makes color and all the lovely things.

She watches the little girl and loves her at first sight, grateful Mac has allowed her this. She so wishes the girl could turn her face and see Jane and know she has a friend. Maybe they could find a way to paint together, beyond roving predators and warring men.

Jane observes her by the river's edge first thing in the morning when the sun lifts ever so slightly from slumber to yawn across the vast plains with her first, feeble rays, until it awakens to soar boastfully overhead, and later when crimson gives way to gold. Jane watches the way the light above shines on the little girl's long, brown hair, casting a copper glow in ribbons from top to bottom, and the way she sings to herself, as if there is no such thing as darkness or shadows.

Jane watches the girl imprint what she sees on canvas, carefully capturing moments that would otherwise be forever lost, each as unique as snowflakes or frost patterns, fingerprints or DNA. Shades of every color aren't overlooked by the girl.

Or Jane.

Jane sees through her eyes, and this makes her feel even more connected to The Land and the young girl, across time and space and logic. They share a way of looking at the world.

And she wonders if the girl detects what Jane does on the breeze here, scents of citrus and lavender, wild jasmine and herbs. She smiles now when she thinks of how the sweet fragrances make her feel. Clean and vibrant and loved.

And so Jane watches the girl walk back to her house fully satisfied in her artwork, before chores, after meals, when she can get away by herself. When she isn't stoking the fire, preparing the grits, sweeping the hearth, stepping outside again to milk the cow and returning with a bucket of warm, foamy milk—and there is beauty to be found in these simple tasks, too.

When the girl isn't inside the house hiding from dark things.

Or caring for her sick parents.

And when she isn't painting anymore, and the skies are only gray.

Jane sees loneliness and fear, too, and she hurts for the girl without siblings, for who will comfort her when her parents are gone? It now occurs to Jane that perhaps it's best not to be alone, even if those around you can't be what they ought to be for you. At least knowing there is someone else cut from the same cloth is helpful, even if they are really so very different.

There is purpose to Mac's methods, behind what he shows her. This young girl, Agnes, is someone with whom Jane shares a bond similar to the one that makes The Land so special. It was pretty clever of him to show her The Land first, to cause her to fall in love with it, to sense a connection before introducing her to the people here.

Anyone with visions like Jane's would sense the same. And anyone who did have such sight and failed to ponder possible connections in real time would be daft. And yet, there is something about the experiences that allows them to stand alone. In their own right, they are sufficiently removed from any correlation to her real life and serve, at the very least, to offer glimpses of things to come. Anyone who failed to ponder the connections to the future would also be senseless.

But beyond that is a nebulous area, a foggy picture contrasted against the clarity of paint. Why here? Why the repetitiveness of such visions, or visits, or whatever they are?

Could her visions be allegory for what she's missing in her own life?

The Land representative for what could be created in the void?

Is the family here—this girl—only an act of kindness? Mac's response for what she lacks—the missing connection with a sister, uninvolved parents, the absence of friendship on multiple levels?

What am I supposed to be learning here?

What am I missing?

"I am overthinking things," Jane groans out loud.

Maybe all of it really is a product of my wild imagination.

But the symbolism, oh, the symbolism!

The Land is significant, it has to be. It's hers as much as anyone's. The girl and she both live here, if only in Jane's mind. The connection is real, and the fact that the girl paints her world, just like Jane paints what she sees, is further proof as far as Jane is concerned.

The only problem, outside of Mac's vagueness, is Jane's inability to control access. Getting here cannot happen enough, and especially now that the picture is becoming clearer and more muddled all at once. While these experiences and subtle revelations have been increasing in equal measure, the mystery of it all rules, and the ramblings of her mind continue in proportion to the movement of paint-dipped brushes.

"Will you ever tell me what all of this means?" she asks Mac.

"What all of what means?" His placidity rattles Jane.

"You know what I mean," she insists.

"Meaning?"

"Mac! Stop it!" Jane shouts, exasperated. "Stop messing around!"

"Who says I'm messing around?" At least he looks serious now.

"The things you show me. The Land, The House, the people here … is all of this a replacement for what is lacking in my own life, or a method by which I am to learn something?" And then a thought pops into her mind she hadn't considered before. "Is Agnes me?"

"No."

"Well, that was the fastest, most definitive answer you've ever given me."

"How can she be you?"

"You know that's not what I meant. I meant, is Agnes allegory for who I am?"

"Now that's a question," he says with a smile.

"You won't tell me?"

"What do you think?"

"I think you're impossible."

"Nothing's impossible."

Jane groans. "Can't we please visit this place more regularly?" she asks, conceding the first round.

"What do you mean, regularly?" Mac asks, his grin expanding.

"You know what I mean. I want to be able to anticipate them, the visits. They shouldn't be something that happens at your whim only. I should be able to control the frequency, at least, if not the content. I should be able to schedule them, like I would any trip, and not be surprised by them," Jane challenges.

"Why?" Mac responds, puzzled, which only further irritates Jane. She's beginning to lose her patience. In fact, she's been losing it for a long while now.

"Why?" Jane mocks thunderously. "Don't give me that crud, Mac. I've been a pretty good sport over the years. I've not made any demands. I've listened and watched and humored you with …"

"Humored me, you say?" Mac interrupts sternly, his radiant smile dropping as quickly as the temperature in a polar front. Not that Jane would know anything about this firsthand. Yet. Mac could very well whisk her away to the North Pole at some point.

"Yes, humored! I mean, c'mon, I've gone along with this, whatever *this* is, and I've only asked a bare minimum of questions. I've played the game. Obeyed your rules. Now, I have a right to more information."

"I see." No evidence of a smile, just the further effect of gravity on his face.

What's with him?

"No, I don't think you do. C'mon Mac, what's the problem? Why can't I have a say in any of this?"

"You're missing the point entirely."

"Really? And what might that point actually be? Because right now, it's lost on me. In fact, I am sick of all this!" Even as the words are out of her mouth, she regrets them, because a strange, neutralizing calmness has gathered itself around her. At once, a gentle wind deposits wisdom from her head to her toes and into the deepest parts of her. It settles into place, like fine silt on the ocean floor after having been kicked up and stirred. It finds rest again where it began, and she knows.

Mac continues gently. "You're missing the fact that it was never my *game* or my rules. And you were never meant to be in control. Neither one of us were. Of this, anyway."

How Jane knows this truth intuitively is not something she's ready to concede yet. But deep down in her core, inside bones made of that same silt, is understanding. The answer had been spoken from within her before she'd even finished her sentence, yet she still felt entitled to ask it, as if she should be allowed to examine her own deception up close and personal, to hold the contrariness of her own reason in her hands for inspection. To sift the dust there.

Like believing beyond the visible, she need only see what's really there. And like panning for gold, expose those veracious nuggets for separation from miry deception. Because somewhere in the midst of it all is the issue of timing, the vagueness of which is hers to discover, hers to unravel and keep wound in intervals, its linear workings something understood outside of her and within her, too.

Which is to say, Jane comes to terms with her limitations. Inwardly, she confesses she can't possibly expect to have all things her way.

And yet, she presses. "Mac, work with me. Why all the secrets and evasiveness? Why not just come out with it? Does it all have to be so— mysterious? Is any of this even real?"

"You knew from the beginning you'd need to persevere. So, do it."

"How wonderfully helpful. Thank you," she replies. "Answer this though: A few days ago, I saw other, uh, beings with you surrounding the

O'Donnell's cabin—what was going on there? Who were they? You explain that to me."

Mac purses his lips, but not in an unpleasant way.

"Please."

He still says nothing.

Jane shakes her head and continues, "And while you're at it, why is there so much—violence and sorrow? The wolves, the gangsters, the fighting and scalping and—the sickness—all the hardship and suffering I see now. Why is there such grief if there are unseen forces at work to protect the people there?"

His eyes remain locked on hers, his face eerily stony.

And suddenly, Jane has another, more alarming thought. "Mac! What happens to the family? To the girl? Do her parents live, or does she end up alone?"

Mac continues to say nothing. In fact, for the first time Jane can ever remember, she sees sadness on his brow.

"Mac! Who were those men with you? It looked like an army made of giants had gathered in and around that house with you and Nell. Like they were ready to go against those thugs. Like they did exactly that." He doesn't blink. "Mac, they didn't look human."

Mac responds at last. "You've been given what you need to know for now. That has to suffice. In the meantime, I have work to do."

"Wait a minute. What kind of work do you have to do?" But he's gone before she finishes her sentence.

What on earth does Mac have to do?

It would be good if it involves helping that struggling family with the lonely artist on the prairie.

Seventeen

CAPE MAY, NEW JERSEY—1989

The art hanging on the wall of Oliver T. Bean is lovely to look at, even though most people don't. They stop in for caffeine and conversation, not for art appreciation, usually in a rush, in and out and desperate for that first-sip feeling. Those who sit at tables for brief business meetings, heads together and intent, might glance up to notice the rich colors and texture there, and perhaps even a mind or two might flicker with aesthetic awareness, but only for a moment. It isn't as if Oliver T. Bean is an art gallery.

Yet, if anyone were to notice, chances are it would be someone who has time to sit down for a moment or two, someone who has more than just a hot beverage in mind. It would be someone capable of being filled and filling in equal measure because beauty is something one must notice. And when one does notice, it is something that compels response.

Beauty begets beauty.

Jake is one of those people. The kind that takes notice and responds, and especially to beauty because he creates it in comprehending it. Not only does he see beyond average, he takes in every little detail uniquely, of his own world and the planet at large, to recognize what is pleasing. There, he mines for gems. Naturally then, he would be particularly mindful of his own business, just like any committed to the success and well-being of an investment. But Jake would have noticed even if he weren't the owner of Oliver T. Bean and didn't spend most of his time ensuring its success. It's important to him to notice. Jake is a unique human invested enough in life not to miss a thing.

Not the wrinkled, snowy-haired woman who comes in every day for her drip coffee with cream and two regular sugars, who takes the change out of her small plastic coin purse one penny, nickel, dime, or quarter at a time to pay for it, and whose hands tremble a bit as she snaps it closed. The one who never allows Jake to give her anything for free.

Not the old guy with the hunched back who drinks his coffee black with three ice cubes added, and only three, not two or four or six, who always sits in the same chair by the west window to read the copy of *The Wall Street Journal* he's brought with him. The one who says he once worked as a secret government operative but who can hardly stand up now, stooped in sadness thanks to the sudden death of his wife to a heart attack last year. And osteoporosis.

Not the very punctual middle-aged gentleman with the bow tie who waits in his car in the clear darkness of an early morning, and in the driving rain and swirling snow, too, to be the first one in the door every single day of the year without exception. The one who doesn't drink coffee himself but is married to someone who does.

Jake loves people. Especially the artist whose art hangs on his walls. He's enamored with her art, too.

So much so, he's asked an acquaintance who is an art appraiser and dealer to stop by and have a look at the sample collection. He'd also managed to convince Jane to display a few more recently created landscape pieces, including his personal favorite, *Elevated*. Jane had outdone herself with a giant sky brushed wide with pink clouds resembling four large, gilded wings taking flight over a thin, gray horizon.

He resolves to confess what he's done, anticipating her displeasure. He doesn't waste time with small talk but cuts right to it as Jane walks in the door on a cold, December afternoon.

"I had someone who knows art look at your collection here this morning," he says carefully.

She sets her backpack down on the desk and begins to take her coat off, eyeing him. He continues. "He's the acquaintance of a guy I went to school with at Temple U, a private art dealer in New York who had some business in Atlantic City. He was close enough to stop by."

Jane says nothing as she hangs her coat on a hook by the door and extracts the scarf from around her neck. Only then does she turn to look at him, waiting for him to say more. When her eyes meet his, he sees a flicker of hope there. Though she won't admit it, though she refuses to let her guard down, he knows she's glad for it.

He runs his fingers nervously through his hair, feeling the seconds tick by in heavy measure. She finally decides to give in. "Well?"

"Well. His name is Michael Bingham. Here's his card," Jake replies, handing Jane the contact information.

"Well, what? What did he say about it?"

Jake chuckles. Her reaction is priceless. If only he could push a pause button to hold this moment and her expression a little longer. Oh, how he loves to look at her face, authentically unknowing. She's stubborn all right, but pure. And he's smitten, but not that selfish, so he doesn't keep her waiting. "He said it's terrific."

"He did?" Jane releases a smile.

"He did." Jake smiles back.

"Specifically, what did he say? Every word."

"*Specifically*, he said it's terrific. In fact, he said he'd love to see more. He wants you to call him. Thinks there's a gallery in the Midwest that might be interested."

"What else?" Jane's voice gives way to excitement now. It's finally sinking in. For the first time, she begins to believe she could actually be good at what she does.

"What do you mean, what else?" he teases.

"C'mon Jake, what else did he say specifically about my work? So, he wants me to call him, so he's interested, so he knows of a gallery that might be, but what did he say about the paintings themselves?"

"I think he said something about 'quality'. He may have also mentioned something about them being 'enthralling'."

"Enthralling," Jane repeats, releasing her breath. She closes her eyes as she covers her face with her hands. "Thank you, Jake," she says, dropping them to look at him. "I really don't know what to say."

"Just say you'll call the guy."

"I will. I absolutely will." She means it.

Jane's attitude regarding her paintings is changing.

Regarding Jake, however, she is still ruefully stubborn.

"He's in love with you, you know," Lucy says from the doorway where she's standing to observe Jane at work. Putting the finishing touches on her latest painting, Jane daubs white on the end of her brush and sweeps it along her canvas to create a sky powdered light with wispy patterns. She stands back to take a look at her progress then resumes her work. Finally satisfied, she sets her palette down, squeezes black paint from a tube onto its surface to join a collection of colored smatterings, and choosing a different, smaller-tipped brush to complete the work, adds her signature in the lower right corner. Just plain *Jane*. Nothing else.

"You do know that?" Lucy persists.

"I do know that," Jane finally answers, pausing to look up at her friend.

"So, what's the problem, then?"

Jane shakes her head in dismay. "He's a great guy, really. The best. I just can't see ever being any more than friends."

Lucy blows on the hot surface of the porcelain cup she has cradled in her hands then takes a small sip. The teacup is French Limoges, Haviland, made in France and painted about a hundred years ago with little pink flowers gilded and stemmed thin with olive green. Its saucer rests on the kitchen counter.

The treasured teacups and saucers had belonged to Jane's mother, and before that, someone else. Her mother had purchased them at the only antique store she'd ever stepped into, as far as Jane knew. Jane had been young at the time, but she'd been fascinated by the lovely porcelain. She had desperately wanted to hold those delicate cups in her hands and sip from them!

But Elise had never so much as looked at the little sets once they'd been paid for, boxed up, and removed far out of sight, relegated to the top shelf of a cabinet in the laundry room. The acquisition had been a mystery to Jane's mind. It still was. Her mother was not prone to fanciful purchases of any kind, let alone antiques.

Why did she purchase them if she wasn't going to use them?

Jane, a fanciful girl herself, hadn't allowed them to disappear from her sight, her mother's strange aloofness regarding the collection all the more intriguing. In her imagination, Jane had hosted a dozen garden parties with them, sharing the dainty pieces with friends as if she were sharing the most delicate parts of herself. Oh, how she'd pestered her mother to unearth them when she was a kid. But in the box they'd stayed. "Please, Mother," she'd begged. "Let me have a tea party with them!"

"Maybe when you're older," Elise would say. "They're delicate." As if Jane didn't already know that. As if she wasn't convinced that she, although not quite as lovely, was delicate, too.

Since Jane spends so much time at Lucy's apartment, it's a good place to finally enjoy them, she had reasoned, after extracting them from the house. Sneaking them out had made her feel like a cat burglar. She smiles now when she thinks about the nerves it took to get that dusty box down from the cupboard and claim them. "It's far easier to ask forgiveness than permission," she'd said aloud.

Now, released from the container they'd been secreted away in for so long, those teacups and saucers painted with pink roses are being enjoyed, and Jane only feels a little guilty about it. Actually, she doesn't feel guilty at all. She makes a mental note to come clean to her mother about it.

She switches her attention back to the subject at hand. "I don't know what to do about it. I don't want to hurt him. I just can't get there with him." She moves past Lucy with a fistful of brushes as she makes her way to the kitchen sink. Lucy follows, trailing scents of Earl Grey down the hallway.

"I'm not saying anything," Lucy protests, still blowing on her tea.

"But you are," Jane counters. She knows how Lucy feels about Jake. In fact, it wouldn't surprise Jane if her friend had a thing for her boss, what with the way she talks about him all of the time. She wants Jane to make a decision. Perhaps one Lucy could act on. Leggy Lucy, who is naturally beautiful and gracefully lithe, with gigantic, perfectly set blue eyes and long, thick blonde hair, who can saunter into any room and turn every head, and who could have any male eating out of the palm of her hand and following her, lovestruck, to the far ends of the earth, is interested in Jake. Her Jake.

But that's just it, he isn't *her* Jake. He's simply her friend. And her boss.

"He's all yours, love," Jane tells Lucy. "Just be careful with him. He's one of the good ones, so unless you're serious, don't mess with him."

"I would never do that," Lucy protests, but the smirk she wears proudly now says otherwise. "Besides, he's not interested in me. It's you he wants, most unfortunately. And even if he were to change his mind and suddenly notice I'm alive, I couldn't. Girl code and all that."

"Whatever. I told you we're just friends, so whatever you choose to do is fine by me." Jane finishes drying her brushes on a paper towel, passes Lucy to walk down the hallway, and returns the brushes to stand tips-up in their place in the studio. "Thanks again for letting me hang out here today."

"It's such an inconvenience," Lucy teases.

"I can't wait for that to change. I'd like to have enough cash to foist myself on you, make you take on a legit roomie."

"We've been through this already. Please stop giving it any thought. You are always welcome."

"Maybe my financial situation really will change one of these days. When I'm a successful artist, or just plain successful."

"You'll get there," Lucy assures her. "And I'm glad for the company in the meanwhile."

"I don't know if I believe you, but I appreciate you." Jane pulls on her coat and grabs her purse. "Now, I'm off to the dreaded family dinner."

"How droll."

"Totally. The absurdity will be the pretenses, not just the conversation," Jane says as she heads out the door for home. "Home is never where the heart is."

Jane does her best to avoid the house she grew up in, and there isn't a soul complaining about it. Mother's caseload has been heavy, and Father's engineering firm has projects all over the world, which means he's traveling a lot, which means Jane sees him even less than before. He's weathered the depressive economy.

Swell for him.

Any time it takes a plunge, her father is only slightly concerned, as far as Jane can tell. Engineers are like lawyers; society needs both for stability.

Society's need for an artist, not so much.

She hopes the jet-setting professionals will be too exhausted to do anything other than eat tonight.

When Jane arrives home, a green salad and loaf of crusty, store-bought bread are already on the table, her mother pouring wine into a tall, stemmed glass. She looks up as Jane walks through the door. "Are you hungry, dear?" she asks sweetly enough.

"Yes," Jane responds wearily. "I'll be down in a minute," she calls over her shoulder as she makes her way upstairs to her room. She throws her things on her bed before slipping into the bathroom to wash up. Across the hall in Jess' room, "If You Don't Know Me by Now," courtesy of Simply Red, is blasting from the boom box Jess keeps in the corner of her room. The volume causes every wall in the house to vibrate. No wonder Mother is already drinking.

Jane finishes up quickly, and catching a second wind, races downstairs to the table before Jess can arrive to herald controversy. She suspects she has just two minutes alone with her mother, and for the first time in a very long time, Jane feels it won't be enough. It would be nice to have a real conversation.

"How did today go?" Mother asks as she pulls out a chair and sits down.

Well, we're off to a good start.

She looks good, Jane thinks, as always. Just the right amount of makeup, not a sprayed hair out of place, and the perfect accessories in gold jewelry, the latest courtesy of Joan Rivers who's been hawking a line of costume jewelry on QVC. She hands Jane a glass of ice water, and then taking another sip of her own beverage, Jane watches her eyes close as she appears to savor the way it feels on her tongue.

"Same old, same old," Jane answers honestly as she takes a sip herself, and what could she tell her mother anyway? That she'd heard from a New York art dealer who's interested in the collection her mother doesn't know about, or if she does, never asks about because she is either too busy or too busy pretending she doesn't know? Of all the subject matter they could discuss, that seems the safest, actually, even though the last time Jane had broached the subject, her mother had shut it down quickly.

"By the way," Jane continues, "you know those teacups, the ones painted in pink roses?" Jane imagines somebody else's grandmother—someone who did everything high society had once expected of her—from needlework in embroidery to traveling around the world with a big black steamer trunk—painting those cups. It's what girls who moved in proper circles did. At the turn of the century, painting flowers on porcelain would have been the equivalent of crocheting purple flowers. Only better. Much better.

"What teacups?"

"The ones you bought at the antique store on the boardwalk when I was a kid." Jane is beginning to have second thoughts about admitting her recent appropriation, but it's too late now.

"Those old things? Of course, why do you ask?" her mother asks, puzzled.

"Oh, I'm just wondering if you know why they were painted? I mean, of course you can't know, but what do you think? Do you think they were painted because it was all the rage to paint white china in the late 1800s, or do you think the addition of flowers to the cups was a personal touch?"

"I have no idea," mother says, clearly irritated despite the wine. "I never really thought about it. What's this all about, Jane? I haven't taken them out of the box in years."

"Actually, you have never taken them out of the box."

"Okay. Why does it matter?"

"Oh, I don't know. I was just thinking why paint a white tea cup already beautiful in simplicity?"

Elise sets her wine glass on the table and looks at Jane quizzically. "Really, Jane. This is so odd." Jane begins to feel she's painted herself into a corner. She had wanted to do this, eventually, but in an effort to make conversation, she'd gone there before actually being ready.

"I'm just curious is all. I realize we'll never know, but I like to imagine the woman who painted them. I wonder if she felt compelled to do it because everyone else was doing it. Like maybe she felt pressured into fitting the norm. Or maybe she painted because she loved the china but felt she had to fill the white with color. Or because she simply loved to paint."

"Everything is about painting to you. You do have an imagination. And I wouldn't know. Maybe it wasn't even a woman who painted them," Mother says, ever the pragmatist, or killjoy, taking another sip of wine. "I've never thought about it." She pops up from the table suddenly and walks into the kitchen, as if to cue an end to the conversation. The subject of art is always one of consternation, Jane observes wryly, watching Elise don an oven mitt to pull a casserole from the oven.

Jane tries another angle, gathering nerve. "I found them. On the shelf in the laundry room," she continues, raising her voice slightly to be heard. "They were still in that box you wouldn't let me open when I was a kid. Remember how I used to beg you to allow me play with them when I wanted to have tea parties?"

"I remember," Elise admits, raising her voice, too.

"It used to make me so disappointed," Jane confesses. "It seemed such a waste. No one ever used them, at least in this house."

"I didn't want them broken and discarded with all your other toys," Elise continues to call out from the kitchen.

"I just wanted to hold something lovely enough to make me feel special, I guess." Until now, Jane hadn't realized the truth of this.

Ignoring her daughter's emotional revelation, Elise moves beyond it. "Jane, really, this is all very random. What's it about? Certainly, you haven't become obsessed with some secondhand crockery you haven't laid eyes on in years." Her mother returns from the kitchen with a steamy dish she places on a trivet in the center of the table. Elise rarely cooks, so this is impressive.

"I told you; I have laid my eyes on them, and I was thinking they should be enjoyed, is all. It isn't as if anyone else wants them."

"Anyone else wants what?" Jess asks as she arrives in the dining room and pulls out a chair, and only now does it occur to Jane that the household had decompressed into golden silence only moments before. So much for peace. Jess grabs a glass and fills it to the rim with Chardonnay. Evidently, neither restraint nor manners will be on display by the underage tonight.

Why do they allow it?

"Nothing," Jane quickly answers. She'll have to follow through with Mother later. "Where's Father?" she asks, turning her attention from Jess to Mother, pleased to now change the subject herself.

"He called to say he's running late. He told us to start without him," Elise says. However, she's just finished her sentence when the door opens abruptly, and in one swift move, Everett is in with his briefcase dropped to the floor. He goes to the kitchen to wash his hands. On the way to the dining room and without greeting his family, he passes the bar, grabs a glass and a bottle of Scotch, and pours himself a double shot.

As he sits down at the table, he looks at Jane pointedly. "We need to talk."

"Oh-kay," she responds slowly, already put off by his tone. *Good evening to you too,* she wants to say. He's clearly in one of his moods, but how does that concern her? How does it ever concern her?

"A police officer called me today ..."

"A *police* officer?" Mom cuts in loudly, returning again from the kitchen with tongs for the salad bowl.

"Well, not an officer but an investigator with the police department," Father repeats. This time Mother waits, transfixed. "He called me at the office looking for Jane."

"What does a police investigator want with you, Jane? What's happened?" Evidently, the wine hasn't inhibited her progression toward hysterics. Jess, however, is as quiet as a mouse before it jumps on its prey. Jane isn't given a chance to answer before Father continues.

"He wanted to update Jane." Everett eyes his daughter quizzically. "On the status of his investigation," he continues.

"What investigation?" Mother trills. Jess remains stoically silent.

"Apparently, an investigation into the theft of one of her *paintings.*"

"Why would anyone want one of her paintings?" Jess pipes up.

"I'm sitting right here, Jess. You don't need to refer to me as *her,*" Jane counters hotly.

"I'm confused," Mother puts in. "What paintings?"

"My thoughts entirely. Jane, I thought we'd discussed this notion of yours. Painting will get you nowhere."

"I didn't realize you were still doing that," Mother says, looking at Jane.

"Yes, well, she is," Father answers for her, "and it needs to stop." He looks from Elise to Jane. "Not only is it an inane waste of precious time, Jane, you are now compromising an overburdened system at the expense of fellow taxpayers with all this nonsense of enlisting the help of public investigators to find a missing painting. It isn't as if a legitimate crime has been committed, for heaven's sake!"

"How can you say that?" Jane asks, her fists balled up in knots in her lap. "Something of mine was taken, and in a public place. And Mother, I tried to tell you about it …"

"From a public place?" Elise interrupts. "What exactly is going on here?"

"Oh brother," Jess interrupts. "She's been displaying her artwork on the walls of that greasy coffee shop she works at." Turning to Jane, she addresses her disdainfully. "That's what this is all about, isn't it? One of your paint-by-number creations disappeared, and you've gotten all wadded up."

Jane slams her fists on the table and leans forward toward her sister. "I've taken about as much crap from you as I am going to!"

"Is that so?"

"Girls!" Mother intercedes. "What is going on between you two?"

"Let me tell you, Mother, if you care. Jess showed up at my place of employment to antagonize me!"

"I most certainly would do nothing of the sort!" Jess shouts back. "I wouldn't think to lower myself."

"What has this to do with the painting?" Mother asks.

"She's probably the one who stole it!" Jane yells.

"That's enough!" Father roars, cutting them off. "You two need to work things out between you. You are adults, or nearly so!" he says looking at Jess. He turns back to Jane. "You are, anyway. Act like one. And stop all this ridiculous kindergarten nonsense about painting, or it will be the ruin of you!"

"The ruin of me? The ruin of me is this family!" Jane shrieks before throwing her napkin down and racing upstairs like a petulant child. But they pushed her to it!

She will show them, if it's the last thing she does!

Chapter

Eighteen

LEAVENWORTH, KANSAS—1867

Twelve-year-old Agnes Rose is alone in the world. Cholera has taken her parents, Seamus and Nell O'Donnell. After all their hard work to keep their land and to survive on it, it has come to this.

"How could you allow this to happen?" She yells at God and she continues to shout at the heavens until she has no sound left in her, until her throat is raw and dry as a summer drought. At last, she concedes she will need to find help.

"I guess it's just you and me this time, Thunder," she tells her father's plow horse as she saddles him and strokes his cheek softly. The gentle gelding seems to understand.

The two leave at sunrise, traversing the ten or so miles between the cabin and the nearest assistance in good time. They stop only once to the drink water from the canteen she'd brought along and to share the buttered biscuit she'd wrapped in cloth and tucked inside the pocket of her long skirt. But the girl and the old horse both know the real reason for stopping is to avoid moving too fast.

The future promises more rapid change.

In 1867, the first city in Kansas, Leavenworth, is just over a decade old and is now a "jumping off" point for settlers heading further west. While there are some visible paths being worn in the earth by travelers passing through, Agnes' trek is uniquely hers this day. With no obvious wagon ruts or telltale markers to guide her, she relies on intuition, memory, and the sun overhead, as well as Thunder's instinct.

Mercifully, their journey over loamy soil and towering stems presents contact with no one, neither animal nor human, other than the numerous birds in flight overhead. No wagons or riders or natives to be seen. No wolves, either, thank the heavens. She can't say God is looking out for her, though. If that were true, this trip would be unnecessary, but she is grateful for whatever force provides her safety this day. Where is that man in the white suit that visits her now?

She'd been to town only a handful of times with her parents, who found no compelling reason to visit aside from the need for occasional supplies. Her parents had chosen to worship their God from home even though she'd heard protestant churches had followed the earliest missions, and the Sisters of Charity had brought her family's familiar Catholic faith of Ireland to the area. They'd even founded a hospital here.

It is to that hospital Agnes goes for help, for it seems the best place in which to find some, and find some she does, returning home with a willing nun and several of the more agreeable townsmen. Sister Mary Ross has enlisted their help to bury Seamus and Nell, and it is no small doing, what with fear of cholera contagion, but people are brave here. The recruits cover themselves with handkerchiefs tied in triangles around their faces as they mount their horses, one of them offering the use of his wagon for the pleasure of the ladies, who also have handkerchiefs on the ready thanks to Sister Mary Ross. She sits behind the reins, Agnes in the back.

"Sit up straight, girl," Sister Mary Ross says in the way of conversation over her shoulder, and it seems there is no kindness of emotion permitted over the strident efficiency of what needs to be done. It's the way of mercy in these times.

Once Seamus and Nell are in the ground, their side-by-side rock mounds a testimony to defeat in a place that seems to demand it, Agnes teeters on the brink of hopelessness. The loss of her parents seems an exercise in futility, and where is Divine help now? What about the secret place of the Most High referred to in that Psalm? Was it all a lie?

And yet, her dreams and visions speak of something more. Though land as big and wide as the earth itself makes her feel abandoned, and her refuge and fortress seem vanished into thin air, she knows deep down inside she is not alone.

However, satisfied the girl *is* alone, to the extent that she will no longer be able to live on the family's property, Sister Mary Ross insists Agnes return to town with her. When the girl digs her heels in, the nun does, too, enlisting the assistance of the men who buried her parents in their very own earth. Their daughter will be forcibly removed from it if need be.

With no other choice, Agnes gathers the family Bible, a few of her mother's books, and her own clothes. She closes the door firmly behind her, knowing it will be a long time, if ever, before she is able to return. She rides into town in the back of the wagon with the nun on the buckboard tightly clutching the reins and Agnes tightly clutching her worldly belongings, presently tied up in a bundle on her lap. Among the things left behind are her paintings and art supplies, for she can see no point to them now. There is no coloring with a broken heart, and only now does Agnes begin to understand her mother's own wounded desire following loss and the fading of expectation.

As she makes the bumpy ride back into town, Agnes considers her predicament. She knows she has ample ability where living off her land is concerned. Her parents made sure of that. She needn't be a charity case or dependent upon anyone, yet even as these thoughts occur to her, good sense does, too. The Kansas prairie is a difficult place to live and especially challenging alone. A twelve-year-old girl doesn't have the physical competence to endure all the adversity that would surely come her way, particularly from humanity. There is always good in spite of evil, but she can no longer pretend evil isn't stronger. She has no choice but to give in.

Someday I'll return, she promises herself.

The nuns, though stern, provide for the girl. They take her in until a local family agrees to allow her to live with them. With the help of a benefactor, Sister Mary Ross also arranges for a trust to be set up which will allow Agnes to keep the land Seamus and Nell had fought so hard for. It will be hers again on her twenty-first birthday.

Or so she believes.

The Richardson family is only practically generous. Agnes is expected to labor to earn her keep. She'd been raised to hard work, and doing so now—even if it is for strangers who are cold, unkind, and terribly selfish—allows Agnes to release pent-up sorrow, anger, and disappointment like a teakettle releasing steam.

She'd rather have stayed with the nuns.

To make matters worse, everything she'd ever owned or been entitled to is now the Richardson's. They had taken the cash for the sale of the cow and sweet Thunder. The farm equipment they'd confiscated from the barn. What was left in the field, what the garden had produced, what remained in the root cellar detached from the little home. They'd taken it all.

However, as far as Agnes was aware, they'd not entered the cabin to thieve anything from within. Maybe they'd assumed there wasn't much of anything valuable there. And there really wasn't. The stash of paintings her mother had done, as well as her own, had been destroyed, found under the bed her parents shared and hauled outside for burning, too. The remaining supplies, including the interior contents of the home, probably weren't worth claiming, especially if they had been contaminated. The Richardsons were undoubtedly afraid the plague still lingered in the air. Perhaps it did.

Meanwhile, Agnes determines they will have nothing else from her, and a roof over her head and meager provisions must be practical compromise. Any real part of herself or consideration of what might have been or will be must be reserved for another day.

Chores, which begin with the lighting of the fire in the stove before sunrise and prior to heading out in all kinds of weather for the milking of two cows and returning to start breakfast for the family, end when the dinner dishes are washed, dried, and put away. Agnes' days are long and busier than ever. She also must care for the Richardson's two children, William, four, and Lucinda, seven. There is no time to learn, let alone paint. Not that she has any inclination to. It's her mother's lessons she misses. Even on long workdays, Nell had set aside time to read to Agnes from an assortment of books she'd brought with her from Ireland.

Meanwhile, Agnes' dreams at night continue despite exhaustion, the man in the white linen suit dearer to her now than ever before. He's become her lifeline to a better world, an odd friend. He doesn't communicate as well as she'd like, and he could visit more regularly, but at least he shows up. His faithful visits in a world lacking love, or even gratitude, are helpful.

It's good to have someone who sees you.

He doesn't have to come right out and say it, but he likes her. He has to, or he wouldn't continue to appear, Agnes reasons. He wouldn't keep showing her things, the most important of which is her land. He takes her there, as if he understands her love of it. As if he shares her sorrow in separation from it.

As tour guide, he shows it to her undisturbed and furnished, in its natural state and all its forms. As she left it, with her beloved cabin upon it, and also with a red chimneyed white house she doesn't recognize, and it's lovely, but alarming, too. Is this the future, or only what could have been? Does her destiny now belong to someone else?

Why has she been shown these things, and others, like a girl with long brown hair standing deep in the grasses and an old woman painting by the sea? These are mysteries the man in the white suit won't elaborate on.

For now, real life is perplexing enough, and Mrs. Elmer Richardson, a sour woman, makes it tedious. Any emotion the woman exhibits is as tight as her pinched face. She appears to be constantly suffering the effects of unpleasant odors, which cause her waxy nose to appear as if an invisible clothespin is affixed to it, and the tightly wound black and white knob at the back of her neck highlights this severity of countenance.

She is nothing like sweet Nell.

The regular demands of Regina Richardson, who fires out directives like a commander at sea, make Agnes feel as though she has been enlisted in a military brigade. Only her companions are no soldiers, and Mrs. Richardson is no leader.

The children are like their mother, never ceasing in their needs, and unlike their docile, bird-like father who chirps a little input now and again but whose small mouth contributes little to nothing to family discourse. It's Mrs. Richardson's voice that directs things while her husband generally flies out the door for his office down the block as soon as he's slurped up the last drop of coffee from the cup between his thin, talon-like hands.

Inwardly, they are Mr. and Mrs. Crow to Agnes.

Both children are ill-mannered and entitled, but it's Lucinda that assumes an air of superiority in a home that seems to brim with it. "Brush my hair, Agnes," she cries from her bed as soon as her head rises off the pillow each morning.

"Coming!" Agnes responds one day as she places the cast-iron cover back on the pot of porridge she's been stirring. She sets the large wooden spoon down on the table near Mrs. Crow's cup of tea, which causes her mistress no small agitation.

"Agnes!" she screeches, nearly upsetting her tea as she whisks the saucer and rocking teacup closer to herself in grand gesture. "Wipe that spoon clean before you set it on the table!"

"Yes, ma'am," Agnes kindly replies, picking up the spoon and wiping it on her apron.

"Oh, for heaven's sake! Not on your apron! Are you daft?" Mrs. Crow shouts. "Dip it in the wash bucket and dry it on a towel."

"Agnes! Are you coming?" Lucinda continues to bellow.

"Yes, of course! Just a minute." Agnes does as Mrs. Crow has bid her, washing and drying the spoon properly before replacing it on the table away from the heat of the stove. Mrs. Crow watches her do this without further comment, then continues to gaze out the small, mottled window while slowly sipping her tea.

"What took you so long?" barks Lucinda when Agnes enters the room.

"I'm sorry," Agnes replies, for she has learned quickly in the weeks she's been here it's best not to argue with one of the Crow People and least of all this young girl, who's entirely accustomed to the planet's revolution around her being.

"I want my hair in a braid today," she demands, sitting up in bed to present herself for grooming.

"All right," Agnes replies evenly.

"But hurry, my bowl needs to be emptied, too, and I just can't stand the thought of it being in my room a moment longer than necessary." Her little brother across the room in his own bed begins to stir.

"I will get to it as soon as I am finished here and have served your breakfast," Agnes replies.

"No, see to it immediately," Lucinda charges. "After you do my braid, that is." After Agnes finishes with the hair styling, Lucinda hops down from the bed and runs toward the front room to have a seat at the table. Agnes follows with the chamber pot from under the bed and heads outside into the chilly morning with it. When she returns from having rinsed it at the pump outside, she finds Lucinda with a scowl to match her mother's and impatience so obvious, it seems to thicken the air. "Hurry!" she orders.

Agnes briskly walks to the bedroom and slides the chamber pot back under the bed. She returns to the kitchen, dips her hands in the pan of warm soapy water she'd prepared earlier and dries them off on her apron. She spoons hot porridge into bowls for the children and sets them down on the table, Lucinda's in front of her clasped hands. "You'll need to let it cool a moment," she instructs the girl.

"I'll need a spoon," Lucinda hotly replies.

"Yes, here it is," Agnes says calmly, handing it off. Next, she pours milk into a couple of tin mugs and sets them on the table as well, before heading back to the bedroom to awaken William.

Mrs. Crow still doesn't look away from the window. She continues to sip deliberately while Agnes takes care of her children and her home for her, seemingly lost in thought. And so, Agnes is afforded no such luxury as contemplation of any kind.

However, later that night, Agnes gets a reprieve when the man in white appears again to spirit her away to the place she loves. Her land. There, she wanders through tall grasses under heaven's light by degrees, under the clouds that weaken to part again and a sun that returns to burn brightly, too. Where darkness seems weak and good feels strong, and the ever-changing sky reminds that light is always behind what is not; it can never be extinguished. Color, a product of that light, must be where her parents are now.

These experiences are like songs sung for her, and she longs to paint them, to transfer the melodies she sees, hears, and feels from air to brush to canvas. Naturally, then, she begins to regret leaving her paint supplies behind, just beyond the graves of her parents.

Now, the only way to paint them is to dream them.

Chapter

Nineteen

CAPE MAY, NEW JERSEY—1990

"My story isn't tragic," Jane protests. "Full of frustration. Maybe a little opposition. But missing any riveting drama."

"Jane, we all have stories. You need to own yours."

"What, that I am surrounded by people who don't give a crap?" She shrugs it off with cynicism. "Most people feel unsupported by those closest to them. I'm not that special."

"I disagree," Jake insists, his eyes searching hers as he takes a bite of a Reuben sandwich.

She's agreed to join Jake on neutral ground. A local soup and sandwich place is less threatening than his condo. Or the home she still lives in with her family. She swallows hard and looks away. "I also realize many of the most successful people in the world are those who had a force of opposition they conquered."

"Thatta girl! Believe it!"

Jane rolls her eyes, but she is resolved to believe. Galleries love a good backstory, and she needn't back off from some of the truth. Her parents will never know just how transparent she's been where their disapproval is concerned. They'll undoubtedly never pay her collection or her story any attention.

Private art dealer Michael Bingham has such a keen interest in Jane Campbell's work, he's not only negotiated with the well-known Downtown

Gallery in Kansas City to display it, he has convinced the owners to hold a private showing without having even exhibited it first. He has also purchased three pieces from the full collection Jane unearthed from confinement.

She'd agreed to part with them knowing full well she will be selling many, if not all, of the others once they are on the walls of the gallery, and she's come to terms with this. Presently, she has around forty pieces that are good enough to show and has been told she stands to make a reasonable sum of money from the sales, even with the gallery's commission. Bingham didn't take a percentage, as Jane's work doesn't fit his niche. He reasons it's only a matter of time before her work attracts buyers with deep pockets, and he himself will be in possession of painted gold.

After all, Jane's work will soon grace the same walls that once held some of the country's most well-known twentieth century art, such as Midwest standouts Thomas Hart Benton, John Stuart Curry, and Grant Wood. Paintings that had gained recognition in places like the Chicago Art Institute as well. Not that Jane's is on the same level, but it absolutely blows her mind that it's in a position to be displayed where great art in her genre once had.

It goes without saying, a kinship must exist with all of those artists who surely have understood the longing to create as much as to breathe, to design as much as to live, as if the expansion of lungs and the beat of a heart depended upon it.

But do all artists feel the way Jane does? As if her art is a reflection of what is sacred within her, a secret place revealed? Because what originates there and courses through her veins as rich nutrient to every part of her body *should* be shared. *MUST* be shared! Art must be, then, in its purest form, evidence of a soul released into tangible medium, an expression of thought and feeling birthed as matter.

I just don't understand it."

"Understand what? Your work is good!" he replies before taking another bite of his sandwich.

"I am not sure it deserves the honor of a private showing in Kansas City's Downtown Gallery," she insists, conflicted.

"I'm telling you, you paint magic onto canvas!"

Jane dives in to more of her cheesesteak sandwich as she reflects upon this. There is so much she could tell Jake, so much she would like to share with him. Though she still desperately needs a friend in whom she could deeply confide, Jake can't be that person.

Really, is there anyone who could be?

She's never come around to broaching the subject of Mac with anyone; she's not ever been tempted. Because sharing anything that's happened between them seems forbidden. Still. Besides, is there any one person who would actually believe her?

Lucy would. Maybe.

Jake would. Wouldn't he?

"I just paint what I see in my mind," she says finally.

"Have you ever been to the places you paint?" Jake asks. Jane considers her response carefully.

"No." It's the truth. "I guess I just paint what I've seen." Also the truth. And then she thinks to add, "On TV, movies, or in magazines." Still the truth. She's seen many places similar to what she paints outside of her visions. "I can't explain how I know what I paint. I just do."

Nothing else about my life has ever been so easy.

Come to think of it, getting my work into this gallery was breezy, too!

"I don't know how you do it, but there's a quality to your work that's different than anything I've ever seen." His smile seems to go through her as he speaks. He is pure in a way unlike anyone she's ever met.

Safe.

Jane nods, taking another bite of her own sandwich, her favorite turkey on rye.

Jake continues. "What do I know? Only enough to understand I'm in line with an art expert who appears to feel the same way I do!"

Jane takes a moment to swallow her food. "I appreciate that, I really do! I'm stunned, honestly," she admits reluctantly. "And not just a little excited," she adds with a giggle.

"So, the gallery in KC is a big deal, then?"

"The Downtown? It really is. They've hosted a lot of amazing work. I couldn't have imagined in my wildest dreams they'd be interested in anything I've done! I mean, no artist's work is just like another's, but mine doesn't hold a candle to the outstanding Midwestern art they've exhibited in the past." She'd stopped by Professor Randall's office at school to fill her in and to dredge up as much information from the art history teacher as possible. As it turned out, her professor had been a wealth of knowledge on the subject.

"How so?" Jake sets his sandwich down and wipes his mouth with his napkin, leaning back to listen.

"That gallery is known for showcasing a certain type of Midwestern art—famous painters in that genre. The work of those artists is rooted in realism. Basically, realism is the idea that paint on canvas can capture a moment as adequately as a camera's shutter. It doesn't have to be beautiful, or even appealing."

"So, realism is all about real life," Jake confirms.

"Exactly. What I paint is real, but there is a touch of romanticism to it as well. I know that, and yet it's as authentic as it can be, in my opinion, because that's the way I see it. I paint what I see. I merely translate my vision to canvas, and what I see is full of color. It's the way my romantic heart is wired." She bites her lip as soon as the information is divulged.

Why did I reveal that last part?

Fortunately, Jake doesn't ask her to elaborate on any heart revelation. "That makes sense," he says, and Jane is grateful. He is certainly more engaged than anyone ever has been. She's never processed these feelings out loud—not even with fellow art enthusiast Lucy, and it feels really good to finally talk about her work with a friend.

Smiling, she continues. "So, I can't compare myself to any of the great masters; I really can't, and yet if I were to, of the three that stand out to me, Curry's is the style I paint more like, I suppose."

"What does his work look like?" Jake crosses his arms and leans back farther still.

"Hmm," she says, delighted he's so interested. "It's more vibrant than that of other Midwestern work, which is to say it looks less monochromatic and more hopeful. Whereas realism might look like a life of neutralities, you know, tan skies and brown grasses with iron horses, the kind that speaks of labor and strength and the fight to tame life, I choose to see the end result …"

"The redemption there," Jake affirms before she can continue.

Jane beams. "You're right!" She shakes her head as if in disbelief. Does anyone understand her like Jake does? "Wow. You get me," she says laughing, but then realizing what she just admitted might be too much, she hurries to finish her long-winded lecture. "Curry's work is actually unappealing, if you ask me—sort of dark and unexciting, even though I like some of his skies."

"Not colorful enough for you?" Jake teases.

Yes. Exactly.

"You're right. But there is this one piece I do like. It's of a farmer in a field of golden wheat under a blue sky with puffy white clouds. Two children stand at his sides, and you can see they're standing in wind, their hair whipping around their faces. It's a little impressionistic, so I guess that's what appeals to me. There's romance in a picture that's just slightly out of focus."

"But your work isn't really impressionistic."

"Yeah. It's more detailed, but romanticized a bit. I use a little fancy," she fibs. "I paint—a different reality, I guess." Jane wanted to stop but she can't be quiet. Jake continues to eat, nodding to encourage her.

"I see possibility. It's there, like gravity," and as she speaks these thoughts aloud, Jane begins to come to grips with her own candor.

Jake is smiling wider now. He really does understand her, and this makes her happy.

It's incredible, really, Jane thinks, as she plans her visit to Kansas City. Everything is falling into place, and quickly. She is both excited and terrified. But the ability to get away is what intrigues her the most.

She hasn't done much traveling, practically speaking, that is. Her family vacationed when she was young, but as the girls had grown older and their parents had worked more with a rare inclination to take time off or slow down, even minimal travel as a group had subsided. Unlike Everett and Elise Campbell, Jane hasn't been anywhere in years, and she's never been close to the Midwest. Realistically, anyway.

"When are you planning on heading out?" Jake asks her at work one day in February when the world is spray-painted in white and frost adorns the windows. The warmth of the coffee shop has drawn a lot of customers.

"I don't know. I'll wait until the school semester is over, of course. In the summer," she tells him. "The show is planned for early July."

Jake nods as he steams the milk for the drink he's preparing. "How long do you think you'll be gone?"

"Hmm, I don't know," Jane says. "Oh, did I tell you the gallery will work out all the details regarding the transportation of the paintings safely? That's a good thing considering my inexperience!"

"That is!" he replies enthusiastically.

"I'm so excited, I feel like telling my parents!"

"You should. Can you imagine? They'd have to eat crow."

"Not at all. You don't know my parents."

"But surely they'd be happy for you, even if they refuse to admit it."

"I'd like to think so …" Jane's thoughts take her into fancying their responses. "But no. Not a chance."

"I'll bet they would!" Jake insists.

She places a lid on the drink she's finished and casts a sideways glance at Jake, envisioning her father's remorse.

Jane, I must admit I was wrong about your art. You obviously have talent.

Her mother's attention.

Oh, Jane, I had no idea! What marvelous news!

Or even her sister's attitude.

I guess you're okay.

Unfortunately, all she can come up with at the present are the more likely responses.

Don't get carried away on the winds of delusion.

It's really time you buckled down, dear.

You think I give a crap about your trash?

"I appreciate your encouragement more than you know, Jake." She sighs. "I don't know, I'll need to communicate with them at some point, but that will be at the last possible moment. I'm too high right now to jeopardize being pulled back to earth by the naysayers in my life."

"I understand, but I don't know how you keep it to yourself, and especially in light of what your wicked sister did." Jake is now the one shaking his head.

"See, that's another thing. I feel as though I'd jinx myself in letting Jess know."

"What, like she'd do something to stop it? She's not that powerful, Jane."

"You say that like I'm some delusional narcissist or something, gosh."

"Not at all." Jake smiles. "I know who you are. *You* need to know who you are. There is nothing that can stop you but you."

"If only life were that simple, my friend," she says with another sigh.

Jane has a dream that night. In it, her sister returns to the coffee shop and pulls all her art off the walls. She tosses them into a pile and then sets fire to them, right in the middle of the store. The customers watch them burn. Jake is nowhere in sight.

Later, after she's awake, Mac returns. "Where have you been?" she asks, not just a little perturbed.

"What do you mean, 'where have you been?'" he answers nonchalantly.

"Mac, you exasperate me! You've not visited me in well over a month! You've never been away that long! And it wasn't as though we parted under good terms last time."

"You're wrong. We parted under fine terms," Mac pauses before continuing, "and you don't set the terms."

"Oh, really? Who sets them? Because you are correct, I surely don't."

"Is there something I may help you with, Jane?" Mac inquires, changing the subject.

"Yes. I told you. I want to know more than you're currently allowing me. There are so many questions I could ask, but I don't. I confine my inquiries to the most important, and given my self-control in this regard, I would think you would have the grace to give me a little more than you've done so far."

"Okay."

"Okay?"

"Okay."

"All right. Let's start with the dream I just had. What does it mean?"

"Could it be Light's revelation?"

"Why is your answer to a question so often a question?" Sighing, she moves on. "Okay, let's talk about what you show me, shall we? The Land and the girl there. Who is she? What happens to her?" Jane exhales audibly while waiting for a response but Mac gives none. He just looks at her.

"Well?" Jane presses. Mac doesn't respond.

"Is any of this even real?" she pleads. She has been vacillating on this subject far longer than she should. Though her experiences seem legitimate, what if they are really long-term delusion?

Perhaps she really should seek medical help.

Before she can consider this any further, she begins to smell the great outdoors again. Scents of wild sage and coriander fill the room but then suddenly give way to a metallic smell again, causing her heart to flutter with foreboding.

Jane is back on the property. This time she observes the girl, Agnes, standing above a grave. Jane watches as Agnes closes the front door to her cabin and leaves the beautiful land in a wagon with others, one of who appears to be a nun.

"Nooooo!" Jane cries. Where is she going? What will be her fate now?

Why are you showing me this?

It seems so terribly unkind of him, and yet, it's appropriate, given her recent demands. She wants to know, needs to know what happens to this girl now!

"Reality is more than you know," he says softly, still standing next to her this time.

Next, Jane sees a group of men on horseback. From atop a knoll and fairly hidden in the long prairie grass, the men watch the wagon disappear over the horizon. Once it has, they move toward the cabin and surround it.

Dark shadows follow them and sulfurous odors rise from the bog beneath them, causing Jane to gag. She is forced to turn back to the grave site, where a fresh breeze strokes her face. It fills the air with something herbal and fragrant. Slight but unmistakably sweet, like wild jasmine again. With the back of her hand, she wipes long tear trails from her face.

Jane is so preoccupied with her condition, she doesn't see the Native American woman step from behind a tree on the property to reveal herself. She wears a long gray skirt over laced-up leather boots and a frill-neck, buttoned blouse of white with long sleeves. Her thick hair is highlighted by silver strands and caught by the sunlight.

Also caught by the sunlight is the long trail of tears that streams down Running Feet's dark-skinned face.

Twenty

LEAVENWORTH, KANSAS—1867

Agnes wants to paint again almost as much as she longs to return to what is hers. But can her land ever truly be home without her parents? She wants to dream again, too, and not just at night or beyond her range of vision. She wants to believe life, liberty, and the pursuit of happiness for herself.

She wants to matter here, too. To be seen in real time.

Images of her parents traveling across the globe for their land crowd her imagination. They'd stood their ground, worked, and loved with a passion, and left a legacy, even if it turned out to be more of mind than body. And maybe what King Solomon said in Ecclesiastes is true, that everything is meaningless. What do people really gain from all their toils under the sun? And what about Psalm 91? Protection was assured for those who love God. Her parents did. So, what happened to that promise?

The only gain for Agnes is the recollection of their love, she realizes. That's really all there is to take from life, and maybe this existence is not meaningless after all. The people who loved her and whom she loved back were real. Their love was real, and she resolves to keep alive the kind of love that can never die, ensconced in a place inaccessible to the rest of the world. No one can take it. No one will thieve those mental pictures, and this makes her feel she may have a little control left after all. Oh, she must fight to keep the memories, but the connection to the light there makes her feel a little meaning may be known yet.

Someday she'll return. Someday she'll paint again, because canvas has the potential to hold what isn't too far away. The transfer of mental images into substance is to gather what is just out of reach for keeping, to hallow time. It means continued company with the parents she will always love in a place where the earth remembers.

Though there had been struggle on The Land, the wonderful overshadowed it after all, and remembering that was poultice for her soul. The earth Agnes will always call her own holds her flesh—that of Seamus and Nell O'Donnell—and not just materially. Maybe she's only sentimental, but to her the soil is still wet with their tears and sweat, and the wind still perfumed with their devotion, and to see it all for the purpose of something bigger than she can hold onto is to touch the sky.

Could the heavens look down upon what had been known there?

Do Seamus and Nell O'Donnell exist somewhere, still feeling and thinking and experiencing the world around them?

Meaning.

Or are they simply gone, no longer filled with thoughts such as these?

Meaningless.

The soul knows. If the former is true, that her parents live beyond the grave, it would have to be so much better than here, and she hopes this is the case as she looks up their favorite scripture. It says God is a secret place and a fortress. Maybe that is where they are. With Him.

As she stands on her own, not a parapet in sight.

Given these musings, she asks The Crows to return home to The Land occasionally. Just to see it, to stay in touch with those remembrances, as if they might fade too quickly otherwise. "There is no time for such foolishness, Agnes," responds Mrs. Crow, always quite firm about this.

"But couldn't we make time, ma'am?" she pleads, unwilling to give up. Agnes would never dare if it wasn't critical. She's fully aware of a proper waste of time. Mrs. Crow makes sure of it.

"Certainly not! It would take us a full day just to make the round trip, and that's time I can't get back." She plops down on a stool by the hearth. Acting quite inconvenienced, she grunts loudly, "Hand me my fan."

How well I know, thinks Agnes as she complies. She will never have her own time back.

Then one day she overhears The Crows talking about the property. How could that be? Why would they be talking about her land, especially considering any such talk is "foolishness"?

But they are, and when Mrs. Crow catches Agnes listening, she admits it. She abruptly turns from her conversation with her husband and addresses Agnes unashamedly. "Where is the key to the house?"

"What do you mean?" Agnes asks politely. Could The Crows actually be considering her request?

"The key. To the cabin on your parents' property. Where is it?" The words are no sooner out of Mrs. Crow's lips when those lips are drawn back in, and puckered, as if they've sucked vinegar out of the air. "It must be on the property since you did not bring it with you."

"There isn't any key," Agnes answers slowly.

"There must be! Why wouldn't there be a key?" Mrs. Crow demands through the ever-tightening hole in her mouth.

"There was no need for one. In fact, my father had only just put a handle on door before he passed. Before that, we'd simply closed it with a string and latched it from behind." Agnes shifts her gaze between the two adults, who now exchange conniving glances, which is odd indeed. This is a couple who doesn't look at each other. And they rarely talk. Agnes imagines black feathers starting to sprout from their beady-eyed faces.

Mr. Crow squeaks up. "The only way to lock the home was from the inside?"

"Yes, sir. Well, before the handle was put on. The bar was put in place only when we were home. We never locked up when we left, which wasn't often. It wasn't necessary. We only ever had one visit from a native, and he was polite. Others had run-ins, but we didn't. We had trouble with the Ruffians—"

Mrs. Crow cuts her off. "Ruffians?" she snorts. "Unjustified labeling. I'll not hear that word in my house!"

"My parents told me—"

"Your parents knew nothing," Mrs. Crow interrupts again. "People like your parents, foreigners with inappropriate opinions, had no business attempting to stop what had already been put in motion. It was none of their affair. It was folks like them that caused so much of the trouble here."

Agnes doesn't respond. She has no idea what really transpired when she was very young, but Mrs. Crow's opinion doesn't surprise her. Still, she hadn't anticipated such a forceful rebuke. Hearing this ornery woman disparage her beloved parents causes her eyes to sting. She realizes she will have to proceed carefully.

Mrs. Crow observes her indifferently, waiting. When Agnes remains silent, she barks again, "Well, where is it?"

"Like I said, we didn't have one," her lips beginning to quiver. "I wasn't lying to you. Why do you ask?"

"Never mind," Mrs. Crow snaps, clearly exasperated. "Get back to work."

Agnes returns to peeling carrot skins into a tub near the stove, but not without an ear open to the continued dialogue in the front room. "Tom says it's tighter than a tick on a dog…no way in…" she hears Mrs. Crow say.

"Can't he just break the door down, a window even?" Mr. Crow asks, clearly exasperated. Agnes glances up to find both of them watching her. She quickly looks away and continues to peel faster, imagining plucking black feathers until the room is full of them.

Why would The Crows care about access to her parents' home? And wasn't Tom one of those Ruffians she heard them talk about?

Agnes doesn't daydream as much anymore. She can't. She doesn't have time to. But nights are still different. She has plenty of dreams then, and in between them, the man in white returns. It seems as though what she experiences with him are dreams, too, but dreams don't feel so real.

He doesn't say much, but that's okay; Agnes doesn't have much to say herself. Actions speak far more than words. But she does press him for his name again. When he doesn't reply, she decides to give him one. It doesn't take her long to come up with a moniker that feels right.

She calls him The Knight.

Her mother used to tell her stories of knights from faraway kingdoms, promising one day when there was enough money, they'd send away for books of Agnes' very own, with more tales of men of valor. Of brave, chivalrous men who fought for justice and honor and beautiful maidens, and it's easier to pretend her visitor is a knight than anything else.

Agnes needs a knight in her life.

Yes, it's the perfect name.

And so it happens, after deciding this, that Agnes is whisked away to her own land again. She first hears music playing and smells delicious things—sweet, earthy scents and unidentifiable floral bouquets. And then her own knight takes her high above the trees and grasses to look down upon it all. Absorbing her land from a lofty perspective for the first time, she grasps the greatness of what seems to be endless miles stretched out in all directions, gathering to her sight the unbroken plains that ripple toward an endless horizon. The little log cabin and its roof of twigs and thatch, the happy creek that runs near it where she used to paint, and the one, lone tree she used to skip around beyond.

Now, like good birds in flight, she and the white-suited man dip and glide through the air across miles and miles. They leave the swelling plains to cross a great desert and finally rocky land on a coast far away. Agnes wants to fly like this forever; it feels perfect.

On the coast, they skim the tops of the tallest trees Agnes has ever seen, while a vast, sparkling ocean capped white near the shore and blended blue with distant sky makes her feel as light as a downy feather in the wind. And then, she begins to feel herself descend.

Dropping to squeeze in between giant conifers, her feet float gently down to touch a blanket of pine needles. Agnes suddenly feels very small, and yet a part of something very big. As the prairie seems to stretch to the ends of the earth at home, these colossi appear to reach for the sky, causing Agnes to feel significant in insignificance. They've trunks so large, many people could stand around the base with arms outstretched!

"Where are we?" she asks The Knight, though she isn't quite certain she asked him but rather thought the question. Perhaps out loud?

He doesn't say a word but smiles in response and then proceeds to look around him. Agnes takes the hint and does the same because she loves that about him. The fact that they don't need dialogue to pass between them to understand one another is good for a girl who always enjoys being alone with nature, and when she looks back to where he had been standing a moment ago, she finds he has gone. She is alone in the woods, but she isn't frightened. The unfamiliar trees comfort her, making her want to stay a while.

Sometimes it's the unfamiliar that can feel familiar.

Maybe these tall trees are God's fortress that psalm referred to.

There's a cabin in the woods, beckoning Agnes to walk toward it. It's made of the same redwood logs that abound here, with a chimney cocked to one side that billows smoke in gray puffs, adding another layer of rough comfort in a fine mist that descends to the forest floor, and it's strange. It's almost as if she has found home again. But how can that be? This is not the prairie. This is not her cabin.

Reaching the front porch, she stretches for the door but feels herself pulled back. She again moves forward, and this time is able to grab the doorknob. She twists and turns and pulls on it, only to find it locked. Why she wants access so badly, Agnes cannot say. She begins to pound on the door. "Let me in," she says. "Oh, please, let me in!"

She awakens to find she is still pounding, and though it's only her pillow, her hand hurts terribly.

The exchange with The Crows about the door on her parents' cabin must have bothered her more than she had realized, Agnes thinks as the picture fades and she sits up in bed to consider it while it's still fresh.

The following night the nightmare arrives. In it the earth trembles and a great chasm is opened, swallowing the cabin and tall trees in the woods. It feels real and terribly frightening, but Agnes doesn't fret about it. She does wonder in her own life, however, what The Crows are up to.

Their interest in her cabin is very strange, especially since her property is far enough away to be considered "time-consuming." But maybe time-consuming shouldn't be considered all bad. Consumed time must be considered by the manner in which it's spent, and some activities are worthy of expenditure.

And speaking of, it was high time she was up to get the fire lit for breakfast! She grabs her boots from the corner of the attic room and, careful not to wake the family downstairs, eases herself down the ladder one rung at a time. The kindling of straw and small sticks she'd set aside the night before she now tosses into the stove to light, thankful there are benefits to living in town where supplies are plentiful.

Once the fire in the stove is going, along with a small lantern for her own use, Agnes finds her coat on a peg by the door, grabs the bucket on the floor, and steps out the back door into frosty air. As she does, one small, lone pine needle slips from her hair onto the floor.

Agnes confirms Tom Crawford is the man who showed up at her parents' cabin when she was younger by listening to The Crows' hushed discussions. He's a past slave catcher and the current town drunk. That much Agnes would have gleaned on her own. Tom's reputation precedes him. He's mean, loud, ill-mannered, and most of the time staggeringly intoxicated.

What she learns now is that Tom is also Mrs. Crow's brother. The information comes largely courtesy of a much-disapproving Lucinda who, no matter the family connection, has no problem vocally acknowledging her uncle's disrepute. At least the child has some decency about her.

Agnes knows she shouldn't do it, but she eavesdrops one late night. She hears The Crows talking in the room below, and motivated to listen in by the couple's sudden interest in her property, she slips quietly to the top of the ladder to hear better. "Your brother is a menace to society and a blight on this family's reputation," she hears Mr. Crow say. What reputation? Agnes muses.

"He isn't, either. He's an unfortunate soul whose selfish wife has no compassion, kicking him out like she did," his own wife squawks.

"Good grief, Regina, you'd have had no trouble doing the same to me if I'd behaved that way." Inwardly, Agnes had to agree. "There's nothing unfortunate about that man, and you know it. Everything he gets he has coming to him. Beatrice should have removed him long ago!"

"Why, Elmer, that is an un-Christian like response!" Mrs. Crow maintains shrilly. What does that woman know about being Christian? Agnes wonders.

"It isn't and you know it! It's no surprise the judge told him to find another place, what with his being drunk all of the time and hitting those kids."

"She brought him to it, I'm telling you—"

"Stop making excuses, Regina. He's a bad seed," Mr. Crow says, as if he knows a thing or two about bad seeds.

Mrs. Crow tsks loudly. "I suppose it is for the best he gets away for a spell. He's not one to take kindly to any missives given him. I'm surprised, though, he suggested the O'Donnell cabin. Usually, he's not one to stay in a fight long." Hearing this part of the conversation alarms Agnes. Did she hear that right? Nasty Tom has designs on her cabin? And what fight?

"Then we agree. He needs to be gone. Was he able to gain access?" Mr. Crow's voice begins to trail off, such that Agnes is having a hard time picking up all he is saying. He is clearly tired. "I would think … beat down the door … kick it in … after all …" She thinks she hears a yawn.

"No. It's the strangest thing. He told me today he was heading back out to the place, so it might be a while 'til we hear more." Agnes doesn't hear Mr. Crow respond. Presumably he's already dozing off. Oh, why couldn't he stay awake a little longer? Agnes just has to know more. Why *her* land? "It's a day's ride up and back," Mrs. Crow had said. Could that foul man be inside her home right now? The thought of it makes her physically sick.

But that's just the half of it.

What Agnes doesn't know but soon will is Tom Crawford's evil plans are more revolting that she could have guessed.

If he can't have The Land, no one will.

Chapter

Twenty-One

KANSAS CITY—1990

In late June, Jane boards a flight to Kansas City, Missouri. She'd have preferred to drive, making a grand adventure of a road trip on her own, but The Downtown's owner has offered to provide a rental car at the airport. Either way, detaching from all things familiar is an adventure beyond her wildest imagination.

As she steps off the plane, Plain Jane inhales the sweet air of freedom for what feels like the first time in her life. Until now, she's done nothing out of the ordinary, her life so basic; were it not for the transportive dreams and visions within such a mundane existence, her life would be aimless.

The Kansas City airport is remarkably small and quaint, so unlike the metropolitan complexes she's experienced back home, and she smiles thinking of how perfect this is for a place like Kansas. It's only a moment before she catches herself. She's not in Kansas! Kansas City straddles both sides of the state line, and the airport is on the Missouri side. Why does she think of this area as strictly Kansas? It must be the state's mention in the city's proper name.

Her luggage is up for claim within minutes after she's off the aircraft, and her rental car is easily found. She tosses her suitcase in the back of the vehicle, and once seated, glances over the map that directs her to I-29 for travel into the downtown area.

The ride offers a sweeping view of a dominant sky over wide spaces blanketed in green. This isn't what she'd expected. The expansiveness, yes. The green, no. There's so much of it! Though her unusual experiences had been mostly green, this area to her mind had been mostly brown.

Kansas City's downtown area isn't as large and commanding as some of the East Coast cities she's visited, but it's impressive, with its art deco, terra-cotta, and Gothic styles that combine to create an attractive skyline. Situated high atop a commanding hillside, the city affords a wide view to the confluence of the Kansas and Missouri Rivers, their bluffs, and the flatlands beyond. However, what strikes Jane more than anything else in this location is the wonderful way it smells. The rich scent of coffee coming from the Folger's plant nearby is enough to awaken her senses, especially after a long period of sitting. She gladly fills her lungs with the warm air and aromatic scents. Coffee could make most places seem charming, and so far, KC is absolutely alluring.

This is going to work out just fine.

She's parked in front of a bar and grill just a couple of doors down from the gallery's front door, so her stomach begins to rumble in response to the other aromas that waft out to the street. Eating is definitely on the agenda, but only after she checks in. And after her heart stops its wild thumping.

Stepping inside The Downtown, she sees some of her collection is already up and in full view, and this causes her to feel a little overwhelmed. This is really happening!

An attractive, slim, middle-aged woman in a smooth suit of lavender pops up from behind an executive desk in the back corner and walks briskly toward Jane, her large smile leading the way. "Hello, Jane!" She beams, holding her hand out.

Jane laughs, already disarmed by the woman's charming manner and rosy cheeks but feeling a little unworthy in common blue jeans and a loose cotton blouse, a backpack for a purse slung over her shoulder. Bland by comparison. Always plain.

"How did you know it was me?" Jane asks, blushing. The woman's sophistication is no match for what Jane perceives as her own insufficiency. Before her is a stunning creature with golden hair twisted up in a style to match the strand of pearls around her neck. Pearls!

For heaven's sake.

"Michael sent a photo with your bio." The woman chuckles, extending her hand. "I'm Glenda. It's so very good to meet you." Glenda is certainly personable. Jane relaxes.

"Glenda. Well, that's a name you'd hear in Kansas!" Jane thinks aloud.

"I hear that a lot, actually," Glenda says, warmth increasing the illumination in her face. "My parents were big Oz fans. A lot of people here are. We can't let it go. If you live on the Kansas side, as I do, you own the Wizard of Oz story."

"Oh, that's right. I keep forgetting! We're in Missouri. I don't know why I have Kansas exclusively on the brain. Please forgive me."

"It's not a problem. I'm personally non-proprietary."

"I guess if you've never been to Kansas City before, you tend to have a few pre-conceptions about the area, based largely on the *Wizard of Oz* association. I saw a lot of touristy Oz things for sale at the airport. Do people on the Missouri side feel the same way about the association?"

Glenda continues to giggle. "That's astute of you. The answer is, not so much. Though the Kansas City area belongs to both states, long-held animosities still exist." Jane's puzzlement is obvious, so Glenda continues. "Though it's been eons since the Border Wars, it's as if a strangeness has lingered in the air ever since. Basically, it prevents either side from acknowledging anything meritorious about the other."

"Oh," Jane manages to say, absorbing this.

"Simply put and generally speaking, people living here together as part of the same area are still strangely loyal to their own sides of the state line. I'd say they're definitely proprietary. Most Missourians groan at the idea of Kansas and Dorothy and all that. But enough about it. We just finished getting some of your work up and are so happy you are here!"

"I am thrilled to be. I have to tell you, though, I am feeling a little out of my league. This is my first exhibit," Jane admits.

"No worries at all! Let's get you settled in, and then we'll talk over dinner. How does that sound?"

"It sounds just fine." Jane decides she'll pinch herself when she gets back to the car. When did all of this turn? The apprehension she once felt in showing another human her work, let alone promoting it to the public, has now given way to gleeful anticipation. Jane feels as though she's dreaming. Big.

With Glenda leading the way, she finds The Raphael Hotel on the Country Club Plaza just a short distance south of city center. It's an elegant, vintage retreat built in the 1920s, and Jane is immediately delighted with its European style and old-world charm. When Glenda leaves her to rest for a few hours, she kicks off her shoes and falls back to the bed. A minute later, however, she's much too excited to sleep and still hungry, so she dons her sneakers and heads outside. The quaint, outdoor shopping and dining offerings next door hadn't escaped her attention on the way in. And, the air is thick with mouth-watering smells.

She stops by the concierge's desk to learn access is just over Brush Creek via a bridge across the street from the hotel. The Plaza certainly wasn't what she'd expected to find here. Mediterranean architecture!

Wait. What about the tornadoes?

The windmills and grain silos and blowing tumbleweeds?

This certainly doesn't look like Dorothy's Kansas, Jane muses. Oh, right, it's Missouri. Kansas, technically, is just over five miles away.

The visions she's been treated to of the Midwest all these years—she's never imagined it like this. Maybe she'll take a drive into the country soon and see for herself if there are any déjà vu similarities.

She meanders past all sorts of window displays in the City of Fountains, admiring the few she passes, along with the upscale stores and trendy boutiques. Settling on a unique coffee shop, she purchases a hot latte and a blueberry muffin to take outside. Corner Coffee isn't Oliver T. Bean, but it's pleasant. From a table in the soft, descending sun, she enjoys the play of water in a nearby fountain.

And the heeled lady who moves at a fast clip, handled bags marked "Halls" swinging over her arm, the sound of her footsteps a tattoo on the sidewalk; the teenaged girls, who saunter out of a clothing store and past the group of cute boys headed inside, their giggles encouraging a second look; the crying toddler who just toppled the scoop of ice cream off his cone, his young mother reassuring him she'll get him another.

The woman, the young girls, the small boy—they are all so beautifully normal, but different, too, Jane thinks, wondering what their lives are like, what living here feels like, and she begins to create scenarios for them in her mind. Jane giggles aloud, thinking of her imaginative younger years.

How often do I laugh anymore? It isn't often.

Before leaving, she'd told her parents everything, of course. Mostly everything. She'd explained the offer from the gallery without fully disclosing the great feedback she'd received and had downplayed her own expectations. It was better for all Jane if appeared to be grounded, not too serious about it. Heaven forbid they think she'd gotten carried away on the winds of delusion.

As a result, her father had said little. What could he say? He doesn't approve, of course, but he seems to be coming to terms with her status as an adult who is intent upon making her own decisions. A little grace from him would be nice, but Jane understands that would be an unreasonable expectation where he's concerned. He'd have to admit he'd been wrong about her work, and the stubborn man would never do that. Truth be told, it isn't as if she's making a living from it. Yet. But she's hopeful. Perhaps one day, should she really make a successful career out of it, her father could be proud of her accomplishments even though they hadn't aligned with what he'd initially wanted for her.

Surprisingly, it was her mother's response to the news she would be headed here that was most troubling. Mother seemed the most disappointed. In fact, she appeared greatly saddened. Melancholy, even. Was it because Jane was actually pursuing a career in art, or had it been because Jane was traveling by herself? It couldn't be because she would miss Jane's company.

Jane finishes her coffee and continues her walk, tossing her cup into a trashcan on the street. She catches a playful couple taking photographs in front of the sprays, the falling water a lovely backdrop for their obvious affection, and something causes a dull ache within Jane's heart. Close by, an exasperated mother fights to hold on to her young daughter who is squealing as she reaches over the wall to splash, while a gray-haired couple walk by hand-in-hand. Jane's ache grows from dull to throbbing.

It would be so nice to have a hand to hold.

Jane is no sooner back in her hotel room when she is suddenly transported away again, this time to witness a tremendous blaze race across The Land. She watches fire catch grass, hissing and crackling like an old witch as it greedily consumes dry stem and stalk. Wind rushes rise and fall to energize the flames like bellows, growing the boundaries of hell as the mass accelerates to the horizon, where a molten sun seems to offer collaboration in kinship.

Jane watches in horror as the meadows of her land—what had been the O'Donnell's land—are devoured.

Fire consumes each growing blade, leaf, petal, and trunk, the living things and the spent ones, too, and she is powerless to halt what rages over it. It will reach the cabin soon. "Mac! Can't this be stopped?" she pleads.

"It can, but who will do it?" he calmly replies.

"You. God. I don't know!" She throws her hands up in despair.

"How could *I* stop it?"

"I—don't—know. You could stop the scene somehow. Please! I don't want to see this if nothing can be done about it." Mac doesn't respond as he watches what is unfolding. "I know you have control over things. I—" She turns to look at him and catches a strange look of satisfaction there. She gasps, "This is supposed to happen. And you want me to see it!"

He doesn't disagree with her.

"Why?" she asks, horrified.

He turns to meet her eyes. And still says nothing. Jane feels hopeless. But if the situation really is hopeless, why such intentionality, as if she should be able to do something? "I feel as though …" Her voice drops to fade.

"You should be able to do something," he finishes for her.

"Yes! Oh Mac, what can we do?" she insists, rallying. "This fire must be put out! It's growing so large and there's nothing to stop it! What about all the life? Shouldn't those, those—guardians—I saw intervene?"

Mac pauses to watch the scene in front of them for a few moments and then continues. "Have you considered the possibility it's not supposed to be?"

"Supposed to be what? Stopped?" she demands. He couldn't have meant the end to growing, living things here. "Well of course it's supposed to be stopped! The fire is destroying everything in its path, every breath of life beneath it!"

"Yes, it appears so," Mac replies again.

"What's wrong with you? For heaven's sake!" Jane screeches.

"Yes, indeed," he says again softly.

"Mac, I don't understand!"

"You will."

"Ugh! I am so tired of hearing this! Just tell me! Interpret all of this for me now!"

"Patience, my dear. I told you years ago you'd need to persevere."

"I don't want to persevere. What does that mean anyway? Doesn't any of this disturb you? Why do you always appear to be so void of emotional response?"

"Perspective is often reality." The corners of his mouth turn up. Mac is so serene, it's appalling.

"You are absolutely exasperating. You know that?" Jane is quite angry now.

Mac smiles. "I know."

"How can you smile at a time like this?" Jane roars over the noise of the fire, which seems to be gaining momentum, she realizes. "Mac, it's headed in our direction!" Never has the environment felt so tangible to Jane before. Her body feels more physically responsive, her mind more present than ever before. The air around them thickens with unbreathable heat. She begins to cry.

Mac softens. "I can smile because I am not smiling *at* a time like this. I am smiling *over* a time such as this."

"Is this what you'll do when the end of the earth arrives? Will you show me that, too?" Her voice is hot and angry.

Mac remains quiet, his face impossible to read.

"What if I don't want to see it? Shouldn't I have a say?"

"What if it's not supposed to be stopped?"

Jane interrupts him. "You said that."

"Hear me out," he says as Jane pauses, fuming. "What if it's not supposed to be stopped except by *you* in alliance with truth?" He looks at her with an intensity that could bore a hole through steel.

Whatever does he mean by this?

"What if you are meant to see what may be stopped, but only after the greatest good can be known?" His voice sounds different now. Smooth and hypnotic, it melts all over her, leading her into a place of utter peace. "What if you are supposed to see what may be altered with your partnership?"

And then Jane finds herself pulled back from the scene and taken up, fresh air filling her lungs, the fire extinguished. This vantage point allows her to look down upon the land, seeing the direction the blaze had taken. The flames are gone and the smoke has cleared to reveal an unusual sight. The fire appears to have created a charred pattern of some kind. It appears to have moved eastward from the log cabin a distance, then westward, double backing, north to south. Jane gasps. She sees now it looks like a branding has been scorched in the earth there. Something that looks like a sword has been burned into the grass!

What on earth?

At the end of the tattoo is a molten tip where the fire is still in the process of burning itself out, the image one of newly extracted metal from a blacksmith's forge. Jane watches as the tip cools, turning black, and the fire is snuffed out, the forging complete.

It's a powerful impression, Jane concedes. "Do I dare ask what this is all about?" Jane asks, meeting Mac's beautiful eyes.

"You can dare," he says, with another complimentary smile.

"But I don't get an answer, do I?" Jane presses, and she can't help but feel immensely relieved and surprisingly giddy at once.

"That's up to you," he answers.

"And how on earth do I partner with it?" she asks, shaking her head. Mac only nods.

Back at her hotel room, Jane finds her hair full of cinders and her clothes reeking of smoke. She quickly takes them off and phones the front desk to inquire about laundry service, then jumps in the shower before Glenda arrives to puzzle over her state, or worse, ask questions Jane can't possibly answer.

Chapter

Twenty-Two

LEAVENWORTH, KANSAS—1800S

The small room on the upper floor of the Widow Sedgwick's home was perfect for a girl on her own, the sanctuary Agnes claimed the very moment her eighteenth birthday arrived six years ago. Her parents have now been gone twelve years.

The opportunity to distance herself from The Crows and her role as their unpaid laborer couldn't have happened soon enough, and the moment she'd realized the freedom to do so, Agnes had bundled up the few belongings she'd possessed in the world and walked out the front door without so much as a word to the people she'd lived with for six years.

The Crows had been livid, but what had they expected? That she'd stick around to slave for them indefinitely?

"Where do you think you're going?" Mrs. Crow had screeched as she watched Agnes gather her things and head for the door. "Out there, you won't be able to find the provisions you've known under this roof." The statement was made with such contempt, Agnes could only stare at her so-called benefactor.

"No, I guess I won't," she had almost retorted, but then she had thought the better of affirming such a curse. Instead, she considered the hidden blessing in the pronouncement and held in all the things she'd wanted to say in response, those that had been accumulated and stored over the years for such a day. It was her birthday, after all. It had been another year without a mention, let alone a celebration. But Agnes had held her tongue. There would have been nothing to gain by using it.

Indeed, she hoped she would not find the provisions she'd been given here. She hoped for more!

If Agnes had any regrets at all, it was the absence of any remorse for detaching from Lucinda and William so severely. The Crow Children, however, were incapable of demonstrating affection, they were so much like their parents. They had surely missed an opportunity to enjoy the sweetness of a sibling-like relationship with Agnes—a loss Agnes understood from the beginning where her own fate was concerned. Though Agnes would have loved them with the devotion of an older sister, she had been nothing more than their servant, and this meant any tender feelings she might have allowed herself were kept under guard, stored away in the place she relegated other hurts.

In fact, the cultivated indifference Agnes felt in leaving was remarkable considering all the anger and resentment she could have allowed to build up over the years, like a plaque on the smooth surface of her heart. The lot of them were horrid, selfish individuals without a care for others and especially for Agnes.

For The Land, though, their feelings were different. They seemed to care very much for that. What was the real story there? Why was it so important to Tom? What was his strange fixation, and why did his sister and brother-in-law feel the need to be a party to it, to encourage it? Agnes had ultimately learned The Crows had been in on Tom's attempt to steal The Land, something that still puzzled her.

He'd been delusional. That much was clear. Two years into the Civil War, President Lincoln had opened up parts of the West to those who could qualify—those who had never taken up arms against the United States. Tom couldn't qualify. Instead, claiming squatter's rights on a piece of land held in trust for a teenage girl had been his best option. "Possession is nine-tenths of the law," he told his sister. The girl hadn't used the property. She probably wouldn't even care.

No amount of effort advantaged Tom Crawford where the O'Donnell land was concerned. In fact, it seemed as though he was up against a strange, unseen force at work there.

First, he'd been unable to access the cabin. It was the strangest thing, the way the door seemed to possess the solid strength of a boulder and the sides of the home unyielding steel.

He'd finally settled for living in the original dwelling dug into the ground, following days of trying to hack his way into the cabin, his shoulders sore and throbbing from hefting an ax high above his head. To spite the fury he'd raised, only nicks and scrapes in the little home's exterior had appeared.

As a last resort, he tried the abandoned dugout a short distance away, but it was unwilling to permit him quarter either. It had caved in on him the moment he'd stepped inside, rousing a copperhead from its nest in the process. Adding more drama to the miserable situation, that darned snake had come after him. When Tom had finally located that blamed ax again to kill it, it had slithered back into the earth. It was probably waiting for him even now.

In fact, every other residence he attempted to construct for himself on that blasted land was thwarted by the winds of the plains and came crashing down to dust, and by the beginning of winter, with no shelter from the harsh conditions, he had been forced to return to town to wait things out while his sister Regina had no other choice but to provide a degree of rescue. More for her comfort than for his sake, and because she knew of no other way to keep him away from her own home and children for the duration.

It had been Mrs. Crow who funded the room he rented in town above the wholesale liquor house. Next door to the saloon, Tom seemed to be right where he was destined to be. His sister worried for her own repute in association, but anyone who knew Regina Richardson was much more impressed with her disagreeable disposition than her brother's disagreeable behavior.

Five years passed before Tom Crawford gave up the idea of possessing the land that belonged to Agnes. He had no fruit for maximum labor, and Tom, not inclined to work, labored greatly. More than at any other time in his life. Having been aggravated in turns by wild beasts, dry skies, wicked storms, and finally, marauding natives which reached crisis level across the state in '67, Tom angrily cast his hopes aside for conquering the O'Donnell's land as his own. He planned to set off for California soon to cast his fortune in the hunt for gold.

But first, he'd set The Land ablaze.

If he couldn't have it, no one would.

However, as peculiar as his inability had proven regarding the securing of dwellings there, so too was his inability to keep the fire going. *Any* fire going. As soon as he'd get one started, the wind would snuff it out. Even when there was no wind. This just made him angrier, and fuming himself, he used every last bit of his camphene to make a blaze.

He poured the dangerous concoction of alcohol, turpentine, and camphor oil on the fences which surrounded the cabin and sloshed what was left in his last can up on the walls, hoping a blaze would easily catch hold and spread to the brittle, October grasses. But the dangerous mixture came to nothing from Tom's effort. Though the more affordable whale oil substitute easily caused many a lamp to explode, Tom couldn't so much as light a spark with it.

Hell-bent Tom, despite laziness, wasn't one to give up easily, so he rode into town for help from his unsavory pals. The war had caused the number of available men to dwindle, but two remaining drunkards, Rusty and Clive, were eager to oblige Tom in his quest to retaliate. Anyone who had ever sided with the abolitionist cause, dead or alive, was fuel for their anger, and Seamus and Nell, even posthumously, remained cause for effect. Their land would be retribution one way or another. It was strange how obsessed the Ruffians had remained.

At length, Tom and his small gang were able to get a fire started with some whiskey and corn husks tossed around the perimeter of the cabin, and finally a spark and then a flame and then a roar resulted.

"See, all ya needed was a little dedication to the matter," redheaded Rusty blandished as they looked upon the grass fire they'd managed to get going. Indeed, it was finally happening, and Tom grinned so wickedly, his companions felt cold shivers.

"I hope it burns a path as wide as Sherman's to the east," he snickered. "I'll be heading away from it."

The men watched the blaze accelerate into a sweeping inferno before parting ways and kicking their agitated horses into a gallop. Tom headed west, while his associates moved fast to the east, alarmed the fire seemed to run after them toward Leavenworth. Winds usually blow across the plains from the west. But as the pair crested a rise on the prairie to look behind them, they watched the blaze double back to the sun, and unnaturally fast, as if in hot pursuit of Tom. Before the men continued on their way, they watched the devouring of tens of acres, and what appeared to be Tom as well, his brimmed hat whisked away to swirling madness in the hot wind. Later, when the pair had returned to find the fire extinguished and cooled, there was no evidence of bones. If Tom had, indeed, been overcome, his final resting place would remain unidentified, incinerated to black earth. Stranger still was the pattern viewed from the top of a rise. From what they could tell, it resembled a scabbard.

The greatest mystery, however, was that the cabin had been passed over by the fire. Not an inch of it had been damaged. The men rode back to town, resolved to avoid whatever presence was hovering over the O'Donnell land.

Agnes learned most of the details regarding her property from Lucinda, who heard it from her mother, who heard parts from Tom and later,Rusty. Before he'd taken off for the hills of California, Tom had stopped by to tell his sister what had prompted his decision to move on. He couldn't make that cursed land work for him. Later, Rusty had been the talk of the town with his news about the strange blaze. No one had believed the town fool or his accomplices, and no one cared now whether Tom was dead or alive. It's been years since anyone has heard from Tom, and even his own kids consider that a fine thing.

Where her land was concerned, Agnes had found herself pining less for it in recent years. Not that she didn't still love it and imagine living there again one day. But if Agnes has learned anything best, it's the ability to wait on the rightness of time. Age has a way of growing one away from the foolishness of youth, if not from the sentimentality honed there.

In short, she met James.

Tall, brawny, and superbly handsome, James Arthur Henry II is the son of a merchant who relocated from Chicago to provide supplies to the ever-increasing population of eastern Kansas. James Arthur Henry I, the elder, does a lucrative business as the owner of the Mercantile of Leavenworth, one that James Junior is eager to take over someday. Long after he marries the beautiful Agnes, he resolves.

Where twenty-four-year-old Agnes is concerned, twelve years of waiting are now over. She spent the first six years following the death of her parents with The Crows and another six with Cora Sedgewick, the owner of the boardinghouse where she had taken a job as a cook and dishwasher. Her duties covered her room, board, and more. In addition to being her landlord, Cora is a dear mentor, mothering not just Agnes but all who live under her roof. Mrs. Crow had been all wrong. Agnes had never been more provided for.

"You have the biggest eyes I've ever seen," James had exclaimed from behind the counter at the mercantile the day they'd met. He had been mortified at the slip. "Forgive me. I didn't mean to just blurt that out, it's just, well—they're very—nice," he finished awkwardly.

Agnes, who'd only just looked up from a bolt of cotton she'd been evaluating on the counter, blushed. "Thank you," she had replied, coyly. "I will take a yard of this, please." She thought him much more attractive than the fabric.

"Yes, Mrs.—" James inquired.

"*Miss* O'Donnell," she'd encouraged him, and she had known then and there James was the one. They had fallen in love in his parents' store that day, in between bolts of fabric, jars of buttons, containers of salt, and sacks of flour, her list of supplies most gently attended to.

At the time of their meeting, James had only recently joined his parents after finishing school in Illinois. Agnes was one of the first people to catch his eye in the little town, and he'd resolved immediately to have her. He enjoyed the way her hair lightened in the sun that had shown through the glass windowpanes, and how the dimples in her cheeks played joy across her face, making him feel like a kid swinging by rope over a creek, anxious to let go. He fancied the way her long lashes were beautiful frames for the light that danced in her eyes, like fireflies in a night sky, something to try and catch. She was satisfying and pleasant, like never-ending summertime.

For her part, she loved the way he was devoted to his parents and their enterprise, and how meticulously groomed he kept himself. His beard was always clean, and he smelled fresh—so unlike her father, who had worked outdoors all of the time. While there was nothing wrong with the way her father lived, the contrast was nice and new, and James was nice and new, too, especially in his nice, new clothes. He didn't plow or sweat all of the time, but his form was muscular and well-built just the same, thanks to all the heavy lifting his job required.

She could begin a new life, with him.

The couple is married in a white church in the small town when everything is new. The world is in bloom again, and the meadowlarks are singing, and this seems to Agnes a foreshadowing of what will come their way. Springtime all of the time. She enters the important date in the family Bible.

They move into a newly-finished home just a short distance from the mercantile over which his parents live—a small, single-level clapboard just off the main street—good and new, too. It isn't her precious land, but Agnes couldn't be happier.

She had to let go of it to find this happiness, this springtime all the time.

Thoughts of her property and the return to it lessen all the while, and it's just as well. James has little thought for the countryside, and isn't life adventurous enough out here in the West, in this budding little town? There is no way he is going to give up the business his father has so diligently invested in, especially now that the elder plans to make their partnership official, and especially now that it's thriving. James' destiny is in retail, definitely not in the earth. There things can bloom, too, and his dreams must be hers as well.

And then, as it happens sometimes, a person isn't who you think he is, and you only learn you've misjudged him after it's too late to do anything about it. Spring never lasts. Summer passes. Winter always returns.

So it is with James for Agnes. Believing her destiny included happiness in marriage, the kind she had once observed for a short time, something selfless and unconditional, a thing that would grow in strength to the big horizon, she saw nothing but possibility in James, which is to say she saw what she wished to see there. What she had hoped for.

Agnes had hoped James truly loved her. More than anything else.

And it seemed he did. At first. But James Arthur Henry II doesn't see the earth the way Agnes does. He doesn't see it in color. He doesn't even see the light in Agnes' hair anymore.

Now, he doesn't have time to see the lovely things.

He works too hard. He is too serious. And he never laughs.

"Each of us loves in our own way," Agnes says to herself in consolation. And she resolves she will be no less herself in endeavoring to need less from him.

Fortunately, at the age of twenty-six Agnes gets another chance to experience the fullness of life. She becomes a mother. She has heard people talk of being born again, and she finally understands. To look a newborn in the face is to see the face of God and to know destiny! So, when Leo James Henry comes into the world on April 18, 1881, Agnes is changed and new again. She feels as though she's waited a lifetime for this—where love gets yet another chance. As a child, Agnes had found true love on the plains. Now, in the soft skin of her baby is the best of all promises. Humanity, new again, holds the light in living color.

Were it not for her son, Agnes would not know the degree to which this is true. If it weren't for her lovely stranger in white, she would have no adult with whom to validate this.

Were it not for the paintings she creates, she would have no way to express it all. A person needs a way to express these things.

"Paint the good you see," The Knight tells her. And so, she does. With a merchant for a husband, she has access to all the supplies she needs.

With her husband, she doesn't convey her feelings of loneliness that grow as their house expands. She doesn't tell her knight either. She knows he knows. Her stranger is fully aware of what she lives and thinks, and this would be unsettling if it weren't so oddly comforting.

He takes her traveling again, this time to a coastline where wispy grasses grow in clumps on dunes and a breeze blows warm off the sea. She's hundreds of feet up in the air before she is lowered, bare feet into the sand. The sun sets at her back, settling itself beneath a blanket of shadows to cast pastels across the water. It's a different coast this time. Not the craggy one covered in scrubby vegetation and pine. The waves giggle along the shoreline in foamy patterns that make her feel alive, a part of a Grand Master's painting, another one in a collection that includes her land back at home.

"Where are we, Knight?" she asks him. "Why have you brought me here?"

"There is no such thing as coincidence," he calmly replies, but provides no further information.

"I've never seen such a place before," Agnes says.

"I know," he responds.

"You won't tell me where we are?"

"This is your future, but not your home," he says, still looking forward to the ever-darkening sea.

"Must you always speak in riddles?"

"Must you always know everything?" he asks.

He doesn't tell her where they are.

Neither does he tell her The Land in Kansas no longer belongs to her.

Chapter

Twenty-Three

KANSAS CITY—1990

Jane is already in love with Kansas City. Is that possible? To fall in love with a place?

Well, of course it's possible, she reasons. She feels the same way about The Land. Never has her passion waned. Feeling emotion for KC is a healthier alternative, truthfully. At least this place is real.

Or, real in present time.

The private showing for her work at The Downtown gallery will take place on Wednesday evening, the fourth of July. It seems an odd date to host a show, but Glenda assures her it's a perfect fit for Jane's work. What better timing than Independence Day for the official revealing of a collection that speaks of hope and freedom? Jane has no choice but to agree.

Glenda, fast becoming a good friend, is persuasive for all her charm. Jane has only known her a week now, but they've covered a lot of ground in that space. Jane knows Glenda to be authentic and fun, someone she can talk with. The consummate professional as well. Jane trusts Glenda's expert perspective on what needs to happen regarding the showing of her work. Technically, it's Glenda's husband Patrick who owns the gallery, but the creative brain behind the business belongs to her new friend. Patrick is rarely in the office. Glenda seems rarely to leave.

"Which do you like best?" Glenda asks Jane after watching the gallery's associate director put the finishing touches on the last painting he's hung. The entire collection is officially up. Bob, also Glenda's handyman, steps down off a ladder to stand beside both women in admiring the biggest piece on display.

Like *The House* that went missing, this one is also a thirty-by-forty-inch panoramic landscape of the prairie in hues of light green dusted with gold under a giant sky of the fairest of blues. It feels like summer, but it also speaks of things beyond understanding for the immensity it illustrates, as if eternity could be represented on canvas. The House is missing; in its place in the foreground is one pale sunflower, its jade stem bent gracefully, as if bowing before heaven. In the distance, the horizon is only an impression for focus on the wildflower in front. It's one of Jane's favorites, a glimpse of what the prairie looked like in its original state before the plow, people, or structures. Jane has given it the name "Summertime."

"I guess the one I like best is this last one," Jane answers, looking up at the large painting on the wall in front of her. "After the one that was stolen, that is."

"What? You had a painting stolen?" Glenda exclaims.

"Yeah. I mean, it went missing from the coffee shop wall where it had been hanging," Jane says wistfully.

"You've got to be kidding me! You didn't tell me that!"

"Well, it's embarrassingly painful, actually," Jane admits.

"Well of course it is! Wow, I'm so sorry!" Glenda says soothingly.

"Give us the condensed version," Bob says, resting his arm on a ladder rung as he waits for Jane to say more.

Glenda nods in agreement. "Please don't leave us in suspense. What exactly happened? What painting was taken?"

Grateful for their polite interest, Jane gives them a short description of the painting, and then explains how she'd been encouraged by her boss at the coffee shop to display her work—how she'd been reticent to do so for fear of failure and what an emotional risk it had been considering her family's perspective, which she elaborates on slightly. It's undoubtedly too much information. However, Bingham had intimated as much in her bio.

"Hmm. A house," Glenda muses, intentionally leaving out the personal information Jane had disclosed. "The fragments of which are evident here," she continues, gesturing to the collection.

"Yes. It's one I imagine belonging to land so wonderful," Jane says.

"You imagine? Come to think of it, how did you come to create any of this?" Glenda asks with a sweep of her hand toward the walls. "You've never been to the Midwest before? Because, oddly, you even speak like a Midwesterner."

"What do you mean?" Jane asks, puzzled.

"You don't have the East Coast accent I expected." Glenda shrugs.

How strange. Jane has never heard that before. "I—just—I don't know—I just see it in my mind," Jane answers truthfully.

"Like, in a vision or something?" Glenda asks excitedly.

"I guess, a little like that," Jane admits. Again, too much information.

"Well, maybe it means something!"

"Maybe it does," Jane agrees. "And then again, maybe it means nothing." Inwardly, Jane knows it means something. Of course it does. Why would Mac continue to take her there if it meant nothing? Maybe it was a way to spark the creativity she would need to be standing here now.

"I get it. Oftentimes we paint what we know, but other times we draw from a collection of thoughts and pictures accumulated over the years. Before we know it, something new appears on canvas."

"Do you paint then, Glenda?" Jane asks, suddenly surprised. Why hadn't she thought to ask the proprietor of an art gallery before now? Of course, one would have to be artistic to be in this business!

"Me? Heavens no!" Glenda insists, chuckling. "I didn't inherit the ability. My father was the artist, or printmaker. He was pretty good, actually. And not only did he create in me great appreciation for his own work, he empowered me to look at what others create with an eye for it. He used to schlep me to a variety of galleries in my youth. When The Downtown hit the market last year, I nagged my husband mercilessly to purchase it until he gave in. Since we don't have kids, it's become my baby."

"Oh, so you've only owned the gallery a year then?"

"That's right," Glenda beams.

"Do you have any ideas about why your painting was taken?" Bob redirects, obviously quite interested.

"I haven't a clue. It just wasn't in the shop one day. No one saw it go missing. None of my coworkers even noticed it was gone. It was my boss that noticed and called the police."

"Someone probably felt they had to have it," Bob says, gently.

"Did they find out anything?" Glenda asks.

"No. Nothing. Unfortunately. It feels weird, knowing my precious work is out there somewhere—as crazy as it sounds."

"It doesn't sound crazy to me," Bob says. "I don't paint either, but I can imagine if I did, it would seem pretty personal."

Glenda nods in agreement. "Do you have any others like it? Because if it turns out that your collection is as successful as I believe it will be, that missing painting could one day be worth some cash."

"I love that you believe in me! But, no, I don't have any others like it. It was one of a kind," Jane admits. "I suppose one day I'll try to recreate it."

Maybe. If I have the heart to.

"You totally should," Bob insists. "You already have us intrigued, and if it's anything like what you have here, it would be great!"

"It's nothing like I have here. What you see in front of you is the exception. As you know, my work is mostly fragments of a greater picture, pieces of a panorama." Glenda and Bob nod together in understanding. Jane has written as much in the collection's description, each piece a lovely representation on its own.

"I still can't get over how you've managed to so beautifully capture the native charm here without ever having set foot on this land, how this kind of creativity happened for you remotely," Glenda says, surveying the walls around them. "Remarkable."

"I guess it is," Jane agrees without saying any more.

"Well, I love your fragments, as you call them," adds Bob. "Fragments of a Greater Picture."

All now on display in the illustrious Downtown.

Each one exactly right and enough to change the greater picture of her world entirely.

Glenda's connections are impressive. The Sunday edition of *The Kansas City Star* does a full-page article in the arts section on the upcoming opening of the exhibit. Jane is tempted to send a copy home, but thinks the better of it. There can be no convincing people who don't want to be convinced. Besides, the support here in KC is more than enough. She does plan to call Jake, however. It wouldn't be right not to keep him in the loop.

He beats her to it. It's the day before the opening, and Jane has just enjoyed an early, solitary lunch at Houston's on The Plaza. She doesn't mind eating alone; in fact, she relishes solitary dining because there's something about sitting by oneself without the need to keep conversation going that allows for a better appreciation of good food. That's what she told herself, anyway. The truth is, she would have loved some company.

She has just returned to her room when the phone rings. She throws herself across the bed to reach it, and soon Jakes voice brightens the room. "How's it going out there?" he asks.

"Oh, Jake, I love it here!" she tells him, sitting up to look out the window. A couple strolls leisurely along Brush Creek.

"Fill me in!" he says, as cheerful as ever.

She tells him about the gallery and her new friend Glenda, of the downtown streets fresh with the smiles of locals and filled with the smell of coffee, the way the sun lasts so long spread out against the expansive horizon and the way the world is so green. And, saving the big news for last, she tells him of the paper's advertisement of her show.

"That's fantastic!" he says.

"I know it! And I have you to thank for it all."

"Totally unnecessary. It would have happened one way or another. It's your destiny!" he assures her.

"Well, you put my destiny into motion!" Jane says laughing. "And I'm so grateful for—that." She almost says you, but catches herself. She must choose her words wisely. Words have a way of growing larger than they should at times.

Jake laughs, too. "I'm just glad I can help. Have you talked with your parents since you've been there?"

"My mom called yesterday."

"And?"

"We didn't talk long. She just wanted to make sure I was okay. She asked me about the city but not about the exhibit."

"You've got to be kidding me! She didn't ask you how things were going at the gallery?"

"No. Maybe she doesn't know what to ask. It's out of her league. She can't possibly understand my involvement here, which is really very little." Jane pauses. "Glenda and her staff have everything under control. My mother has no idea I arrived well in advance so I could take a break from home and have a little fun."

"Well, she could at least feign a little interest by asking a few questions about the process. And about how you feel," Jake tells her.

"Feelings aren't usually our mode of operation," Jane admits with a sigh.

"Did you at least let her know about the write-up in the paper?"

"Nope. I wanted to. Just couldn't. I guess I'll leave a copy out for my parents to stumble upon when I get home."

"Well, I for one can't wait to see it!" Jake is so genuinely happy, he makes up for the disappointment she feels where her family is concerned.

"You're the best," Jane says, and changing the subject asks, "What's new back home? Anything juicy? Are Heather and Leslie still arguing about who's on bar? Bill and Chloe still flirting?"

"Did the sun come up this morning?" Jake chuckles again.

Joining him, Jane realizes she doesn't miss the coffeeshop in the least. Maybe she misses Jake, though. Just a little. But not enough. Not enough to have brought the subject of flirting up.

What was I thinking?

She mentally smacks herself on the forehead. Fortunately, Jake knows not to go there, surely. Especially now. "Yeah, same old, same old. I swear though, if those two girls don't stop bickering, I am going to have to threaten to fire them!"

"Do it! You can't have the customers seeing their antics!"

"You don't have to convince me!" he assures her. "They are this close!" Jane imagines his accompanying hand gesture, and they continue to giggle together until their laughter trails off into awkward silence.

Jane is quick to the rescue. "Well, I should let you get back to work and save you from any further outrageous long-distance charges. I really appreciate your checking in with me."

"Of course! I had to know how my favorite artist was faring."

Jane blushes. "I'll let you know how the opening goes tomorrow night."

"It will be a smash!" he says with a warmth that grounds her, making her feel more connected to life in the present. It really is wonderful to have such a friend.

"You've made your first sale!" Glenda greets her with a grin nearly as wide as her beautifully-tanned face as Jane walks through the gallery's front door. Glenda's skin always appears aglow, thanks to the tennis she plays regularly at her local club. Jane has learned it's about the only thing the woman does outside of working at the gallery and absorbing everything she can regarding a variety of art forms. Glenda knows more about art and art history than most university humanities professors.

"How can that be? Shouldn't the buyer have waited for the show tonight?" Jane follows Glenda toward the back of the gallery. She is early, but she knows Glenda doesn't mind.

"We had a client who loves your work stop in early. It happens. Sometimes buyers have no problem passing up the champagne and appetizers to be first in line."

Jane doesn't think this method is exactly fair, or fun, but supposes if she were the buyer, she'd operate the same way. "What did he, or she, buy?"

"It was a 'he', and *Summertime*," Glenda answers. "Oh, and you got your asking price."

"Go figure. I didn't think anyone would go with our asking price!" Jane exclaims. Inside, she feels her stomach tighten.

I need to let go.

"What did I tell you?" Glenda says, elbowing Jane as she moves back to her desk, still smiling like a child at play. "It's a good thing we priced it all the way we did, especially considering my handsome forty percent cut!"

"Yeah, what with you gouging me and all," Jane teases. She already feels as if she's known Glenda a lifetime. "What was the guy like that bought it?"

"Does it matter?" Glenda glances at her sideways.

"Well, no. I guess not. Just wondering. Old or young? Upper or middle class? That sort of stuff."

"Young, if you must know. I don't know his financials."

"Like, how young?"

Glenda lifts an eyebrow and says nothing.

Jane shrugs. "Just thinking about the kind of person my work would appeal to, that's all."

"I already told you," Glenda assures her, "Your work appeals to all kinds of people."

She had decided to wear a seamless black tank dress with a scoop neck, though she'd have preferred to wear something colorful in her favorite hot pink color. But that probably would have been too flashy here away from the coast. Better to keep her own look simple, the focus on what's hanging on the walls. However, the thick serpentine of 14-karat gold around her neck, along with the gold bangle bracelets on her wrists and the large hoops hanging from her ears are eye-catching.

So much for Plain Jane, she muses as she catches her reflection in the gallery's glass window.

She's worn her thick hair down and loosely curled in waves and has even used a tube of red lipstick liberally. Not so plain tonight. She actually feels beautiful for a change.

You can do this.

She observes Glenda making the final preparations for the evening and feels helpless, her part already done, aside from the small talk she will be obligated to participate in this evening. She clutches her small black handbag tighter.

Glenda has arranged for a caterer to provide a variety of hors d'oeuvres and drinks, but Jane determines she'll not partake of the elegant offerings. She'd probably only embarrass herself with a dribble down the front of her dress or a bit of parsley lodged between her front teeth. As it is, she worries she'll not know what to say should anyone decide they'd like to talk with her about her work. She picks up a glass of ice water so as to have something else to steady herself. On second thought, a glass of bubbly might be helpful, but before she can think any more on this, a customer arrives.

He's early but appears blasé regarding his timing or any obvious signals of the event's impending status as Glenda and her staff busily work to finish setting up. He looks to be mid-thirties and sports a sandy-colored mullet and matching mustache under ruddy skin. He's wearing high-top Reeboks and black and white parachute pants with a neon orange shirt that most definitely doesn't match, and acting nonchalant, or unaware, he turns to his right, puts his hands in his pockets, and begins to inspect one of the pieces on the wall.

"Winter Tree," a painting of a lone tree on a windswept prairie, has caught his eye. It's one of her more monotone offerings in tones of grey and brown, but Jane has always felt there was something elegant in the allegory of that tree surrounded by nothing but grass and set against a magnificent sky. It's one from her visions, one she's noticed in its constantly changing environment. While it transforms to accommodate its surroundings, it appears less inclined to give up its identity as the grasses that surround it do, less willing to be overcome by circumstances. That tree represents resiliency. Triumph. The symbolism is empowering.

But she feels awkward now, watching the lone visitor eye it, and this, again, seems too personal. She realizes, of course, this kind of thinking is impractical for an artist aspiring to be successful, so she shakes it off by turning away in search of an engaging task.

She makes a beeline to the table covered in white linen laid out with sparkling glasses and enticing appetizers and again opts for another iced water. Better safe than sorry. Best to run to the ladies' room all evening than to have a sluggish mind, dragon breath, or worse. Much worse.

That would totally happen.

Besides, her stomach is in no condition for food right now. She takes a sip from her glass and catches sight of a flutter of activity as Glenda flies across the room. Ever the consummate hostess, Glenda is by the visitor's side in a graceful flash. As she occupies him in conversation about the painting, Jane remembers the criticism component to all of this. What will she do if she hears it tonight?

Just keep sipping.

She'll have to fight to keep Glenda's advice secure. And then she thinks of Jake. Perhaps she should have invited him to attend the show! Ugh, that would have ratcheted up *personal* beyond her own comfort level. Still, she finds herself missing the safety of his companionship.

Glenda finally excuses herself from conversation with Parachute Pants and then steps to the back to resume her last-minute touches. She'd already instructed Jane to just take it easy. Jane should prepare only to mingle and smile and to be herself. There will be introductions, naturally, but she should simply walk around and engage when it's appropriate to do so. And enjoy her evening.

But that's harder said than done!

Thank heavens for the glass in her hand. She looks down to it now, pressing her fingers into the condensation and removing them again to create a lacy pattern around the outside, her elbow an iron vice against her handbag. Parachute Pants continues to mill about. As unsettling as this is, it's better he does that than talk with her. But she's no sooner had these thoughts when she feels him making his way toward her.

Oh dear.

She keeps her focus on her glass.

"Excuse me," he says. "Aren't you the artist?"

Jane has no choice but to look up and meet his eyes. "Yes. I am."

"Great! It's great to meet you!" he says, extending his hand toward her. Jane must shake it. "I'm John. John Brown."

John Brown? You've got to be kidding me. What's with all the recycling of noteworthy names here?

"Nice to meet you," she says, although it really isn't nice at all.

Parachute Pants.

Now, can you go away?

"I saw your picture in the paper. You're from the East. How'd you end up painting the Midwest?" he asks pointedly and there's something about this man that makes her feel like she needs a hot shower as his eyes cover the length of her.

That certainly happened fast.

"I don't know. I just did." She shrugs, trying to smile.

Why can't I just enjoy feeling good about myself for a change without attracting things that creep?

"Well, I sure like it! It's some good stuff!" he drawls, still looking at her devilishly. "Sorta reminds me of land my grand-pappy used to talk about."

How do I escape?

"And you're so young, too. Wow!" He says most inappropriately, in his flamboyant neon pants. It would stand to reason his cologne is also overpowering. He obviously thrives on negative attention.

Jane finds it difficult to smile through her unease. Was a revealing bio really such a good idea? She'll have to talk with Glenda about this later, but evidently, the damage is already done.

"How long are you in town?" he persists. "Maybe we could …" And just then, Glenda arrives at his side again, thank heavens.

"Mr. Brown," Glenda says firmly, cutting him off. "How would you like to take a look at the rest of this artist's work?" The business woman really is quite impressive. Parachute Pants nods reluctantly and returns to continue his inspection of the exhibit despite the clattering and shuffling around him as everyone but Jane busily prepares. He has no idea how to read a room.

"Thank you," Jane mouths silently to Glenda once her task is completed. Jane is still clutching her water glass like Linus would his blanket a quarter before the hour when all is finally ready and in place. Patrick walks in five minutes before showtime and Jane finally gets to meet her business associate's husband. To say she's taken back is an understatement.

Patrick is obviously older than Glenda, something that impresses Jane, but what isn't a revelation is his good looks. She expected Glenda would be married to a looker, and boy, is he.

More like blue-eyed silver fox. Patrick's thick mane is brushed back to short, feathered sides parted down the middle, making him look like that actor who played the male lead in the hit TV show *Dynasty*—the show her mother never missed. He's tan and fit, a match for his wife. Jane assumes the crisp, olive-colored suit he's dressed in is Giorgio Armani, given Glenda's slip of her husband's favorite designer when they'd been strolling on The Plaza one day. She said he'd not been able to find what he wanted locally, so he'd taken advantage of shopping in Milan when the couple had traveled to Europe over the holidays. Jane had felt it tactless to ask what he did that allowed for such extravagance, but Glenda had already intimated it was wise investments from family income. If it wasn't old money, whatever it was allowed for shopping trips to Europe and the purchase of a well-known gallery for his wife's amusement.

He must *be wearing Armani.*

"It's fabulous to meet you," Patrick says sincerely when Glenda introduces her husband to Jane. He meets Jane's eyes with respectful attentiveness and a wide smile.

"And you as well," she replies, determining immediately her friend is married to a good man.

When a crowd of guests begins to arrive on schedule, Glenda springs into further action, moving first to greet an elegantly dressed couple who looks to be in their seventies. The man wears a dark dinner jacket, the woman black slacks and a white ruffled blouse, open wide enough to reveal what appears to be a diamond pendant. Her pearly hair is twisted and pinned up in back to more easily reveal the glimmering stones which dangle from her ears.

Behind them are two middle-aged women dressed in stiff blue jeans and tight-fitting white cotton shirts with high-heeled boots and silver belt buckles; a tall, thin, balding man with glasses in a red dress shirt and navy trousers, evidently in honor of the current holiday; and an amorous young couple, hand in hand and clearly on a date. The latter look to be Jane's age and so enamored with one another, they can't be serious. The girl shows off a nice figure in a tight pair of denim shorts with a strapless, floral top; the guy is in a Chiefs T-shirt and jeans. Clearly, they've stumbled into the place in error. They look more in the mood for a movie and popcorn than for art.

Jane eyes the champagne glasses now filled, lined up, and sparkling on the table. Like Jake, she is noticing all the details tonight.

The small space fills nearly to capacity in no time, and now more potential buyers enter. The latest are several men who look to be ranchers dressed in Levi jeans and pointy leather cowboy boots. All wear western hats. Two appear to be in their fifties, but a third is considerably younger. He's in his early twenties and has that John Travolta, *Urban Cowboy* look, something Jane finds startlingly appealing. All are clean-shaven, and well fit, and from the looks of it, spend a lot of time outdoors. Urban Cowboy considers her intently. She turns, blushing.

The early evening is warm but comfortable, the sun making its slow way to the horizon, as if to demonstrate there's no hurrying tonight. Fireworks displays are still hours away. It couldn't be lovelier.

Jane makes for the table to refill her water glass. She needs something to do! She's just put the pitcher down when she feels the soft touch of a hand upon her shoulder. Turning with a start, she finds Glenda standing with the group of cowboys she's evidently gathered for introductions. All eye her now with great interest. "Jane, I'd like to introduce you to a few people," Glenda says in her most charming voice.

Jane smiles, genuinely this time, thinking she's never met anyone before that's made an immediate impression like the attractive young man in front of her. She tries to appear as interested in his companions.

"Gentlemen, I'd like you to meet our artist, Jane Campbell," Glenda purrs. *She does have a way about her.*

"Jane, this is Ed Hawkins, Doug Wainwright, and Derrick Copeland."

"Hello," Jane says warmly, extending her hand to each of the men in turn. "It is so nice to meet you. Thank you for attending my first show."

"These men are some of my best clients, but shh, no telling the others that!" Glenda says playfully as she elbows the man named Ed.

"I wouldn't say that, darlin'," says the one introduced as Doug. We don't get into the city near enough." Turning to address Jane directly, he continues, "We were motivated to make the trip in tonight after what we'd seen in the paper."

Jane doesn't know what to say but manages a grateful response. "Well, I appreciate that Mr.—"

"Wainwright," he helps her.

"Wainwright." She hopes her jitters aren't too obvious. Her sudden need to use the restroom doesn't help.

"It's a great collection. You really have a way of capturing the beauty of the plains," he continues.

"Do you have anything in particular you're looking for?" the always helpful Glenda inquires.

"Not really," Ed pipes up. "Did like the landscape I saw in the paper."

"Which one was that, Mr. Hawkins?" Glenda asks.

"The one called 'Summertime,'" Doug replies for him.

"I'm sorry to say that particular piece has already been purchased. But there are quite a few others available tonight. Why don't I let you get started?" she says, gesturing toward the collection.

Honestly, if I'd signed my name to a coloring page, Glenda would find a way to sell it.

"That sounds like a plan," Ed says, accepting champagne from a passing waiter, who balances a half-dozen glasses on a tray.

Glenda leads two of the group away but the Urban Cowboy, Derrick, lingers. He hasn't yet said a word, but Jane understands he is definitely interested, and not just in her work or the crab-stuffed mushrooms passing through. He hasn't taken his eyes off her since he'd arrived and he keeps grinning. Surprisingly, Jane doesn't mind.

She takes another sip of water, this time to cool down, but she nearly chokes on it when she sees Mac saunter by, just behind Derrick.

Mac is here?

A groan escapes her lips.

"Are you okay?" Derrick politely inquires.

What a great way to open a conversation!

Jane feels heat rise to her face. "Just fine," she says, straining forward in a way she hopes isn't obvious.

Derrick laughs. "It looked there for a moment you'd seen a ghost."

She shrugs it off with a feeble chuckle as she rotates to survey the back of the room where she'd just seen her old friend headed. Sure enough, he's there. Mingling! He's never appeared in a crowd before, never interfered with her real life until now. That she knows of, anyway.

What in heaven's name is going on?

She'd like to head to the back of the gallery and confront him immediately but turns to Derrick, feigning a wider smile. He starts to say something when she whips around to take a look over her shoulder again. Surveying the room of art enthusiasts rapidly, she finds no trace of Mac this time. Finally, she responds, "I thought for a moment I saw someone I know."

Wonderful. Now is a fine time for my imagination to be acting up.

Derrick laughs out loud. It's a merry, musical laugh that warms her to her core. "Shouldn't you know people at your own art show?" he asks, still grinning.

"Yes, well—" She really doesn't know what to say to the stranger before her. "I guess I was startled for a moment," she responds lamely.

"Oh? Is someone bothering you?" he asks, suddenly concerned.

"Oh, goodness, no! Please forgive me," Jane hastens to add.

"May I get you another drink? I see yours is empty." Jane looks down to her glass.

"That would be nice. Thank you," she says.

"What are you drinking?"

"Water. But champagne would be nice," she says, forgetting about everything else.

Chapter

Twenty-Four

LEAVENWORTH, KANSAS—1900

In the year 1900, the woman once known as Running Feet is ninety-two-years old. Her hair is still thick, but silver highlights long white strands; her skin remains a most beautiful brown, but rivers run through it. She is no longer able to run herself but is able to walk fast on her own legs, and because of this, she is a legend in the town in which she lives. Today she rides high atop her favorite gelding, a young man seated protectively behind her.

"Well, shall we get down, Grandmother?" he asks, surveying the plains before them and the cabin in the distance, nearly concealed in its folds.

"No," she says, shaking her head slowly. "I don't need to."

"Then why did we journey all the way out here?" he asks gently.

Contemplative at first, she finally answers, "I needed to take another look before my time on this earth is gone, and I return to the Great Spirit."

Her great-grandson says nothing. He waits. She continues.

"You must not be sad when I leave, my love. When He calls for me, I will be ready. And you must be as well. It should be a time of great rejoicing for you because I will be home, finally."

"And this place reminds you of home," he says, comprehending.

"It does," she nods, seemingly lost in thought. She turns to him. Do you not feel it?"

He inhales deeply before scanning the horizon. "I will admit there is something special about this land. I do feel that. But I am unable to say definitively that heaven reigns more strongly here than in other places."

"I have experienced things here of magnificent wonder," she says. "Here, under the big sky, the veil is thin." She pauses again in quiet contemplation, her companion respectfully still. A soft breeze stirs the grasses. "I believe there are places in this world where earth and sky blend together more easily than in others, and in such places exists an opening in the fabric between this life and the next."

"And this is one of them," he says at length. He has grown up on his great-grandmother's tales of Manitou's protection and the portal to heaven she had found here. And yet, he foreknew what they would find upon arrival. A place of immense importance to his great-grandmother, but one that had failed to resonate for other family members the way it had for her. His father and grandfather, his aunts, uncles, and cousins had accompanied Grandmother Ruth here on occasion. Few had come away with the sentiments she had.

And yet, he could feel a presence here. Maybe if they waited long enough, he would sense more. As the midday sun begins its descent to the other side of the horizon, a soft breeze grows to a mighty wind, causing the grasses to bow as if in reverence, like a parting of the sea. A floral scent perfumes the air. The birdsong increases.

"It's time to go," she says with a sigh, leaving the young man to ponder if there wasn't some part of heaven here after all.

In the year 1900, eighty million public acres have been parceled out to humans, who, making good use of hope, have staked claims. Not all of what has been made available is accommodating. Not all of the claimants have been, either.

There have been verdant years followed by dusty "drouth" ones in cycles. There have been wars and fires, bitter cold and scorching heat, wicked storms and wicked men, and in all seasons, trails of tears. But in all of those things is victory. This is Kansas.

Agnes has been married to James for over twenty years. Their oldest, Leo, is nineteen already. It's been two years since their daughter, Edith, now fourteen, began having unusual dreams. In them a dark-skinned man in white linen comes to her and shows her things beyond her wildest imagination.

Though mother and daughter are close, Edith initially holds back from telling Agnes this but finally confesses, knowing she can keep the secret no longer. She senses her mother is also relieved with the confession, but Agnes is quick to point out they must admit their *travels* to no one else, and certainly not to Edith's pragmatic father.

"They must be real!" Edith says, anxious to explore the subject at length. "Don't you think?"

"Yes," Agnes admits. The snow is softly falling, and the women sit by the fire to do their mending. James and Leo are at work in the mercantile, where James' parents remain involved in the ever-expanding business. James is the official proprietor of the family store now, a financially lucrative arrangement for all. As the population increases, supply needs expand, and the Henrys work diligently to meet demands. James and his son, now following in the family business, are rarely home.

"But I can't get that man to tell me anything. Can you?" Edith asks her mother.

"You mean The Knight? Yes, well …" Agnes begins.

"What?" Edith exclaims.

"Yes. That's what I call him," Agnes continues, giggling. "He didn't give me his name, so I gave him one." She shrugs.

"Did you ask him? Because I did and got nothing."

Agnes continues to laugh, nodding. "Yes, I did ask him, and yes, he was the same way with me. He's dodgy, that one!"

"Isn't he though?" Edith chuckles, too. "So, you named him. Heavens!"

"Yes. And he didn't protest! Though he would never confirm it's acceptable." She shrugs.

"But why choose that name for him?"

"Well, your grandmother used to read to me a lot. First from the Bible she'd brought from Ireland—it was rarely out of her sight, you know. She also had a few other books she considered treasures, but the tales she told from memory made a great impression on me—those handed down for generations by word of mouth. People used to be much better at telling stories when they didn't have access to books or the ability to read them. The tales of a king named Arthur and his Knights of the Round Table thrilled me."

"The Knight," Edith says, still mulling over the nickname.

"Yes!" Agnes continues, "We couldn't afford to send away for books like we can now. My mother had a vast memory she could tap into for most of her stories," she remembers wistfully. "Anyway, I love the idea of heroic people, like knights, who lived in castles and according to a code of honor and chivalry and who nobly loved and defended women. I found it romantic, especially as a young girl without any friends living alone with her parents on the wild frontier!"

Edith looks pensive. "Mom, what do you think it all means?"

Agnes glances up from her needlework to consider that for a moment. "What? The Knights of the Roundtable?"

"Our Knight!" Edith says, shaking her head. "He's so—."

"Unusual," her mother finishes for her. "Yes, indeed. He is rather elusive, too."

"Exactly!"

"I haven't the faintest idea. When I was your age, it never occurred to me he was anything more than someone who came to me when I needed a friend. And, obviously, someone who confirmed there is more beyond what we can see."

"Another reality," Edith offers.

"I believe that's it, but there's so much I don't understand. So very many things he and I have seen together since he first began visiting me, which was when I was twelve, just like you, I now realize."

"I should have told you sooner—I don't know why I didn't. I wanted to! I just didn't think I was supposed to." Edith pauses, needle in hand, to look her mother in the eye.

"Oh, I understand that entirely. There's something so—private—about the experiences." Agnes nods in agreement as she continues to stitch. "And mystical. Truly, what would people think if we attempted to describe what we see? They'd believe us mad."

"Yes, that's true," Edith agrees, still pensive.

"But I was the one who should have broached the subject a couple of years ago, you know, to see if you were experiencing anything unusual, especially when you dropped hints about your dreams occasionally. I guess I just rationalized that you couldn't possibly be seeing what I was seeing. It just wasn't possible. Or normal!"

"Do you think there are other people who have the same experiences?"

Agnes shakes her head. "I couldn't say."

"I think there has to be a point for us, since we are seeing the same things independent of one another." Edith continues without taking a breath. "Maybe there's a reason you named him The Knight. Maybe he is really protecting us."

"I don't think so," Agnes sadly admits. "My parents used to talk about protection and a fortress and shadows—a secret place talked about in a psalm found in their Bible, but I've not experienced it. Not entirely, anyway. I have felt little protection from anyone. I know God exists—I have seen the evidence, but most days He seems a million miles away. And as far as our Knight is concerned, he went missing when I needed him most."

"Did Grandma Nell talk about having visions or anything?" Edith says, steering the subject in a safer direction.

Agnes stops stitching and sits still for a moment, gazing out the window. She appears lost in thought as she watches the falling snow. Edith waits patiently. "She *must* have seen something. I was so young when she began painting ..." she says trailing off into a whisper.

"Grandma painted?" Edith asks softly. Considering her own urgency to paint right now, this is interesting indeed.

"Yes," Agnes says, turning around, "as did I." She watches her daughter's face gather in disbelief, and seeing the confusion in her furrowed brows, Agnes takes a deep breath. Sorting out the details in her own mind, she plunges ahead.

"You have to understand, there was so much work to do then. Little free time. But I do remember, vaguely, that she had made an effort to paint for a while. And then she just stopped." Edith holds still, watching her mother as she closes her eyes in concentration. "I think—I think it had something to do with my father. He was angry with her. No, that's not it. She was angry with him!"

"Why would she have been angry with him over her painting?"

"That's right! I remember now! It was because he lost her favorite painting!" Agnes says excitedly. "How had I forgotten that?" She appears momentarily lost in thought.

Edith leans forward in her chair, dropping her own work in the process. She picks it up without taking her eyes off her mother and sets it aside.

"He'd taken it to show someone and had come back without it. Those were the days of war, and he was out fighting. It was at that time the painting went missing." Her voice softens with emotion as she recalls this.

"He took a painting with him to fight?" Edith states in disbelief. "Why would he do that?"

"I know it sounds odd, but I believe he did. I think he wanted to show it to someone."

"Okay, so then he lost it and she was furious, no doubt. But why would that cause her to stop painting?"

"I can't say," Agnes says wistfully.

"And why did *you* stop?" her daughter asks pointedly.

"I—I wanted to keep at it. But it was impossible. As you know, your grandparents had died suddenly and I was devastated. That was part of it. The reality was the family I was sent to live with would never have permitted it. Just after I married your father and had access to supplies, I started up again, but then found I hadn't the energy to continue." Agnes has told Edith little about her youth, choosing to spare her daughter and instead fill her with beauty of the kind she'd been denied herself. Edith really knows little about her mother's history or her roots and certainly nothing of the awful Crows.

It's better that way, Agnes had reasoned. Free of the past, the love and friendship she's lavished on her only daughter has fostered an unusually intimate connection between the two and an optimistic outlook on life in general for them both. It's an investment that's paid off. Not that she hasn't tried with Leo. Her son's affection for others often mirrors his father's.

"What did you do with your work? What happened to hers?"

"It was burned and—I never went back to the cabin," Agnes stammers. "I should have gone back!"

"What cabin, Mom?" Edith realizes there is so much more her mother hasn't disclosed and this astounds her. Whenever Edith has probed into her mother's past, she has been told only that her grandparents died when her mother was young. Nuns had placed Agnes in a home in which she lived before finding a room with the sweet woman who had passed away when Edith was young. Edith only vaguely remembers meeting Cora.

"The one I believe still belongs to me," Agnes responds, realizing how full of regret this makes her feel.

In the summer, after the snow has melted and the spring mud dried to solid earth again, Agnes decides to broach the subject of her land with her husband. She'd spent a winter ruminating about it and is now resolved they should take a ride out to the cabin on The Land that belongs to them all. She can't wait a moment longer to discuss this.

The dinner dishes are dried and put up, Leo out for a dance being held by the local Methodist church. James grabs his pipe and begins to load it. Edith is sitting in her favorite chair reading that "modernized fairytale," *The Wizard of Oz*, thanks to a father who has access to literature others don't and who managed to secure a newly-printed copy for her. The dimness of candlelight is challenging, but she refuses to set it down.

"Why on earth would you want to head out there now? You haven't been to the place in decades!" James roars after Agnes explains what she has in mind. She had expected such a reaction.

Edith looks up with concern but quickly puts her head back down in her book. She's accustomed to her father's temper. As is Agnes.

Generally, Agnes would tread lightly, but this is important. Why she just now feels this way after so many years of indifference, she can't say.

"It's still mine, isn't it? My inheritance for such a time as I use it or sell it?" She knows not to aggravate her husband, particularly when she needs him to agree with her, so she attempts to disarm him with a pleasant tone.

"Well, the truth is, I don't know," James admits reluctantly.

"What do you mean you don't know?" she shouts before stopping herself. She softens her pitch. "My parents left that property to me. James, it was land they'd worked so hard for—"

"But you see, Agnes, even land held in trust has its limits. There's the matter of the property taxes—"

"Which you've been paying," she interjects.

"Which I'd stopped paying years ago," James confesses.

"What? Years ago!" Now Agnes is most definitely shouting. "How could you stop paying the taxes? Why would you have made that critical decision without discussing the matter with me? Why wouldn't my parents' lawyer advise me?"

"He did. I thought you'd lost interest. You stopped talking about it!" His retort is gruff.

"What? We were advised?"

"The letter was delivered to our post office slot. I opened it and decided not to bother you with it. Again, I'd assumed you'd lost interest."

Agnes can't believe James would have been so utterly selfish as to stop paying the taxes or to keep from telling her he was planning to do so. "I was raising children. Doing what you expected of me. You can't actually believe I'd given up that dream!" Agnes cries.

"I didn't even know you had a dream!" James roars.

"I have plenty of dreams! Have you ever thought to ask me about them, or did you just assume my dreams were to support all of yours?"

"Weren't babies enough?" James roars.

Agnes tries to keep her voice from trembling. "You all have been my priority, James. You know that. But my land was a birthright I always imagined I could reclaim! How could you be so cavalier with my feelings?"

"You knew I would never live there! You understood that before you married me. It's worthless to us. Let someone else deal with it. It's hard enough to make a living out here, let alone in the wilderness. We've got it about as good as it gets. Look around you! We're set up better than most folks around us."

"And *you* had to know I would never want to let it go! I just don't know how you could live with yourself, not saying anything to me about it."

"I don't know how *you* wouldn't say anything about it then," he said. "I'm sure the government has appropriated it by now. Sold it even."

"Appropriated?"

"You know, allowed someone else to buy it. To farm it. That's why land has been given out in the past, Agnes. It's been conditional. We've not met those conditions. Don't be ignorant."

From her corner, Edith grimaces.

"I'm not ignorant!" Agnes yells. "My parents paid for that land! I can't lose it because of a failure to pay taxes!" Agnes has never been so angry in all of her life, and she's had plenty of things to be angry about. She'd never imagined this would happen. Sure, she had known the potential, but still, she'd pushed it from her mind, preferring to avoid the discord associated with any half-hearted attempt to face the past there.

And she'd trusted her husband. More than she'd been willing to confront him because Agnes detests conflict. Yet, she recognizes she's often to blame for some of it by refusing to meet it head on before it becomes unmanageable. How had she not fought for what her parents had given their lives for? For what they'd produced from their dreams?

What a fool she had been.

James refuses to respond. He reaches for a box on the hearth and, opening it, begins to transfer the tobacco inside to his pipe in small pinches.

"What happens if the taxes aren't paid?" Agnes asks. James remains silent as he lights the pipe between his lips.

"What happens, James?" she insists.

"I already told you. I think the bigger question is what happens when the land isn't cultivated. That's the bigger issue. Land was meant to be used," he says, taking a sharp draw from the pipe as he lights it.

"I'm going out there. I'll hitch up the team tomorrow myself and head out to *my* land to have a look at it myself. Then, I'll head to the city clerk's office to see what can be done about making sure my claim is intact."

"I'd head to the clerk's office first, if I were you, and besides, it's a lost cause."

"I'm going to the property, James. You can't stop me."

He eyes her for a moment, assessing her resolve. "Fine, but you aren't going anywhere without me," he says.

"We leave before sunrise," Agnes orders, surprised at her newfound confidence.

Two mornings later, Leo readies the wagon for the journey, hitching up the family's ten-year-old thoroughbred horses, Major and General, who've served them faithfully over the past years. Purchased about the time the railroad arrived in town, they've proven the ideal horses for moving supplies from the line to the store whenever new shipments arrive.

This morning, the flatbed is equipped with the food, water, and other necessities for their twenty-mile roundtrip journey, including the blankets and pillows the women have piled up in the back for their own use. Leo, who has volunteered to join them, sits on the buckboard next to his father, reins in hand for the first leg of the journey. Under stars beginning to fade in the pink light at their backs, the Henrys set off.

Agnes holds the map she'd secured from city hall the day before, for it would have been impossible to rely on a memory so far away from the present; thus, the two-day delay in getting started. And miracle of all miracles, she'd learned no one had legally claimed her land in the time she'd neglected it.

The travelers make good time. After heading west from town about five miles, they turn with the creek to head northwest for the remainder of the journey. They don't stop to water the horses and arrive at the property in about three hours. Not bad timing, all things and unknown terrain considered, and Agnes can't help but recall her own journey from the property to town just after the deaths of her parents. Or the last ride she'd made after saying goodbye to them at their gravesites here.

The grass, tall and green and brushed with golden highlights, seems to welcome her home. As if in merry greeting to the travelers, it seems to rise and fall in swells like waves at sea.

It's just as she remembers it, though evidence of a long extinguished fire remains.

The cabin remains a short distance from the creek and the big nut tree, still framed by oaks rooted lovingly in place by her parents. Once saplings, the proud torsos now impressively flank the cabin at a distance, sentries on their way to becoming massive trunks, their leaves fluttering in the wind like flags of arms. Seamus and Nell had told her they'd carried the tiny sprouts, wrapped in burlap, from a tree farm back east. Those transplants had beaten all odds to survive. The vulnerable newcomers had held strong, defying the desires of a powerful prairie, one ever intent upon reclaiming its natural bluestem and tall grass.

Leo pulls the team to a halt and sets the brake. Agnes is out of the back of the wagon before the rest of the family and running to the front door before anyone else can take a breath. "I can't believe it's still here! I can't believe it's standing!" she exclaims, running her hand along the exterior.

Close on her heel, Edith follows, overwhelmed by what she sees. "It's just as I've known it," she whispers once she reaches her mother's side, for she too had begun to experience visions of the cabin in recent days. Agnes turns to meet her daughter's gaze with an intensity of emotion the others miss.

James finally steps down from the wagon, attempting to wipe some of the dust from his pants. He pays no mind to his son as Leo unhitches the team and leads them to water.

"This sure is a pretty piece of property," James admits.

"Isn't it though?" Agnes sighs. "It's definitely special." She takes a few steps and stops again to take in the view around her. There are so many memories here. So many stories. As she reaches the front door and rests her hand on the doorknob, she pauses to take a deep breath. "This place. Can't you feel it? It's like life is more, I don't know—vibrant here."

Edith, in her mother's shadow, places her hand on her mother's shoulder, prodding her gently. "Well Ma, are you going to open the door?"

"Yes, of course, but—" Agnes looks down at her feet.

"But what? We've come this far. Why are you hesitant now?" James asks impatiently. He is now a few feet behind the women.

"It's just that, well, how is this cabin even here after all these years?" Agnes whispers. "Several decades have passed since I closed this door. I guess I didn't expect the old place to still be standing."

"That's right," James agrees, as if only now considering this. "Are you sure it's the same cabin?"

"It is. It's what my father built himself. This is the door my father crafted just before he passed. I know every crack and crevice here, each splinter too. I had all the time in the world to explore, and with no siblings to distract me, when chores were done there were endless opportunities." She doesn't mention the creative ones.

The porch boards beneath her groan under her weight, but the flooring holds, encouraging flashes of memory with their sound. The many footsteps here, of kind visitors and hostile intruders, intent men with guns and intentioned women in black, the neighbors' boots, the native's moccasins. And beyond the porch—she remembers the night sounds of cricket and coyote, the day sounds of cicada and crow, all under the observation of a big, always-shifting sky.

"I know you must all think me overly sentimental," Agnes says, and turning to her children adds, "but you have to understand how important this place was to your grandparents, how hard they worked to possess property of their own. They came from a place where owning land was impossible for them. This was their dream realized."

The group remains silent, so Agnes adds, "It really *is* a dream." Turning the handle, she finally pushes on the door. It won't budge. She tries again, this time shoving her weight against it. It moves ever so slightly, as if weighted to bar entry. She tries a third time, throwing her right shoulder into it, and finally the door gives way.

As it whooshes open, the years unsettle. Sudden movement releases dormant dust motes in galaxies that swirl up from the dirt floor to dance in the light. To Agnes' mind, this is a victory celebration, filtered through years of accumulation. The room could be considered murky nothingness to the other observers, but to the woman who feels a little girl again, triumph is weightless to rise and float like congratulatory confetti. She feels welcomed home.

Though the cabin is small and rudimentary, it possesses a beauty rooted in love. Although it's been over thirty years, the interior looks as if it had been only yesterday she'd left.

It's exactly the way she left it.

Precisely the way she left it.

"How is this possible?" she asks herself out loud.

"How is what possible?" Edith asks, still taking in her surroundings, but she thinks she knows. A black kettle hangs on a crane pulled away from the fireplace, a matching pot on the hearth. A meager wooden table sits in the center, clear of all but a small, white ceramic vase, while a twin bed, covered in a multi-colored quilt, is pushed up against a corner of the room. The adjacent corner is noticeably empty, as if something had once occupied the space.

"What's missing from the corner over there?" James asks, pointing to the space.

"My parent's bed," Agnes says matter-of-factly. "They died in it. It was hauled outside for burning." James says nothing. Edith is sorry he asked. Hearing footsteps on the porch just then, the group turns to observe a man and teenaged boy charge in through the door. Without a moment's hesitation, the man bellows, "How in the tarnation did you get the place open?"

"I just opened it," Agnes calmly replies, and in the notable absence of a proper salutation, returns the demand in kind. "Who are you?"

"The owner of this here property. Who are you?" the man fires back gruffly.

"The owner of this property," Agnes retorts indignantly, even as James steps forward to touch her arm in warning.

Whether the man is aware of James' signal is immaterial. "Well now, how can that be? Seein' how I've lived here goin' on ten years." The teenager next to him smirks maliciously. It's clear the pair aren't the sort to be intimidated.

"Then you've been living on land that doesn't belong to you, Mr. —" Where Agnes is concerned, pretenses are unnecessary.

A few seconds pass before he answers. "Brown. Harold Brown. This 'ere is my son, Raymond." The pair is dressed alike. They wear mud-encrusted boots and stained, unwashed clothing in neutral colors. Atop sooty heads, each has a well-worn leather hat with a high crown and pinched front that's generally preferred these days. They've pulled the brims down low over their foreheads.

Attempting cordiality but standing her ground, Agnes continues evenly, "Mr. Brown, my parents purchased this land thirty-four years ago and built our home here—the one you are now standing in. When they passed away, it was willed to me."

Harold Brown's eyes narrow to slits and for a moment all present feel silent tension building. "Have ya never heard possession is nine-tenths of the law?" he asks, confirming Agnes' suspicion. The Browns are squatters.

"I mean no trouble, Mr. Brown," Agnes proceeds, hopeful. Her eyes begin to water. "But this land belongs to me."

"Where ya been, then?" Harold demands. It isn't as if Agnes didn't expect something like this, however, she'd hoped against hope she wouldn't have a real fight on her hands. There'd been enough of that here. With all the wide open, unclaimed land in the state, why was hers the one happened upon by squatters?

Meanwhile, guilt or indifference, or both, causes James to remain uncharacteristically silent, which allows Agnes to handle this discussion on her own. "Mr. Brown, I was a child when my parents died in this cabin from cholera. I am here now." She manages to keep her rising emotions under control.

"Well, yur too late. Me and my boys live here, and we don't have a mind to move, seein' how long we've been settled in." The boy standing beside him, Raymond, shifts his weight and snickers.

"I can certainly appreciate that," Agnes says, softening her tone. "Where are you living on the property?"

"On the other side of the creek. We couldn't never get that damn door open!" Harold concedes. "We built a sod shanty. Never could get enough good timber to construct nothin' else, so I thank you now for presenting us with a better option."

"Now see here," James finally interjects, but before he is able to continue, Leo returns and weighs in.

"Not so fast! This is *our* family property, so I believe *we* will determine who will live here and who won't. In fact," Leo asserts. "I plan to spend some time out here myself, beginning immediately."

Agnes is stunned. This is sudden news, indeed. She doesn't dare look her son's way, resolving to stay her direction in the conversation. It wouldn't do to give away any hint this wasn't the plan all along. Thankfully, before James can give away their hand, the Browns storm out.

"You aren't removing us from our land," Harold holds over his shoulder, "But you can keep your old cholera cabin." The two march off in the direction of the creek but not before young Raymond turns around with a vulgar hand gesture.

"Wonder why he changed his mind so suddenly on the cabin?" Leo says, shaking his head.

"What are you thinking, Leo? You can't possibly live out here and work with me," says James, finally coming around to speak on the matter.

"It seemed the right thing to say at the time," the usually detached young man offers. "But now, I don't know, I think it's a good idea. Someone needs to live here to keep the property."

"We don't even know if that's possible," Agnes intercedes. "Back taxes may prevent us from reclaiming it."

"Yes, let's not be hasty. We must think rationally," James bellows.

"I would think," Leo chuckles, "in a worst-case scenario, we should be able to reclaim it as squatters ourselves. In the best case, we can afford to pay what's owed."

"But they've lived here so long," Agnes laments. Now that she's set foot again on this marvelous land, she never wants to lose it again. Shame washes over her anew. How could she have allowed this to happen? How is it her son is so enthusiastic?

"Leo, have you lost your mind?" James demands. "You can't live here! Not and work in town!"

"Why can't he? Why can't we all?" Edith interjects. She is far too enamored with the property and much too excited about the remote prospect of spending time here not to push in a way she hasn't before. Generally, she wouldn't dare to offer an opinion in opposition to her father.

"I do wish we could come up with a way," Agnes says wistfully.

"There is a way. I've just come up with it." Leo takes a deep breath and turns to his father. "Now is as good a time as any. The truth is, I'd prefer to try my luck at farming here. I appreciate your bringing me into the family business, Pa, but I've been feeling lately a little off about it."

"A little *off* about it?" James roars. "How can you say that? Think of what your grandparents have done to provide us an opportunity to run such a viable business. One that will only continue to grow! It's yours, Leo, or it will be one day."

"Yes, and think of what my maternal grandparents did to set us up with land. Land our ancestors only dreamed of, Pa. One hundred and sixty acres of soil that could be owned and coaxed into producing life, and not just for those who live here, but for those destined to benefit from it."

"What are you saying, Leo?" James barks.

"You know what I'm saying," Leo says. I'm out of the mercantile business and into the land business. I'll head into town to square things up legally and collect my things. I appreciate the opportunity you've given me, but I feel I am supposed to do this."

Edith, though inwardly thrilled, is equally concerned as she looks to her mother for direction. Agnes' face reveals hope and apprehension in equal measure.

Oh, what have I done? Agnes wonders if she has just torn her family apart.

Chapter

Twenty-Five

KANSAS CITY—1990

Jane Campbell's artwork produces a reaction in people, something that takes them to an experiential place that causes them to realize what had formerly been unrealized. Something best explained as an awakening.

Jane's brushwork never ceases to result in a refreshing of her own soul, too. Like a blossom unfurling, what innate knowledge she liberates seems fragrant incense—something not wholly her own doing. Something she is supposed to share.

What she has translated to canvas unlocks access to what is intrinsic but sealed tightly, as if secret treasure maps hidden high on a dusty shelf accessible only by ladder have been pulled out for display, and maybe this was what Mac was talking about when he referred to partnership.

There is so much revelation in the human experience!

And hope is color on canvas.

There is an ancient knowledge made known by whatever draws her to The Land.

What is it with that specific location on planet earth?

On one level, Jane understands she speaks a universal language. On another, she senses she's afraid what she speaks is far from collective. And once again, she is spiraling. Or spinning in place!

But Mac had to go and show up when he did. At the gallery. Briefly, and without preamble, and Jane is again thinking he may, in fact, be a delusion after all. Until his presence at her showing at The Downtown, he'd never crossed real-time boundaries to interact in this dimension. Naturally, then, she must again seriously consider the malfunctioning of her own mind. Oh, the roller coast she rides there each day!

Yet her experiences with him have been as real as the gray carpet beneath her feet and the yellow papered walls around her now. As real as the blue Kansas City scene outside her window and the purple lilacs printed, framed, and hanging on the wall in the hotel room in front of her.

But how real is that color, if only recognizable in light?

Does color fail to exist in darkness? Does darkness eradicate it altogether, or is it still there, hidden, just waiting for exposure?

Jane isn't far into thought when Mac arrives. He's here, in front of her, in her hotel room.

So much for my imagination!

This time he doesn't whisk her away to any other spot but stands to face her in real time. And she doesn't smell any of the prairie's earthy scents in announcement of his arrival. It's only the soapy cleanliness of her recently-made-up hotel room that envelopes her senses now.

A new tactic, bold and clear, and there can be no doubting her perception in the present. Startled at the sight of him, she sets a trembling cup of coffee down on the table and steadies herself against the back of a chair.

"That was a terrific show last night," he says coolly.

"I suppose I should ask you if you'd care to join me for a cup of coffee, now that you've just appeared in the middle of my hotel room in the light of day."

He ignores her sarcasm. "That won't be necessary," he replies. "But thank you."

"Mac! What are you doing here, now?" Jane roars, but before he can respond, she continues, "And why were you at the gallery last night?"

"It was my way of assuring you that you were right where you were supposed to be." He beams.

"Couldn't you have told me that earlier rather than shocking me wobbly with your sudden appearance in the middle of my real-time event?"

"Jane," he says shaking his head, "you know me well enough by now not to overreact."

"It was a big night for me, and I was unsettled as it was!"

"You are stronger than you think and on your way to breakthrough." He smiles radiantly, like a proud father, and something stirs within Jane that isn't objectionable.

"You mean great success?"

"I mean what I say," he replies evenly.

"Which is?" Jane looks at him quizzically.

"Dependent upon the way you define success." His eyes twinkle radiantly, as if electrically charged, but simultaneously convey an intensity Jane is unprepared for.

"Must you always speak in riddles?" Jane sighs, exasperated. "What did you think?"

"I'm glad you asked. It's not what I think but what you think."

"You see what I mean?" Jane throws her hands up in the air and sits down in the chair beside her. "You are absolutely impossible!"

"Nothing is impossible," he says evenly, but still grinning from ear to ear.

"I swear—"

"You shouldn't swear," he interrupts. "Okay. The show was wonderful," he says, changing the subject. "Your paintings are a delight."

"I don't think you've ever told me that before," Jane says, backing down and now grinning herself.

"I believe in you," Mac says affectionately. "You know that."

"Yes. And I appreciate you. You know that." A seriousness stills the room.

"From the moment you were created, you were believed," Mac continues, meeting the emotion in her eyes with his own.

To Jane, discussions with Mac are like journeys themselves. Sometimes they're winding and uphill, sometimes they're straight and level. Where Mac is concerned, regardless of climate or circumstance, any destination appears perpetually out of reach, and forward progress seems a dance in circles. Lucidity, if there can be such a thing in his world, is something bubbling out on the horizon for another day.

And then Jane is transported away from her hotel room in Kansas City. Just when they were getting somewhere, a change of focus, and swiftly. Now, the sweet and spicy smells of coriander and grass pollens. Of sage and wild sumac. And wet earth.

The grass is thick and high presently, full of seedy tassels that surround her waist. She runs her palms over the tops of them, blinking in the bright light of the sun which rests high overhead. Individual shafts stream through cloud cover, scattering rainbow prisms across the meadows as she makes her way to the cabin straight ahead. The colors seem to have grown more vibrant since her last visit.

Two oaks stand nearby, set a good distance out from the sides of the cabin and Jane can see someone has planted a variety of flowers along the front porch. There are bells of blue and clusters of lavender, starbursts of yellow and rushes of orange, all in neat rows. White bundles are scattered in fistfuls across green, too. Even the sky is brushed in many hues. Rainclouds move close to swell with purple; background yellow lightens azure to turquoise beyond, and bird song has never sounded quite as melodious as it does now. It's like heaven again. What she imagines heaven to look like, anyway.

Could it be?

As if on cue, an orchestra begins to play, with violins and wind instruments she can't identify, a piano's keyboards touched lightly in occasional accompaniment. Never has Jane felt so perfect.

This is a perfection that can only exist supernaturally, apart from the anchoring of humanity. Jane has never really given the idea of a such a place—heaven—much consideration, Mac's initial visit notwithstanding. Why bother when depictions like the movie *Heaven Can Wait* show heaven as a place to float aimlessly on puffy clouds. A monotone existence. Being stoned out of her mind. Galaxies of white and tedious, unproductive existence set to the music of harps and monotonous bliss, which could only clarify earth as much more interesting. Even in all its imperfection, she has seen its splendor.

And yet, logicality demands she consider heaven not only exists but could function beyond her scope of limitations.

It may even be accessible from earth.

That would be some fairy tale!

However, she doesn't pursue these thoughts as she catches sight of a gathering around the cabin. Again, an army of giants appears, all dressed in armor of some kind and standing at attention, shoulder to shoulder with hands on their sheaths, as if ready to do battle—something Jane knows instinctively as she witnesses this.

The scene shifts further as the most gigantic member of the group now emerges to stand before the others with a stature like nothing Jane has ever seen before. The man must be at least twelve feet tall and appears to be floodlit, his face an illuminated marquee. With skin aglow like bronzed tourmaline, he is eerie and inhuman. He is also dressed in a suit of armor of some kind but looks to be without weapon, as if his large hands are sufficient armament.

She watches this giant address the others, and after some dialogue between them which Jane is unable to make out, the group disperses, vanishing into the air as quickly as they'd initially appeared. It's long enough for Jane to gain a lasting impression. She knows intuitively the glimpse was intended for her alone. It was something she was meant to understand. It takes only seconds, but it's enough time.

Once the militia has departed, another group of men come into view. Though of great stature themselves, these men are smaller than the others and dressed differently in light colored robes of some kind. They're tending to the trees and gardens; several are sweeping the porch, stairs, and gravel path up to the home. One sits down on the steps, his hands folded in his lap. Another leans back against the trunk of an oak, his arms at his sides. Still another holds a small, wounded bird, unable to fly, cupped in his hands. He brings it to his mouth, kisses it, and releases it to fly up and away.

Who are these people? Why do they work in the unseen?

"Your eyes have been opened," she hears a voice say, though where it came from, she cannot be sure. "See," it says.

Jane blinks, and the scene before her changes again. Gone are the flowers and the caretakers and the sunshine. The purple clouds darken, glowering in place momentarily, and within a minute, night has descended, though a gray mist can be discerned hanging in chilly air.

Through an uncovered glass window, Jane can see inside the home, where she recognizes Leo reading peacefully at a table. A candle lamp sits beside him.

Outside, two men dressed in ratty overalls and patched, long-sleeved shirts creep steadily into view from the back side of the house. They are armed with torches in their right hands and large rocks in their left. Once they near the window, they hold flames to a material wrapped around the rocks. They ignite the rocks into flame, then hurl them through the small glass window. A loud crashing sound is heard as glass splinters. The men take off as Leo scrambles to his feet to put out the fiery missiles. He grabs a gun on his way out the door.

Meanwhile, Jane sees the two vandals head for a field of wheat. She watches them douse the field with liquid from cans found stationed there, and once satisfied, lower their torches to the tall stems. Jane shudders when she realizes what they are attempting.

What is it with people trying to cause harm to The Land and its occupants with fire?
And why would they warn Leo first?

Jane's horror at this sight grows to astonishment and then amusement as she realizes the fire they are trying to set isn't catching. Though she knows little of primitive flame-starters, it's no trouble to deduce whatever they've doused the field with is highly flammable.

But ineffective.

Until the older man's pants are ignited with a whoosh and he drops to roll on the ground. The younger man only watches, visibly unsure how to react, until he begins to kick dirt on his companion, and the scene would be absolutely hilarious if it wasn't so infuriating. And scary.

It is only then that Jane recognizes the men as Harold Brown and his son, Raymond. Perhaps they only wanted to scare Leo off with the forewarning, not ruin the property completely.

A group of giants then comes into view. They are surrounded in the field by what appears to be a barrier of water, as if they are standing behind the thick and steady cascade of a fall that forms a wall. Their forms behind it are blurry but unmistakable. They appear to be protecting the field. As an added benefit, the spray from their cascade puts out the fire on the pants of Harold Brown and he is up running away from the scene in a flash, his son chasing behind him.

Leo arrives and finds nothing out of order, so he returns to the cabin. He doesn't even notice the mud on his boots.

Jane has quite a number of questions for Mac now. Clearly, he wants her to know this property is unique. She's always known that. From the first moment he had brought her here.

And he wants to emphasize its supernatural protection.

But why?

And what, if anything, does that have to do with her?

Finding herself suddenly back at the hotel, Jane changes her damp clothes before heading out.

When Derrick calls her room the next day to see if Jane will have dinner with him, she isn't surprised. She had been expecting he would reach out (hoping more like), considering the efforts she'd made to drop hints, like admitting to loving The Raphael when he'd asked how long she'd be in town. She had intentionally emphasized the name of the hotel knowing that doing so would increase the odds he would make a call.

She'd made it easy for him!

She had certainly taken advantage of what little time had been made available during their short conversation at the gallery show, and she'd understood perfectly her own flirtatiousness. No, she'd not been shameless about it but had implied he should call, knowing he would, also foreknowing this would surely invite complication.

I'm so out of my league.

But oh, the chemistry there! No denying it. What could a little coaxing hurt? He'd started it, after all. Or had she been imagining that?

Hopefully he isn't playing me!

He certainly could be. Though his good looks make him seem confident, she senses humility, too, and this resonates the most with Jane. His properly unassuming way makes her feel happy.

She sighs. She's never felt these emotions so fast before. She's never responded to anyone, ever, this way. She doesn't even know the man! She doesn't even know what he does for a living!

She forgets about her so-called plainness.

This could be a problem.

She'd initially planned to fly out the day after the show but had an inclination to change her flight reservation to one that would allow her to enjoy a few more days in Kansas City, and now she can't help but congratulate herself on the decision. It isn't as if anything pressing awaits her at home, although she senses Jake is most eager for her return, and not because he's short-staffed at Oliver T's. She feels a twinge of guilt.

Jane's mother has only checked in a couple of times and her father not at all. Jess couldn't care less what her sister is doing, and it's a great relief. Taking her time on her first business trip is a pleasure.

Derrick suggests an Italian place on The Plaza and she agrees to meet him there at five in the evening. It's a short walk across the river and a couple of blocks over on a balmy, July evening when she sets out, wearing comfortable but high wedged leather sandals with a white, puffy-sleeved cotton sundress that highlights her tan. Walking so many places during her stay here has meant a lot of time outside, and she feels more physically invigorated by the sunshine on her skin than she has in a long time. A bright pink lipstick makes her feel pretty, actually.

It isn't long before she finds him standing at the entrance. Glowing, more like.

Sheesh. This could be a BIG problem.

He's left his hat at home and has dressed in blue jeans and a button-down white shirt himself, as if they'd coordinated to take photos. His brown hair is parted in the middle and feathered back to the sides. He's also wearing sneakers, so maybe he's not all cowboy after all, Jane concludes. No matter what he's wearing, he's absolutely gorgeous. She vows not to appear overly eager.

"You look beautiful!" he says, beaming, and there is something about the way he says this that is so genuine, it takes her breath away. She realizes she need not worry about her own enthusiasm. He has even more than she does, it seems.

"Thank you," Jane replies slowly. It's the first time anyone has ever responded to her in this way. Anyone she's interested in, anyway. "So do you," she says, fully aware of her awkwardness. "I mean. You look great."

"I appreciate that!" His smile widens. "We're eating underground tonight." He motions the way. She now realizes the entryway amounts to a set of stairs with an iron railing that leads down to restaurant doors below. "It's cozy, and the food is terrific."

Cozy? Oh dear.

"Yeah, I just noticed that," Jane says lamely as she carefully negotiates her way down the flight of stairs, regretting the height of the wedges she'd chosen to wear and praying she won't stumble on her way down to the small patio alcove. As she reaches the bottom, air thick with oregano and garlic invites them in, and she's suddenly aware she's famished. But how will she be able to eat in front of this man?

Once she and Derrick are seated and the ice water served, Jane settles into a more comfortable breathing pattern. He makes a few recommendations, and before long, the seemingly laborious task of ordering is behind her, a loaf of warm bread and plate of olive oil at reach between them. "So, what's it like to live on the East Coast?" he asks, breaking the bread to offer her a piece.

"I'll tell you," Jane answers smiling, "But then you'll have to tell me what it is like to live here." She dips her bread in the oil and takes a nibble.

"Deal," Derrick says, laughing. "Although, I'm afraid I'll have an easier time of describing things to you, since you're already here. I've never traveled to the East."

"Well, before now, I'd never traveled to the Midwest!"

"Then how on earth—"

"Don't even start with that," Jane cuts him off.

"Start with what?" he asks, puzzled.

"I know what you are going to ask," she says laughing.

"Oh, you do, do you?" he teases, with the most beautiful, slightly lopsided grin Jane has ever laid eyes on. The energy between them might just kill her.

"I do," she responds, more at ease now than she had expected to be. "So let me answer your question for you. It's all right here," she says, pointing to her temple.

Jane has no trouble describing life on the coast, her job, schooling, and even her family, though she doesn't elaborate on the latter, and he doesn't press for more information. She enjoys sharing her passion for the seashore and her favorite places, like the Lobster House restaurant she frequents and the cheesesteaks, hoagies, and calzones she loves. Pretty sad when the best thing about your hometown is the food. God knows it isn't the company there.

"Wait, I thought you had to go to Philly for a cheesesteak." Derrick says.

"How did you know that?" Jane laughs.

"Every guy knows where to find things that satisfy him," he says, and then adds, blushing, "That statement didn't turn out the way I wanted it to."

Jane laughs. "No problem. I knew what you meant. I just find it interesting you know what a cheesesteak is—and that you're aware Philly is known for them."

"Like I said, men are all about their stomachs." Realizing he's not improving communication, he adds sheepishly, "I'm not doing any better, am I? I may need to just shut up now."

"You're fine," Jane assures him, giggling. She's feeling so much better now. "And, no, Philadelphia may be known for cheesesteaks, but you can find them many other places besides South Street. There are plenty of places that make a decent sandwich in the Northeast."

"I guess I'll have to pay you a visit and find out for myself."

"Don't you trust me?" Jane teases.

"Don't you want me to visit?" he volleys back.

Jane isn't sure how to respond. The short answer is, yes. Most definitely, yes. "Of course!" she says, but she knows he can't be serious.

"Of course, I am serious," he says as if reading her mind. "I've only just met you, but I have no intention of letting you go." Jane blushes at the statement but suddenly finds herself hoping he's for real. He could be a liar, but there's something about him that's true-blue. Her gut is feeling better.

"Tell me about your job," she says, changing the subject.

"Hmm, well, it isn't that exciting. I'm a reporter for *The Star*."

"*The Star*?" she asks, and then thinks to add, "Oh, *The* Kansas City *Star*. I'm sorry, that must seem so ignorant. I'd only become aware of your paper after the great write-up the gallery received."

"You mean the great write-up your collection received!"

She blushes. "It was amazing!" she admits. "And all thanks to Glenda."

"Glenda may have pulled some strings, but your collection was what garnered the attention. You really are amazing, you know," Derrick says.

"How did you learn about it? I mean, why were you at the show?" Jane asks as their food is served. She wonders how she might steer the conversation back to his work or family.

"So, you don't think I'm immersed in the art world?"

"That's not what I meant." Jane reacts nervously, seeing no way to avoid the topic.

"No worries," he assures her chuckling, "I get it. Actually, the men I was with are fans of your work. In fact, one of them, the tall one with the salt and pepper hair—Doug—has some pieces in his collection that look a lot like yours. He and Ed had already worked with Glenda at The Downtown before, so when they read about your opening show, they resolved not to miss it."

"Oh," Jane says, not sure what else to say. "Do you know what other pieces they acquired from The Downtown?"

"You'd have to ask them that. I'm not sure where Doug got all in his collection, but he's been an art enthusiast for quite a while. Long before I knew him. But as far as I can tell, it's limited to the same genre as your work. Is that right? Genre?" he laughingly asks. Jane has a difficult time not getting distracted by his dimples.

It's a shame I've booked a flight back home so soon.

"Well, if you mean different types of art, I suppose there are endless ways to classify art. There is even a genre called genre art, or scenes of everyday life," Jane tells him. "Following the Renaissance, when people became obsessed with re-creating what they had experienced in real life, and they had time to do it for the first time in, well, forever, since they were no longer struggling to just stay alive, art began to thrive. That's when classifications were made." She stops abruptly, aware she is probably boring him. "That's undoubtedly too much information!"

"No, it's not! I'm fascinated!" he assures her, still showing off those impressions in his cheeks. Jane looks away.

"So, what does your friend collect, specifically?" she asks, nervously dabbing the corners of her mouth with her napkin.

"Landscapes, primarily, which shouldn't surprise you, considering he is so drawn to your work."

"Is that what you like? I mean—" Jane stutters. "I don't mean to presume you were there yourself to view my work."

"Of course I was!" Derrick interrupts. "Duke was there to do just that, and I was interested, too, only reporters don't exactly make the bank farmers do."

"Duke?"

"Oh, I'm sorry. Doug's nickname is Duke."

"Oh. So, Doug, or Duke, is a farmer?" she asks, again steering the conversation away from herself.

"He is, and a really successful one. He grows a variety of crops and raises sheep and other livestock, but it's his cattle ranch that does particularly well."

"Wow. I've never known anyone that's done that before."

"You meet a lot of people in the Midwest who are farmers."

"You don't meet a lot of people in New Jersey who are!" she says.

"So, really though, tell me about your family," he continues.

"So, really though, tell me about yours," Jane calmly redirects.

"Okay, I get it. Family is a discussion off the table for now." Derrick grins and picks up his glass of water to take a drink.

Jane looks down at the napkin in her lap, unknowingly attempting to smooth the wrinkles out of it. "Not necessarily off the table. It's just not my favorite dinner conversation."

Now Derrick is chuckling. "That bad?"

"You don't know the half of it." Jane laughs, attempting to lighten her mood. She wonders if perhaps she is overreacting or if her family really is more dysfunctional than most. "What do you do for fun?"

"You seem more like the investigative journalist here than I do," he says, still laughing playfully. She waits for his answer as he considers a response. "I write, obviously, and I like to run. My favorite food is Mexican, particularly tacos, and my favorite color is green. Do you have any hobbies?"

"I like to paint," she says, laughing. "And I enjoy reading. I also love tacos, but give me a cheese pizza any day."

The two spend the rest of the meal avoiding serious subject matter. After Derrick pays the check, they take a walk outside, window-shopping and taking in the sights on a pleasant evening. They eventually find their way to the ice cream shop she had noticed on her first visit to The Plaza when she'd witnessed a mom promise another treat to the little boy who'd lost the scoop off his cone. When she'd imagined what life might be like to live here.

Now, Jane is wondering what life here in Kansas City would be like more and more.

It's late when Derrick suggests they might go on to another place for a drink, and Jane is encouraged by this. He must really like her, and she's feeling intrigued.

Though she knows she should decline the offer until she has gotten to know him better, she agrees.

Chapter

Twenty-Six

LEAVENWORTH, KANSAS—EARLY 20TH CENTURY

Agnes would have done just about anything to keep her precious land once it was returned to her family, but she would have given it up in a heartbeat if it meant she could have her only son back instead.

Leo had given homesteading a good run before he died.

He had stood his ground, keeping the angry squatters at bay by refusing any expenditure of energy where they were concerned. Focused on steadily making improvements to the land, he had lovingly invested in the soil and waited patiently in the balance, his constant vigilance finally tiring the gruff Harold Brown and his son, who had given up and moved on after numerous verbal altercations and strange, supernatural setbacks. The fact that Leo hadn't appeared to suffer the trouble they had was initially the cause for an all-consuming belligerence that gave way to reluctant defeat.

Leo had tenderly planted saplings and scattered grass seed to join with the native varieties, and he had turned the earth with respect, one small section at a time, intentionally avoiding careless consumption. He'd planted corn and soybeans and wheat, and this provided well for the young man, once he'd gotten a couple of years into the process. The Land was finally beginning to prosper again under his capable hands.

The little cabin there had come to life, too. Leo had whitewashed the interior, complementing the fresh look with white cotton curtains he'd ordered through the family store, and he'd secured a shipment of wood with which to craft a new bed, table and chairs, and other adornments. Whenever the family would visit, Agnes was amazed at the organization and cleanliness her son had dedicated to the enterprise. The only thing missing to her mind were regular vases of fresh flowers, and in the spring, summer, and fall, she always made sure to stop for wildflowers on the way out to the property. It had become standard procedure to fill the porcelain vase that had once belonged to Nell. This renewed in her a desire to paint wildflowers again.

But she never got the chance.

When the U.S. declared war on Germany on April 6, 1917, Leo enlisted to fight overseas. Though he was already past the prime of his youth, he felt he had to do it. As far as he was concerned, freedom was freedom, and even if it wasn't your own land you were fighting for in the moment, it very well could be your own in the next.

Leo James Henry didn't last long on foreign soil. He died in the first U.S.-led assault near the French Somme in a small village called Cantigny. He was thirty-six years old and had never been married. His land had been his only bride.

His mother had never painted those flowers.

Agnes was devastated. His father was, as well. But it was his sister, Edith, who suffered the most. She would not consider any other option but to move to the homestead on the land her mother had once loved, to pick up where her brother had left off. She had no trouble convincing her husband to do this. She was, after all, not one to back down from a thing once her mind had been made up, and the land itself didn't mind. Neither did her husband.

Edith had fallen in love with Jack Bell because he was agreeable. Actually, there was more to it than that. Jack was also tough and rugged and nothing like her father. It wasn't that she disliked her father, but she had realized his human limitations from a young age. A person should marry the one who shares her dreams, something her mother had failed to do. Jack was willing to come alongside Edith's ambitions. He was supportive of what excited her, and she was madly in love with him, so they became husband and wife in 1908.

Together they had six children. Opal Rose was born in 1908, followed by Violet May, Lily Helen, Iris Louise, and the twins, Arthur Paul and Albert Jack, who arrived just before they'd learned the news about Leo. Edith will forever regret not naming one of her sons after her beloved brother. Meanwhile, her father, James, was already preparing his grandsons, her own boys, to one day take over the family store.

Edith's dreams had always included children, just like every other woman she knew, but motherhood wasn't where she envisioned her life ended. No, she had every intention of crafting an existence beyond what made her happy in that way. Hadn't she already experienced possibilities well past the status quo? And she had no intention of laying aside any of her desires to fulfill a man's, either. She watched her mother do that. Not that she wouldn't or didn't support her man, she just expected his feelings would be reciprocal. Her aspirations would be every bit as important as his. To them both.

And maybe someday there would be a future for this land.

Now, her mother has no heart to return to the homestead she had been robbed of. This was something that bothered Edith, particularly given the otherworldly experiences both women had been treated to. They'd nearly always been centered around their piece of property, as if to underscore the importance of it. The subsequent paintings between them had been a byproduct, but Agnes had never resumed what she had so long ago begun. Maybe this was why her mother's visions waned now.

Edith supposed it was too painful, the connection between the loss of her parents and then her son too much to bear even with an understanding that life consists of more than meets the eye. Eventually, Agnes had come to terms with helping run the family store, especially when James' parents had also passed. Now she helps her husband train up their twin grandsons in the way of things.

To Edith's mind, she had compromised too much.

Edith has no intention of giving up on her maternal ancestors' dreams, or her own painting, now that she's resumed it. She loves The Land. Outside of motherhood and tending to the needs of her family, painting gives her more joy than anything else in the world. Her fierce loyalty matches a fierce love.

Jack is a hard worker. He'd been in construction until such time as Leo passed, when Edith insisted the family relocate to the property. Jack was agreeable enough and in love enough to go along with his wife's request, no cajoling necessary. After all, space was good for a family, and land was good for wheat, and whatever was good for his wife was good for him.

As it turns out, The Land and the wheat it produces is good for the both of them. In fact, in the 1920s, wheat is the gold of the prairie, the cash crop of the Midwest, and Kansas is called the Breadbasket of the World. As early as 1888, *The Topeka Daily Capital* had announced, "All parts of Kansas grow good corn but in wheat, Kansas can beat the world." However, it took winter wheat to turn things around because in the beginning, wheat didn't grow well here. Planting in the fall for harvesting in the spring was a game-changer.

Now, investors hungry to turn a fast profit have begun buying up land in vast tracts, including the acreage all around them, but not before Jack is able to increase the size of his property to three times the original one hundred and sixty acres. Nell and Seamus O'Donnell's original property has now expanded quite lucratively. The bank still owns a large majority of it, but the note will be paid off in no time.

So, when those slick cats from the East arrive for a piece of the pie, reaping the high profits of demand by hiring out to work the land without so much as laying a hand themselves to a plow, it doesn't bother Edith or Jack in the least. Winter wheat is profitable for them, too, and they mind their own business. Jack is able to hire on help and even supports Edith in her dreams of building a new home on the property.

But then the dust arrives, and the wheat piles up, and the cash dissolves.

The Great Depression comes upon them all.

From far away, another woman watches the family in and out of their happy times and during those that aren't so.

Jane sees evidence of prosperity and knows the struggle, too. She sees the faces of many happy children at play on The Land, at first as oblivious to scarcity as to plenty. As they sing and dance and chase each other in the wind,

Jane catches glimpses of guardians that fly with them, too. Against the backdrop of shattered dreams is sweet hope that dances in the breeze, like the scent of wild jasmine on an early morning.

Like the faces of the guiding spirits only she can see.

Chapter

Twenty-Seven

KANSAS CITY—1990

The couple wastes none of the time Jane has left in Kansas City, filling every moment of it together as if they are both tourists on vacation.

They visit museums, see a Royals game, and take a hike on a nature trail followed by a picnic Derrick packed himself. They see a late-night movie. They hit every coffee shop in the area.

"I was thinking for your last night in town we could have dinner at my place." Derrick grins hopefully as he studies her.

Jane meets his gaze earnestly, amazed at her own self-confidence. They've just finished breakfast at a lovely café with outdoor seating. At this point, she hates the idea of leaving Kansas City. And Derrick.

"I'd like to make you dinner," he continues. "And, I have some artwork you might like to see." Jane finds his awkwardness charming as he extends the invitation.

"Hmm, that's what they all say," she says, teasing him. He laughs. She continues, "But, sure, I'd love that. The old farmhouse you've described sounds delightful." Inwardly, she'd been hoping for a drive out to the country.

"Well, don't be too impressed. I spend most of my time working in the city. I'm always lamenting my predicament: I don't live in the country. I only sleep there. When I'm lucky! And speaking of work, I'm going to have to drop you off at your hotel for a bit while I get a story filed. I've pushed my deadline as far as I can, and my editor is chomping at the bit."

"Oh, my goodness, I am so sorry! I have monopolized your time!" Jane says, genuinely concerned.

"You have! And in a good way!" Derrick assures her. "Please don't give it another thought. My job is flexible enough to permit some juggling. I was able to call in a few favors over the past few days to avoid getting new assignments." He takes note of her sudden disquiet and adds, "Hey, no biggie! I'd already done most of the research necessary. I'd only put off the writing. It won't take long."

"It must not be breaking news, then," Jane says, relieved.

Derrick chuckles. "Like I said, I got some slack this week."

"I suppose I should pack up anyway. I'll get everything ready to go for my flight tomorrow, and this way I'll be able to fully enjoy the evening."

"Sounds like a good plan! Okay if I pick you up at six o'clock?"

"If you're sure it's okay."

"Absolutely!"

"Then that sounds marvelous," Jane tells him truthfully.

What isn't marvelous is how unsettled she feels right now.

"You've got to be kidding me!" Jane declares as they take the long drive out to Derrick's house in the country. "You live this far out from your office?" Though they'd encountered some traffic heading out of the city, they'd been driving for thirty minutes and hadn't yet reached Leavenworth, where Derrick said he lived. "I mean, it's gorgeous out here, don't get me wrong, but you drive a long way to work and back every day!"

"I do, but it's worth it. There's nothing like the countryside!" he says, glancing her way. "I prefer nature's peace to city hustle, even in a relaxed metro area like Kansas City. Most suburbs here are pretty wide open and spacious, with plenty of farmland all around and in between, but I prefer to be in a place where the sky is unbroken."

"It is lovely!" Jane agrees, thinking of her travels with Mac. The drive is becoming increasingly more interesting. "I have never seen so much green in all my life, or so much wide-open space!"

Not in reality, anyway.

Derrick laughs. "I'm glad you understand why I make the effort."

"I do, indeed!" Jane smiles and leans back against the headrest. The late afternoon sun seems in no hurry to descend. As it settles comfortably into position above the horizon, Jane begins to feel drowsy. Even so, she keeps her eyes open so as not to miss a thing. The occasional red barn and silo, a number of old, whitewashed farmhouses, and sprinklings of cows in clusters with their heads bent to pasture are all like a picture book. Their black and brown accents on a tapestry of varied textures makes her want to paint everything she sees.

It would be foolish of me not to consider a connection.

As the languid miles pass, swards of green form and flatten, like ripples in great sails slackened and pulled taut by moody winds. "There's something oddly satisfying about watching the movement of the grasses," Jane says as she gazes out her passenger window. "And the trees. There are more and more as we head north, as if they are better at challenging the alpha grass." She laughs.

"No wonder you're an artist. You notice the world around you," he chuckles.

"I have a friend at home who does this much better than I do," she admits.

"An artist?"

"No. An observer. He's taught me it's the little things that are big!"

"Yeah, I guess that's true. Even in what appears to be mundane or ugly. I should take you to the areas that aren't so nice. Believe me, we have those, too."

"I'm sure you do."

"But come to think of it, they're few and far between," Derrick says, obviously reflecting. "There is always a lot to be appreciative of here."

"Yes! Like the color green! And you have so many more trees here than I'd imagined."

"If you come back to visit again, we should take a drive out to the Flint Hills west of here," he says enthusiastically. "It's flat and rolling and covered in nothing but prairie grasses to the ends of the earth that change colors through the seasons. But you must know that from the way much of your work looks."

Jane doesn't know how to respond to that, for a couple of reasons. "You'll have had enough driving once you make the loop to get me back to the hotel later," she says instead.

He chuckles. "It's really no big deal. You're also worth it, so please don't give it another thought," he assures her. Jane blushes.

He soon exits the highway and negotiates a smaller, two-lane road, and after another mile or so, pulls off pavement and onto gravel. It's a slow and bumpy ride, and through grass higher on each side than she's ever observed before, while occasional fields of cornstalk grow walls taller than she can see over. The dry earth beneath the tires kicks up a plume behind them that could surely be seen from outer space.

They've covered another long mile on gravel when he lowers his speed to a crawl and points to an old farmhouse on their right. "That's it," he says as he uses his left hand to steer the truck onto a short, gravel driveway.

The house is a small, white clapboard structure that looks to be a hundred years old but new landscaping around the perimeter makes it seem fresh and welcoming. Just one story with a front porch that appears weathered and bowed with age; two big picture windows grace each side of the front door. A chimney stands at the right side of the house, while a collection of ancient trees provides plenty of shade all around. Jane thinks it absolutely charming. Deep down, she's a little disappointed. Had she really thought she would find the white house of her visions here? Of course not, but the area looks similar to The Land Mac has treated her to! Is that possibility what has drawn her to the man next to her?

Derrick brings the truck to a full stop and hops out of the cab quickly. "Come meet my dog!" he happily calls over his shoulder.

Before Jane can open her passenger door, the most beautiful German Shepherd she's ever seen comes bounding down the steps from the porch to greet them, his tail flapping merrily. "Oh, my goodness! You have a German Shepherd! I've always wanted a dog like this!" Jane exclaims, now out of the truck. "I used to pester my parents like crazy for one, but I could never convince them."

"This is my pal, Rufus. Rufus, meet Jane," Derrick says, rubbing the dog's head, who, suddenly finding himself satisfied, breaks away to bound toward Jane. She gladly obliges his need for further attention by continuing to scratch the top of his vibrating black head, his tail at a faster wag now.

"Hi, Rufus," she says. Rufus couldn't be happier.

"Let's head inside, shall we?" Jake also appears he couldn't be happier.

Jane is feeling pretty joyful herself. "Let's," she says, looking up and around, still taking in her new surroundings. She notices the porch wraps around to the west side, beyond the chimney, where a small wooden table has been set out with two chairs. A vase of wildflowers sits in the middle.

"I thought we'd grill out, but don't worry, everything is prepared. I just need to throw the steaks on, and dinner will be served up in no time." Derrick holds the door open for her. Rufus follows.

"How on earth were you able to work, get back here to set everything up, and then get back into the city to pick me up in so short a time?" Jane asks incredulously.

"Oh, I have my ways," Derrick grins mischievously. "I even got in a short run."

"Braggart."

"You're darn right. Do you know how dangerous it is to do that in the country? Dogs out here are serious about protecting the land they are assigned to."

"Okay. You win. I'm impressed."

"C'mon," he says grinning. "Follow me."

Porch boards creak loudly beneath their feet as they make their way inside, but the old hardwood complains only mildly. Scents of woodsmoke and the past, those typically associated with an old house, greet her soundly. They aren't unpleasant.

"Oooh. This is lovely!" she exclaims.

The living area is small but decorated surprisingly well for a single guy, and she doesn't know whether to be impressed or worried. Then she catches sight of the painting hanging prominently above the fireplace mantle. It's one of her own landscapes, "Summertime," which had sold before the show. She only now realizes Derrick had been one of her buyers. Of course, he'd said as much. She should have known. Maybe she did on a subconscious level, but either way, she doesn't know how to feel about it.

Glancing away quickly so as to lessen the self-consciousness of such a discovery, she takes the rest of the room in. The hearth bricks are painted a neutral beige, creating a soft look, while a couple of complementary tan leather couches decorated with colorful throw pillows face one another in front of the fireplace. A glass coffee table framed in bronze and set atop a light-colored wool rug, is placed in the middle with a big, colorful coffee table book entitled *The History of Art* resting strategically in the center. A set of bronze torchiere floor lamps set at angles from one another adorn the end of each couch, completing a cozy, inviting look. Every wall is decorated in a glossy, dark wainscoting. "This is beautiful, Derrick!" Jane exclaims. "Did you decorate it yourself?"

"I can't say that I did. This," he says with a sweeping hand gesture, "is a woman's touch, wouldn't you say?"

Jane laughs a little nervously. "Should I be worried?" she teases, and then almost slaps her hand against her mouth.

It's way too early for such statements!

But now that the words are out of her mouth, she realizes she *is* a little worried. She shouldn't be, for heaven's sake! She'd only just met this guy!

Of course, he's known other women! He looks like a Hollywood celebrity, for crying out loud!

And yet, his obvious interest in my work unsettles me. Why?

Derrick laughs as Jane pushes her assorted internal conflicts aside. "You can be worried if you'd like, but you really shouldn't be." She cringes. He continues. "The woman that put this all together for me is Karen. My second mom." Jane tries not to appear relieved. "Not the wood décor, obviously. That was done by the original owners. Come with me to the kitchen, and while I get dinner ready, we can talk about our families," he says roguishly, knowing she most certainly will protest.

"I'm all ears," Jane plays along, following him.

"So am I," he says.

She rolls her eyes as he glances back at her.

The kitchen is set back beyond the fireplace and is nothing more than a small room with an even tinier nook near a back door. It's tight but functional; the walls and cabinetry are painted a light eggshell color, which helps to foster a feeling of space. Storage is maximized by the hanging of pots and pans from hooks attached to a steel rack suspended by cables hanging above the stove.

"For drinks, I'm afraid you don't have much of a choice. It's pop or water, but I did pick up some Perrier," he says as he opens the refrigerator and begins pulling out the food.

"Just regular iced water would be great for me," she replies.

He sets a premade green salad and a bottle of Italian dressing on the counter, then places a glass dish next to them in which the steaks appear seasoned generously and ready for cooking. He steps out the back door, calling over his shoulder, "I'll just get the grill started. Be right back."

Jane has two glasses of water filled when he returns. "Is there anything I can do to help?" she asks, still amazed as his ability to multitask.

"Not at all," he replies. "Why don't you grab your drink and join me outside for a minute?" He locates a large set of tongs in a drawer next to the stove, and tucking them under his arm, heads out the door, motioning for her to follow. Jane trails him outside to a small patio where Rufus has already contentedly repositioned himself.

It's a beautiful evening, and as she's already learned, not too oppressively hot like July evenings can be here. A light breeze ruffles the leaves on the tall, shady trees that enclose the backyard, and the smell of freshly cut grass and hickory chips on the grill sweetens her senses. The cicadas are warming up, but they only add to the uniqueness of the evening on the prairie. She feels herself mellow.

"So, who's Karen?" Jane asks as she pulls out a chair in the shade of a tall oak and has a seat.

"Karen is the woman who raised me after my mother died," Derrick says, continuing to prepare the grill.

"Oh, Derrick, I'm so sorry," Jane says, startled. "I had no idea."

"So, you want to talk about our families now? I thought—"

Jane interrupts. "Gosh, you must think me so awful."

"I don't," he says, interjecting softly.

"I am *so* sorry," she continues. "My selfishly-constructed wall wasn't fair to you. Just because I didn't want to talk about mine didn't mean you were relegated to silence yourself. I'm just so—insensitive!"

He smiles. "It's quite all right. Be right back," he says, heading inside for a lighter.

When he returns, she is contrite. "Would it be okay to tell me now?"

He takes a seat next to her. "My dad took off before I was born. I never knew him. My mom was a local waitress in a small coffee shop, and though we didn't have much, we had enough. When she was waitressing at The Grind, a diner here in town, she met Duke Wainwright—you remember him? He was one of the guys I was with at your show."

"That's right, the one introduced as Doug," Jane says.

"Yes. Doug is his real name, but everyone calls him Duke."

Jane nods, encouraging him.

"Well, Doug, or Duke, used to visit that diner every morning meeting with a few of his farmer friends. Over coffee, they'd talk about crop prices and that sort of thing. He was a regular, so Mom got to know him well. When I say he was in that shop every morning, I mean every morning. And every morning, he left a big tip for my mom. He knew she was a single mom forced to take me with her to work. She had to be there before my school started, and I was too young to stay home by myself. Apparently, the owner of the restaurant was all for having me there. I got to know her too—Margaret was her name. Both Margaret and Duke always tried to make conversation with me, but it was Duke I was drawn to. Maybe that was because I already had a mother. I was missing a father."

"They can be overrated," Jane blurts.

"I'd like to hear about that when you're ready," Derrick replies gently.

Jane nods. "Go on," she encourages him.

"Well," he pauses, and then inhaling deeply, continues. "Mom and I were headed to work one morning when she fell asleep behind the wheel. I was only five at the time, but I remember it. She'd often stay up late at night studying, and that morning she was exhausted, as she usually was. I noticed she was beginning to nod off, and I wanted to yell, "Mom, wake up!" But I didn't. That's the last thing I remember thinking before finding myself across the road from the accident scene. She ran a stop sign, and we collided with a trash truck."

"Derrick, it makes me so sad to hear this," Jane laments. "What a horrible thing to have to go through."

"I appreciate that," he says, standing up. "It happened just a block from The Grind. Duke was one of the first on the scene. Interestingly, no one knows how I got out from that vehicle to be found sitting across the street from the accident, least of all me." He turns to the grill to begin stirring the coals. "I'd like to think I have a guardian angel."

This makes perfect sense to Jane. "Why, you must be right!" she agrees enthusiastically, yet any inclination she might feel in this moment to share her own similar experiences is tempered by an understanding of the newness of this friendship.

"Do you believe in spirit guardians?" Derrick asks as he closes the lid on the grill and rejoins her at the table. "I mean, it's sort of a weird thing to contemplate, but I have, obviously." He turns to face her. "I can't think of any other plausible reason for why I was in that vehicle with my mother just before impact, but just after that was sitting safely away from the scene on the other side of the road as an observer. I was found well away from the accident and my mother, and I was in a daze when the first responders arrived on the scene. I got there somehow. I wasn't ejected through closed windows, and since others have suggested it was the work of something supernatural and people have talked forever of 'guardian angels,' I opted for that theory over some sort of time wrinkle."

"Hmm. A time wrinkle. Guardians. Very interesting."

And very possible.

"Isn't it though?"

"For sure, but I don't think the idea of you having an angel that stepped up to assist you is as strange as you might think I would."

She smiles inwardly, thinking of Mac. Naturally, she'd considered the possibility Mac might be something like an angel, a guardian of some kind, but he'd never really seemed that interested in protecting her or even invested in her welfare in general, for that matter. Still, the visions she'd had of those guardians on The Land was compelling. They were protectors of some kind. Their kind existed.

Derrick smiles. "I don't know if I would go so far as to call them angels. That seems so, I don't know, cliché."

Again, Jane nods in agreement. "But fun." She giggles. Called to mind are the gothic, one-dimensional, gilded depictions she'd seen in art history class as well as Peter Paul Reuben's fleshy Renaissance cherubs. Neither seem remotely plausible.

Mac was something different entirely.

Derrick continues. "So, here was this guy Duke that I already sort of knew. When he and his wife offered to adopt me, I begged the social worker I was assigned to convince the judge to allow that to happen. The rest is history, as they say."

"Duke is your adopted father?" Jane asks, surprised.

"Yep. Sorry I didn't let on earlier. I just knew telling you would have opened a box you weren't ready to delve into."

Jane remains quietly remorseful for a moment. "And let me guess. Duke's wife's name is Karen?"

"You got it!" Derrick says. "They didn't have any kids, so they gave me all the love and affection I could have asked for. They really are special people. I consider them my real parents."

"But at five, you must have been so sad, missing your mom."

"Oh, I was. Let's just say it was a very difficult time," Derrick admits.

Worse than having dysfunctional parents was not having any at all. "Did your mom have any family?" Jane asks gently.

"Not that we know of. I have vague recollections of her mentioning Native American ancestors, but she was disconnected from any family we might have had. It was just the two of us."

"Wow. That is rough. You must have felt so isolated."

"Honestly, not really. I mean there are occasions in which it's easy to let your mind wander a bit, but the Wainwrights were good to me, and still are. I have never felt I was missing anything."

"Have you ever felt as though you wanted to do any research? I mean to find out if you have any blood relatives around?"

"Honestly, not at all. When you have a real family as good as I've got, there's no need to go digging around in the past. Let stay buried what is already underground. Although, I do think my dark eyes and ability to tan easily could mean I have Native American blood in me."

Jane smiles. She understands leaving well enough alone, and yet, she'd probably dig. If for no other reason than to get out from under her own familial circumstances. To excavate for better.

"I hope you don't mind me asking, but why didn't you take their last name—the Wainwrights?"

"I kept the name Copeland to stay connected to my mother who never took my father's name in marriage. And no, I don't mind you asking."

"Do they live close by? Duke and Karen?"

"They sure do. In the area but outside Leavenworth, to the west. Just a short drive from here. They have a big place on a lot of acreage. Maybe I'll show it to you the next time you're back in town." He certainly seems confident.

"That sounds lovely," she says, hoping she really will be able return to the Kansas City area, and soon.

Once the coals are ready to Derrick's satisfaction, he lays each steak on the hot grill, causing them to sizzle immediately. Jane feels her stomach growl as he returns to sit down again. She knows she should probably now tell him about her own family life. Honestly, hearing his story, she realizes hers isn't so bad. Maybe. It's just that she has never felt as loved as the way Derrick has just described being loved by his adopted parents. She's never felt truly wanted. But, at least she has a family. Or something like one.

"So, tell me about that beautiful painting I have hanging above my mantel," he says, taking the conversation in another direction, and suddenly Jane doesn't feel so uncomfortable anymore. In fact, she has a sudden desire to share the joy she finds in her scenes.

"What do you want to know about it?" Jane asks, meeting the intensity she sees in his eyes. She wonders where to begin.

"You sure are different than most," Derrick says, shaking his head.

The smell of the grill works in complement to the balmy evening and Derrick's disarming way. Jane is beginning to feel very relaxed. "Different?" She swallows hard.

"Yeah. Most people want to talk about themselves, their work. Especially those who've created something. You know, authors want to blather on about their books, composers want to boast about their music, and I would think most artists want to talk about their paintings—where they've gained inspiration, why they've chosen their subjects. But not you. You clam up every time I bring the subject up."

Jane considers what he's just pointed out. He's right. She sighs. "That's very shrewd of you. Okay, I give. Let's talk about my family," she says, giggling.

"You see what I mean?" Derrick says, getting up to check on the meat. He makes a couple of flips, satisfied at what he sees.

"How much time do you have? Because once I get started, I may not be able to stop," Jane says playfully.

He considers the question for a moment and then says, "I have all the time in the world. But first, give me a hand." He motions for her to follow him inside, where he pulls already baked potatoes out of the oven and instructs her to serve herself some salad. Once the plates are piled high with loaded potatoes and dressing-covered lettuce, they head outside to add the sizzling meat from the grill.

"I guess I've intended to be evasive," Jane admits, taking a seat. "But my family isn't the most enjoyable topic for me to discuss." She cuts a bite of steak, and blowing on it slightly to cool it, carefully puts it in her mouth. It's still quite hot but delicious. "This is so good! Wow!"

"I'm glad you like it," Derrick says, and not to be deterred, continues his line of questioning. "Why do you feel that way? I mean, please don't think I'm pressuring you. You don't have to share that with me if you'd rather not."

"I don't mean to be melodramatic. It's not like that. In fact, it's really no big deal. I just—haven't had the closest relationships with my family. I have a mom who's an attorney and a dad who's an engineer. They've always been much too involved in their careers to be interested in a meaningful relationship with me. Emotionally, anyway. Growing up, they were great little micro-managers when it came to dictating what they felt would be suitable activities and ultimately career choices. They were all about me then." Jane sets her fork down and picks up her glass.

"And did you end up choosing anything they recommended?" Derrick asks earnestly.

Jane laughs. "Heck no!"

"They aren't big on art, then?" He reaches for his own glass.

"Not at all. Not by a long shot."

"So, what do they think of your visit to Kansas City? Are they not excited for the show at The Downtown?" Derrick asks directly, waiting for her answer.

"I mean, I'd like to think they care more than they let on, but I guess the best way to sum up their reaction to all of it—my choice to paint, the show, everything—can be boiled down to one word: indifference. They are completely unmoved by my work," she says matter-of-factly.

And me.

"But that is better than openly hostile, which had been the case."

"Wow. I am so sorry," he says. "Because you didn't follow the career path they'd imagined for you?"

"Yes. That's part of it, anyway. The other part is their self-absorption."

"What had they envisioned for you?" He takes another stab at his meat and biting it off the end of his fork, chews deliberately as he waits again for her answer.

"I guess a career in engineering. Or law, even. I don't know, anything blatantly lucrative," she says reflecting.

"Sounds like they didn't come from money," Derrick observes.

"You are right! They didn't come from money. How did you know that?" Jane is stunned by how little she needs to say. Derrick already understands so much.

"Well, if one comes from money, one generally doesn't obsess about careers necessary to keep it coming. It's usually a foregone conclusion. Money produces more money, usually. Investments handled well and all that. But new wealth dictates strategies for perpetuation."

"That's amazing. I never even considered this. I guess I've been so anti everything they've suggested, I've had no curiosity regarding the origin of their perspective."

"What about their parents, your grandparents. What are they like?"

"I don't know. All of them are gone except one grandmother, and she lives out of state in a nursing home somewhere."

"Interesting," Derrick says as he picks up a pitcher of iced water to add more to their glasses. "And you don't know her?" he asks gently.

"No," she answers sheepishly.

Deciding to venture into safer territory, he asks, "Do you have any siblings?"

"One. But I can also boil my relationship with my younger sister down to one word: strained. No. Even that isn't adequate. Strained is giving our relationship more grace than truth. The truth of it is my sister hates me," Jane discloses. Now that she's gotten started, she can't shut up!

"Aw, it can't be all that bad," Derrick responds softly. He reaches down to the side of his chair where Rufus waits to be included and gives the patient dog a piece of steak.

"Yes, it can be. It is," she confirms. "Like I said, no big deal, but better not to put too much stock in it. Which is to say, it's best not to talk about it."

"I don't know about that," says Derrick, shaking his head. "I think it's good to talk about things now and again."

"It won't change anything." Jane shrugs.

"It might help you feel better, though. Talking to a friend about it could be affirming." Derrick's smile doesn't wane as he eats his food. His calm assurance is magnificent. He exudes humble strength in a way she has never known before now.

"You could be right. I've learned over the years to keep my feelings to myself, so this is new to me. I mean, I do have a couple of really good friends back home I can talk to. Jake and Lucy are good listeners, but I try not to burden them, or anyone, with my problems, and truthfully, they really aren't problems anyway. Obviously, I am doing what I want to do right now."

"Are Jake and Lucy a couple then?" he asks pointedly.

Jane laughs hard now. "No. Lucy is a friend, and Jake is my boss at the coffee shop. They don't really know each other, but Lucy has mentioned she'd like to know Jake better! Again, you are quite insightful, especially for a guy!"

"Especially for a guy, huh?"

"That's right. You're … sensitive, I can tell. But so is Jake. You two are two of a kind, for sure." Jane gobbles another bite off her plate. She hadn't realized how hungry she'd been.

"So, you and Jake are close?"

"Yes. He's one of my best friends," Jane admits.

"Oh," he says disappointedly. "I'll bet he really misses you right now."

"See what I mean about you? You're right. I'm sure he does miss me. But it isn't like you think it is. Jake and I are just friends." Jane leaves off the part about knowing her best friend is in love with her. How did Derrick do that? Like Jake, he reads the world around him, too. But it's more than that. Derrick comprehends what isn't visible, too. Also, Derrick has the charisma Jake lacks. She immediately feels ashamed for thinking this.

"So, circling back around, what I'm hearing is that your parents didn't want you to invest yourself in your artwork, but you did anyway, and though you haven't felt supported by them or your sister, you're resolved because you're doing what you want to do, and in doing so, affirming yourself."

"You are exactly right!" Jane agrees. She takes another bite from her plate, and feeling no need to elaborate further, remains quiet. She's never felt so naturally close to anyone, and so fast.

"You know, you don't have to meet anyone else's expectations for you. You only need to meet your own," he says seriously. Jane nods appreciatively. "Really though. Tell me where you get your inspiration. How did you discover you wanted to paint, and is there anything else you've considered doing, or has painting been the only longing of your heart?"

"You sure ask a lot of questions."

"Just keeping pace with yours, my dear. Besides, I am a reporter, remember. It's my job to ask questions." He laughs and wipes his mouth with his napkin, clearly waiting for the answer he's been aiming for all along.

Jane takes a deep breath. She really would love to tell him. He seems so understanding. Wise. "Why do you want to know so badly?"

"I suppose it's because I love your work."

"But why? Why does it appeal so much to you, Mr. Reporter?" Jane recognizes her response hints at annoyance, but she can't help it. His interest in her work is suddenly a little bothersome.

Why is it so necessary to glean the source of my inspiration?

Why does that trouble me?

And why is he so good-looking?

And then, suddenly, a new thought occurs to her out of the blue. This irritation she feels isn't really irritation, but a reaction to what is happening here. Her own inexperience.

Yes, that's it!

She shouldn't be annoyed but flattered! It's only seconds before she realizes her reactions are emotionally inappropriate, and worse, she's reacted this way before. She groans inwardly as she instantly comes to terms with how she's treated Jake. He had only been trying to reach out to her, assure her of his concern for her, but she's treated him similarly. And she's doing it again, getting unnecessarily touchy with someone truly interested in who she is. How is she just now coming to terms with this?

Still, maybe it's her gut's own warning system.

"I guess I should show you something you might find interesting," he confesses, seeing she's finished her meal. He puts his fork on his plate and his napkin on the table. "Follow me," he says.

Intrigued, Jane readily agrees. "Where are we going?"

"Back inside. I want to show you some more of my art collection."

"You have an art *collection?*" she teases, trying to make up for any edginess he surely perceived.

"Indeed, I do. It's not expansive, by any means," he explains. "But Duke and Karen sort of raised me to consider such things. They have a collection themselves. I guess you could say I was raised on it—appreciating and collecting art, that is."

"Do either of them paint? Do you?" She now thinks to ask.

"Nope. Not at all." He chuckles loudly again. "We're grateful there are people who are able to do what we can't."

Back inside, he leads her past the kitchen to another part of the house, and Jane suddenly feels panicky, realizing they're headed back to where his bedroom must be.

What is he up to?

In the short hallway, she passes a bathroom on the right. "Mind if I make a pit stop?" she says. She's already resolved to avoid any rapid acceleration of this relationship, and her flight out the first thing tomorrow keeps things in perspective. Where Derrick's mind is, Jane can only speculate. A bathroom break will give her a few minutes to collect her thoughts.

"Not at all. Just meet me in the kitchen when you're finished," he says, seemingly unconcerned. Jane takes her time freshening up, and when she's finished, she finds him cleaning.

"Let me help you," she says, picking up a towel.

"Don't. Just leave it for now," he says, turning from the sink. He shuts the water off and dries his hands. "I told you; I want to show you something." His eyes hold mischievous twinkles as he says this, causing her stomach to catch butterflies. He reaches behind him for her hand, grabbing it before she can protest. "Follow me."

"Derrick, I think we ought to have a discussion—"

But before she is able to continue, he whirls around to place his strong hands on her shoulders. Something in his eyes takes her breath away as he bends close to place his lips tenderly on hers. As he closes his eyes to kiss her, Jane feels her insides begin to liquify.

"I didn't mean to do that just now, but I couldn't help it. And don't worry, that's not where I was headed. I'd like to. Believe me. But later."

Again, Jane doesn't know whether to be impressed or worried. He turns to continue his path, and she dutifully follows him, this time without feigning an excuse for bailing out. He opens the last door on the right, ushering her into his bedroom, and she now sees what this is all about.

On the wall next to a set of French doors that open out to the yard, across from his neatly made bed, is a portrait of a woman.

Who looks exactly like her.

More astounding, Jane's doppelgänger is standing on a piece of property that looks very much like The Land she visits with Mac.

And she's dressed in a white sundress that looks *exactly* like the one Jane wore on her first date with Derrick.

How can this be?

Jane moves closer to inspect the painting, feeling an odd pull to it. The style and strokes are so like her own, it's uncanny.

Think, Jane. What is happening?

Chapter
Twenty-Eight

LEAVENWORTH, KANSAS—1932

She sets the newly-arrived wooden easel up to her satisfaction, positioning the blank canvas on its support at just the right twenty-degree angle for optimal ease of work. She then applies colors to her workspace, squeezed from tubes and ready for mixing and transfer to creation.

Satisfied all is in order, she picks up a palette knife and combines deep blue with white, and once she has the achieved the hue of her mind, she sets the knife aside and picks up a brush, dipping it into the paint puddle. After sweeping a powdery sky across the top length of the canvas in up and down, back and forth strokes, she stands back to admire her work.

"What do you have a mind for this time, Edith?" a smooth, baritone voice behind her asks. Beaming, she turns to her husband, who is also smiling as he holds two mugs of steaming coffee. He sets one down on a table beside the easel, careful to keep it a distance from her current range of motion.

"Something different, Jack" she tells him. Her eyes dance with merriment.

"Is that so?"

"It's time to get the house down," she says, baiting him with a grin that begs him to ask for more information.

"A house? Whose house?" Jack asks good-humoredly.

"I think you know the one." She winks, resuming her work.

"Something you've seen in town?" Still playing along, he is the one now baiting her. He is perfectly aware of Edith's desire to build again on their property. Furthermore, he knows how much his wife loves the subject of architecture. Rarely is a trip taken into town or beyond without her observations voiced on the various styles and construction methods she observes, whether the oldest structures or latest building projects. She's been talking about creating her own for years.

"No. It's actually something I keep imagining." She giggles.

"*You* imagine?" he asks, chuckling, too. She isn't going to let this go.

"I think it belongs here." Edith sets down the palette to pick up the coffee. She takes a sip, looking over the rim of the mug at him mischievously.

"So, my wife is now an architect in addition to being an artist," he says laughing.

"I am glad for your support," she observes. "Because one day, this might just happen!"

"Keep at it, my love," he says as he starts to walk way. "I'll not crush your dreams. Not now, anyway," he teases mirthfully.

"Or ever," she sings over her shoulder. "We will one day build our house Jack. We will!"

In the blink of an eye, the children have grown and moved out. Why is it necessary to construct such a large, beautiful home? Edith asks herself again and again, though she already has her answer. It's always readily forthcoming. It is supposed to happen.

Someday, those grown kids might return with their families. A worse depression could hit than the one they are working through now. People she loves could need a place to stay. However, she prefers to believe the current state of things will change for the better, and the house she sees in her mind must be a fulfillment of destiny. A place her grandchildren could enjoy.

We will build in the gap, prepare for another time, she resolves.

Fortunately, her husband agrees. It will be a help to the community to hire local people to get the job done.

Massive dust storms have been plaguing the Midwest and Southern Great Plains for the last few years, and folks are becoming uneasy, even here on the east side of the state. Drought conditions are far worse in Western Kansas, and Edith can only pray for their oldest daughter, Opal Rose, and Opal's husband who decided to head west to begin a new life. He's a strangely possessive man. Edith misses her daughter terribly.

Presently, all of her kids are close to being married off and dispersed, though their youngest—twins—are still just twelve years old. Albert and Arthur are living and working at the family's mercantile with their elderly grandparents. None have an interest in staying on the farm.

None have mentioned any unusual dreams or visions.

Edith's mother, Agnes, is now seventy-seven and still insists on running the front counter. The family's store has been a lucrative business, something they were all appreciative of when wheat had ceased to turn a profit. Prices dropped over thirty-one percent last year alone, down from $1.41 a bushel to ninety-six cents a bushel. Now, it's plummeted even further, selling for just forty cents a bushel. Wheat farmers are in a bad way. Many small farmers have packed up and moved along with the earth, nearly everything in a constant state of flight. The mercantile suffered, too, but not nearly as much as others. People still need supplies. Often that means they must barter for them, and the Henrys have been as decent as possible about it.

Jack Bell thinks they'll be all right here on the farm. For now. They've enough saved in a safe in the basement in spite of the downturn and own their property outright. If need be, they can always sell off extra acreage, he reasons, but he keeps those dire thoughts to himself. Instead, he pulls out the big family Bible and reads Psalm 91 aloud to the ever-decreasing household. He's been led to this verse repeatedly in confirmation over the years, and at the end of the days, at the end of all days, trust will always be most lucrative. He and Edith pray this over the names of their family members, all listed in the big Book.

For her part, Edith also paints and dreams.

Because hope can be painted.

So, Edith does, in all the seasons. She paints the tall trees and the faraway girl with the hair highlighted in ribbons of copper. She paints the seashore with the long pier and the waves as they crash, too, and all the places she's visited from the plains of Kansas.

All the good things.

She paints other things, too, like green leaves on white plates and curling vines on white vases to join the Limoges porcelain teacups her mother gave her. Pink roses on white china make her feel happy. She'd painted those, too, years ago because white begs for intercession.

She doesn't paint darkness or the Black Sunday that comes for them.

She doesn't paint her children, who disappear one by one, their faces vanishing from her mind as surely as they leave, and later, she wonders why this never occurred to her.

She doesn't paint the casket her beloved mother is laid in when her time comes, or the little ones lined up in front of the old, white church following so many deaths from dust pneumonia. The starved cattle, the carcasses, too. The decimated crops, the desolation of it all. The brown. The gray. Everything in between.

The absence of green everywhere, but in paint and mind and even dirty canvases can be painted over with color.

The green will return. It has to.

Surely it is beyond what cannot be forever. Surely there is white canvas there to work with again.

Chapter
Twenty-Nine

LIBERAL, KANSAS—1935

Opal isn't initially aware of the looming black mass of clouds behind her as she's working in her garden. However, an abrupt drop in atmospheric pressure startles her, causing her to look up from her work. What she sees frightens her motionless.

A black mountain has emerged where none had been before. At an alarming rate, it grows larger and accelerates as it heads toward her, threatening to blot out sun and sky.

She drops the spade she holds and jumps up, frantic. "El! El! Where are you?" she screams spinning around, but any sound she makes is lost to the growing wind. The child had been right behind her a moment ago!

Opal is held, motionless. She knows she must hurry, but she can't move! Terror holds her in limbo; it causes her arms and legs to turn to stone as she watches the monstrous form stretch and retract in dark, billowy intervals. It moves closer, its fringes licking at the laundry on the line before it begins to suck it straight up into its hungry field. Fabric fights to hold on until the line snaps, sending a whirling collection of small sails airborne into obscurity.

Opal manages to right herself, and regaining function, sprints to the farmhouse. To her great relief, she finds her daughter and the bulldog,

Gretchen, playing safely inside. She quickly shuts and bolts the front door and then races to pull the shutters on all the windows closed while instructing the little girl to grab the dog and get under the table, fast. The two-year-old is frightened by her mother's unusual command and begins to cry, but her mother has no time for coddling. She repeats her directive, albeit this time more gently, as she pulls the final latch closed on the window in the kitchen.

"Mommy needs you to hide under the table, sweetheart. Get Gretchen and hide for Mommy. I will join you in a minute," she says, grabbing a quilt from the sofa. She tosses it under the table as she races to the back door to scan the horizon.

The temperature falls as the darkness grows. Within minutes, there is little left of the sky, and then, in a flash, all daylight is gone. A monster looms, gaining width and altitude hurriedly, all the while becoming louder. And rushing. It sounds like many ocean waters over a fall.

Her husband is nowhere to be seen. Floyd should be finished in the barn following afternoon milking chores! Where is he?

Opal deliberates making a quick run outside, but just as she resolves to do so, she looks out the back window to discern his opaque form sprinting toward the house. She sighs with relief as the atmosphere grows darker still, the growling black mass now circling above as if it plans to devour the small dwelling and its occupants.

She rushes to the back door while her toddler runs to the hem of her skirt. The little one has returned to grab a fistful of the material and now tries with all her might to pull her mother from the door. "Mommy, Mommy, come, please Mommy," she screams. The dog remains under the table, whining and scratching at the blanket the woman had tossed there.

Holding the door open against an iron wind with one arm, Opal manages to slide the child behind her with the other. She holds her there while waiting the seconds it will take her man to reach the threshold. She hopes he's been able to secure the barn doors and the chicken coop. She hopes the animals will know what to do.

"Please God, take care of them out there," she pleads aloud, her words inaudible to anyone else in the wind.

Floyd makes it through the door, and together they fight with all their might against the force to push it closed. The moment the latch is in place, a gritty gust scratches against the other side with the sound of a million small rocks and mineral particles unleashed. It's followed by another, more powerful force which slams against the home, causing it to tremble. It wraps around the structure, snakelike, squeezing and scraping like a beast trying to work its way inside.

Floyd motions for his family to get down under the table, and once he's covered it with more blankets, he joins them. "It snuck up on us this time," he yells angrily. He motions for his wife and daughter to draw nearer, and once they're huddled together, the small dog settled in the child's lap, he pulls the quilt around them, the noise outside still deafening, the room shrinking further.

There is no point in attempting a word, but if she could, Opal would say, "Floyd, I don't think I can do this anymore." The house continues to quake as the noise of a hundred freight trains bears down upon them.

As if he knows her thoughts, Floyd holds his wife firmer. As if their little one understands, she squeezes her mother's hand tighter. The dog shivers. Time stands still.

The dust storms had begun nearly five years before. Without warning, they'd descended upon the land with a vengeance, destroying all life in their pathways. Raging across the land at speeds as high as sixty miles an hour and ascending heights hundreds of feet in the air, the risen earth had taken to ungodly flight time and again. Those storms had sucked the breath out of the living things, and scattered the dead things, and had made hell of the plains. Now, it feels like the end of all good things.

Farming was to blame. And greed. And other factors, too. But mostly, it was a gluttonous shift in agricultural practices and nature's response, and it wasn't true what they'd said, that rain would follow the plow, because all that had followed strip farming on such a massive scale was deficiency and ruin and the earth a desolation. The loosened topsoil had nothing left to anchor it when life-giving water evaporated.

It wasn't as if the signs hadn't been there all along.

The weather, unpredictable, had given warning, but humans don't usually pay attention to past cycles in the present. And so, another rounding of another cycle during which time the skies dried up again, meant the plow's contribution to catastrophic death.

And homelessness for a half a million people. The federal government now calls this land "sub-marginal" for living.

Western Kansas is among those places hit hardest, where tons of earth was blown eastward to re-sculpt the land, depositing dirt from as far away as the Oval Office. At least that's what people say, but how can one be certain it was Kansas soil on the desk of the president and not just the dust of Maryland or Virginia?

One thing is for certain: there is now more land where there had been less, and less where there had been more, and so much dead and buried here and asphyxiating dust everywhere.

No, there's no end in sight, and it's only getting worse. This day in April, when spring showers should be watering the land for color restoration, after so many days and weeks and months of praying an end to all things parched and brittle, it's only black dust that falls down from above and all around. The worst duster is upon the land, what will soon become known as Black Sunday.

It is two days before the bawling passes and the little family that held itself together in the dark and under patchwork can venture outside. When there is finally light, it reveals only gloomy devastation.

Once everyone has climbed out of a window and onto a dune blown up against the house, they see their blanketed home, covered coop, and partially masked barn. The wheat in the fields is gone, burned to a charred crisp. The bodies of scattered birds, buried chickens, and stranded cattle, few with life remaining in them, are too much to bear.

"Floyd," Opal says, shaking her head in dismay, "We can't—" She sighs, unable to finish her sentence. She's exhausted, so worn out she fears she has nothing left on which to operate. Even inhaling is laborious.

He finishes for her. "I know," he says, and not gently. "I know." Frankly, he feels the same way, so much of his hope gone now. He'd moved his family to Liberal from Leavenworth, from one side of the state to the other to cash in on wheat profits, but what had been difficulty is now impossibility. They both know it's finally time to cut losses and move on. No words lamenting the ways they'd tried and failed, no statements of regret, no offers of apology are necessary.

"I say we continue west to California," Floyd says. "It's time we leave Kansas behind."

"I say you're right," Opal agrees. "It's past time."

Chapter

Thirty

CAPE MAY, NEW JERSEY—1990

Jane's trek home had been uncomfortable.

Though she'd found a straight flight between Kansas City and Philadelphia, the two-and-a-half-hour journey seemed never-ending. She hadn't been able to get relaxed in her seat or to fall asleep, and the child and his father who had been playing cards on the tray table behind her seat—Slapjack, of all games—didn't help matters.

On the ground, her luggage was slow to appear at baggage claim, and she'd been irritable and exhausted before getting behind the wheel for the late-night drive home to Cape May. After coughing up her life savings to pay for parking at the airport for the two weeks she'd been away, she had driven her rusty brown 1980 Corolla the ninety minutes home through bleary eyes.

Now, finally in her own bed, she is no less irritable and plenty wearier. She'd arrived to find no one waiting up for her—not that she'd expected anyone would be pleased enough with her return to forgo sleep. That was just fine. No human to communicate with meant no further precious energy expended. But when she finally lays her head on the pillow, she finds her mind far from ready to shut down. Though her body feels as though she could sleep through the rest of the week, contemplations batter her mind like a steady rain hitting a tin roof.

Jane left Kansas conflicted and is now oddly relieved to be home. She needs time to think about how she feels about Derrick, about how fast things had moved, about the magnetism the Kansas City area has. She also needs time to process how she feels about Derrick's art collection, which seems all kinds of weird.

Where on earth could that portrait of me come from?

It certainly looks like me.

And does Derrick's interest in me have something to do with the portrait?

She groans aloud when she considers the scene she had caused in his bedroom. She had overreacted when she'd laid eyes on it. She'd made a fool of herself, extinguishing the sparks of mutual enthusiasm with an emotional bucket of ice water. She'd jumped headlong into conclusions, none of which were flattering to Derrick. Or herself for that matter.

But she'd been suddenly suffocated! Immediately hysterical. She'd acted like Derrick was obsessive. A stalker. Like he was another Pete. Yet she'd been more bothered by Derrick being a stalker, for some strange reason.

Jane had asked him to take her back to her hotel. Straightaway. They had talked little on the way. It had been so awkward!

But the truth of it was that deep down in the pit of her stomach, she knew when laying her eyes on that painting of Derrick's there was something beyond normal. The connection to him and to Kansas, not to mention another dimension, was obvious. Even so, she'd felt queasy about it. Unsettled. She just couldn't put her finger on what her gut already knew —something her mind hadn't yet caught up with. And swirling thoughts had made her dizzy, catapulting her into fight or flight mode.

Flight had been the easier choice.

Ultimately, she'd made Derrick the proverbial scapegoat, covering the peculiarity of the situation with subterfuge that made things clumsier than they'd needed to be. She was tired, she'd told him. Her flight was early. She needed to get some rest before leaving, though she'd already moved the flight back to an afternoon departure. They'd parted clumsily. He said he'd call.

Maybe he would.

But would he? Her behavior had been slightly neurotic.

I've basically intimated he's a stalker.

And acted like I was a complete wacko.

But shouldn't she be weirded out by what seemed to be a bit of a fixation with her art, and subsequently Jane herself as the artist? How strange it was that painting looked so much like her! In the very dress she owns, or one that looks like the very one she owns. The very one she wore on her first date with him. If it weren't for the way things are with Mac, it would be so much easier to dismiss what she'd seen as weird coincidence.

But it can't be coincidence.

Can it?

Is anything coincidence anymore?

Naturally, she'd considered the possibility that there was another woman, another Jane—as if some cosmic practical jokester was at work, viewing her from another dimension just as she was given myriad opportunities to see beyond her own reality. And if that were true, the idea that she might not ever be alone was also disturbing. Even more so was the fact that Derrick's possession of a painting that looks just like her was not something he had been readily forthcoming about. This was also true of the one he purchased at the opening. Why couldn't he have been up front with her from the beginning?

What exactly was he after?

He could have been honest with her about it! He could have at least told her he owned a portrait of a woman who resembles her. He could have been frank about the reasons for his appearance at the show to begin with. It hadn't been just to increase Duke Cunningham's collection, or that other guy's—what was his name? Ed. That's right. Ed's collection. And Duke—he hadn't even told her initially that Duke was his father by adoption. However, it was the omission of the portrait that was the most glaring concern.

But, to be fair, just how could that disclosure have gone? And when? On their first date? With him saying something like, "Oh, by the way, I think you should know I have a painting of a woman who looks like you in my bedroom."

Creepy.

She wouldn't have gone out with him.

Despite his looks.

Probably.

She'd be more freaked out if he'd told her right away than she is right now.

He should have said something. He should have made some effort to warn me he already had a shrine of sorts.

Of me!

She cringes at the thought.

But what about Kansas City? Is she drawn to it because it is so dreamily familiar? Or because her family isn't there? It couldn't be because Derrick is there. Not as uncomfortable as she feels about him now, she decides, having worked these thoughts through.

Should she forget about Kansas City? The show, the gallery, the atmosphere?

The people?

What is it about that place?

She'll stay in touch with Glenda, naturally, but the rest of them? Better to give it some time. And space. She resolves to talk about it tomorrow with Lucy. No, with Jake. He'll understand best. She's missed sharing with her good friend. And then, as Jane finally begins to power down her mind to drift off to sleep, it's Jake she is thinking of.

"Well, there's a face for sore eyes," he shouts over the steamer's high-pitched whine as she enters the coffee shop the next day. The air is thick with the aroma of freshly ground coffee, and she inhales deeply, enjoying the atmosphere she realizes she's missed.

"Hello there!" She waves softly.

"You sure took your time getting back," he says wistfully.

"I'm so sorry. I had a hard time coming back," Jane yells over her shoulder as she heads to the office. He follows her, a look of disappointment on his face.

"I want to hear all about it," he says, pulling up the chair at his desk. He motions for her to sit, but she shakes her head.

"I'd prefer to remain standing for now," she protests. "I've had a lot of sitting lately."

"No problem," he says, leaning against the desk. "Really, leave out no detail."

His company feels nice, she thinks. More than she remembers it ever feeling. In contrast, at home earlier, there had been only a perfunctory acknowledgement of her arrival.

"The gallery was great. They handled everything extremely well. I love the owners, but especially Glenda, who is the consummate professional and dearly loves her work, as you know." Jake nods encouragingly, so Jane continues.

"I sold a number of pieces the night of the opening, and they're still selling. I'm not sure what the total is now, but I think it's somewhere around twenty so far."

"That's fantastic!" he says. "About half your collection!"

"Yes, and Glenda thinks she'll have no trouble selling the rest. She wanted to commission more of the same, but I told her I would rather wait and see what I come up with." However, as Jane says this, she ponders a strange loss of enthusiasm for painting.

"This may sound like an odd question, but did you see the people who purchased your paintings? What kind of clientele did you find there?"

"No, it's not an odd question, actually, because I was wondering how they would look, too," she assures him, and then proceeds to describe the people she saw at the opening, including the weirdo in the parachute pants. She leaves out a specific description of Derrick, but is forthright about the group as a whole, telling him about the trio of cowboys who turned out to be enamored with her work.

"I am so happy for you, Jane. It sounds like you need to make the best use of the rest of your summer and get right to work!"

"I would love to, but I need to pay the bills, too, you know," Jane answers, placing the black apron over her head.

"It sounds like you already have them covered for the time being."

"I haven't technically received my first check, yet. So, I guess I'll stay on here, if you'll have me," she teases him.

"I have really missed you," Jake says bluntly.

"I've missed you too," Jane responds, realizing she means it. Jake is someone she can trust. The *only* one she can trust. She forces thoughts of Derrick out of her mind and allows thoughts of Jake to take over. Jake is normal. Safe. This time, she isn't the first to look away.

"Your friend Lucy stopped by a couple of times," he says casually.

"Oh yeah?" she asks, a sudden knot in her throat.

"Yeah. I guess she missed you, too." Jake picks up his cup and looks Jane in the eye. She doesn't look away.

"How did that go?" she asks nonchalantly. She doesn't care how that went. Why should she care? She'd dated, too.

"How did what go?" he asks, puzzled by her intonation.

"C'mon Jake, you know she has a thing for you." Jane rolls her eyes.

"No, she doesn't. I mean, she does?" he asks innocently.

"Yes, isn't it obvious? You must know that. It was no accident, her dropping by the store while I was away." In all fairness, Jane did tell her friend she should go for it, she recalls. What was she thinking? Not that Jane is interested herself, but encouraging her two best friends to get together? No. That would be a terrible idea. Way too complicated.

"No, it really isn't," Jake assures her. "I thought—" he begins, and she can see the emotion in his eyes is more intense than ever before. She supposes it's time to face the topic head on.

"You thought what, Jake?" she encourages him, feigning more naivete than necessary.

"I thought you knew I have a thing for *you*," he says, still keeping his eyes on hers. "I mean, you have to know that."

My absence sure encouraged him out of his shell.

"Jake, you're my best friend. I haven't wanted to jeopardize that," she says honestly.

"Wonderful. I'm being friend zoned." He says this as a matter of fact, as if he's resigned to it, as if he expected no other response from her.

"You know that's not true," Jane objects. But it is true. She waits for him to say more but he doesn't, so she continues. "Jake, I don't know what to say. You are so very dear to me—"

"But not in that way," he finishes for her, wounded.

"I'm sorry, but I don't want to lose you as a friend," she says, hearing herself through her own ears. She doesn't have the right words. She doesn't have the right feelings.

Do I?

She feels a shift developing but can't identify it. Jake is good. She cares for him. Deeply. The thought of Lucy dating him makes her queasy. Angry, even. And he's been so very patient, waiting for her, not Lucy.

But is anyone right for me?

And then something prompts her to ask, "Do you think maybe we could grab dinner later? I mean, do you have plans tonight?"

"No, I don't have plans. So, yeah, let's grab something to eat tonight," he says dully, as if platonic friendship is now a painful compromise.

He'll snap out of it, Jane reasons. He's not one to pity himself.

But will I snap out of it?

Because as soon as she recognizes the position she's put him in, it's herself she feels the most pity for.

Chapter
Thirty-One

LOS ANGELES, CALIFORNIA—1942

The ten-year-old is up well before dawn, pulled quickly from her bed with a pillow and blanket to huddle with her family in the center of their small, stucco home. It is safest to be as far away from the windows as possible tonight.

This is déjà vu for the child and her parents, Opal and Floyd. Here they are again. Taking cover. Fearing the unknown outside these walls. Hiding in the dark.

Air raid sirens palpitate glaringly across a city on the verge of hysteria. The Office of Naval Intelligence warns of an imminent attack thanks to a citizen who reported seeing a Japanese submarine heading south after it fired upon targets on the coast near Santa Barbara yesterday. The citizens of Los Angeles believe the Japanese will bomb their city. If a Japanese sub was easily able to attack the Ellwood Oil Field without immediate repercussion, why wouldn't the bigger target of LA be in its scope? The city is the fastest growing metropolitan area in the U.S. with numerous factories producing supplies necessary for war.

So the family huddles again with lights out, this time with thick, light-obscuring curtains drawn. The air raid wardens will be working hard tonight to make sure everyone is complying with the total blackout order.

The girl squeezes her mother's hand hard in her right, her father's hand in her left, as she sits between them in the middle on the floor.

It's always the middle on the floor. She's always in between them.

True for black twisters and savage dust storms. True against marauding bands of thieving highwaymen that roam during depression times, and the relentless rain that follows long periods of drought when clothes are threadbare and stomachs are cold and the world seems as though it has moved away from the sun to run in liquified rivers to eternity.

The girl is so very tired of being frightened, which is most of the time. Living in migrant camps after fleeing Kansas only made things worse.

Hope wasn't enough.

Fear was bigger.

And then the war. It brought them here to Los Angeles, where her father now works in an ammunitions factory. Though there is food, the rations of wartime better than anything she's known before, it doesn't satisfy tension or ease the darkness there.

The world is still full of shadows.

Though she can't see her father's eyes in the dark, she doesn't have to in order to know his gaze is on her. "It will be okay, El," he says, but not gently. Never gently. "This too will pass." He turns to his wife. "You didn't see this in your visions, did you Opal?" It isn't a question as much as it's an accusation, and for Opal, it cuts her own warm heart.

"No, I didn't," she replies sadly. Her gift for seeing beyond to another world is no match for this one.

Opal Rose knows she should not have shared what she had been seeing with her husband—the things the man in the linen suit showed her. Floyd only thinks her crazy. And maybe she is. Maybe they all are.

But Opal's mother had understood. About the time of her twelfth birthday, Edith had looked at her eldest daughter with a gleam in her eyes. "Have you had any unusual dreams lately?"

"It's funny you should ask that," Opal responded. "A beautiful man with dark skin has taken me out of this world!"

"I knew it!" her mother exclaimed.

"How did you know, Mama?"

Edith had never looked so radiant to Opal as she answered. "He's appeared to me too, and your grandmother as well. I imagine he was also in contact with your great-grandmother Nell, though she died before Grandmother Agnes could talk to her about her own experiences."

"So, it wasn't a dream?" Opal had asked pensively.

"No, my love, I don't believe so." Edith's smile could have lit the room were it not for the sunshine exploding through the open window. "Your grandmother told me not to breathe a word of what I'd seen to another human, but I was fine to discuss our experiences between us. It was your grandmother who gave him the name of The Knight. She loved medieval stories."

"I shall call him Gladius!" Opal decided then and there. She didn't know why, but the name seemed to fit. "Gladius seems a fit name for a knight," she declared, well pleased with herself.

Edith laughed. "I think he'll rather like that name," she said. "But who knows? He's not very responsive about such things."

"I know! But sometimes the corners of his mouth turn up in a confirming way. It seems to speak a thousand words."

Mutually encouraged, Opal had asked her mother to explain all she knew. "Tell me everything, and don't leave anything out!" So Edith had, as her mother had before that. The accounts allowed another generation to speak about the mystery, if only between those who had experienced it directly.

However, their experiences weren't proprietary information, as far as Opal was concerned. Emboldened by the conversations she, her mother, and grandmother had shared regarding their mutual experiences, she'd subsequently not held back from telling her husband about her visions. Warned by her mother that there was little chance anyone would believe her and that she mustn't discuss what she'd seen, she'd done so anyway. There could be no harm in telling her husband.

Floyd thought Opal was daft. Her disclosure that her mother and grandmother had received the same sorts of visions, or experiences, hadn't helped matters. Floyd had wanted distance from the rest of the family from the start, and the revelation only motivated him further. California, a better choice than Kansas, facilitated greater distance.

And now trouble has found them here in the Golden State, too, threatening to burst open and swallow them all. Loud sounds tear up the night like paper, slashing peace to shreds, as machine gun fire destroys the last vestiges of hope and sleep alike.

"Mommy, will they bomb us?" El asks worriedly.

"Shush, now. Don't you fret about such a thing," her mother assures her, but El's gravelly voice is almost too much for her mother to bear. After all they've been through, now this.

"Let's lie down and try to get some sleep," her father is quick to respond.

In the middle of the machine gun fire and anti-aircraft shelling taking place in the skies above the City of Angels, Gladius arrives, just like a knight in shining armor, to whisk Opal away to a better place. He sets her down on a boardwalk next to the sea, a long pier before her. The skies are gray with clouds stretched thin in cotton-like whisps, just enough descending light at her back to cause delineation.

She observes a woman walking toward the water carrying what appears to be a very large framed painting. The woman is dressed in a straight, knee-length navy dress with a light gray raincoat belted at the waist. Her high heels are not ideal for negotiating the coarse planks of the pier, and soon one gets lodged in a gap, causing her to stumble forward. She catches herself and mutters under her breath before resuming her stride. At the end of the causeway, she leans over the railing to dangle the painting above a churning sea. She seems to hesitate but then releases it, turns and walks away.

Opal watches the painting bob up and down on agitated swells. There, awash in cold water, is the clear depiction of a white house on the plains of Kansas. It had been many years since she'd been home, but she notices immediately how very like her family's property the scenery appears to be. Though the land seems familiar, the house is foreign to her. With two red chimneys and a red door in the center and a gabled window paned in white at the top, it is a beautiful house.

It was a beautiful painting.

She watches as it rolls over a swell and down into a shadow, until a wave crests and swallows it whole, and it is lost to the darkness.

She's startled when she realizes Gladius is still beside her. "The darkness won't prevail," he says, and somehow, she already knows this is right.

She also knows it is right to think about going home to Kansas again. California was never supposed to be her home.

She resolves to return, unaware it is already too late.

Opal will never make it back to Kansas.

Chapter

Thirty-Two

CAPE MAY, NEW JERSEY—1992

"**M**arry me!" he says as they sit on the boardwalk against the setting autumn sun. He looks longingly into her eyes. "I love you."

"I love you, too," Jane says, feeling the truth of the words. Because with time, Jane realized what her soul knew from the beginning, from their first meeting. It just took some time for her heart and mind to catch up.

And it took a trip to Kansas City to make this obvious, though consciously Jane has yet to process through all of the reasons for her shift of heart. Recognizing she had felt out of balance removed from Jake made her see things differently, and maybe she'd finally begun to see through his eyes, noticing everything as if for the first time.

Noticing him. Paying attention to the way he made her feel. Safe. She squeezes his hand in hers as they sit together on a bench at the Jersey Shore. The early September evening is unusually mild, and people are out strolling. A light breeze glides across the shore without bothering the clouds set in whispers across the sky.

Jake releases her hand and reaches for the picnic basket at his other side. Unlatching the top, he fumbles around, keeping his back to her while she continues to watch the way the light dances on the waves.

"I'm not doing this the right way," he says, and she turns to find him with a small box. He pivots to drop down on one knee in front of her. "But hopefully you'll still say yes." He opens the box to display a beautiful, one-carat solitaire set in a band of 14-karat yellow gold.

"Jake, oh my goodness! Yes, yes. Of course!" She throws herself into hugging him, and then pulls back to examine the ring. "It's gorgeous! Wow!"

"I hope it's what you like. I had to guess, but I wanted to surprise you."

"It's exactly what I would have chosen. Thank you." She wastes no time in extracting the ring from its velvet bed, then changing her mind, she hands the box back to him. "You had better do the honor of putting it on my finger for the first time."

"It would be my great pleasure," he says, taking it from her. He rises to sit again on the bench beside her as she holds her left hand out to him. He takes it, sliding it on easily. It's a perfect fit.

"How did you know what my size was?" she says, looking down to admire her beautifully adorned hand.

"I noticed," he says simply.

"Of course. You never fail to notice anything." Jane laughs, still admiring her gorgeous ring.

"Nothing about you, anyway," Jake says, gently grabbing her chin to pull her closer to him for a kiss.

"I never thought I could be so happy," Jane says. "But you …" she leaves it there, resting against the bench as she looks up to the sky. She holds her left hand up and rotates her wrist, allowing the facets on the diamond to catch the last of the sun's rays. The gem sparkles magnificently in the pale, pink light. "Why do you love me, Jake?"

"Let me count the ways," he says. Jane giggles. "I love you because you're unassuming. Unlike anyone I've ever met, you're not out to convince the world, or yourself, that you are special, and yet you are. So special. You just don't know the value of your worth." He turns to look at her with a smile.

"I'm not just Plain Jane?" she teases, already knowing what he'll say.

"You know you're the farthest thing from plain, Jane."

"That's nice of you."

"Are you kidding me? It's the truth. And the fact that you are so capable in spite of a lack of affirmation during your formative years is remarkable. You are my remarkable, beautiful, non-pretentious, talented Jane."

"And the reason I love *you*," she responds, finding it easier to shift the focus to his attributes than to deal with all that praise, "is because you are the truest, nicest, most agreeable man ever to walk the earth. You never fail to notice everything about everyone in each environment you find yourself in. It's inspiring."

"Well, I appreciate your kind words, my love," he says, and this time she leans in to kiss him. "I am so excited you finally gave in to me."

"I am, too," Jane teases as she throws her arms around his neck. "I am glad I have someone to share life with," she says, knowing there is so much of her life she can't yet share with him.

"I still don't understand why your love of painting evaporated," says Lucy as she and Jane sit cross-legged on the rug in front of their coffee table to devour a three-cheese pizza from the Italian restaurant across the street.

"What are you talking about?" Jane dismisses the question. She's focused on extracting a hot, gooey slice from the box.

"When was the last time you lifted a brush?" Lucy persists. "Really. You have lived here with me for a year, and I have not seen you do it once." Lucy is always direct.

Jane doesn't want to talk about it. It's been over two years since her show at The Downtown in KC, and since then, she's not been able to regain the enthusiasm for painting she once had. Even her relationship with Mac, if you can call it a relationship, seems strained. "Why does it matter so much to you?" Jane asks, a little annoyed.

Lucy reaches for a second slice, looking up to the wall to catch sight of one of the few pieces Jane has left of her work. This one, entitled *Seeing*, highlights blush clouds that look like feathered wings against a pale, colorless sky. "Because, your work is extraordinary! You know I hate to see you give up on it. Therefore, I intend to go on bothering you about it."

"Of course you will," Jane says, laughing. As intrusive as that could feel, it's Lucy's unique, laid-back personality that makes everything good. She is never overly reactive but overly supportive. The biggest testimony to this truth was the way she'd taken Jane's announcement about a blossoming relationship with Jake. When Jane had finally confessed, Lucy had exclaimed, "I knew it!" And then she'd jumped up and down with excitement for Jane. In Jane's life, there are only two types of people. Those who are all in for her and those who aren't.

"Then you knew it before I did!" Jane had giggled.

Lucy had rolled her eyes. "Gosh, you two have always been so obvious."

Jane disagreed. Things had been floppy and one-sided early on. But Jake, like Mac, has always been dependable. That's where the similarities end, however. Jake, who operates according to schedule and who is as reliable as a Swiss watch, is most definitely not like Mac. Mac comes and goes as he pleases. Mac seems anchored to no one and certainly not to Jane. Jake has always been anchored to Jane.

Jane still counts Mac among her closest friends, even with their falling out. Or her own falling out. And she's still not breathed a word to anyone about their *arrangement.* It seems the loyal thing to do, and Mac is definitely loyal to her. Though he gives off the non-committal vibe, he maintains the friendship and their travel together. Jane concedes her disposition isn't always agreeable, and her zealousness to discover the motives behind his attention has waned.

On his last visit, he took her to a forest blanketed by redwoods in Northern California and the nearby Crescent City's rocky coast; the week before that, they had visited the tall grasses of the Konza Prairie west of Kansas City. To date, most of their visits are filled with an airy peace and beauty, however, there are still rough scenes—those that have the potential to tear her heart out, particularly because she has no ability to react or help anyone in the moment. However, that a supernatural presence works amidst human choices has become more evident over the years. That much she gets.

So much of life is free will.

So much is something else.

Still, she experiences her land, The Land, and she remains in love with it because there exists a real soul connection there.

And yet, she feels less inclined to paint it.

For some reason, it hurts now.

Jane and Mac are standing in front of the beautiful white house with the gable and symmetrical chimneys, the familiar rush of the prairie's pleasant fragrances all around them. All these years, this spot of earth and its landscapes have been featured as significant. She's finally learned to be content with the wonder of it.

"You will have your answers when you ask the right questions," he says softly, still gazing ahead.

She nods. "Clearly, this land is special. What I've seen makes me think this is a portal of some kind. One of many, perhaps." She looks over at him, but he keeps his focus on the house before them. "Am I getting warm?" she asks.

To her amazement, Mac turns to look at her. Squarely meeting her eyes, he continues slowly. "You are still considering *what*. Have you considered yet *Who*?

Jane ponders this.

"After everything you've known, including what I've shown you, have you ever stopped to consider the most important question? The *Who* that leads to everything else?" Jane continues to think about this silently as Mac continues. "It seems that is where you should begin."

"Ugh. Isn't that working backwards? How can I know that without knowing exactly *what* is happening here or *why* it is happening? Remember in the beginning, you told me to ask why?" She pauses to consider his question further, then asks, "Is it you?"

He frowns, narrowing his eyes in dismay. Her question has plainly displeased him. "You aren't asking the right questions yet."

"Why did you send me to Kansas?"

"What makes you think I sent you to Kansas?"

"You exasperate me," she says, raising her voice.

"You exasperate me," he says, lowering his.

"So, you are saying all this time you've been waiting for me to ask the right questions?"

"This is much bigger than me," he replies in that impactfully monotone way of his.

"Could you give me a clue as to what the right questions are?"

"I already have."

"So, I should know?"

"Why wouldn't you?" he asks, disappointedly. "It seems most logical."

"Mac, I learned a long time ago, from you, nothing is logical."

"And I learned a long time ago you weren't one to question logic or to adequately shift through what isn't obviously so."

Before she can give this last statement any further consideration, the skies open, releasing a deluge upon them. It falls steadily, and when its accompanying thunder and lightning catch up, Jane looks for cover.

Mac makes no move to take shelter or to remove himself from the storm. Neither does he move to shield her, so she takes the initiative to run toward the white house. But before she reaches the front porch, thunder cracks above her head and she finds herself drawn to the magnificent tree nearby, where an odd shaft of light has broken through the clouds.

The Tree she's always been drawn to is now highlighted in a way that makes her feel the heavens have parted to revelation above them. Refuge beckons under its branches.

Chapter
Thirty-Three

Los Angeles, California—1944

"I hate you!" she yells. "It's all your fault!" The girl runs into her room and slams the door, her mother fast on her heels. "You are the reason he left!" she screams into her pillow.

"El, you know that isn't true," Opal pleads, blanching from the hurtful words. "Please, be reasonable." She sits down on the bed.

"I want my daddy!" The child cries, beating fists into her pillow.

"Honey, I would give anything for you to have your daddy back here, but he made the decision. Ultimately, there was nothing you or I did to make him leave." Opal places a hand on her daughter's back, but the girl shifts away, keeping her head buried.

"That isn't true. I've heard you fight. I know what it was about," El says through muffled sobs.

"What, then?" Opal calmly asks, though she already suspects.

"Your lies!" the child yells.

Opal remains quiet for a moment. "I think—" she begins at length, desperately searching for the right words. Surely El will understand once her upcoming twelfth birthday arrives. Opal sighs again deeply and responds the only way she can. "I'm so sorry," she says sincerely.

"No, you're not. He kept telling you to stop, and you kept doing it."

Opal considers this for a moment. "I told your father the truth, El. He just didn't believe me. I guess you don't believe me, either," her mother says sadly.

"I believe Dad." There is no reasoning with the child now, thinks Opal, but she can't leave things the way they are.

"Sometimes," she says softly, "we believe the wrong things." El starts to object but Opal cuts her off. "Now, hear me out. Your father believes he is right. In this case, my right is wrong to him, but that doesn't make him right or me wrong." El is quiet. Opal takes this as a good sign and continues.

"What I am saying is, he believes I haven't been truthful, but I was. I am. Just because someone doesn't want to see or accept what I have to say doesn't make me a liar. Everyone is entitled to perspective, but truth is non-negotiable. Truth doesn't change to accommodate perspective."

"But his perspective is truth!" El retorts.

"He is entitled to his view, but I am not obligated to it," her mother tells her. "Truth is absolute. It's above viewpoint, opinion, and even understanding."

El doesn't respond so her mother continues, "People may define it differently, but that doesn't change it. For example, how about you tell me what the color of the sky is."

El rolls over and looks up at her mother through red, puffy eyes. "Ugh, Mom, everyone knows it's blue."

Opal smiles. "Maybe to you. But as I look outside the window right now, I see gray, as it nearly always is along the coast. If it were that simple, if we could assume a constant state of blue as defined by one specific hue, it would be easy. But there is a matter of perspective. Our viewpoints don't make either of us wrong." Opal can see El is thinking about this. "The sky is many different colors. Sometimes it's purple when the rains come, and sometimes it's pink in the clouds that hold onto the sun. And sometimes it's gloriously red as the day says goodbye."

"I guess that's true," El sniffles, looking out the window.

"My mother used to paint the changing colors of the sky," Opal admits wistfully. "I miss her. Terribly."

"Is she still in Kansas?" El can't remember meeting her grandmother. They've lived away from Leavenworth for so long now, she'd stopped thinking of the possibility of relatives, and oddly, she now realizes they've really not discussed this. "If you miss Grandma so much, why don't you ever talk of her?"

Opal stares out the window. Only a leaden sliver of the heavens is visible above the flat roof. "It was impossible to keep in touch during—all we've been through. When we can afford a telephone, I am going to try to call her. She's probably still in Kansas," she says thinking on this. She realizes she should never have permitted the distance to widen between them. Between her father and her siblings, too. There had been some hard years, but she could have made an attempt to stay in touch through writing, particularly at the beginning when they'd had a permanent address. In spite of pressure from Floyd to stay detached. Feeble excuses, she knows now. She could have dropped a letter in the mail without expecting one in return.

Turning back to the conversation, Opal picks up where they'd left off. "Anyway, as you've just learned, where things get complicated is that some truth is difficult to know."

"I guess, but what does any of this have to do with Daddy?"

"I just want you to see that we can both have opinions, but the truth is that I never lied to your father." Opal decides not to defend herself any further, and mercifully, El doesn't press her in the moment to expand upon the statement.

Later that night when El is fast asleep, Opal pulls out her precious paint supplies, and since materials are hard to come by, lays an old, white sheet out across the table on which to work. She stretches the makeshift canvas the length of it and using clothespins, fastens it flat and taut across her workspace.

Then, she begins to paint home.

Chapter

Thirty-Four

CAPE MAY, NEW JERSEY—1992

Jane awakens to find green leaves in her hair and what looks to be grass seed in her bed. She will never get used to her unusual travels or the souvenirs she returns with.

"Thanks Mac," she calls out sarcastically.

After making herself a cup of coffee, she curls up in a chair by a window that overlooks the street from the second story apartment she now shares with Lucy. Beyond the fully loaded branches of a large oak in a robe of auburn, she watches a boy pedal by on his bicycle with a backpack slung over his shoulder. A woman dressed in a warmup suit steps out from a brownstone apartment building to grab her morning paper. They have no idea their world is much bigger than it appears to be. A small blue bird flies down to a low-lying branch to perch.

Jane sips from her hot mug, holding still as she watches the lovely bird hop to a branch nearest the window to sing. She observes it turn its head varying degrees before chirping out a few more high notes. Then, satisfied with what it had to say, it flutters away with a freedom Jane envies.

Suddenly, thunder booms over her head. "That's odd," she mutters aloud. There are no clouds this morning. She steps to the window for a better look at the sky. It's pale blue as far as she can see, the morning light a gilding influence. Thunder cracks again, this time shaking her apartment.

What in the world?

A third boom is heard, rattling the walls and ushering in the aroma of perfumed earth, as if cedar and sage burn in wispy coils of incense nearby. The room dims as powerful scents continue to grow, and the view before her changes. She finds herself on The Land.

Mac is nowhere in sight. Gone too is The House.

Before her is a battlefield.

Where tens of thousands of magnificent soldiers on the wide, windswept plains are engaged in fighting.

How thrilling and terribly unsettling!

Jane takes in the height and bulk of the warriors as Greek gods of antiquity come to mind. They're dressed in what appears to be a metallic mail with pairs of feathered wings attached to their backs. The largest, most distinctive of them must be forty feet tall with wings that are covered in—eyeballs! Hundreds of irises of blue and gold, lidded and lashed, cover his feathers in a variety of colors. Jane stares in bewilderment.

Their faces are half-human, half-animals of many kinds. Some have the appearance of wolves, some of eagles. Some look like rams with crescent horns, and others resemble bears or badgers with unusual markings. Still others are like no animal she has ever known on earth. A few have the countenance of men, such as the one with the seeing eyes the length of his wings.

They outnumber their opponents. Overall, the opposition seems to be a collective dark mist in which the giant creatures are only knee-deep, more shadowy bog than sentient beings. Nevertheless, Jane can see movement within the mass. It appears to be comprised of individual creatures of varying sizes whose facial features remain largely obscure, though momentary flashes reveal grotesque visages. Some are twisted and contorted. None seem to be any match for the good giants who effortlessly push them back with the palms of their hands and wings.

They unfurl wings in pairs of two and four, and when the wings begin to beat, the enemy is blown away, as a fierce wind would do to a small, black column of smoke against a big sky. Shadows disintegrate like dust blown away on a breeze.

"Mac!" she cries, feeling very exposed.

But it isn't Mac's voice that replies. "You are safe here," the Voice says.

Where did that come from?

She looks all around her to see nothing but the giants now, standing at attention, shoulder to shoulder against the prairie sky. They are frightening to look at, but they smile, and Jane can't help but smile back.

"Where is here, exactly?" Jane asks, expecting no answer but secretly hoping for one.

Where the battle had just been, a shroud of chiaroscuro contrast remains against a sky above that widens, becoming bluer. Her senses accelerate as everything around her is suddenly bathed in golden light.

"Who are you?" she cries.

"You know. You've always known."

The Voice causes her to look around again, but she sees only her favorite tree a short distance away. The Tree! It signifies something! But what? Maybe it's a regal sentinel of the seasons, a natural statue made to commemorate the determination of humankind here in this place. Presently, it's full of form, each branch laden with bright green leaves and nuts.

Upon closer examination, Jane sees someone huddled near the base of it. She moves closer to find it is a small, dark girl with long hair. Dressed in soft leather, she's hugging a portion of the trunk, as if for dear life, and Jane immediately discerns remaining shadows just before several Native American men come into view.

They intend to harm the child!

However, before their murderous thoughts turn physical, confusion overtakes them. They stop and begin to look around, left and right, bewildered. One pivots around in a circle. It seems they've lost sight of the little girl! In fact, they seem obliviously unaware of the tree's refuge.

"You are safe with me, Running Feet," the gentle Voice says to the girl.

Running Feet moves farther back behind the tree as thunder rumbles, shaking the ground. It's followed by a crash of lightning, which causes Jane to shiver in the good power there, the power that seems connected to the light and the tree and this land in a marvelous way.

Neither the girl, nor Jane, is afraid.

The men shake their heads, then grumbling, leave. Jane again glances over to the base of the tree where radiance surrounds the girl. A small bluebird sits on a branch. What looks to be a gathering of men and women in white linen surround her, too.

Mac is one of them, but an even more beautiful man in an illuminated white robe with long, dazzlingly-white hair stands in the middle of the group. All the hosts around him bow in reverence to him before dispersing. He alone remains, looking not at the girl but at Jane with the most overwhelming love she has ever known.

Jane finds herself back in her apartment chair, cradling her coffee mug in her hands. Its contents are still hot. As she continues to sip, she smiles, paying attention to the way the warm liquid feels as it goes down. It's comforting. And so is contemplation of what she has been shown.

Not even when she had painted had she allowed her mind such exploration as she does now. Instead, she had delighted in the ability to recreate what she'd experienced, to bring it forward with her into the present and within the parameters of her own reality. There was peace there. That was it!

Why had she run from painting then? Why had she stopped doing the thing that gave her the greatest joy? It couldn't have been Derrick. Not entirely, anyway. What exactly had she been afraid of?

Painting had permitted Jane the luxury of simply living in two moments at once, lavishing the ability to select the things that made her feel good without contemplation of any emotion produced from what was not.

Any knowledge beyond that had felt uncomfortable. In spite of her persistent questions and pestering of Mac to know everything, she finally concedes she hadn't really wanted to know everything.

It would be so much easier not to know both good and evil. So much easier to pretend only an understanding of what assists and supports. What makes all things right. The good and only that. So, she'd kept the disparate knowledge at bay, like a forbidden fruit she wasn't supposed to consume, and she imagines pitching every last piece of what it offers over the fence and outside of her own time.

But truth isn't limited by time.

And this reminds her of something Mac had told her in the beginning, when they'd first met. He'd said time was running out. That the world would end soon.

He'd also said she would need to persevere.

Hadn't she been doing exactly that?

Hadn't she accepted the terms of engagement?

Ugh. I have to get off this merry-go-round of thinking!

It can't be rocket science, for heaven's sake. She knows there are things that occur beyond what she can see. That there are forces of good and evil at work there. Everyone knows that, as well as knowing there is a possibility of carrying what is chosen here forward into eternity.

We've all had evidence.

And suddenly, it comes to her. The thought that has been at the forefront of her mind all along but thoroughly unexplored.

God exists.

It's not as if Jane has been a fool. Any person with a pulse knows there has to be a power in the universe bigger than what exists here. However, with all the suffering in the world, a loving God seems light-years away. He seems elusive.

But didn't Mac say something about partnership?

How does that happen, exactly?

The wild beasts and fighting, the wicked weather and suffering. Death, hunger, deprivation, struggle. Her own turmoil at home. So very much sorrow. The things she can't paint. How could a God exist that would permit all of it?

And yet.

The color.

Without a Master Painter, we would all live in a monotone, sepia existence. Color is evidence. Even in the depths of the sea where no human eyes are able to venture, life exists in forms, textures, and colors that celebrate creativity, as if what is out of sight is as much for His pleasure as for ours.

And our pleasures are too numerous to count.

She decides she must no longer hold back from sharing these things with Jake. She must tell him everything.

But for some reason, she doesn't.

"Good is what you make here on earth," Jake says when she leads him into a theological conversation later that afternoon.

"Yes, but what about its origin?" she prods him. "Where does good come from?"

"If you mean good comes from God, I don't think so."

"But how can you say that? Shouldn't good have a source?"

"If you argue that, you would have to argue for the source of evil, and then wouldn't God be the source of that, too?" Jake reasons.

"No. What if evil had a different source?"

"Then why wouldn't a good God stop it?" he counters. Before she can answer, he continues. "Listen, in life we create good and evil. It's humans that do that. If there is a God, then he would have to be one who stands back and watches it all unfold."

"But what if it was never his desire to have us exposed to it? What if humans chose to know it, and he is trying to help us overcome it?" she maintains.

"You sound like my parents," he responds.

Jane lets the comment go. She's too focused on his perspective—something that unsettles her more than she'd prepared for. In fact, Jake's deistic approach is something she'd not considered.

How could he be so kind and yet so … faithless?

"But what if God isn't standing back to observe? What if he's actively involved in combatting evil? What if he offers us an alliance in doing that?"

Jake pauses a moment, his brows creasing in thought. "That is an interesting perspective."

"But what if it's true?"

"Then it would change everything," Jake admits.

The phone by her bed on the nightstand is ringing, startling her awake. A glance at the clock reveals it's 6:01 a.m. Wow, she slept hard last night without any travel to interrupt it. She should be getting up now anyway. She's agreed to have coffee with Jake's mom this morning. Sue is sweet and gentle and so unlike her own mother. Jane appreciates the ability to nurture a good relationship with the woman who will soon be her mother-in-law.

Fumbling with the receiver, she picks it up backward. After smacking herself in the head with it and groaning aloud, she manages to turn it around and speak into the right end.

"Hello?" she says groggily.

"Jane?" The distraught voice on the other end startles her awake.

Jane turns over and sits upright in bed. "Yes? Sue?" She recognizes the voice at once.

"Oh Jane," she moans. "Jake was in a traffic accident on the way to work this morning. He's been transported by ambulance to the hospital. The officer who phoned wouldn't give me any other information." Sue's voice is on the verge of breaking. "I wanted to call you first. Will you meet Jeff and me there?"

"Yes, of course," Jane responds, already bolting out of bed to find her clothes. "Tell me where they're taking him." She scribbles down the information Sue gives her, and she's in her jeans and a pullover sweater in seconds. Running a quick brush across her teeth and another through her hair, she slips on a pair of sandals and grabs her keys. "Please, please let him be okay," she begs the universe aloud. "Mac!" she thinks to add, "Help us, please!"

Fifteen minutes later, she's pulling into the parking lot next to the signs that say EMERGENCY at Regional Medical Center. She has the door open before turning the engine off but enough presence of mind to grab the keys and her purse before shutting the door behind her. An ambulance is parked in front of the double glass sliding doors, blocking her line of vision as she sprints toward the entrance. Is he already here? Are Sue and Jeff?

As she nears the entryway, the doors open to release a rush of cold air. Jane bounds in and looks around quickly, panicked she can see no one she recognizes in the adjacent waiting room. Her mind feels oddly disconnected from her body.

A couple of police officers standing at her right glance at her momentarily before resuming a discussion in hushed tones. EMTs wheel a gurney and equipment back to their truck with no words exchanged between them.

Jane moves to the front desk, where a receptionist sits behind a glass partition.   "May I help you?" she asks mindlessly, as if she were at work in the department of motor vehicles.

"My fiancé was brought here," Jane says, nearly hysterical. "I'm Jane Campbell," she adds. It's a wonder she's able to get the words out of a mouth that feels like cotton. She puts her hand down on the counter to steady herself as the receptionist looks at a computer in front of her.

"Just a moment, please," she states coolly, and Jane feels her joints turn to jelly. After a moment the woman looks up and says, "He isn't here. He—"

Jane interrupts. "How do you know? I haven't given you his name."

"Ma'am—"

"Don't!" She shouts, holding up her palms. The receptionist is taken back. Jane softens. "What I mean is, I want to make sure we are talking about Jake Nash." Her teeth begin to chatter.

"Yes. He's the only patient we've received in the last hour. But he's been transferred."

"What do you mean? He isn't here? This is the only hospital in Cape May!"

"Yes, well, I'm sorry, but he's has been airlifted to a hospital in Philadelphia." Jane thinks she might collapse. Breathe, she tells herself. This will be okay. "Why?"

"We don't have what is needed here to treat the injuries he sustained," the woman says, now letting down her guard enough to show a little concern. "I am sorry," she says gently, at last. "He will be in capable hands at a Level One trauma unit in Philly."

"Can you tell me what hospital that would be, then?" Jane asks, thinking of the length of time it will take her to get there. Undoubtedly Ed and Sue are already en route. With no way to have reached her when she'd been driving here, they'd not have waited.

"Just a moment. I will find someone to help you." She rolls her chair back, and as she stands, another woman in scrubs walks in the room to stand beside her. The receptionist turns to speak with her for a moment in whispers. The nurse steps forward.

"Miss, would you meet me over here?" she says, motioning for Jane to step over to the door next to the counter. All Jane can think of are the precious seconds she will waste in taking the time to stop now. She should be on her way already.

The door opens and the nurse steps out. "If you would like more information, I can call the doctor who met the ambulance crew."

Jane is already stepping back and shaking her head in protest. "No, I really need to get on the road if I am to drive to Philadelphia right now. Just tell me the name of the hospital he's been sent to."

"I think it important that you take a deep breath and—"

"Don't!" Jane shouts, holding her arms out, palms up again. "Don't patronize me! I don't need to do anything but see my fiancé as soon as possible." Jane feels herself start to spiral out of control. Keep it together, she tells herself.

"Neither of those things are my intention," the nurse says, in a firmer tone than before. "We just don't want to see you take to the road in an agitated state."

"You are increasing my agitation," Jane snaps. She's trembling now. "Please. Just give me the information."

"I need you to calm down," the nurse insists.

"Good grief!" she roars. "All I want to know is the name of the hospital he's been transported to. Why are you making things so difficult?" Jane can no longer hold back a dam of emotion. Tears begin to stream down her face.

"May I help you?" says a deep voice from behind. Jane whirls around to find one of the officers who had been talking near the front door now in front of her. He's young with kind eyes and a nice smile. Thank God.

"Yes," Jane says relaxing. "My fiancé has been transported to a trauma unit in Philly. I just need to know which one so I may get to him."

"Of course," the police officer assures her. "Let's see if we can get that information for you. What is the name of your fiancé?" She's mildly aware he didn't use the word patient. What a relief. She will remember to look back on this man fondly, if she can only get through this moment.

"Jake Nash." She says, exhaling through pursed lips.

"Okay. I was one of the first officers to arrive on the scene of his collision, Miss—" He waits for her to give him her name.

"Jane," she finishes for him. "Jane Campbell." Now, she hopes he won't divulge any details from the scene. She couldn't handle it.

"Miss Jane. I believe he was transported to Penn on Market Street. Do you know how to find it?" he asks kindly. The nurse remains in place with arms at her sides and her eyes still fixed on Jane.

"Yes. I do. Thank you very much for your kindness," she says as she begins to turn toward the doors.

"And Jane?" the officer says, "do make sure you drive carefully. Okay? He is in the best possible hands. Rushing won't change that."

"Thank you," she says. She knows he's right. Even so, she can't help but feel she is already out of time.

Chapter

Thirty-Five

PHILADELPHIA, PENNSYLVANIA—1992

Jane takes the back roads to Philly, vaguely aware of speed limits or the consequences of exceeding them. All the while, she fights to hold on to her tears, refusing to let them go. She won't give in to the isolation, helplessness, or fear they would acknowledge.

What is this life that allows for such terror and heartache?

Who is God, really?

And where is Mac?

The Pennsylvania countryside is lovely this fall day, with leaves dancing in colors of purple, orange, yellow, and red. Occasional wind gusts carry them from outlying areas to the road in front of her where they rise and fall in swirling patterns to be gobbled up under her tires. The bold proclamation of the end of glorious things seems miserably allegorical.

She keeps the radio off for a silent drive, but her mind is loud with thoughts of Jake. All the best parts of her life are because of him, and even as she thinks this, she knows that isn't altogether true.

The drive affords her the exploration of memories. The tender ways he's loved and cared for her, made her believe in herself. The manner in which he sees, truly sees the world around him, noticing everything, taking it all in. The way he takes nothing for granted.

Jake has helped her view the world differently. The planet is so much better for his place on it, even though there are things beyond it he has refused to address. She swallows hard, immediately regretting that last thought.

The tears sting her eyes now. "God, where are you?" she cries aloud. "*Who* are you?" She doesn't even bother calling for Mac. What would be the point? She reaches for a tissue on the passenger seat and wipes her face, and as she drives, she begins to feel nudges of peace, but they quickly flee, eddying and spinning to be caught up with the wind like the fall leaves reclaimed by the earth.

"Everything will be okay," she says aloud, resolving to believe it.

When Jane pulls up at the hospital in Philadelphia, everything seems painted in dread. She parks again near the big red letters spelling out EMERGENCY and races inside the doors to the front desk behind glass where another receptionist sits. This causes a trembling within her to resume, making her feel unsteady. Before she makes her appeal, she does a quick survey of the room, and to her great relief, she spots Jake's parents. Jeff and Sue sit close together holding hands, their heads leaning toward one another. She runs to them.

"Jane," says Jeff, standing up. His wife joins him to embrace Jane. "We're sorry you had to make the trip alone. We had no way to let you know."

"Please don't give it a second thought. How is he?" Jane only now realizes how she must look with no makeup on, her skin blotchy and red from giving in to tears. She doesn't care.

"We don't know. We've only just arrived ourselves," Sue says as she reaches for her purse. Her eyes are also rimmed in red, her lids swollen. She pulls a tissue out and wipes her nose, offering another to Jane.

"Do they know we're here? The hospital staff, that is?" Jane hears the edginess in her own voice. She's sure Mr. and Mrs. Nash feel as impatient for answers as she is.

"Yes," Jeff assures her. "They know." His voice betrays his lack of confidence in the situation. "Perhaps we should pray."

"Good idea," Sue adds.

These people pray?

Jane had no idea Jake's parents were the religious sort.

Why hadn't this topic been explored?

Jane has never prayed with anyone before, and she's immediately concerned. What will *that* be like? She's never attended a church service, doesn't know anyone who has, at least in her inner circle. Worse than any embarrassment she might feel in joining in to expose her inexperience, the adrenaline coursing through her body right now suggests no peace for it. Could they just check in again with the hospital staff?

Nevertheless, she nods mechanically at the couple in front of her. She follows Jeff's gestures for a group huddle, and as she reaches out to grasp the hands offered her, she considers the boldness of such an intentional appeal to the Creator.

Here.

In public, for all to see.

Believing in what can't be seen.

For her part, she's made appeals to God in the past, of course, in those times when she felt threatened or misunderstood. But those where more like petitions to the universe at large, not intentional requests to a God who would hear and respond to them with specific help. Those appeals had been casual, floating out from the periphery of her mind like aimless arrows shot at the sky. Mac was more reliable, and that wasn't saying much.

And yet, she's known good at work. One can trust good is available without having to know its source, right?

The rain falls.

The sun rises.

Sleep comes.

Good is something we accept and want more of. Like Jake said, good exists no matter the appeal for it.

But to pray directly to a God who seems a little hands-off and galaxies away?

They huddle closer. Jeff and Sue bow their heads. As Jeff begins to speak, Jane is aware of how little she knows about her new family.

"Father, we ask you now to heal our son. Give the medical team the wisdom and knowledge they need; guide their hands as they work to fix him. Please God, don't take our boy. We trust you, Jesus. Amen."

Well, that was fast. And painless. Sort of. Jeff's voice had begun to crack on those last words. Sue had begun to audibly sniffle. Jane had begun again to lose control of her own fortifications.

Oh God! If you are there, please answer our prayer!

The moment is broken by the arrival of a doctor in scrubs. "Are you the Nash family?" he asks softly.

"Yes," Jeff answers, his voice heavy with anticipation. Jane feels as though her heart might beat its way out of her feeble chest.

Now's your chance, God. Prove you are real here.

A serious look on the doctor's face makes it difficult to read what he might be getting ready to say. No matter what information he provides them, he has to look that way. There can be no emotion attached to his words. "Would you step over here so we may talk privately?"

"Certainly," Jeff says. The women are speechless. The group follows the doctor to a corridor off the emergency room waiting area.

"We did everything we could …" His words hit the walls of the hallway, the adjoining rooms, the roof.

"… everything we could …"

"… everything we could …"

They echo down chambers and brush by the people waiting here like rogue missiles looking for a target. They zoom haphazardly over each doctor and nurse and technician and administrative professional to return to Jane's chest. There, they find their mark.

"… everything we could …"

But they don't reach her mind. No, not really. Because her mind refuses to accept them, refuses to accept what will surely follow those words, words too difficult to bear.

"… however …" she hears the doctor say.

However means unfortunately, regrettably, catastrophically …

"… your son's wounds were too extensive …"

"… too extensive …"

"… too extensive …"

"… too extensive …"

"No!" she hears someone cry out. Is it Sue? Or herself? "Noooo!" the voice says audibly, loudly. It originates in a place between her sternum, as a knot like a fist works its way up her esophagus to her throat to hover there before it bursts.

Where are you now, God?

You can't be real. You had your chance to prove yourself!

Without looking behind her, Jane runs down the hall and outside the building to her car out front. There, she cries until she feels dried out, moaning aloud all the while.

"Jake! We had so much to talk about! How can you leave me now?" she yells until she has no voice left and until Jake's dad knocks softly on her window, urging her outside the vehicle and into his arms.

Jane doesn't sleep for two days following the nightmare of Jake's passing, and Mac doesn't visit, either. That's fine. She doesn't want visitors. He has to know that. In fact, she doesn't care if she ever sees Mac again. She doesn't even want to live. She pushes Lucy away, her parents, too, in their awkward attempts to say something nice. But oddly, there is a strange sense of peace that comes over her.

She doesn't feel like she will live, but she knows she will. She doesn't want to be optimistic, yet she senses hope within her. It's dim in this moment, but it's there. Understanding exists beyond her periphery, just out of sight but not fully out of reach. And serenity, though elusive, is attainable. It's in the distance, like a mirage she will walk toward and find. In the wait, there is no disappointment because there is no realization of being right or wrong. That would be too much to consider.

Until three days later, when the fragrance of spices alerts her of a change of scenery, and she steps into another experience. This time, she's alone, Mac nowhere in sight.

Coward.

She's on The Land at twilight, standing in front of the old, white house. Golden light flows from the windows and onto a soft, new snow.

This time, she walks straight up to the door without any hesitation. She doesn't knock or wait to be invited in but just turns the knob and enters.

The home is dressed in its Christmas best with a variety of greenery strung all around as the day's end transitions into a deeper, pink twilight. Flickering candlelight within combines to create a charming greeting card effect. Sprigs of white baby's breath and red berries within verdant bouquets decorate an entry table as well as a dining table across the room, while garlands of evergreen climb the staircase and doorframes in curly vines. The scents of apples baking and meat roasting, of cinnamon and nutmeg, make the air heavy in a good way.

Even without the trimmings, this house would be heavenly, Jane thinks, beginning to shed the sorrow she has draped around her shoulders. She has so wanted to come inside and now, finally, the opportunity has come.

The home appears empty but prepared for the impending arrival of guests. What will she do if the people who live here return while she is here? Will she pretend to be a specter, hovering about like a mist, or pull back to flatten herself against a wall as if she could truly be seen? It doesn't even matter. She undoubtedly walks in a dimension apart from detection.

And oddly, it seems the home has been readied for her visit.

Then Jane has another thought. Could someone else be experiencing the very same perspective concurrently? Someone in another realm of the unseen? And what of the guardians she has seen on this land before? Are they still at work here? Beyond this vision or within it?

Jane moves farther inside, noting the smoothness of the hardwood beneath her feet. The floor is lovely, as is all the woodwork within the home, from the hand-carved banister to the mantel over the hearth. The wainscoting and molding. It's all breathtakingly beautiful, as she'd known it would be, and despite the overwhelming scents of the season, traces of new paint are powerful.

It's all so fresh and alive.

Jane begins to move farther back to the kitchen to the right when she hears music begin to play. Turning left, she steps into the parlor to find an old phonograph on which a flat record spins. The needle appears only recently set upon the recording, as it's placed at the beginning of the grooves. The rich, angelic voice of Ella Fitzgerald fills the room with "I'm Making Believe."

Who could have done that?

She looks around warily, seeing nothing, no movement of any kind, though she can't help but feel she is visible to someone.

> *"I'm making believe that you're in my arms*
> *though I know you're so far away ..."*

The grainy lyrics grip her heart as never before. It feels as though a vice holds it in a way that wrings melancholy from every part of her, here in this place of merriment and sentimentality where generations will celebrate such moments as are prepared for this time. And life will go on, and—why? Why now must she feel this place and know what she's longed for here?

Connection.

But why does she crave it so? What's with the magnetism? What is so special about this place? Over time, over decades, over centuries, that she has found purpose here?

And what exactly is that purpose?

It's sore and raw. A production of longing, as if what can be known can only come secondhand, and it hurts, the blues that rush her like floodwaters across the plains.

> *"Making believe I'm talking to you*
> *wishing you could hear what I say."*

If she didn't know better, she'd think someone with a really bad sense of humor put the record on to play so as to take advantage of her emotions.

Or worse, ghosts could exist that have orchestrated this. The ghosts of the past. The ghosts of the present or the future. The ghosts of her mind.

Could this be a way for Jake to send her a message? In a vision from the other side?

But what exactly is the other side?

"No!" she hears a voice say. *"Don't follow the promptings of darkness."*

She immediately thinks the better of her musings. She knows intuitively there can be no talking with the departed in this life. She'd once had a conversation with Mac on this subject. She'd understood his minimalist response very clearly. Any convo with the deceased was off the table. Not to happen. No can do. Somehow, she knows this is right. She probably couldn't handle it anyway.

She'll have to wait to cross that bridge for herself. She'll have to wait until this life is passed for any further connection with Jake, and that's what makes the pain so unbearable. Pretending otherwise is not only unfruitful, it's demonic. She's seen these things firsthand. They're in the shadows.

At least she knows there is life after this. Humanity is limited. What is out there beyond it is not.

That hope will fuel her forward.

Please, God, help me. If you are there.

Chapter

Thirty-Six

CAPE MAY, NEW JERSEY—1993

He hadn't come to her. When she had needed him most, he hadn't been there.

At the time of Jake's passing, Mac went missing. Now, months later, she still doesn't know why he remained aloof when he did, though fragmented understanding is beginning to come together, forming a colorful mosaic of sorts. The big picture is ever-increasing, even with cutting shards among those that tell the story.

She's spent the past year crying herself arid.

She's spent the last three years away from her easel, despite now working in an arts and crafts supply store. It's enough.

"I called for you," Jane says, her voice heavily burdened when Mac finally shows up again. "You didn't come."

"I know," he'd replied evenly. "And—"

"And?" she sniffled, spoiling for an argument.

"And. I heard you. And. I was detained."

"I needed you!" And as Jane says this, she feels her heart fold in on itself. The pain is almost too much to bear sometimes.

For the first time since she's known him, Mac seems full of emotion as his misty eyes meet hers. "Oh, Jane, my dear, don't you know you shouldn't be calling on me?" No smile causes his eyes to crinkle at the corners, no playfulness dances, twinkling. He is completely serious.

"What are you even talking about, Mac? Shouldn't I be able to depend upon a friend?" Tears spring to her own eyes as she says this.

"Yes," he replies gently, "that's exactly it. I am a friend. And I do care for you very much."

"Mac, for the love, be clear. I *need* you to be clear." She wipes her wet face with the back of her hand, prompting Mac to pull a handkerchief from his breast pocket.

"Don't worry, it's clean," he says as she eyes it suspiciously. She accepts it and gently begins to press it under each eye. She hands it back to him.

"Let's talk about coming clean. No more mystery swathed in allegorical words or works. No more cloak and dagger crap. Give it to me straight."

Mac looks down to smooth the lapel of his always clean and pressed linen suit, flicking away imaginary lint as he does. "I've neither played tricks nor cloaked my communication with you," he says looking up again. "I've simply expanded upon what you know in your heart with additional information in an attempt to guide you toward truth." Now, he doesn't take his eyes from her. They seem to bore a hole clean through her chest. She shakes her head.

"I don't know. I don't—"

"You already have the answers," he continues.

"Then answer me this, Mac. To whom do I call on, if not my friend? When I had no one left in the world, and I do mean no one, once Jake had left me, you were the only one I could truly count on. You went missing. Please help me with this, because for the life of me, I do not have the answer for that."

"You may not have all the answers, but you have all you need."

"Do you see what I mean?" Jane roars. "It's always the same with you. Nebulous tones, mysterious statements. I am so done!"

"Are you, then?" A grin finally appears, exasperating Jane so much, she feels she might choke him. Or at least try to.

"Ugh! You are impossible," she shouts, shutting her eyelids to begin the release. Tears course down her cheeks in salty streams until she tastes them. "Yes, I am." She places her fingertips in the corners of her eyes, attempting to cut off the flow. "And if you won't answer me—"

He cuts her off. "You are always answered. Close your eyes." She refuses. "Close your eyes," he instructs again. Already halfway there, she complies, squeezing them shut tightly, her lips an iron vice. "Take a deep breath," Mac directs her. She does. "Now, what do you feel in your heart?"

Jane considers this and realizes she doesn't have the words to adequately describe the rawness she feels. Pain and sorrow, disappointment, frustration, and more consume her.

"I feel—incomplete." It's the first word that comes to mind in spoken form. "Heavy, yet empty at the same time."

"Yes. This is good," he replies.

"Good?" she shouts again, opening her eyes. "How can you say that is good?"

He stops her, holding up his hand. "Just a minute. Keep your eyes closed," he instructs firmly. She does. "You are incomplete because you must be filled." Before her lids can flutter in protest, he continues. "What is the best way?"

"You tell me."

"You don't need me to tell you," Mac assures her. "The knowledge is written within you," he says before departing again.

"Just when you think things can't get any worse, why do they always get worse?" Jane asks Lucy as she sweeps the kitchen floor.

"Oh, I don't know. It's the law of nature, I suppose."

Jane groans. "The question was rhetorical, silly. I didn't want an answer."

"I know it, but it still doesn't change things," Lucy responds truthfully. "Life sucks, and then you die," she adds with a smile, as if the gesture is enough to keep them both from spiraling into a mutual pit of despair.

"You can't really mean that," says Jane despairingly.

"Of course I do. Here I am a single, nearly broke artist who waitresses at a broken-down grease trap, and there you are, a—" Lucy can't bring herself to finish the sentence. She'd gone too far.

"Yeah," Jane finishes. "Here I am." Lucy stops ministering to the kitchen counter she'd been feverishly scrubbing to look at her friend intently. She's at a sudden loss for words, so Jane rescues her. "I have to believe we aren't here on this planet to live a life that sucks, even though mine has certainly seemed that way."

"Oh honey, I'm so sorry," Lucy says, recomposed. "I meant to be funny. I just wasn't thinking." Her eyes become misty.

"I know that. It's okay," Jane assures her, setting her broom aside to move toward her friend for a hug. "Though life is full of pain, I have to believe we were meant to live it well."

"I want to believe you're right," Lucy admits.

"I want to believe I'm right, too," Jane says.

It's been over a year since the passing of Jake, and though suffering moments continue, peace grows oddly bigger all the while. She's glad for it.

But sometimes, near meltdown again, a voice tells Jane she is all wrong. That her mind isn't right, only prone to imagination as it had been in her youth. Sometimes that other voice attempts to convince her she really is mad, that her visions are delusions, and there is no beyond.

That she has never known love.

That she never will.

She will always be incomplete.

But then she remembers to banish the voice of deception. Much like the clashes she's borne witness to in in real time, she realizes her battles may not be what they seem.

What Mac had said all those years ago was true.

The end is in sight, but it's nothing like she'd envisioned. Not that she'd greatly deliberated over the end of the world. The future has always been too much to deal with in the present.

Lest she return to dust before giving the present all she has, Jane works to restore life here, to end the old and bring on the new. She tries more diligently to communicate with her parents and to be kind to her sister, despite their ever-present lack of support and disinterest. Still.

She asks Jess to meet her for lunch, but Jess still wants nothing to do with Jane. Jess delivers a half dozen excuses for her lack of availability, saddening Jane's heart. "Okay, well, how about we get something on the calendar?" Jane persists.

"I don't have my calendar in front of me," Jess insists. "I'll have to call you back," she says, audibly irritated.

Unwilling to give up, Jane phones their parents at work, inviting them to dinner. "What are you doing tonight? I thought it would be nice to connect over a meal," she says, adding, "I'd be happy to pick something up so we can eat at home, if you would prefer."

"Dad and I are leaving for the city this morning, but your sister should be at home. Why don't you two dine without us?" her mom suggests.

"She's busy. I already asked her," Jane says glumly.

"Let's do dinner when we return this weekend," Elise says. "I'll call you later to talk about the details. I do have to run now."

"Okay," Jane agrees, thinking it will be another night of pizza at home with her roommate. Not that she minds, necessarily. She's just getting bored with it.

And bored with a family that will always remain detached and far away. Maybe that won't change in this lifetime, but it won't be for Jane's lack of effort.

Meanwhile, she can't get that beautiful man robed in white out of her mind. He had been standing at the tree, just behind the Native American girl.

He'd been waiting for Jane. Not just Running Feet.

With that look! His eyes held acceptance and devotion and love. Intense, beyond words love!

It had been me he was waiting for!
Right?

Why did she keep putting off the truth? What was she waiting for?

Later, when she stops by Bruno's to pick up her standard thin crust three-cheese, she spies Jess in a corner booth under a trellis hung with Chianti bottles and fake grape vines. She's with a man whose back is turned to her.

Good for her.

Jane grabs her food and rushes out the door toward her apartment.

Jane finally decides to paint again. She throws out the old, hardened brushes and buys new ones. She purchases fresh paints in vibrant colors and gathers a collection of canvases of various sizes together by driving all over town to hit sales on art supplies. She attends art auctions and visits galleries, even stopping into thrift stores and boutiques to collect materials. At Blessings Abound Thrift she finds a gilded Rococo frame; at the Pickled Cucumber, a blue fog linen apron to use as her new smock; and at the local Goodwill store, *The Natural History of the Palette*, a coffee table book with gorgeous photos of art objects over the centuries in rich colors. While there, she also picks up a vintage teapot with pink rosebuds on it to match her teacups. It's an amazing find.

She wants to live the beauty again. To see it and paint it. Everywhere.

To focus on the good again.

She remembers the many ways Jake noticed small details, how he never missed the big in the little. He never failed to take note of the moods that flashed across faces, the emotion attached to words, the statements made in clothing, the way a person stood. Nothing was overlooked because he took time to look.

The seemingly unimportant and the noteworthy. The big and the little.

The here and the now.

But how had he missed God? Had he even thought about an afterlife?

Faith was the one thing they couldn't negotiate.

Why hadn't we?

Was it because Jake was too focused on the here and now?

Was it because she was too protective of her own supernatural experiences?

Had I been too selfish?

What is holding me back?

Thirty-Seven

FAIRWAY, KANSAS—1994

"**J**ane," says Glenda over the phone one crisp fall day. "You need to come by today. I have a new piece I think you'll want to see."

Nine months after relocating to the Kansas City area last winter, this is easily accomplished. Fairway, Kansas, just across the state line, is only a short distance from The Downtown gallery.

"Oh yeah?" Jane yawns disinterestedly.

"Oh, yeah," her friend confirms, her voiced laced with amusement.

"What's this all about?" Jane is awake and more curious now, despite not yet enjoying her first cup of desperately needed coffee. It will take a few minutes to shower and dress. "Give me a little something to go on!" She laughs, acknowledging her friend's clever maneuver.

Refusing to budge, Glenda chuckles. "Nope. Come on. Get a move on it."

Jane hasn't had a second official showing since her move to the KC area, not that Glenda hasn't tried to convince her to do one. Perhaps this morning's call is simply a ploy to get Jane to agree to another event, but income is no longer a concern. Jane provides the gallery a trickle of pieces for which a handsome commission covers expenses, even without Jake's life insurance policy payout, which had been hers even before their abruptly-canceled nuptials. Not only that, the proceeds from the sale of the coffeeshop were hers, too. He'd thought of everything, guaranteeing she was well provided for. At least for now.

Jane is free to paint, and she doesn't do much more than that. She rents a quaint, little studio apartment attached to an old home with big floor-to-ceiling windows. It had been a large, attached sunroom, but Doris Eldridge, the elderly homeowner, had decided to convert it into a separate living space. Doris was in need of companionship as well as extra rental income to supplement her paltry social security benefits. With the ideal lighting, the studio awash in white is mutually beneficial for the women.

On the way to the gallery, Jane stops at a local coffee shop, opting to walk inside as opposed to running through the drive-through. Scents of the season hang in the air—cinnamon and nutmeg along with the heady aroma of freshly ground coffee. The combination dredges up hard memories. Recollections of Oliver T. Bean's, and the accident, make her chest feel windswept and barren. Her own spirit often feels as though it could be pulled from her like those beautiful fall leaves separated from branches, spent and loose and swirling in ribbons. Like the earth itself, she fights constantly to hold on to what is hers.

Hot pumpkin spice latte in hand for herself, along with an Americano without sweetener for Glenda, Jane returns to her car and sits behind the wheel for a moment. She removes the top on her own cup to blow on delicious foam while contemplating what Glenda might have in mind. She hopes it has nothing to do with commissions for weird clients. There is that one that gives Jane the creeps, John Brown, the insistent one who wore the parachute pants to her opening and who hasn't given up on his attempts to contact her, sending emails to the studio addressed to her, babbling on about how his family's roots in the area go "way back." Glenda helped her get set up on the newly-created AOL. Thank heavens Parachute Pants doesn't have her private email address.

But today Glenda said she had something to *show* Jane. It didn't sound disagreeable. Jane takes another sip of coffee then places the drink in the holder next to her before backing out of her parking space.

She finds Glenda behind her desk at the back of the gallery. She is on the phone but holds an index finger up to Jane, indicating she'll be just a minute. Jane places Glenda's coffee on her desk, and then takes a seat, continuing to sip her own. While she waits, she scans the space, looking for something out of the ordinary. She doesn't see anything.

Her latest canvas, a work entitled "Testimony," is featured prominently in the center of the gallery's west wall and highlighted under track lighting. It's a large landscape, thirty-six by forty-eight inches, and features her signature prairie with a wide, gray canopy parted blue by radiant light in the upper right corner. It's one of her new favorites. She almost hopes it doesn't sell so she can hang it in own her studio.

"Thank you so much for your inquiry," she hears Glenda say. "I hope you have a great day." Glenda places the receiver in its cradle and turns to face Jane. "Hey! Thanks for the coffee," she says, taking note of the cup on her desk. "Sorry to have kept you waiting."

"No biggie," Jane responds. "So, what's going on?" She uncrosses her legs and leans forward.

"I didn't want to keep you in suspense, but there is no way to describe what I am about to show you." Glenda rises from her chair. Jane waits patiently as Glenda walks to the back room. She disappears for a moment, returning with what appears to be a framed painting in hand. Glenda has positioned it facing herself so Jane can't see what it is that's caused such a fuss.

It isn't large, perhaps sixteen by twenty inches, and vertical, from the looks of it. Jane guesses it might be a portrait of some kind. "Well, are you going to turn the thing around?" she asks her friend who now positions herself in front of Jane with dramatic pause.

"Of course," she says, rotating the painting so it faces Jane. There on the canvas is what appears to be a portrait of Jane. In fact, the likeness is so uncanny, it feels as if Jane could be looking into a mirror.

The young woman in the painting is clothed in a long, white dress with puffy shoulders. She is a brunette, and like Jane, she has copper highlights in her hair. She has Jane's dark chocolate eyes and long lashes, her rounded nose sprinkled with freckles, the same dimpled chin. She is standing on land Jane recognizes. Her own land. *The* Land.

It's the very same painting that had once hung on Derrick's bedroom wall.

"Where—" Jane can't finish. She must sit down to allow her brain time to catch what she sees.

"Derrick Copeland brought it in. He wants to sell it. I told him to leave it here, and I'd think about it. It seems to be very old, so I had it appraised." Jane remains silent. Glenda continues, "Do you want to explain?" Glenda knows very well Jane had connected with Derrick when she'd been in Kansas City for her first show three years ago.

"This was the painting Derrick had on his bedroom wall," Jane admits, offering no other commentary.

"On his *bedroom* wall?"

"Yeah, I saw it there, and I was pretty freaked out, to tell you the truth."

"Well, let me tell you, this is about to get freakier—"

"Wait, you say it's old?" Jane interrupts. What do you mean, old?"

"It's over a hundred years old. An antiquities expert evaluated it. I wanted that to happen before I called you."

Jane puts her hand to her head and begins to comb through her hair with her fingers. "I haven't told you everything yet," she says with a sigh.

"I'm listening."

"Not only does that portrait look like me, I think—and you are not going to believe this—I think it is me." Jane watches Glenda's face change as she registers what Jane has said.

"That's impossible. This painting was done sometime in the middle of the last century."

"Yes, well, I know, but you see—"

"I'll admit this is really weird, but it's also really impossible," Glenda says, staring at the painting. She looks back at Jane.

Jane attempts to finish the sentence she'd begun. "You see—that dress is one I own. I actually wore it on my first date with Derrick."

"What?" Glenda exclaims. "No. No way," she says, shaking her head. "The date has been authenticated."

"See, that's the thing, Glenda, when I saw it there in his room, I was overcome with—I don't know—this strange feeling. It did look just like me, and I wondered if he could have commissioned someone to paint it of me, though I immediately understood there would have been no time for that. I also considered the possibility that he had seen a photo of me that could have been provided to another artist long before he met me in person. He is a reporter, after all. He'd have contacts."

"But the dress—" says Glenda.

"But the dress—" agrees Jane. "There is no way he could have come up with that. NO way. I had only bought that dress just before arriving in Kansas City. I'd never even worn it before, let alone been photographed in it." Jane now inwardly considers all her supernatural experiences. Mac, the visions, what had inspired her own painting. Anything was possible.

Could the painting truly be of me?

And how did Derrick get a hold of it?

She could let Glenda in on some of her secret—the part she was murky on herself. She needn't divulge her own experiences in the process.

"There's more," says Glenda, breaking Jane free of her thoughts. "Did you happen to notice the signature at the bottom?" Glenda eyes her quizzically.

Jane shakes her head. "There's a signature?"

"In the standard, right-hand corner." Glenda's hesitation to comment further on this makes Jane shudder.

"No. Why?"

"Take a look for yourself."

Jane moves closer to inspect the small signature at the bottom.

It's signed, "Jane."

Chapter

Thirty-Eight

LEAVENWORTH, KANSAS—1970

The big, white house is hollow, its hardwood floors swept clean for echo. There are no dishes in the cupboards, no rugs on the hardwood floors, now scratched and dull. All furniture has been removed—anything that would indicate occupation here, though a few belongings have been left behind, including a broom in a closet, a family Bible forgotten in a space under the stairs, and on a top shelf in the kitchen, a few old teacups. Outside, a rusty Radio Flyer wagon sits near the front porch, nearly swallowed by the overgrown, reedy grass. The child's toy is really the only visible trace a family had once called this place home.

A "For Sale" sign is posted near the road.

The wind stirs, creating a leafy rush between the tall oaks flanking the home; the rustle is melodious, a collection of gentle chimes. Day crickets pipe their song as the sun climbs the sky, and the distant sound of tires on gravel increases, growing a dust plume that moves closer to arrival.

A brown Ford Maverick pulls up in front of the home and begins to make its way down the long driveway. It's followed by a tan, paneled Buick station wagon, which moves at a pace to put a little distance between its windshield and the cloud of earth that arises from beneath the tires of the car in front of it.

In the driveway, the drivers turn off their engines and step from the vehicles. Out of the Ford pops a stocky, middle-aged bald man in a tightly-fitting gray polyester leisure suit. Out of the station wagon steps a young couple dressed in blue jeans and T-shirts, the man, a gentle giant of sorts, unfolding himself from confinement. He's broad shouldered and attractively rugged with a strong jaw and square chin. Jane watches him lovingly reach for the slight, blonde woman's hand. She has rosy cheeks and a clear complexion that shines. Together, they walk toward the businessman.

Jane thinks the couple lovely.

The woman seems unable to keep her eyes from the house. "It's just as I imagined it would be," she says dreamily. The man beside her nods in agreement.

"Yes, as you can see, the land is stunning," says the bald man Jane now discerns as a real estate agent, especially as he steps forward to unlock the door. "Wait until you experience the interior. It's every bit as alluring." He fumbles with opening a lockbox attached to the door handle. Once the key is inserted into the door lock, he jiggles the handle and gives the door a hard shove. It opens more easily than he expects, sending him tumbling forward.

The couple looks at one another and smiles.

"Well, that certainly opened more easily than the last time I showed the home," he says in the way of an apology.

"Have you shown the house to many people?" the tall man inquires.

"Yes, there are a number of others quite interested. I expect multiple offers within the week." The couple exchanges knowing glances. Real estate agents always say such things. He continues, "Until now, each time I've shown the property, this door has been most perplexingly stubborn." He dismisses this with a laugh and waves them in, still eyeing the entryway with a look of puzzlement. The smiles on the couple widen as they step through it and into the foyer.

As they enter, a most interesting thing happens, a thing which doesn't escape the attention of all present. As they cross the threshold, the home seems to embrace them, pulling them in quickly, as if saving them from peril. The dwelling now seems their personal place of refuge, like a warm blanket on a bleak night, instead of an empty old home unaware of strangers or summer winds.

This is most welcoming because the couple now feel as if they have, indeed, arrived home safely. They aren't the first prospective buyers to feel tingly when encountering their home for the first time, when there is something in the air that says, "You belong here," but in this moment, the experience seems uniquely theirs. The woman looks to the man and meets his eyes. He knows exactly how she feels.

"Well, let's have a look," he says. His voice is powerful in the surrounding void, and she squeezes his hand as the agent leads the way, babbling over his shoulder. It's the agent's responsibility to cover all the obvious amenities even though the couple aren't really listening now.

The rooms are small but airy enough, offering sufficient space. Traces of woodsmoke linger in the walls and the old paper that covers them in places, but it's not unpleasant. Good, pleasing, and comforting, the interior smells like the residue of antiquity, a record of lives lived.

"As you probably know, the house was built sometime in the 30s, to spite the depression. The original owners did well in wheat, affording them an opportunity to take advantage of their position. They only recently decided to part with the property."

"So, the original owners are the sellers?" the man asks.

"Their children are offering the property for sale," the agent responds.

"I wonder why they decided to part with their childhood home," the woman questions aloud.

"My understanding is after the couple passed, none of their children were interested in keeping it."

"That is too bad," the woman says sadly. She means it.

"I'll leave you to inspect the place on your own," the agent tells them, stepping back toward the front door. "I will be here when you have questions."

"Thank you," they say before resuming examination of their newly-found treasure. The agent begins to busy himself with the paperwork he carries in his hands.

The woman grabs her husband's arm, sidling up next to him. She whispers in his ear, "I love it already."

He smiles. "Yes. I knew you would."

Chapter
Thirty-Nine

How on this blue planet could there exist a painting of Jane painted a hundred years before she was born? And wearing the very same dress she'd purchased all those years later?

And why, for the love, was it signed by someone named Jane?

Was all of this part of some masterful illusion, or was there an explanation for it? Naturally, Jane's ponderings center on Mac and his supernatural revelations.

He's got to be tied up in this somehow!

"Mac! Please tell me what's going on!"

Naturally, she hears nothing in response.

Glenda has hired another art expert to evaluate the painting, now entitled *Jane*, further. Jane nearly groaned aloud when she learned this. She would have preferred her friend not dub the painting with anything that might tie her to it or to garner her any attention where it's concerned. Okay, so maybe she's overreacting. Maybe she's a little fascinated by the portrait. But still, any real or imagined connection makes her nervous. Fortunately, since the work was verified as authentically vintage, Jane hopes no one will think to connect her to the woman depicted, despite the uncanny resemblance she bears.

No one, that is, except Glenda and her husband.

And Derrick.

Which is why she knows she must reach out to him. Perhaps he will tell her more than he was willing to share with Glenda. It's time to get in back in touch with him and sort all of this out.

He could be married by now. That could be another reason for his willingness to part with the painting. After all, it had been hanging on his bedroom wall.

But then she thinks the better of that last thought. No, that would give the painting too much prominence. They had dated. A few times. Nothing had happened. That was all.

Oh, right. She had freaked out over it.

Now, over three years later, Jane must assume he'd moved on. The consignment of the painting in question has nothing to do with it. Hopefully, the latest expert evaluator will be unimpressed.

Doris is out for an early senior bingo night at church when Jane places the call. Derrick could have a different number, she considers upon dialing, but an answering machine picks up, and she hears his voice. Deeply smooth and comforting, Jane finds herself hoping he's still single. Her cheeks blush at the thought.

"Please leave a message, and I'll call you back. Maybe," Derrick says in jest. She hears the beep prompting her to record her response, and she freezes for a second. What should she say? She almost hangs up.

"Hi, Derrick. This is Jane. Jane Campbell. I—I hope you are well." She cringes, knowing she sounds awkward.

What a dork!

Fighting the impulse to hang up, she continues, "I'm wondering if you wouldn't mind giving me a call? I want to talk with you about that painting you've turned over to Glenda. I'm here in Kansas City, now." She leaves her number and hangs up without "looking forward to your call," because that would have been weirder. She also leaves off a "bye" to end the message. She just hangs up, feeling more in control this way.

Well, the ball is in his court. If he's involved with someone, she had said nothing to preempt a response. Nothing that could have left an impression that the call was about more than just a painting.

Of her.

Nothing that could give any hint of her own surfacing feelings, those far from annoyance or discomfort.

Glenda phones later. "You are not going to believe this …" she tells Jane.

Jane interrupts. "You found another painting."

"How did you know?" Glenda is astounded.

Jane rolls her eyes inwardly. She was only kidding. "I didn't. It was a lucky guess," she answers truthfully. "But really?"

"Yes. You need to come in and take a look at it."

Wonderful.

"Okay, but first, please tell me it isn't a portrait of someone who looks like me!"

"That I can tell you," Glenda assures her.

"Okay," Jane agrees warily. "I'll be right there."

She's at the gallery in good time, even with the fight for a parking spot out front. Glenda greets her with the painting in hand, again facing toward her and away from Jane. It appears to be of medium size, around twenty by twenty-four inches, as far as Jane can tell.

"This one our antiquities expert dates from a later date, circa late 1920s, and it isn't signed by a woman named Jane."

"Oh-kay—" Jane responds expectantly. Silently, she thanks the heavens.

"What makes this painting unique and something I felt you would be interested in is the content, not the technique." Glenda pauses.

"You're killing me," Jane protests. "Would you just stop with the suspense?"

Without another word, Glenda turns the painting around. It is a seascape. Gray ripples are highlighted by foamy breaks, a sky dark and menacing with the sandy seashore light contrast. A pier on the right side is one Jane immediately recognizes. In fact, she would know this shore anywhere. It's Cape May.

How did Glenda make the connection?

And then it dawns on her. "This—" Jane doesn't know where to begin. She looks to her friend, wondering how crazy what she is about to say will sound. "This, I recognize. It's my hometown, Cape May. I would know it anywhere."

"Are you sure?" Glenda asks, frowning.

"Completely. I know the pier well." She pauses, taking a deep breath. "But what I have to tell you next is, well, odd," Jane continues, her eyes still on the painting.

"Oh dear. I knew this was somehow connected to you. I recognized the house!" Glenda says as she looks to Jane for further explanation.

Of course you did.

The woman depicted on the pier appears to have just thrown a painting into the sea. The painting within the painting appears to be the very house Jane has brushed to life in segments on many occasions. The only time she'd transferred the entire house to canvas was years ago, when she'd painted it in all its glory and then had agreed to hang it on the wall at Oliver's.

The very same painting that had gone missing from the coffee shop wall appears to be the very one this woman has tossed into the sea.

Jane reaches for the wing chair behind her and sits down. However will she explain this to Glenda? To herself?

"How did you recognize the house as one I had painted in segments for the collection?"

"It has characteristics which were easy to identify," she says, setting the painting down on her desktop to reach for the magnifying glass beside it. She holds the glass up to the painting within the painting. "It has those two red brick chimneys, which you once told me were positioned symmetrically on either end. Here, they are positioned exactly that way." She looks to Jane quizzically, but Jane remains stoic. Glenda proceeds. "Then, there is the red door and large porch, and most striking, the gable at the top, center, with the windowpane that looks like a white cross. Those things are hard to miss, even separately. You've painted them all."

Jane still says nothing. She doesn't know what to say.

"They all come together in this house and all look exactly as you've rendered them individually. It helps that the land it sits upon looks very much like your subject matter."

Glenda certainly has an eye for small details.

"It's your house," she continues.

"It appears that way. Not mine, but the one I painted."

"Not a real home, but one you've imagined?"

"Yes." Jane bites the corner of her lip.

"C'mon, now. You don't expect me to believe this." Glenda's eyes implore Jane to confess.

"I don't know what to believe myself," Jane answers truthfully.

"Come clean. It's no big deal. You've replicated someone else's work—a Cape May artist's, perchance?" She says this nonchalantly, however her dewy eyes suggest a perception of betrayal.

"No! I would never do that!" Jane exclaims. "What I paint is mine only! I've never even been influenced by another's work."

"This is the craziest thing I've ever heard of," Glenda says shaking her head. "There is no shame in admitting inspiration gained from another artist, Jane. Everyone is inspired by someone. The work of some of the greatest artists of all time reveal influence."

"I promise you, that's not it," Jane says.

Glenda knows there is more than meets the eye here. Jane's subject matter is far from average, and there are too many fine details that make it impossible to be a coincidence. Furthermore, it doesn't look like any house Glenda has ever seen. "I don't even know where to start with my questions."

Jane beats her to the first in what will surely lead a painful inquisition. One she can't possibly face adequately. She has no idea where to begin but does anyway, taking a deep breath.

"The painting you see within this painting, is indeed one I painted. In fact, it's the one I had stolen from the coffee shop in New Jersey. You know, the one that was never found."

"I don't understand," Glenda says, shaking her head.

"What I mean is, I think *that* is my painting there. Someone painted a picture of my painting within theirs," she says, pointing to the smaller painting within the larger one.

"Jane, darling, it can't be. This painting was done a half-century ago."

Still lost in thought, Jane doesn't answer her immediately. "It means my painting is probably at the bottom of the ocean," she muses to herself sadly.

"Let me process what you're telling me." Glenda speaks slowly, struggling to comprehend. "You are saying, just to clarify, this isn't some other artist's house you replicated."

"No."

"You painted this, this—painting here," she says, pointing to the framed canvas of the white house with the unusual characteristics that someone appears to have hurled over a railing on a pier, hovering above the waves. "And that—this—very painting is the one that went missing years ago, never to be found."

"That is exactly what I am saying," Jane says, still processing herself. She holds still as Glenda continues to follow the thread.

"And again, we have a painting dating to before you were born."

"It appears that way," Jane agrees. "Or it's what we've been told," she thinks to add.

"Yes, this is true," Glenda confirms. "Is this some illusion?" she asks weakly.

"No!" Jane assures her. "Well, at least not on my part."

Glenda eyes her suspiciously, pauses for a moment, and draws a deep breath. "This one was *not* done well over a century ago like the other that appears to be a portrait of you and signed by someone named Jane. However, it is another mystery attached to you in that this one is of your work, done a few years ago, in a painting created a half century ago."

"Yes. I believe that's it."

"This painting also depicts the disposal of your stolen painting."

"Yes," Jane admits meekly.

"This is impossible," says Glenda. "Is this—could this be—a part of an elaborate hoax?" she persists. "Or are you trying to drive me to drink?"

"I don't think it's a hoax, but a drink isn't such a bad idea right now," Jane says kiddingly. Actually, she needs to find a quiet place to think. And to call on Mac.

Glenda props the painting up where they can see it and takes a seat in the large leather chair behind her massive desk. She crosses her arms out in front of her on the desktop. "Please explain this to me, if you can."

Jane thinks a moment before proceeding. "I can't. I have no idea who painted these or why. Neither do I have an explanation for why the woman in the mid-1800s portrait seems to be me, or why this one, done in the early twentieth century, appears to be of my mother."

"Your mother?" Glenda exclaims incredulously.

"Yes. The woman on the pier who likely threw my painting out into the sea appears to be my mother." Jane nearly chokes on the words as she comes to terms with this truth.

"And something else," Glenda declares.

"What?" Jane asks weakly.

"There is a signature on this painting, too."

"Why didn't you tell me this sooner?" roars Jane, catapulting out of her chair. She picks up the painting and again places it on the desktop next to Glenda, retrieving the magnifying glass as Glenda leans in. Together they inspect the signature in the lower righthand corner.

"Opal," she says.

Opal?

"Well?" Glenda asks.

"Well, what?"

"Do you know what this is all about?"

"No." But as Jane continues to gaze at the painting, a faint understanding grows warm. "I have a grandmother named Opal," says Jane. "I've never met her. She and my mother are estranged."

"Is she still alive?" Glenda whispers, as if she's lost the power of her own voice.

"I—think so. I believe she lives in a retirement community in California." Jane's voice begins to crack. "I—don't know much about her at all, but I am now thinking we have more in common than I have realized. I have wasted so much time!" Jane can't stop the tears of shame and regret now pooling in the corners of her eyes. She continues to think aloud. "But how? How did she paint this before I was born? Of my painting? Of my mother destroying my painting?"

But even as she ponders these things aloud, she knows. She already knows the answers to these questions.

Bewildered, Glenda manages another question. "Could you start from the beginning again? I don't know how to sort through all you've just told me."

"Honestly, neither do I, but I am going to get to the bottom of it. If I can."

The woman is so old, she's having difficulty standing to paint. The room is spacious and wide, a large easel positioned in the center. Floor to ceiling windows framed in white reveal the boughs of a large tree just outside and the neatly trimmed green grasses that surround it, while sunshine streams through the glass in bold yellow. Jane watches enviously, savoring the creative atmosphere.

The artist has long, gray hair which is pinned up in a knot, soft tendrils falling like silver streams to the sides of her head. To Jane's eyes, the woman is stunningly beautiful, even in her old age, with soft skin and rosy, clear cheeks. A loose, A-line skirt down to her knees is covered with a button-up smock. She wears flats on her feet and bright, red lipstick on her lips.

Jane doesn't recognize her.

Who is she?

As the woman works, a phonograph plays nearby. This time, the voice of Judy Garland singing *Over the Rainbow* saturates the room, a fitting serenade for the little bluebird that alights a wooden fence in the foreground of a beautifully painted landscape that really could be over the rainbow.

The old woman dips her brush in white to daub light brushstrokes resembling feathers atop the bird's wings, a highlight that gives them light for lift, and song takes flight in accompaniment as she works. She hums as she alternates between sitting and rising, always conscious to reach behind her for her seat before settling into it, great effort required to get upright again. Through each move, she doesn't avert her eyes from the painting. It's almost as if she is mesmerized by what she sees.

Jane can relate. Glancing around the room, she notices a copy of *The Kansas City Star* laid next to a collection of art supplies. Curious, she moves closer to read the date: December 8, 1941. The front page banner is no problem to see from a farther vantage point, the font size slightly larger than the paper's masthead. It reads, "CONGRESS VOTES 470 to 1 FOR WAR."

Repositioning herself, Jane steps from behind the woman and closer to inspect the canvas before her. What she now recognizes propped up on the easel causes her to gasp aloud and the woman stops at this precise moment, her brush poised in front of her canvas as if she has heard Jane's reaction. Jane holds her breath; the old woman continues to work. Jane exhales in relief.

The landscape is one Jane could have painted herself. Why, her subject matter looks just like The Land! Exactly like it, in fact, though her style is a bit different.

Who is this woman? Could she be Opal? No, that would be impossible. Opal would have been in her twenties in 1941, Jane works out in her head. But why is this woman painting Jane's mind? Has she known the same experiences Jane has? Unlike the others she has witnessed painting before, could this artist be re-creating things seen from a distance? Or on site, as one of The Land's rightful owners?

And, for goodness' sake, *where* is The Land? That understanding has never been prioritized.

It's high time Jane sorts all of this out. There have been too many nebulous years. Maybe she hasn't sifted through the information well enough.

Clearly, it doesn't belong to Jane alone. Not that she's ever truly believed that. Others have loved it.

But from her unique perspective? Could others exist outside of time that love The Land as I do?

Has Mac has been treating someone else to his revelations?

She doesn't know how to feel about this at first. Should she be jealous? What she and Mac have shared, what they've experienced between them, has made her feel unique. Special. He has nurtured their extraordinary connection through The Land as sustenance.

However, until now she has never felt inclined to consider the possibility The Land isn't hers alone from a distance. That Mac isn't hers alone outside of time.

It doesn't matter, she resolves. What matters is someone had thought her exceptional enough to treat her to the unique perspective she has been given over the years—that which has impacted her life and taken her thoughts captive, as if it were her own Promised Land.

Now this.

It's minutes before she fully sorts through these feelings, which bring her back around to truth again. The love she feels for The Land is shareable. In fact, her heart is filled with joy in this understanding!

She's also filled with love. She feels her core spread with a warmth that extends to the tips of her fingers. She even feels it for the woman in front of her.

"Mac, who is she?" Jane whispers, afraid she will be overheard, which is strange. It's never happened before. "Mac?" she calls out again, this time louder. She keeps her eyes on the woman and her landscape. This time the woman doesn't flinch but continues about her work intently. Jane sighs audibly. Mac doesn't appear.

She watches the woman work but suddenly covers her mouth, lest she exclaim loudly again. There in the field the woman is painting, is a man with brown skin in a fine, white linen suit. Jane watches, mesmerized, as she adds lustrous white hair. He is small in proportion to the glorious, golden fields and big sky, but there is no mistaking it.

This woman, whoever she is, knows not just The Land.

She knows Mac, as well.

She's painting him, for crying out loud.

When she is finished, she adds "Edith" to the bottom righthand corner of the canvas.

Chapter

Forty

CRESCENT CITY, CALIFORNIA—1994

The retirement community sits nestled above the sea like an ornament mounted within the piney prongs of an ancient redwood tree. It has a wide view across rocky outcroppings to a vast body of glistening water highlighted with breaks in lacy trim. Jane thinks there aren't many places as lovely in the world in which a person can spend their remaining days on earth—her own land on the wild plains aside.

Perhaps she'll get there one day.

She resolves she will. Didn't Mac show her Crescent City specifically? And now she's here.

She maneuvers the winding, coastal road up to the facility with a sense of wonder. She'd visited this place, and the ancient forests beyond, with her unusual tour guide.

As it turns out, this is where her grandmother lives.

Her mother had been reticent to provide Opal's address, but in the end, it was the fear of Jane's volcanic disposition which finally persuaded her. Jane was nearly as angry with herself as she was with her mother for keeping her grandmother from her, though Jane recognizes her own culpability where the distance between her grandmother and herself is concerned.

She should have taken notice of the absence earlier, should have inquired, begged, cajoled, groveled if needed, to see her grandmother. Now, awash in a variety of emotions, not the least of which includes guilt and remorse which press on her like boulders, Jane resolves she will stand down no longer.

Later, she'll address her mother's betrayal. On so many levels.

The theft and subsequent destruction of her painting is something she may very well consider therapy for, and that's probably just the tip of the iceberg.

At least Elise hadn't denied this deplorable action when Jane had confronted her. She'd admitted it! But then, her mother had refused to provide any additional information to Jane. She'd given no excuse.

And no apology.

Jane mulls all of this over as she parks the rental car and exits to make her way toward the stony, camouflaged lodge now serving as a retirement center atop the bluff. A chilly, spring wind kicks up, but it feels refreshing as it hits Jane's face.

What if her grandmother is as stubborn as her mother? The apple doesn't fall far from the tree, as they say. Jane prays this visit won't be an exercise in futility.

Just inside the building, a receptionist looks up and smiles from behind a glass partition.

This is promising.

Jane smiles back, feeling more at ease now. She walks up to the window. "Hi. I'm Jane Campbell, here to see my grandmother, Opal Lawton."

"Good afternoon, Jane. I'm Debbie. Opal is expecting you," she says, getting up from her seat. She pushes a button on her desk that releases a lock on the door, motioning for Jane to move toward it. "Please come in."

Jane steps into a hallway paved in Spanish tile. "How is she?" she asks sheepishly, feeling at a loss for proper words. Debbie must wonder why Opal's family has been absent so long.

"She's doing as well as can be expected, under the circumstances," Debbie answers. "This way." Jane follows her down the hall framed in arched supports. Small insets serve as ledges along the stucco walls which hold potted cacti and other succulents with a variety of colorful blooms. The corridors smell sweetly fresh, like aloe and eucalyptus.

The home's warmth causes Jane to feel the intruder, as if she could be the one to spoil it. What kind of granddaughter would go missing from visiting her grandmother for so long?

What they must think of me here!

"Circumstances?" Jane asks, taking note of her own shaky voice.

"Well, she's a spry eighty-three-year-old, but at her age, pneumonia is difficult."

"I had no idea she had pneumonia!" Jane exclaims. "When I called prior to booking a flight out, I wasn't told she was sick!"

"Yes, well, she is doing better now." Debbie isn't elaborative but she isn't unkind, either. Jane understands entirely.

"Here we are, Room 12." Jane chuckles inwardly as Debbie knocks. Of course. "Opal," she says gently, "you have a visitor."

"Come on in," she hears an amiable voice warble.

Debbie retreats as Jane pushes the door open. She enters to find a beautifully aged woman sitting in front of a wide window overlooking the sea. Her long, silver hair is pulled up into a twist, her soft cheeks dusted in pink, a white shawl draped over her shoulders. Next to her chair is an easel and a side table, with a basket full of paint tubes and a mason jar full of brushes standing upright. Jane wouldn't have recognized her grandmother if she'd passed her on the street.

But, oh, she's wonderful!

"Jane, darling," Opal says with a dazzling smile, holding her hands out. Jane grabs her hands and falls to her knees, tossing her handbag aside.

"Oh, grandmother, it is so awfully good to see you." Jane begins to cry. "I am so sorry," she says, not knowing how to begin.

"What have you to be sorry for, my dear?" Opal's eyes dance with merriment as she says this, calming Jane's nerves. The large-petalled white orchids covering the length of her grandmother's azure blue gown seem happy, and Jane's heart begins to feel like warm jelly.

She shakes her head repeatedly before continuing. "Oh, I just—" She sniffles, then reaches for her purse to find a tissue. Opal beats her to it.

"Here," Opal says, handing her one from the box on top of the cluttered table. Jane blots at her eyes and wipes her nose.

"I should have been better about keeping in touch. I should have insisted."

"Now, don't you go beating yourself up," Opal interjects in a way that seems familiar to Jane. "There are enough people in the world who will do that to you. You needn't do it to yourself." She beams.

"I have to confess, I've been beating you up as well in my mind," Jane says gently.

"I can imagine," Opal says sadly, pausing for further elaboration.

"A million ways I wondered what had prevented you from trying to reach us." Jane is surprised at her own candor. She hadn't wasted any time addressing deep wounds.

"I did try. You must know that," Opal assures her. "But I, too, must confess. I didn't try hard enough."

Jane relaxes further. She feels an immediate connection, as though they hadn't been apart all these years. Loving her grandmother in spite of her humanness is immediate. "Well, for my part, I regret being away for so long. I missed so much of you."

"I regret my part, too," Opal assures her, squeezing her hands. It feels a little déjà vu. "You're here now, and that's enough."

"You knew I would come, eventually." Jane says softly.

"Well," Opal pauses. "I hoped you would. I hoped you would make up the distance between my failures and—" She can't finish the rest.

"Mine," Jane says, finishing her thought. She stops there, too. What words could possibly suffice to make up for the time lost? Excuses would seem ridiculous.

The women exchange deep glances before Jane pulls away to look down at her hands, now clasped tightly in her lap. "When was the last time you saw my mother?" Jane blurts, in a sudden rush to know.

Opal doesn't appear to mind the abrupt transition, but thoughtfully considers her response. "Hmm. That would have been 1964."

"Wow. That's—"

"I know," agrees Opal. "A long time ago."

"Mom would have been, what, thirty-two then?" Jane calculates. "She was thirty-eight when I was born in 1970; forty-one when Jess arrived. I guess that is largely what has made her an absentee parent, having children so late in life."

"Actually, I wondered at first if she would ever marry and have children. It's a shame she has been absent for you." Opal sighs out loud, which causes Jane to laugh.

"I do that too, Grandma." She watches her grandmother's brows knit together in puzzlement, so she explains. "I have a tendency to sigh audibly. Gasp even. And loudly." Jane continues giggling.

"Well, I guess it's a family trait, then," Opal says, leaning in conspiratorially.

"I'm sure it is," Jane must navigate the conversation carefully. It's too early to process her mother's painful emotional truancy in Jane's life. "Why did Elise leave California—and you? What happened to her father? I have so many questions."

"She never told you?" Opal seems disappointed to learn this.

"There is a lot she never told me." Jane can only imagine how difficult all of this has been for her grandmother's mental health.

Opal nods. "El's father left us. We'd had some hard times. Very hard times." She pauses, as if what she is about to say is too difficult to put into words.

Picking up the cue, Jane tenderly offers what little she knows. "That much I surmised. I don't know the details because Mom is pretty closed off. However, I have always been aware she grew up without a father."

"Our family didn't start out that way," Opal explains. "Floyd left when he couldn't take hard anymore. He was always a distant man, a sort of loner. Didn't like being around people a whole lot. That's why we only had one child, which I have always regretted. Shortly after we were married, he convinced me to leave my family to head west. The Great Depression hit, the Dust Bowl filled our lungs, and we came out here, hoping to find work. At first, there was none to be found, and food was scarce. Life was a miserable existence then," she admits, glossing over the intensity of it. "By the time we had another World War on our hands, he was gone. One day he was working in a factory in Los Angeles, and the next he was gone, never to return. El was pretty angry about that. She always blamed me."

"I'm sorry to hear that, Grandma. You never heard from him?"

"No," she says plainly. Jane catches a glimpse of melancholy rush her grandmother's face. "I contacted the police and filed a missing person's report, but I knew it was useless. There was a war on, after all," Opal says, patting Jane's hand. "LA was already becoming crowded, and I was in need of a slower pace, especially as a single mother—something really frowned upon at the time, as if the separation was all my fault. So, we relocated north, here to Crescent City, after about a year. I was able to find day work in a munitions factory while your mom went to school. We rented a little cabin in the woods, to begin with. It was a bit unsettling off by ourselves, but I felt protected there."

"Did Mother not like it there?" Jane asks, already knowing.

Opal smiles wryly. "I think you already know the answer, or you wouldn't have asked the question. No. I don't think she did. But then, I don't think she liked much of anything. She wanted nothing to do with this area. She definitely wanted nothing to do with me," she adds with emphasis. There is no emotion tied to her words, but Jane knows how deeply wounding this must have been. Must still be. Jane has felt her mother's isolationist personality from the other side.

"Well, Grandma, I don't think she's changed much. She doesn't seem to like me, either."

"That can't be true," Opal says delicately. "You know that can't be true."

"It is," Jane assures her flatly. "But I learned early on to be self-sufficient where my own emotional needs are concerned."

"Now I'm the one who is sorry to hear that."

"Grandma, why did she wait until 1964 to leave? Did something happen between the two of you?"

"Well, that was the year the tsunami hit," Opal replies.

"A tsunami hit the California coast?"

"Yes. It followed the 9.2 magnitude earthquake in Anchorage, Alaska. Maybe you've heard of it?"

Jane nods. "Of course, it was an infamously devastating earthquake! But Anchorage is thousands of miles from here. How did it affect this coast so tremendously?"

"Though it was about 1,700 miles away, it still produced the worst tsunami in the history of California. It wiped out twenty-four city blocks and killed eleven people."

"That's terrible! Mom left because of it?" Jane asks. Opal nods. "Why?"

"You see, World War II followed the devastation of the Dirty Thirties, and her father's disappearance came after that. It was one tragedy after the next, it seemed. The tsunami following what El perceived she had already lost was her last straw. She packed a suitcase and left for the east coast with what little she'd saved from working in the DA's office. She hated the West, and there was too much trauma attached to the Midwest. It didn't surprise me she ended up in New York to start. That's where she worked her way through law school and met your father."

"And she never returned to visit you," Jane muses. She can't believe her mother could be so selfish, but hearing this part of her story brings much clarity to Jane's childhood and beyond.

"No," says Opal. "I regret to say her actions are a mirror of my own, more or less. I never got back to see my own family in Kansas, truth be told. I always planned to." She sighs. "The decisions we make affect our generations to come, something we humans are largely unmindful of when we are simply trying to survive."

"Wait. Our family is from Kansas?" Jane asks incredulously. Goosebumps crawl up her arms. How had she missed this?

"Yes. You didn't know that?" Opal asks, incredulous.

"I'd no idea."

Or maybe I did.

Both women become silent.

The Midwest had been vaguely familiar. But the distance between Jane and the past—and her precious grandmother—illustrates Jane's lack of knowledge as culpability. Knowledge intentionally kept from her could have been revelation if she had only asked more questions.

Opal is the first to speak again. "I put Christmas and birthday cards in the mail every year, along with letters for you. Initially your mother would return a short note, but that was the extent of it. She stopped doing that years ago." A funny look passes across her grandmother's face. "You never received any of my cards and letters." It is more of a statement than a question.

As Jane considers a response, her grandmother adds, "I never missed your birthday. It's December twelfth. Am I wrong?"

"No. You aren't wrong, but—" her voice trails off.

"You never knew I was thinking of you," Opal finishes woefully.

"No, I never knew," Jane confirms. Silence passes between them as both consider what to say next. Jane breaks the silence. "I have a photo I want to show you." Opal gives a slight nod as Jane rummages through her handbag. She finds what she is looking for and hands it to her grandmother. "Did you paint this?" she asks hopefully.

Opal adjusts her glasses to look at the photograph. In it is the seascape signed "Opal," depicting Jane's precious landscape being tossed into the ocean waves.

"Why, yes!" she exclaims. "How on earth did you find this? And how did you know I painted it?" Her grandmother's eyes twinkle merrily.

"It turned up at a gallery in Kansas City where I exhibit. The owner, familiar with my work, brought it to my attention."

"It looks like *your* work?" Opal asks, her smile growing wider.

"Actually, it looks like the genre I usually work in."

"You paint?" Opal asks with delight. "I should have known."

"I have to say, I'm a little taken back by your response. I've never had a family member look anything other than grieved about my calling as an artist."

"Your calling," Opal repeats, beaming. "Tell me about your work."

"Yes. Well. I mostly paint landscapes—"

Opal interrupts, unable to contain her obvious enthusiasm. "Of your home? I mean, of the seashore where you live?

"No, oddly. I mostly paint the Great Plains. In my mind, of course, I've never—" Jane stops short there, not knowing how to proceed.

"You paint your visions," Opal clarifies for her. She looks to Jane with one eyebrow cocked knowingly.

"Yes! How do you know that?"

"Because, I have them myself," Opal tells her.

First, Kansas. Then painting. Now the visions themselves. Jane has never been able to talk about these things before. Could her grandmother be intimating what Jane is hearing? That there has been a connection between her family and her visions all along?

"Yes. I have the visions, or experiences, too," says Opal. "And so did my mother, your great-grandmother, Edith."

"My great-grandmother's name was Edith! I don't know what to say. First, I've seen her work in my visions! Also, I've never known anyone who has experienced what I have, but then, I've never talked about it with another soul. Until now, that is."

"Because you've felt you couldn't," Opal suggests, but it's more of an affirmation.

Jane nods, relief flooding through her. "You don't know how freeing this feels, to talk about it with another human!"

"Oh, I think I do know." Her grandmother chuckles.

"This means I'm not losing my mind!"

"No, you are not," Opal continues, giggling. "But you have been wise in not sharing what you've seen." She grows serious. "Though my mother and I were able to discuss these experiences, I made the mistake of talking with your grandfather, Floyd, about them. Ultimately, my openness is what drove him away, and subsequently what caused a rift between El and me. She couldn't believe what I said was true. Just like her father, who accused me on his better days of lying, and on his worst, of insanity."

"Then, that means my mother never—"

Again, reading her thoughts, Opal finishes for her. "Never had them herself."

"But why? If you and Grandmother Edith had them, and I've had them, then why would that be the case?" Jane asks.

"I believe she must have rejected the idea. About the time she began to have them. Or, perhaps she was never visited in the first place. Perhaps her heart was never right for it."

"You mean, you think the visions are a choice."

"So much is."

"She would have been given the option on or around her twelfth birthday, I'm guessing, like it was for me."

Opal nods. "Exactly. For me as well. Anyway, it's the best theory I have for her attitude. Had she experienced what we have, she wouldn't have accused me of the deception she believed permitted a way for all the evil that seemed to follow us and ultimately drove her daddy away."

"If what you are saying is true, then she missed taking advantage of an opportunity." She pauses. "I am still sorting out what that looks like for me."

Her grandmother smiles wryly. "Me too." More silence settles as both women consider the implications of these words. Opal is the first to speak again. "Life is all about free will. You know what they say, that five percent is what you are dealt and ninety-five percent is how you respond to it."

"I believe that." Jane continues to reflect on this where her mother is concerned, finally gasping loudly again. "That's why she threw my painting into the sea!"

"She did *what?*" Opal exclaims.

"My painting went missing. I never got it back. It wasn't until this painting of yours crossed my path that I recognized my mother as the culprit."

"The painting within my painting was yours? I'm confused, but that is par for the course these days. Please explain."

"I had better start at the beginning." Jane tells her grandmother everything. She shares her childhood, the specific visions she began to have at twelve years of age, her sudden desire to paint, and her parents' response to her love for it. She includes the trouble with her sister, how she and Jess have never clicked. And she opens up about Jake—his devotion to her, his belief in her talent, his insistence she display it, and how all of it made a way for her to exhibit, which ultimately led her back to her grandmother. If she hadn't come across Opal's painting, she might not even be here. Until this moment, Jane hadn't fully understood the role Jake had played in her life. The roles others have played as well.

"First, I must tell you I am crushed your heart was hurt by Jake's passing. Do you know if he had faith?"

Jane grows quiet for a moment. "You mean in God?"

"Yes. Faith doesn't exist apart from Him. Everything in creation points back to the Creator. His song is the fabric of our existence, His color the life of our canvas."

"I don't know, Grandma."

"But you must know, given the sight you've been gifted with, that all humans on earth are given every chance to be so heaven bound, their spirit can be free while on earth to see beyond the veil."

"Wow!" That's perspective," Jane says.

Free. Heaven bound. See beyond.

Jake had never considered these things, as far as she had been aware. And he had not been as stubborn as she. But had she really been pursuing truth? Had she settled on expectations of Mac?

It really wasn't about The Land itself, then. It was about The Land as promise. And as illustration of so much more.

Opal stops for a moment to hold her gaze, returning her to the topic at hand.

"I must say your mother harbors more anger than I'd imagined. What it must have taken for her to do that," Opal muses. "To steal your painting to destroy it."

"Yeah. I don't know how she managed it, actually. But I guess it wouldn't have been impossible during rush hour. She could simply have walked in, taken it down off the wall, and walked out with it, without any of the customers thinking twice about it."

"I suppose that's true, if it was a busy place."

"Yes, it was generally packed in the morning. I assume it still is. Jake's parents sold it after his death. I was his beneficiary, so I am well provided for."

"I am glad to hear that," Opal responds.

"But answer me something. How is it you didn't recognize your own daughter when you painted the scene?" Jane instantly regrets the way this sounds.

"When I painted that particular vision, your mother was a child. At the time, I didn't recognize her as the adult she would later be. Even today, I'm not sure I would recognize her. I haven't laid eyes on Elise in decades."

"That makes sense," Jane says sadly.

"I merely painted what I saw, then put the painting up for sale. I needed the money. It was odd, you know, creating a painting within a painting, and especially one being tossed out to sea. It was a hit, though. The water was oddly magnificent in its turmoil, so it sold quickly, as if I was making some sort of social commentary. People really dig hidden satire. I made a hundred bucks on it, which was a small fortune in the 40s."

"Who did you sell it to?" Jane asks. "I mean, I'm just wondering how it ended up at The Downtown gallery in Kansas City.

"I have no idea," Opal answers. "Before I was hired on at the factory, I needed to put food on the table, so I would set up my easel in town to entice passersby to stop and consider my work. I don't have the slightest remembrance who I sold it to. I sold a bunch of my art in that period of my life."

"That's understandable," Jane says.

"What is hard to understand is how that painting found a way back to you," Opal says. "But then again, I already know how that happened." She chuckles.

"Yes, and now I understand why I am so drawn to Kansas." Jane stops to fully consider this for a moment.

"I have also had visions of the prairie. I've not been there in person since I was young."

"I believe it is our family's Promised Land, or something like that."

Opal considers this. "Why, I do believe you are right. But it's more than that. There is a Creator's allegory in it as a way to draw us closer to Him and to achieve our purpose here." She sighs. "Life is ours to make of it, our destiny a choice, and our wills don't always choose wisely."

"No. I suppose that is true. I wish sometimes we didn't have free choice. It would be so much easier if our God made the most important decisions for us for greatest benefit." Jane takes another breath and changes the subject. "I have something else to show you." She reaches down into her handbag on the floor again and fumbles around until she finds the other photograph lodged there.

Opal smiles. "Let me guess, it's another photo of a painting."

"Yes," Jane laughs, looking at the photo in her hand. "You are right. This one, however, is, well—"

"Just go on and show it to me, then," Opal says, giggling.

Jane hands the photo over to her grandmother and waits silently for her to take it in.

"It's a portrait of you," her grandmother says, clearly puzzled. "Did you paint this?"

Jane shakes her head. "No."

"It looks as though you're standing on our plains. And with lambs. Isn't that sweet? I am assuming this is the family land?"

"Maybe. Probably. But Grandma, this painting was done over a century ago. Not only did I not paint it, but I've no idea who did, or why. Knowing we aren't the only ones to see things, since you said you and your mother had these experiences in common, do you have any ideas?"

"I suppose your great-grandmother Edith could have painted it. It does look like it could be on the property, but again, who knows? I've never seen it before."

"I should tell you, the strangest thing is it is signed by 'Jane.' You can't see that in the photo, of course." Jane waits for her grandmother to process through this information.

Opal finally answers. "My great-grandmother's name was Nell. Nell Jane."

Jane gasps. "Her name was Nell Jane! I've had visions of a woman named Nell! That would make her my great-great-great grandmother! Could it be?"

"I haven't been in Kansas in a long while, but it seems as though it might be possible these puzzle pieces fit." She continues, "I have no idea if she painted." She pauses. "No, that isn't true," she exclaims. "I remember my mother saying she did paint but had given it up."

"If it is the same woman I've seen, she did. She definitely did!" exclaims Jane. "So again, I am thinking that property I've seen and felt so drawn to is, indeed, family land!"

"I'm sorry to say, if it is, the property was sold over twenty years ago."

"Then what would be the point? What would Mac be up to in showing me all of this?"

"Mac?"

"The guy who always shows up in my visions as tour guide," says Jane.

Opal laughs so hard, she causes herself a coughing fit. Jane hands her a glass of water from beside the bed. Opal takes a sip. It helps.

"What does this Mac of yours look like?" Jane describes him and this results in more laughter and more coughing. When she finally regains her composure, she says, "I call him Gladius. My mother called him The Knight."

"Because he wouldn't give up his real name, right?" Jane asks with exasperation.

Opal continues to giggle. "Exactly!"

"Well, when he shows up again, this Knight, or Gladius, or Mac has a lot of explaining to do!" Jane turns to look out the window across the ocean. "You hear that?" she yells out to the sky, where she knows there are plenty listening who will deliver her message to her messenger.

Forty-One

KANSAS CITY—1994

Jane is oddly hopeful when she returns home to find her answering machine flashing with a red-light message. It would be good to hear from Derrick, if only to tie up a few loose ends.

She drops her luggage, and tossing her keys on the counter, makes her way over to the wall-mounted phone above the counter on which the machine sits. She depresses the play button.

"First message, Wednesday, 9 am ..." the automated voice says, just before a long beep sounds. What follows is Derrick's smooth, masculine voice, causing her to heart skip a beat.

"Hey there, Jane. I got your message. I agree, it's time to talk. Give a call when you can. Mornings are a good time to reach me this week." He clicks off without leaving a parting goodbye, just like she often does. Interesting.

And oh, no! Today is Saturday. He'd left the message Wednesday. He'd surely think her indecisive, or worse, flighty again.

But before Jane continues this spiraled thinking, another long beep sounds and the automated voice continues, "Next message, Thursday, 6:26 pm ..."

Another long beep, followed by a woman's voice. "Now, I know you aren't home to receive this message, but I wanted to leave a reminder here and now for you to call me as soon as you get this message. And I do mean, as soon as you get this message. I am dying to hear what your grandmother said about the paintings!" Glenda, of course.

Jane looks at the clock. It's just after 4 p.m. Might as well phone Derrick now, even though he said mornings were best. Before unpacking, eating, relaxing. Returning Glenda's call. All of a sudden, this can't wait.

She picks up the phone and dials, her heart beating soundly in her chest. He answers on the third ring. "Hello?" Just the sound of his voice, melty like drawn butter, causes her to feel things she shouldn't.

"Hey, it's Jane," she manages to croak. "I'm sorry I missed your call. I was out of town. Just got back." She clears her throat nervously. "I know you said mornings were best, but I thought I'd take a chance in catching you—"

Well, that didn't come off like I'd wanted it to.

"No problem." He pauses before continuing. "How are you?"

"I'm good. And you?"

"Great. Thanks. So. Let's meet up, okay?" He certainly doesn't waste any time in getting down to business, but his tone is friendly and reassuring.

Jane exhales. "I don't want to keep you from anything—"

An assignment, a wife …

Jane swallows the knot in her throat.

"Nope. Nothing that can't wait," he says. "I know it's late notice, but how about tonight?"

No plans on a Saturday night?

"Uh, sure. Where would you like to meet?" Jane hopes her rickety voice doesn't give her away.

"That Italian place on The Plaza?"

"The Plaza it is, then, but give me a few minutes to get cleaned up."

"We can wait if you'd rather." And something about the way he says this makes Jane feel as though that is the last thing he'd want to do.

No.

"Actually, I don't think it can wait," says Jane, instantly regretting sounding too anxious.

Derrick overlooks her enthusiasm. "How does six sound?"

"Six sounds good," says Jane, hoping it really will be.

The couple is no sooner seated at their table, the exchange of pleasantries finished, when Jane decides to plunge right into the topic she has in mind.

"Derrick, I reached out to you to find out more about that portrait. The one that, uh, looks like me."

He looks good.

"I figured that was what this is all about." He resettles his napkin in his lap and leans forward, crossing his hands on the table. "What would you like to know?"

Wow. His lashes are so long. How does a man get lashes like that? It's so unfair.

"Everything you know about it." She doesn't give him a chance to answer before firing off the next question. She can't help herself. There are so many answers she no longer wants to wait for. "For starters, where did you get it?"

Stay focused, Jane.

She continues, hardly pausing for air, "Why was it in your house, I mean, what was it that appealed to you about that painting—of a woman who bears a strong resemblance to me? Is that why you asked me out? Because I looked like her?"

Wow. That sounds so narcissistic.

She knows she sounds fully self-absorbed, but at least she hasn't been rendered speechless like she'd imagined on the drive over here.

"Okay, so those are a lot of questions, for starters," he says smiling. "Let me begin by assuring you I am not a weirdo or anything. Not a stalker."

Jane smiles and takes a sip of her iced tea. He'd read her mind there.

How embarrassing.

At least she'd not asked him why he'd chosen to hang the troubling portrait in his bedroom. Thankfully, she'd stopped herself in time, and any migrating monarchs taken to flight within her vanish.

"It's really very simple. I loved the painting the minute I saw it. Obviously, that was long before I met you. There was something about the woman's eyes that drew me in, and if that makes you feel uncomfortable, please accept my sincerest apology. The quality in the painting is superb. It's quite a masterpiece."

Jane nods, encouraging him to continue.

"It might have seemed strange that it was hanging in my bedroom, but I didn't consider it *that* odd, though I'd begun to think differently by the time I so proudly showed it to you. Your reaction told me you thought otherwise, causing me to question my perspective. I could have smacked myself at that point, but suffice it to say I had an empty wall on which to hang a painting I thought very beautiful."

Jane feels herself blush, fully comprehending Derrick's double meaning. He smiles and stops to take a drink himself, creating a natural break for a response from Jane. But she can't bring herself to react, or to smile back, not just yet anyway. She'd already spilled her guts and was still mentally cleaning them up. Instead, she reaches for a piece of bread and dips it in the plate of oil and Italian spices.

Sensing she's waiting for more from him, he continues. "I purchased "Summertime" before the show opened because, well, I had stopped by the gallery after work the day before and fell headlong into it, if that makes sense.

It does. She has merely translated what is already there. Naturally, others will feel something in their souls, too.

"When I met you for the first time at The Downtown, I was attracted to you. You had to know that." Again, he lingers for a response, but Jane remains stoic. Undeterred, he presses on. "In fact, and maybe you'll think this part is weird—" He hesitates before continuing. "Though I didn't immediately connect you to the painting—that part happened later that evening when I returned home, and I noticed the uncanny resemblance —I did feel as though I already knew you, but I don't think it was because of the painting." He looks for her eyes, finally meeting them. She allows him to hold her there a moment before breaking away.

"Does that make sense?"

Jane nods in agreement.

"We had an unusual connection," Derrick insists. "Please tell me that was true. Tell me I wasn't delusional." He looks at her with such intensity, Jane suddenly feels hot. She unconsciously places a hand against her cheek as if to cool it.

His eyes, oh, his eyes.

They aren't just brown—they've flakes of gold dust in them, like gleaming particles caught up in a stream, shifted and panned for exposure.

So, this is how it feels to fall in love at first sight—or instantly, anyway.

Love? Stop it, Jane!

Jane can't deny Derrick's perspective. She feels something now, had felt something before, too. But she had been deeply attached to Jake when Derrick and she had dated—the degree to which she'd been consciously unaware of at the time.

That was it. Wasn't it?

Was Jake what had prevented her from moving forward with Derrick?

No, she'd freely enjoyed her time with Derrick. So much so that she'd fantasized moving to Kansas City, something she'd ultimately done anyway. Derrick had felt right. Exciting. At first.

Why then, had she allowed discomfort in seeing the portrait to cloud her judgment in the moment? Had it propelled her, wrongly, into the arms of Jake? Or had something else been in play here?

Could I have been wrestling a force in the unseen?

She would never regret loving Jake. Their friendship and subsequent relationship were truly the best things that had happened to her—to them both—despite the pain and heartache it had ultimately cost Jane. No matter the price, she wouldn't have missed the dance, as Garth Brook's song attested to. It was good. In the end, it had to be.

But now, far enough removed from what could have been, Jane must concede there had been something missing there. She'd known it from the beginning. Jake had been comfortable but never exciting. And they'd never deeply connected as she'd hoped they would.

Of course, she'd recognized the bond with Derrick at the time. On a subconscious level, anyway, she now realizes. But the knowledge was there, on the periphery, ready for exposure. She'd pushed it back. Because in the moment, it hadn't thrilled.

It had terrified.

Looking back, and in light of the way she is now feeling, she'd been foolish. What *was* her problem? What had startled her so? The mystery of the portrait?

Or the powerful—something—here, with Derrick?

What is happening?

The present clarity is overwhelming. A warm feeling wells up in her chest and begins to spread.

The safety. It's always been here. Here is where she felt led. Could this have been what Mac's clues were all about?

Jake would want her to move on.

Don't rush things!

"I can't deny it," she finally admits, thinking she's already said too much too fast. "I felt it too." Suddenly another thought occurs to her.

Why is he admitting this now? Oh, right, the painting.

"Where did you get the painting, Derrick?" she persists, remembering her mission.

His grin widens. "That's the strangest part," he says. "My parents found it in the basement of their house."

Jane nearly drops her glass. "Your parents found it in their *house?*" she repeats, thoughtfully. "How did it get there?"

"My understanding is the previous owners left it. It dates back to before you were born. Glenda told me it's at least a hundred years old. It's probably worth a bit of money, now."

Jane holds her tongue still, but at last, finally, holds his eyes.

He doesn't look away.

"Then why did you get rid of it?" she asks, smiling in an effort to lighten things up a bit.

"Well." He stops.

"Well?" she persists.

"Well, I hoped it would bring you back in touch with me."

Jane is speechless.

"I know—it's crazy. But it worked, didn't it?

"I will have to get back to you on that," she says, giggling.

"Oh, you will, will you?" he says, chuckling too. "They say everyone has a look-alike or doppelgänger. What a coincidence a painting found in my childhood home looks an awful lot like you. It seems weird. Definitely weird. I don't know how to explain it, but it's true."

Maybe he hasn't noticed any similarity in the way the woman was dressed and the way I was on our first date.

"Oh-kay," Jane says, not knowing what to say next. She needs to think this thing through.

"Even weirder, though, is that you appeared in a white dress when we first had dinner together, do you remember?"

Wonderful. He noticed. Why do all the men in my life have to take such notice? That can't be normal.

"Yes, I do recall that," Jane admits. "That is—" she begins, shaking her head, "so weird." She wonders what is going on in that mind of his. He couldn't possibly be processing through the information the way she is. She doesn't even know what to think herself, but she plans to take the matter to God. Finally. Mac, too. The first chance he gives her.

"So, you see, Jane, I felt it was, well, some sort of cosmic coincidence, or a divine arrangement."

"I can see why you would think that.". Could his parents' house have belonged to her great-great-great grandmother, Nell Jane? No. Nell died just after the log cabin had been built on The Land. One of her other ancestors? Could there be a family tie?

Oh, God, please no! I can't be falling in love with a relative!

Wait a minute. Derrick was adopted.

Falling in love!

"There are no others, that I am aware of, but I believe one of those can be ruled out."

"Oh really? Which one?" Jane laughs nervously.

"The coincidence option," Derrick responds gently, in a way that causes Jane's heart to skip a beat.

She agrees. This—whatever this is— is no coincidence.

"At the risk of scaring you off, I think God brought us together through that painting." His tone is firm but gentle at once, and there is something so pure and honest about his way, Jane relaxes into what she knows must be truth. "I'm thinking God allowed me to acquire this painting to make a point."

God.

"What would that be?" Jane asks.

"You."

Or God allowed a painting of me to be painted a century ago, and somehow it fell into your parents' possession.

So I could meet you?

It's crazy! He undoubtedly already thinks her unstable. Best not introduce other issues just yet. And yet, he seems really into her.

And he has a point.

"I can see why you would think that," she says softly. It's all she can come up with. Then a wildly inappropriate idea occurs to her. Derrick may think it odd, but she voices it out loud anyway. "I would like to visit with your parents, if that is okay. I mean, if your—uh—" She stops, realizing how awkward she sounds.

"I think that would be fine," he says evenly. He doesn't hesitate or ask her why.

That's a surprise.

"You don't have a—anyone in your life that might object to this?" That sounds atrocious, and she knows it.

Good grief.

Of course he doesn't. He wouldn't have said what he just did if that were true. Would he?

"No. I don't have a girlfriend. Or a wife, for that matter. If that's what you mean," he thinks to add. "Not yet." He grins.

Well, this conversation accelerated in a hurry. How did they cover this ground already?

Oh, right, it was my doing.

And then, in the interests of full disclosure, Jane tells him about Jake. "I did. I mean, I had a fiancé. He passed away two years ago in a car accident."

Derrick's face clouds over immediately. "Just like my mom," he says pensively.

"Yeah."

"I am so sorry to hear that." She's wondering if he's doing the math, assessing out how he figured into the timeline.

She helps him out. "I knew him before I met you. He was my friend, my best friend, actually."

"I recall you mentioned him."

"Yes. Well." She hopes Derrick doesn't think she was the one playing him when they dated then. She rushes to explain. "At the time you and I were seeing each other, I was still thinking Jake was just a friend, but after I returned home from Kansas City the first time—" she hesitates.

"You realized he was more," Derrick finishes for her.

He's certainly intuitive.

"I really scared you off, didn't I?" he laughs.

How does he do that?

"How did you—Yes, you scared me!" She relaxes, laughing too. "And no, that's not all true. I scared myself, too," she says with a lightness in her voice she's not felt in a long while.

"Tell me about Jake, or is he off-limits since he was to be your family? As I recall, discussions about family weren't doable," he teases her, but his tone is soft and concerned. Safe. That word again comes to mind.

Smiling, Jane tells him all about the man she lost. In doing so, she begins to shed some of the weight on her shoulders, only now realizing what a burden it has been to hold everything in so long. She talks about Jake's belief in her, the contrast of this perspective to that of her parents, and about how he taught her to look at the world differently. How Mac taught her the same on a completely different level was a tale for another day.

"I—well, I'm just so sorry. And I'd like to see you. To pick up where we left off, if you're comfortable with that." He definitely isn't wasting any time, but his directness is refreshing. "After all, your current living arrangements make this seem a perfect coincidence," he says with a wink. She considers this only briefly before answering.

"Yes. I think I am comfortable with that. But tell me, you've certainly not been single all this time, am I right?"

Ugh. I didn't mean to be that direct myself!

He laughs good-naturedly. "Honestly, I was going to chase after you years ago when you raced out of here, but then I figured if it was meant to be, you'd come back. And you did."

She allows that to sink in. "You must have been pretty confident I would reach out to you again."

"I guess I was, although you made me wait so long, I was getting pretty nervous. Thus, my willingness to part with a priceless painting." He laughs.

"You didn't answer my question," she insists playfully.

"Yes. I dated. But I held everyone up to you, which wasn't fair to anyone. I couldn't get over you." Concerned that might sound slightly intense considering what little time they had actually spent together, he adds, "I mean, you made quite an impression in the short time you were here."

"The portrait and I did, anyway."

A shadow passes over his face until he sees Jane is only teasing him. "We can definitely take things slow," he assures her. "So, let's go meet my parents."

They both giggle together. Meeting parents is definitely not taking things slow.

Chapter

Forty-Two

KANSAS CITY AREA—*1994*

Jane's mind paces like a caged animal, slamming around inside her skull as if in prison. An escape to sleep will be difficult this night.

"God," she pleads, "if you are with me, help me settle down." But her brain only works in overdrive, accelerating beyond rest. As she sorts through years of accumulated disappointment and sorrow, what she's allowed to build up like bacteria formed to plaque around her heart, she realizes so many circumstances have been the direct result of choices.

She's been shown more than most, and—

To whom much is given, much is required.

Yes.

Well.

This is true, undoubtedly, but feelings often triumph over understanding. Despite knowing God exists, he still seems a million miles away most days, somewhere in the Great Beyond.

She's fully aware she has been given more than most in terms of spiritual sight, but what exactly is she supposed to do with it?

Real life is still real. There is still so much loneliness and devastating disappointment, even with knowing there is a Someone who is good and cares enough to show her a perspective outside of her own. Someone to fill the void.

But what is the point? Why does there have to exist such a wide hole to fill in the first place? It seems an exercise in futility, or a sick game. If there is such good in existence, why suffer the bad?

Could it be so the greatest amount of good can be known now, in this time?

Maybe she should dare to let her defenses down and believe good will triumph. And suddenly she realizes the good she wants is Derrick.

The feelings she has for him are suddenly more than she's ever known and certainly more than she's ever imagined or hoped for.

Derrick is a stranger. But one she feels she's always known. Everything about him is dependable, comfortable, and easy. He is another one who takes in every detail about the world around him. What's more, he explores what he knows within the framework of faith to see beyond the material, as well. He is fantastic!

Jane's future is written all over his face.

If not the portrait.

In it, there is a connection yet to be revealed. There has to be.

It isn't Derrick's fault the portrait looks like Jane, or even that it came to be in his possession.

It's as if this were the way it was supposed to be.

But she had run from it. And him.

She throws herself onto her opposite side and fluffs a pillow, curling herself around it. She rubs her eyes, which are jumpy under the lids, too. Concentrating on breathing deeply, and just as she finally feels merciful sleep approach, she hears a noise behind her. Long past being easily startled, she rolls over to find three figures standing beside her bed. She would have screamed were it not for seeing Mac. For the first time, he's brought others with him. A man and a woman. With crowns on. She sits up, the desire to find sleep forgotten.

How weird are things going to continue to get?

A radiant light surrounds the trio with stunning illumination. The woman has ruby red lips and purple irises emphasized by translucent skin. Her glossy brown hair, falling in cascades from under a golden tiara, seems made of light. She's definitely not earthbound. Dressed in a long, silky gown of rich hues resembling watery inkblots of many colors, she exemplifies magnificence. Jane can't take her eyes off her stunning beauty.

The dark skin of the man beside her glows, too, though it's nearly the color of onyx, and like Mac, he has hair that seems made of snow. Only his is curly and closely cropped. His eyes are also white—so white, they seem to glow. He's dressed in what appears to be a coat of malleable mail. It looks like metal but appears breathable and lightweight, as if it could be painted on. His armor includes a breastplate, pants, and belt. He too wears a golden coronet atop his head. It's quite the ensemble.

"Who are you?" Jane asks incredulously.

The woman smiles radiantly, her white teeth matching her companion's eyes, but she says nothing. Mac says nothing.

The dark man is the first to speak. "I am Salazar, and this is Gia," he says in a deep, baritone voice, turning to the woman beside him. "I am your primary guardian, and this is my assistant. It is our great pleasure to introduce ourselves to you formally." Mac beams proudly, as if a proud parent.

"It's—nice to meet you," Jane responds tentatively. She turns to Mac. "I guess—well, I thought—" She has trouble finding the words. "Aren't you my guardian, Mac?" she finally manages to ask. Then turning to Salazar, she thinks to add, "Not that I'm not appreciative of you."

"I am a member of the Malakim," Mac replies humbly. "Though I protect when I can, I am not assigned as one of your guardians."

"Who are the Malakim?" asks Jane, bewildered, as if anything could bewilder her at this point. Mac has never been forthcoming, so why is he encouraging the release of information now? She doesn't wait for a response before proceeding with the next question that comes to mind. "If you aren't my guardian, who are you, exactly? Will there ever be a time you can start at the beginning?"

"Which question would you like me to answer first?"

"All of them!" she exclaims. Perhaps he is finally prepared to answer her queries.

"Your first question concerns the group I belong to, the Malakim." Mac opens his mouth to continue but Jane interrupts impatiently again.

"A group, like a membership?"

"Hardly. A membership implies the joining of a group voluntarily, not something you were created for." Mac is always so pragmatic.

"This is a group you didn't join voluntarily?" Jane asks.

"The Malakim is a group I was created for and appointed to. Similarly, you were created human, appointed to belong to a group of living souls made in the image of the Creator."

"You aren't human?" Jane asks incredulously. "You certainly look human." Sort of. Mac is too beautiful to be human.

"No. I'm not human. But of all the Angelos—to use the Greek word—Malakim, or messengers, are the most like humans."

Jane processes this before asking her next question. "So, the Malakim are also Angelos?"

"Yes. Malakim means messengers. It comes from the Hebrew word, Mal'akh, which the Greeks later called Angelos."

"Angels," Jane whispers. "I should have known. I guess I did—"

"You did. You've always known. You were chosen to know."

Jane looks over to see the guardians now beaming. They possess an unusual, joy-filled peace that makes her feel unanswered questions aren't the end of the world. Contentment is found in trusting revelation from a God of mystery as he sees fit. He knows what we need in the eternal present.

Where did that thought come from?

"They've been with you from the beginning," Mac continues, "and there are others."

"Others—" Jane murmurs, looking at the two guardians before her, who gaze upon her so lovingly, it brings tears to her eyes. She's no sooner said this when a vision within the current experience whisks her away to an observation of herself, years ago. When she'd been accosted by Pete in high school and wondered where everyone had disappeared to, there had been others with her. Salazar and Gia stood ready to act with arms spread wide. As she watches, dark shadows grow long and tall, appearing to rise from within and around Pete. They form human-like figures, who begin to poke him and shout at him, spurring him into action. Jane is unable to discern what they are saying, but sees Pete become angry.

Suddenly, a giant creature steps down from the heavens, his feet thunderous as he lands. His landing seems to rattle the planet, while bolts of lightning emanating from his movement threaten to crack the sky in half. The nearly forty-foot-tall creature has a head which looks like that of a koala, but his face resembles an eagle. His wings span the length of a jet.

The shadows flee. Jane hears screeching sounds as they depart. She watches Pete retreat.

Next, Jane sees herself with her unseen guardians at various locations throughout the years. She watches Salazar and Gia intercede at the gas station on the occasion Pete and his goon pulled up next to her to antagonize, and as she watches the bald man in the suit walk back to the pump next to hers, she spots wings on his back she hadn't noticed before! No wonder he'd smiled at her in a way that had left a lasting impression. Even the officer who had been so kind to her at the hospital following Jake's accident had been affected by their presence. Jane sees a guardian next to him whispering in his ear.

Often, her guardians acted alone to provide assistance; sometimes others of varying heights and features stepped in. One time a man with long black hair and almond eyes joined the two. On another occasion a woman who bore a striking resemblance to Jane, and far from plain, stepped in. And as Jane glances again at the guardian standing closest to her now, she sees the greatest resemblance to herself is found in Gia! And oh, is she … gorgeous!

At no time had Jane been aware. Few times had she even noticed the danger around her, and she'd been in many more significantly perilous situations than those Pete presented her. Many more.

The time she'd had a flat tire at midnight heading home from Lucy's apartment and a nearby gang had been thwarted from heading her way; the time a man had come into Oliver's intending to rob it at gunpoint but had changed his mind. Numerous scenes flash before her eyes. She'd been so unaware!

She'd been saved too many times to count.

There were the countless times her guardians and others worked on her behalf for good. Mac wasn't the only Angelo present in The Downtown gallery the night of her showing. And he surely wasn't the only one with her when Jake passed. Then others joined him, including one who was the most beautiful man she'd ever seen. He'd been full of a love for her she couldn't wrap her mind around as he held her hand.

It was his eyes she had met that day under the tree. He was the One all hosts took direction from. He was the Creator and King. The Son of God. Jane feels her knees begin to buckle.

Oh, my. How was I so blind?

"You have what you need to know," Salazar volunteers. "What exists behind the veil could be a little overwhelming to human eyes."

"It already is!" Jane exclaims. "But in a good way," she adds.

"Suffice it to say, not all Angelos look like us," Gia volunteers. "Some can appear quite fierce."

"But not the guardians or Malakim," Jane again states, considering the appearance of the trio before her.

"It's complicated," Gia says. "The hosts are intimidating, to say the least. They are supposed to be. They are warriors."

The velvety smoothness of Salazar's deep, baritone voice is comforting. "To summarize, you should know we serve the Lord of Hosts and are assigned to protect you specifically. No one else."

"Oh," Jane says, allowing this information to sink in.

"In fact, we were assigned to you the moment your mother conceived. It is our great pleasure to serve you, and it will continue to be as long as you live here."

Mac giggles as Salazar speaks.

Has the man, or Malakim, ever laughed like this before?

"So why are you telling me this now?" Jane asks. She glances to each Angelo in turn, her eyes finally resting on Mac.

"The Kingdom Age approaches, Jane. It's time you prepare for it," Mac says.

"When we first met, Mac," Jane says, turning to him, "you told me the earth would come to an end. You told me to persevere. Is this what you are talking about?" Jane's heart begins to accelerate.

"I said your world would end, and you would need to persevere. The planet was not what I was speaking of. You don't always understand what you hear." He grins. "Your world, on the other hand, is about to change radically. There are some spectacular times ahead."

"But what does that mean? And why me? I'm no one. Why not reveal all of this to a great leader, or to the world at large? Why must everything be so cloaked in secrecy?" But even as she questions these things, she realizes she is not the only one who had been given revelation. There were generations of women before her who had been given it, too. And there are undoubtedly others around the globe in the same position now. The Land, a portal of some kind, is her place of connection. Others would have their own, but she had been given her own symbolic Promised Land, a gift from the One who created it to reveal the majesty of heaven and to share a love beyond measure.

Jane remembers what Mac had said about the scriptures. All of the earth testifies. Even the rocks would cry out the truth of the glory of God if humanity failed to recognize its Creator.

Stand in the ways and see. Ask for the old paths, where the good way is, and walk in it. Jane hears the voice of God say.

There is only One Way.

Mac turns to her. "Jane, beloved, the day is coming when the planet will be more agreeable to truth." She nods. He continues, "And remember, you are anything but plain. You are God's created. A leader. And you are chosen. Not just to see what you've seen, but to do something with what has been given you. The time nears. What you paint is just the beginning of your destiny."

"But how will I know my destiny?" she asks.

Gia touches her arm gently. "You already know."

Do you want to follow me now? Another voice whispers gently beside her, in a way that causes her heart to thaw and warm, like land coming to life in the spring following a long winter. The sound of this beautiful expression vibrates in harmony with the love she witnessed in that man's eyes—the one she had seen by the tree, and she is swept away, soaring with a clarity she hasn't known until now.

"Oh, yes!" she says as she falls on her knees, knowing he is here with her now. Lead me every step of the way, Lord of Hosts. I give my heart to you."

I promise you are whole and safe with me.

Jane feels the difference already. Her heart overflows with the love that fills it to bursting. She feels his Spirit within her. It is a priceless gift.

My Spirit is within you now to guide you toward good choices and the empowerment to enforce them. You will feel my freedom as you are guided into further wonder.

So, this was it. What Mac has shown her, what the Spirit of God has revealed to her: the picture both within and outside of herself and alongside the limitations of society, a masterpiece much broader, and more colorful, than she'd ever dreamed.

She'd been color blind.

Maybe it was her own imaginative mind that had been limiting after all.

There exists a universe of color and harmony without end, accessed innately but enjoyed by choice.

Eternity is permitting one's senses to operate efficiently.

And it is available to all who choose it.

Chapter

Forty-Three

LEAVENWORTH, KANSAS—1994

When Derrick picks her up the following morning, Jane is still floating on the information she has received. The drive to his parents' house is lovely, the early morning light pale and gentle as it yawns across the plains. Tall, copper-colored tassels lean into it, a white fog settled comfortably in scattered patches as the sky gains blue. But all Jane can think about is what she learned last night.

We all have guardians with us. The hosts of heaven are under the command of Jesus. He is our Ultimate Guardian. Wow.

"You're awfully quiet this morning," Derrick observes. "Something on your mind?"

"No. Yes. There is just so much to take in," she says pensively.

"But you are okay?" he asks, concerned.

She turns to smile at him. "I'm wonderful," she says, and means it.

"I am glad to hear it. Oh, I hope it's okay with you, but I told my parents we would meet them at their usual Saturday morning coffee shop before heading out to the house." The look he gives her when he meets her eyes makes her feel she would go anywhere with him right now.

"Coffee sounds wonderful," Jane says, still smiling. Her heart sighs. She's completely at peace. Something has shifted within her to empower her to purpose.

What Mac had said is true. Jane feels brand new.

There is nothing now about Derrick that makes her feel uncomfortable or concerned, and she won't let forces that could be conspiring against her to change that. What resides inside her is much more powerful. It can't be coincidence that she is forming relationships with the Lord of Hosts and this man beside her at once.

"They have a long-standing date with a few friends at an old gathering place in town and weren't quite going to be wrapped up by the time we arrived," Derrick continues.

"Totally fine by me," Jane says dreamily.

The coffee shop turns out to be a quaint, timeworn steepled church, similar to the kind seen in old western flicks. A white, clapboard-like structure with double doors front and center; two large windows adorn each side of a set of railed stairs. A sign above the doors says "Welcome." Surrounded by lacy green trees, it's a charming, paintable picture.

Inside, as Jane's eyes begin to adjust to the difference in light, she is impressed to see quite a few people seated at long, wooden tables under a magnificent, vintage, wrought-iron candelabra which hangs from the center of the vaulted ceiling. The aesthetic is lovely, especially with the earthy scents of coffee and bakery items floating through the air.

A group of people talking in a corner breaks up as a couple detaches themselves to make a straight approach for Derrick and Jane, wide smiles leading the way. As they get closer, Jane recognizes them.

They're older, but there is no mistaking who they are. These are the people she saw at The House! These people bought her house on The Land!

How crazy is this?

Derrick's parents. Of course. It's wild she had not recognized Doug as a younger man, when he and his wife had purchased the property. She hadn't put two and two together at the gallery, either.

"Wow!" Jane exclaims softly, but it's audible enough to cause Derrick to cast a look of puzzlement her way. He steps forward to hug his mother and then to embrace his father with a slap on the back. Turning, he makes the introductions. "Doug and Karen, I'd like you to meet Jane. Jane, these are my parents, Doug and Karen."

Jane is so momentarily stunned, she's unable to do anything but awkwardly stare. Mercifully, she quickly recovers, attempting to mask her strange reaction. "It's so nice to meet you," she says genuinely as she too steps in to hug Karen. Turning to Doug, she says, "It's so nice to see you again, Doug."

"Please, call me Duke. Everyone else does," he says laughing.

And then Jane catches her breath as she realizes recognition isn't as one-sided as she'd believed. The way Karen is looking at her is unmistakable.

Karen recognizes her, too.

Of course. They'd found the now-infamous portrait in their home!

Calm down, Jane.

Thinking back to the opening at The Downtown, perhaps any unusual reaction on Duke's part had been clouded by her own excitement over all that had been going on at the time.

"Would you like some coffee?" Karen asks.

Derrick looks to Jane, motioning her ahead of himself to the barista at the counter. "That sounds wonderful," she says.

As Derrick's parents take seats at one of the tables, Jane wonders how she will be able to sit still. Her mind feels electrified with thoughts of Derrick's family, The Land, and The House. She feels tingly from head to toe.

But just then a peace like she has never known before wraps around her. The Spirit of God is here!

I can feel Him!

Jane relaxes, taking it all in, feeling the contagion of being in His presence with these people. It's absolutely wild! Concerns about anything else fade to a backdrop for the thrill over what will undoubtedly come next.

The drive to Derrick's parents' house is only about fifteen minutes away, he tells her as they leave. "We'll pass the turnoff for my place on the way out."

"Oh, do you live close to them?" Jane pulls her eyes from staring out the window to look over to him. Her heart is beating wildly in her chest.

He meets her gaze lovingly. "Yes. I'm about halfway between their property and the church."

"You are so unusual," she states.

"How so?" he asks, happily frowning.

"Most people want to get as far away from their parents as possible."

"You do, anyway," he says teasing her.

"I suppose not everyone feels the way I do," Jane admits.

"You might give them a chance," he offers, before stopping himself. "I'm sorry. That was presumptuous of me."

Jane sighs aloud. "It's okay. I understand where you're coming from, but I've not been blessed with the parents you have."

"I get that." Derrick keeps his eyes on the road.

"And at times, I wish I was an only child, like you."

"I get that, too," Derrick says, trying to be supportive.

"I don't really mean that, of course." Changing the subject, she says, "I'd love to see more of Leavenworth one of these days. It's charming." She looks out the window to catch old, brick buildings and vintage facades, antique storefronts and paned window displays, all weathered and sweetly pleasing.

"It has a lot of history," he says proudly.

Jane smiles. "I love history, though I've not dedicated much time to understanding it, which is weird, growing up on the East Coast where there is so much of it—you know, with it being the birthplace of our nation. Perhaps now that I'm here in Kansas, I'll make the time." Experiences she still can't share with anybody fuel this desire.

"Sounds like a good idea. I dig it, too. Maybe we can explore a little together. We've got some great museums here. Not like what you find in the East, but still good."

"I love that you're interested in the past!" Jane exclaims. "Most people can't be bothered with it these days; they're so forward focused. But you can't be fully committed to the present or the future if you don't have an understanding of the past. It's what's brought you to this moment," she adds happily.

"Exactly. When you don't know the past, you're doomed to repeat its mistakes."

It isn't long before Derrick is turning onto another gravel road, and once the tires hit rock, Jane is overcome with more electricity. She'd been feeling a little déjà vu, but now the feeling is uncanny. Everything around her feels so familiar.

Acres and acres of wide-open space covered in long grasses; stalk and stem in a variety of neutral tones are offset by the occasional clump of green trees and low blades, despite the descent of winter.

Down a hill and up to the other side, around a small grove and past a creek, and then it comes into view.

Derrick's parents' house is The House.

THE HOUSE is Derrick's childhood home. *Derrick's* childhood home!

She should have known. She dared not hope.

She suspected. Albeit only recently. The knowledge had been deep inside her.

Her Promised Land is real, more than just allegorical.

Jane thinks she has never seen anything more beautiful in all her life. There it sits atop the rise, the white house in all its glory. The sun casts its light from directly above the gabled roof.

There are the red chimney stacks on either end, the red door in the center. The paned windows in white, the gabled one with the cross in the center.

It is just like she's always seen it. Exactly.

It's been here all along. It's real.

As Derrick parks, Jane stares, her mouth agape. She'd known this.

Hadn't she known?

He gets out of the truck and comes around to open her door, but her body feels turned to stone, immobilized in place, her heart the only acceleration as she takes it all in.

The pasture is dotted with puffs of white as lambs nibble what's left of the season's offerings with their heads down. Goats in colors of black and brown butt heads as they play, jumping off a hay mound and then prancing to the top again. From somewhere nearby, a rooster crows. Beyond the magnificent oaks that stand as bookends beside the home is a quaint, red barn.

And there, beyond the structure, a giant tree comes into view. The last of its resilient bronze leaves cling to a wide canopy of branches. The Tree. It completes a postcard-worthy picture.

She struggles to regain composure lest he recognize her bewilderment. Derick can't know, not just yet, anyway. And really, where to start? She wiggles her toes, willing her legs back to life, hoping the rest of her limbs will be restored to follow suit. The length of her is covered in chill bumps.

She looks down to the gravel, placing one foot on the ground and then the other. This is really happening. After years of seeing this land, this home, experiencing it in and out of time, she is finally here.

Fully present.

How many seconds pass before she is able to stand, she doesn't know, but she manages somehow, and before long, she is walking with Derrick. She's only mildly aware he has taken her hand in his.

How did any of this happen? Was it all a dream?

As they walk toward the door and up the wide stairs that run the length of the home and porch, she doesn't know where to look. Down at her feet? At each board and nail, along each window frame, each warbled pane of glass? Or out across the land, to the trees, the grasses, the sky? What unseen things might she view with the proper lens?

No wonder that portrait had been found here. A painter from the past had seen me here. Just as I'd seen that painter.

But how had it gotten here when the painting predated even this home?

Like so many other mysteries, that will surely be revealed, too. If it is supposed to be.

There had always been a connection.

"Thanks, Mac," she whispers under her breath.

You've brought me home.

But as soon as she has this thought, a voice within her corrects.

No. It's my Spirit that drew you here.

Chapter

Forty-Four

LEAVENWORTH, KANSAS—1994

Thrill rushes Jane's body as she steps up to the porch. A sign in black iron above the front door reads, 2012 Running Feet Way.

Running Feet! Wasn't that the name of the native girl who had found refuge by The Tree? How on earth had she been memorialized this way?

And the number 12? C'mon!

Jane tries not to gawk as she makes her way into The House. How many times had she been here in her visions? So many times, she couldn't possibly count them, and yet she'd painted only one complete rendering of it. She'd only been inside once, experientially.

It was as if once was enough, as if to recreate what had been known from afar had been waiting for this moment in the present when all things lost would be restored, and the future would be full of such painting.

It's exactly as she's known it.

And suddenly, this knowledge, like a missing puzzle piece, assuages even the hurt of her mother's betrayal in destruction.

Her mother had rejected her destiny.

Elise's anger had kept her from her own life-changing experiences. This could also be true for her sister, though Jane realizes there is much she will never fully understand. However, what isn't a mystery is Jane's call to action. To begin with, she vows she will do everything in her power to prevent future generations from missing their callings, whether here or elsewhere, for what could it be but a curse in the shadows that would rob someone of her identity?

Jane vows to break off any curses. She still doesn't know what her own destiny is, but she knows, finally, who she is. She is most definitely, most assuredly, not plain. She is seen and valued and has a purpose. And she belongs. To the God of the universe and to a family. Beyond that, she is beginning to get a better picture. And it dawns on her, this is a gift she shares in common with Derrick.

"We are so happy you are here," says a faraway voice. Karen's.

"It's so good to be here," Jane replies, pulling herself together.

If these people only knew how good.

"Brunch is almost ready. I prepared everything earlier, so we'll eat here in a moment. In the meantime, may I get you something to drink?" Karen says kindly.

"Water would be great," Jane answers.

"For me, too," Derrick says. "I'll get it. Make yourself comfortable; I'll be right back." He strides quickly into the kitchen.

"You must excuse me. I need to get the food on the table." Karen smooths an apron she now wears over her dress before following her son.

"May I help you?" Jane offers.

"Not at all! I'll only be a minute," she says, leaving Jane to make small talk with Duke.

Where to begin?

"Please have a seat," he says, gesturing to a number of options in the living room. "Derrick tells us you live in the Kansas City area now. How do you like it?" He lowers himself into a big leather wing chair opposite the sofa. Jane settles herself on the sofa. She glances around the room briefly, taking in the décor. It's clear the same interior designer was at work here as was at Derrick's place.

Derrick is fast on his return with two glasses of ice water, handing one to Jane before sitting next to her. "Thank you," she says. She turns to Duke, who is waiting patiently for an answer. "I love it. The shore is beautiful, of course, but the plains speak to my heart."

Duke laughs. "That's obvious, from the beautiful work you do."

Jane blushes. "I suppose that's true. And thank you." She takes a sip of water.

"Really," Duke continues, "your work is magnificent. As Derrick has undoubtedly shared with you, I have a keen interest in art. Have for years. Can't do it myself, so I appreciate those who can."

Jane chuckles. "I recall you said that! And, I get it. I enjoy seeing others do things I can't."

Duke smiles warmly. "I guess that's what your paintings do for people who don't know how to re-create what you do."

"Well, I appreciate your kind words."

"Duke has quite a collection here," Derrick volunteers. "As you know, he's the one who found out about your show at the gallery. He and Ed were pretty excited about attending and convinced me to join them."

"I see," Jane says.

"He didn't have to twist my arm," he adds quickly, with another one of those long-lashed looks that makes Jane heart beat faster.

"I noticed your street address on the way in the door," she says, hardly able to contain herself a second more. "Running Feet is an unusual street name."

"Interesting you noticed that!" Derrick says, suddenly excited.

"Boy, is that a story," adds Duke.

"How so?" Jane says, casually.

If they only knew.

"I'll let you tell her, son," Duke says, looking to Derrick.

"As near as I can figure it, Running Feet is the name of my great, great, great, great grandmother."

"What?" Jane gasps. "I thought you didn't know much about your ancestry!" Goose bumps crawl up her arms.

"When we first talked, I didn't. But then an article about Running Feet and her descendants turned up, linking me to them through the name Copeland."

Jane is stunned silent. Derrick continues. "She was a native American who lived here last century. Her family was decimated by a band of Comanche warriors, and she was left orphaned, eventually finding her way to refuge on the Shawnee Mission Indian reservation in Kansas. She gave herself the name Ruth Copeland and became quite the figure of perseverance, gaining notoriety among settlers. That's how I was able to connect the dots."

Jane remains speechless as she works through this latest piece of information, managing only a mechanical nod. She'd have more dots to offer him at some point, she realizes. Images of the young Native American girl flood her mind and heart, filling her to capacity with the love of their Creator.

It is only now she finds the words to speak of the painting above a large, stone fireplace. She should have known Duke and Karen would have one, too. On second glance, however, is it one of hers? It certainly looks like one of hers.

"The connections are unbelievable!" Duke laughs, but Jane is no longer listening. She is now so engrossed in the artwork above the mantle, she realizes she must confess her distraction. There is too much to process here, really.

"Is that one of my paintings?" she laughs nervously. "I mean, you'd think I'd know, but—it looks so much like one of my landscapes, and yet, it's—different."

Duke stands up walks toward the painting, motioning for her to join him. "Come take a look," he says.

Derrick stands with Jane, and together they move to join Duke at the fireplace. Upon closer inspection, she can see the landscape is not hers, but it is very similar to her style. She inspects it closely as the others wait.

The scene is exactly like one she would have chosen to paint! More monochromatic than most of her work, this one includes The Tree on the prairie in early winter, its silver branches highlighted by tones of blue and gray. The obvious cold is offset by a sun shining like a brilliant torch in the west. Light emanates from the orb in four distinct, linear directions, causing it to look like the Star of Bethlehem in the sky. It seems to indicate hope for brighter days.

There is no way two paintings done by different artists at different times, apart from one another, could be so alike.

But if I didn't paint this, who did?
And it highlights The Tree!

As if reading her thoughts, Duke offers, "It's signed. Look here, 'Edith Bell'."

Chills continue to rush Jane all over, confirming what she suspected. Dare she admit this? It's all too—overwhelming. But how can she not confess? She'll have to be cautious. She doesn't want to reveal all of the truth just yet. It's more than any of them could process now. It's more than she can process! Furthermore, too many questions remain unanswered. "Edith Bell was my great-grandmother, I believe," she says quietly.

The woman I witnessed painting just after World War 2 broke out!

Duke laughs aloud. "You and your grandmother have an uncannily similar talent."

"We purchased this home from her estate," says Karen gently, who is now standing behind her.

"This is exciting!" Derrick exclaims, waiting for Jane's response to say more. He doesn't seem surprised.

Jane looks at him quizzically. "How did you know?"

Derrick speaks before Karen or Doug can. "I mean, I suspected there was a connection, what with the similar styles between this painting and yours, and the painting of one of your ancestors who looks just like you!"

Yes. Just like me.

"I really don't know what to say," Jane says. She takes a deep breath. "I believe there is, indeed, something going on here. I had no idea my great-grandmother painted, until recently. Until recently, I didn't know my ancestors had property in Kansas." At least that much is true. It isn't as if Jane is intentionally withholding pertinent information.

"This painting has been dated to the early twentieth century," Duke adds.

"She must have done it in her old age," says Karen. Jane nods. "This property was in the family for many generations. It was to our benefit they were willing to part with it, but their loss seems wretched."

"Who was it that no longer wanted it?" Jane asks, heartbroken.

"The kids and grandkids, to our understanding," Karen says sadly.

"Hmm. My great aunts and uncles. I wonder if any are still around."

"I don't know," Karen replies. "We've been here over twenty years. No one in the family has ever contacted us."

"It's amazing that portrait looks so much like you. I'll need to remove it from consignment with the gallery," Derrick says with a wink.

"You know, we found it in the basement with the one hanging here," Karen finally says. "That one is dated to the mid-1800s."

"Actually, I think that one was painted by my great-great-great grandmother," says Jane.

Of me.

"Jane, how could it be that the woman in the painting looks so much like you?" Derrick asks, but she detects a mischievousness in his eyes.

Jane shakes her head. "I honestly don't know. But I recently learned my great-great-great grandmother Nell Jane may have signed her work with her middle name."

"I would have a difficult time following, were it not for ..." Duke says.

Derrick cuts him off. "How strange is it that these paintings done by your family ended up in my family home, which must really be your family home. And that we met up independent of knowing the truth."

"Sort of. The paintings brought us together," she answers slowly, not knowing where to start or how to put her thoughts into words. "I think," Jane begins. She pauses. "I think you were right, Derrick. About us meeting. We were supposed to." Perhaps this is too much, too soon in front of Duke and Karen, despite their encouragement, but by the looks on their faces, they already believe it themselves. Derrick must have discussed his own perspective with them already.

"And I have to admit something else. You may think me crazy, but, well—" She shrugs and sighs. Might as well tell them. What does she have to lose? This is already so unusual. "I've been having visions of this home, and of this land, for a decade. I don't know how to explain it. I don't know how or why. I also don't know how or why I am here now." She swallows. "I just know I am supposed to be."

Derrick places his hand on her shoulder tenderly. "We don't think you crazy, Jane. We've been having visions, too." He pauses. "I mean, to clarify, I've only started having them recently. Karen has been having them ever since she moved into this house."

Karen nods in agreement. "I had a vision of the portrait that looks like you. Not of the painter who created it, but of it being found in a local thrift store years ago. That's all I saw. I assume that is how it was returned back here to this family—to your great-grandmother, Edith. She must have found it and retrieved it, though heaven only knows how it got there in the first place."

"It's a mystery, for sure," Derrick declares in a way that makes Jane wonder if he knows more than he's letting on.

"It's supernatural, is what it is," Duke says, softly.

Seeing tears collect in the corners of Jane's eyes, Karen scurries out of the room. She returns quickly with a tissue which she hands to Jane. "I have something else to show you," she says. She then motions Jane over to a cabinet which holds an assortment of porcelain and fine china plates, saucers, and cups, all of them covered in pink roses.

"That tea set!" Jane exclaims as the group waits for an explanation. "My mother has the same one! Or she did. *I* now have the set, or one very similar to it." She wonders how her mother had been drawn to the old set she'd purchased years ago. If Elise had been estranged from her grandparents, she wouldn't have known about this one. Some things are really no more than coincidence, after all. But the collection had captured Jane's attention, too, and here is a matching set. On The Land.

Karen slides the top drawer out to remove what appears to be an old, leather Bible. She opens the front cover and turns a couple of pages until she finds what she is looking for. Then, she looks up at Jane. "I don't know how this has happened, exactly, but I believe God has brought you home."

Jane is speechless.

"When we moved into this home over twenty years ago, it had been emptied out, of course, with the exception of a few nondescript items. But in a closet under the stairs, we found the portrait Derrick has, or will have," she says winking at him, "the portrait signed by someone named Jane, the painting by Edith Bell, a box with that tea set in it, an old wagon, and this family Bible." She hands the Bible to Jane.

The page in front of her is entitled Births and Deaths. Above that, in beautiful, shaky cursive is, *This Bible belongs to Nell Jane O'Donnell.* The list, evidently only partially completed under that reads: *Our Family.*

On the family tree drawn beneath the title, the names *Seamus and Nell O'Donnell* and *James and Agnes O'Donnell (Henry)* stand out to her. As do *1881—Leo Henry* and *1886—Edith Frances Henry (Bell);* and *1908—Opal Rose Bell (Lawton),* followed by what must have been her grandmother's siblings: *1910—Violet May Bell (Doyle), 1912—Lily Henry Bell (McCusker), 1915—Iris Louise Bell (Minton),* and *1917—Arthur Paul Bell and Albert Jack Bell.*

She can tell by the differences in ink and cursive styles, the list had been added to. Then she finds her mother's name. It's listed last, without a surname or date. Just *Elise.* But it's here, in this family Bible. On The Land.

Jane turns to the front cover and reads:

> *This Bible was carried from Ireland by Nell Jane O'Donnell in 1854. It was recovered from the original cabin belonging to Seamus and Nell O'Donnell on this Kansas property, May 1900.*

This house, the one she has been seeing in visions all this time, The Land, really is her land! She can't get over it. The Spirit of God really is here!

He is hers.

And the people who have lived, fought, and died here are hers, too.

Including the ones that stand next to her now. The past, present, and future are all woven together here.

The Spirit at work had always been beside her, and now within her, and had led her home! Mac had only supported God's remarkable, yet gentle, prodding. She had only to respond.

Finally, she had.

Jane is overwhelmed with understanding. She had painted her own past to find the present and to fulfill the future.

She looks around the room to bask in the beauty of it all, imagining plenty of room on blank canvas in which to create more color.

Epilogue

KANSAS CITY—JANUARY 1, 2012
THE KINGDOM AGE

"It is time," he says tenderly.

"I know that," says the girl, who rubs sleep from her eyes as she sits up in bed. The stranger remains standing before her. Beyond him, beyond the four walls of a bedroom bathed in moonlight, past the long, white gauzy curtains framing the tall window, is a sea of grass that shimmers in the light as if brushed in stardust. A soft breeze stirs delivering sweet bouquet fragrances to her senses. She inhales deeply. The curtains flutter gently.

The man smiles, understanding the girl perfectly. He proceeds. "Today marks the beginning of a new age. Now, you will work in greater partnership and with greater understanding than has been possible before."

The girl remains silent, attentive at first, but then adds, "Today is my twelfth birthday."

"Yes," he says evenly. She waits. He continues, "You were born for such a time as this."

This is no surprise to the girl, either. There are some things that can be felt, and this is one of them. This, and the fact that the beginning of things is imminent. And though she can feel a shift in the significance of this moment, there is much she doesn't yet understand.

"The Golden Age isn't just yours, it's for all the planet." The stranger continues to read her thoughts.

She hopes he can't read what she's thinking now, that he is the most beautiful creature she has ever seen. He must work out like crazy—his muscular frame is evident under the fine linen suit he wears.

"You must be willing to persevere." The girl nods, still admiring his attractiveness, despite his long white hair. His eyes penetrate her with love and devotion, and how could that be? They've only just met. Yet she feels as though she knows him, she's always known him. "You must be committed." She takes a deep breath, waiting for more. "You must be capable of following direction."

"And," the stranger says with emphasis, "You must be willing to love. You already have the Spirit within you. Now, you must let Him better guide you." He pauses to wait for the girl's response.

"Of course. Now, are you going to tell me what this is all about?" she asks, becoming impatient.

"I have."

"No, you haven't. Not really. Would you tell me more?"

"No," the stranger calmly replies. "For this information, you will need to ask your mother. She will be able to fill you in. It is time." The girl looks puzzled now.

"My mother? What's my mother got to do with this?"

"This is not a dream, this is *time*, and you are here to make the best of it while it lasts," the stranger says with a smile. "Jane will explain." As soon as he finishes his sentence, he begins to fade.

"Wait a minute," she calls. "Will I see you again?" The man smiles with a slight nod. Encouraged, the girl continues. "What shall I call you?" He is almost completely vanished now. "What is your name?" she pleads.

"Gabriel. It's Gabriel." He winks.

"But you can call me Mac."

Acknowledgments

Thank you, Holy Spirit, for coaxing me out of my comfort zone to write this first novel and for giving me the words to get it done. I had no idea where we were going with this when we began writing together, but you did. You color my world!

A big thank you to my children and your God-chosen mates. Your love and devotion mean the world to me. Thank you for cheering me on to the finish line: Taylor Brian & Cassie, Kelsea & Michael, Tarah, Connor & Tori, Haley & Kyle, Emily & Ryan L., Rachel & Ryan S., Mary Grace & Matt!

And to my grandchildren whose pure love sustains me: Henry, Abigail, Kyra, Logan, Hudson, Teagan, Alice, and all who will follow you!

I am so grateful for my precious friends and light warriors who have believed in me and celebrated this story through all the valleys of dark shadows—those that held the torch for me so I could see my way out. I couldn't have made it through all the things without you, Roxanne Hayes, Carolyn Searcy, Missy Maxwell Worton, Karen Johnson, Diana Larkin, Patty Teichroew, Ash West, Sandy Cadwell, Holly Hatfield, Cindy Julian, Catherine Wendt, Janet McNeely, Ashley Phillips.

Thank you to my amazing editor, Traci Matt, and to my outstanding proofreader and formatter, Ashley Hagan.

A shout out to my previewing readers: Diana Larkin, Patty Teichroew, Sarah Almanza, Ash West, Karen Johnson, Carolyn Searcy, Missy Maxwell Worton.

And to my guests, viewers, and listeners on COLOR SPEAK Podcast. You have each blessed and inspired me in ways you cannot know this side of eternity.

I am especially grateful for the New York Times Best-Selling author, Francine Rivers, whose eyes were the first to look the manuscript over in rough form. Thank you for your great advice, my friend.

And thank you to my little sister, Jackie Lindemann, who always makes life so much fun, my mom, Sally, and mother-in-law, Jane, whom I love dearly.

Other Books by J.M. Huxley

About the Author

J.M. Huxley (Janet Huxley) is an award-winning author and broadcast news anchor. Currently, she is a morning news anchor for conservative radio and host of COLOR SPEAK, a podcast dedicated to empowering all people to spiritual sight. Formerly, she was an airborne traffic and news reporter, as well as operations director for the San Diego and Kansas City offices of Westwood One's Metro Networks. Later, she homeschooled five of her eight children, milked goats on her farm, and taught high school literature and world views classes. Her memoir, MILK AND HONEY LAND: A Story of Grief, Grace, and Goats, won the 2019 Author Academy Award for Best Memoir and the 2021 Readers' Favorite Gold Medal Winner in the Christian Non-Fiction genre. Her children's book, RAINBOW LAND, encourages children to see God in the rainbow. She enjoys redemptive literature, good company, and adventures in food with her kids and grandkids.

www.jmhuxley.com
Email: JM@JMHuxley.com
Instagram: @jm.huxley
Facebook: https://facebook.com/AuthorJMHuxley